"*The Samurai's Wife* is the latest in Laura Joh Rowland's bracing books about Sano Ichirō, a 17th-century warrior who serves as a detective for the imperial shogun . . . a mixed blessing for Sano is his wife's insistence—virtually scandalous in feudal Japan—on accompanying him in his investigations; but she proves invaluable in what turns out to be a probe into deep duplicity indeed."

—*Seattle Times*

"Unlike historical mysteries that try to dazzle us with research to hide their shortfalls in the story department, Laura Joh Rowland's richly detailed books about 17th-century Japanese samurai-warrior-turned-detective Sano Ichiro are also packed with plot and narrative."

—*Chicago Tribune*

"Rowland . . . uses her fine eye for detail as she creates memorable vignettes of a place and time far removed from this one."

—*The Times-Picayune*

The Concubine's Tattoo

"An exotic setting, seventeenth-century Japan, and a splendid mystery . . . make for grand entertainment."

—*New York Daily News*

"Rowland is a sturdy, persuasive storyteller, and well worth keeping an eye on."

—*Washington Post Book World*

"Rowland offers fascinating glimpses into the culture of medieval Japan, especially into the thankless lives of women. A good choice for fans of historical mysteries."

—*Booklist*

Also by Laura Joh Rowland

The Perfumed Sleeve

Laura Joh Rowland

St. Martin's Paperbacks

THE PERFUMED SLEEVE

Copyright © 2004 by Laura Joh Rowland.
Excerpt from *The Assassin's Touch* copyright © 2005 by Laura Joh Rowland.

Library of Congress Catalog Card Number: 2003062546

ISBN: 0-312-99208-4
EAN: 80312-99208-8

Printed in the United States of America

St. Martin's Press hardcover edition / April 2004
St. Martin's Paperbacks edition / April 2005

St. Martin's Paperbacks are published by St. Martin's Press, 175 Fifth Avenue, New York, NY 10010.

10 9 8 7 6 5 4 3 2 1

To Kathleen Davis, Elora Fink, Charles Gramlich,
Steve Harris, Candice Proctor, and Emily Toth,
in gratitude for their company on Monday nights,
their friendship, and their support

The Perfumed
Sleeve

1

Japan, Genroku Period, Year 7, Month 10 (November 1694)

News of trouble sent Sano Ichirō abroad in the city of Edo at midnight. Clad in armor and metal helmet, his two swords at his waist, he galloped his horse down the main avenue. Beside him rode his young chief retainer, Hirata; behind them followed the hundred men of Sano's detective corps.

Constellations wheeled around the moon in the black, smoke-hazed sky. Cold wind swept debris past closed shops. Ahead, Sano saw torches flaring against the darkness. He and his troops passed townsmen armed with clubs, standing guard at doorways, ready to protect their businesses and families from harm. Frightened women peered out windows; boys craned their necks from rooftops, balconies, and fire-watch towers. Sano halted his army at the edge of a crowd that blocked the avenue.

The crowd was composed of ruffians whose faces shone with savage glee in the light of the torches they carried. They avidly watched two armies of mounted samurai, each some hundred men strong, charge along the street from opposite directions. The armies met in a violent clash of swords and lances. Horses skittered and neighed. The riders bellowed as they swung their blades at their opponents. Men screamed in agony as they fell wounded. Groups of samurai on foot whirled in fierce sword combat. Spectators cheered; some joined in the carnage.

"I've been expecting this," Hirata told Sano.

"It was only a matter of time," Sano agreed.

As the shogun's *sōsakan-sama*—most honorable investigator of events, situations, and people—Sano usually occupied himself with investigating important crimes and advising his lord, Tokugawa Tsunayoshi, dictator of Japan. But during recent months he'd spent much time keeping order amid the political upheaval in Edo. The *bakufu*—the military government that ruled Japan—was divided by a struggle for control of the Tokugawa regime. One faction, led by the shogun's second-in-command, Chamberlain Yanagisawa, opposed a second led by Lord Matsudaira, a cousin of the shogun. Other powerful men, including the *daimyo*—feudal lords—had begun taking sides. Both factions had started building up their military forces, preparing for civil war.

Soldiers had poured into Edo from the provinces, crowding the barracks at *daimyo* estates and Edo Castle, overflowing the district where Tokugawa vassals lived and camping outside town. Although Chamberlain Yanagisawa and Lord Matsudaira hadn't yet declared war, the lower ranks had grown restless. Idle waiting bred battle fever. Sano and his detective corps had already quelled many skirmishes. Now, the city elders who governed the townspeople had sent Sano an urgent message begging him to come and quell this major disturbance that threatened to shatter the peace which the Tokugawa regime had maintained for almost a century.

"Let's break up this brawl before it causes a riot and wrecks the town," Sano said.

"I'm ready," Hirata said.

As they forged through the crowd, leading their troops, Sano recalled other times they'd ridden together into battle, when he'd taken Hirata's competent, loyal service for granted. But last summer, while they were attempting to rescue the shogun's mother and their wives from kidnappers, Hirata had disobeyed Sano's orders. Now Sano could no longer place his complete trust in Hirata.

"In the name of His Excellency the Shogun, I order you to cease!" Sano called to the armies.

He and his men forced apart the combatants, who howled in rage and attacked them. Blades whistled and slashed around Sano. As he circled, ducked, and tried to control his rearing horse, the night spun around him. Torchlight and faces in the crowd blurred across his vision. The armies drove him to the edge of the road.

"Behold the great *sōsakan-sama*," called a male voice. "Have you been demoted to street duty?"

Sano turned to the man who'd addressed him. It was Police Commissioner Hoshina, sitting astride his horse at the gate to a side street, flanked by two mounted police commanders. Fashionable silk robes clothed his muscular physique. His handsome, angular face wore a mocking smile.

"You shouldn't lower yourself to breaking up brawls," Hoshina said.

Anger flashed through Sano. He and Hoshina were long-time enemies, and the fact that Sano had recently saved Hoshina's life didn't ease their antagonism.

"Someone has to uphold the law," Sano retorted, "because your police force won't."

Hoshina laughed off Sano's accusation that he was neglecting his duty. "I've got more important things on my mind."

Things like revenge and ambition, Sano thought. Hoshina had been the paramour of Chamberlain Yanagisawa until recently, when Yanagisawa had betrayed Hoshina, and the police commissioner had joined Lord Matsudaira's faction. Hoshina was so bitter toward Yanagisawa that he welcomed a war that could elevate him and depose his lover. He didn't care that war could also destroy the city he'd been appointed to protect. A lawless atmosphere pervaded Edo because Hoshina and his men wouldn't stop the fighting between partisans.

Sano turned away from Hoshina in disgust. Along the boulevard, more soldiers and ruffians streamed in as news of the brawl spread. Running footsteps, pounding hoofbeats, and loud war cries enlivened the night.

"Close off the area!" Sano yelled at his troops.

They hurried to bar the gates at intersections. The boulevard was a tumult of Sano's forces and the crazed soldiers colliding, blades flashing and bodies flailing, murderous yowls and spattering blood. As Sano rode into the melee, he feared this was only a taste of things to come.

It was dawn by the time Sano, Hirata, and the detectives separated the combatants, arrested them for disturbing the peace, and dispersed the crowd. Now a sun like a malevolent red beacon floated up from a sea of gray clouds over Edo Castle, looming on its hilltop above the city. At his mansion inside the official quarter of the castle, Sano sat in his private chambers. His wife Reiko cleaned a cut on his arm, where a sword had penetrated a joint in his sleeve guard. He wore his white under-kimono; his armor lay strewn on the *tatami* floor around him.

"You can't keep trying to maintain order in the city by yourself," Reiko said as she swabbed Sano's bloody gash. Her delicate, beautiful features were somber. "One man can't stand between two armies and survive for long."

Sano winced at the pain. "I know."

Servants' voices drifted from the kitchen and grounds as morning stirred the estate to life. In the nursery, Sano and Reiko's little son Masahiro chattered with the maids. Reiko sprinkled powdered geranium root on Sano's wound to stop the bleeding, then applied honeysuckle ointment to prevent festering.

"While you were out last night, the finance minister came to see you," Reiko said. "So did the captain of the palace guard." These were two of Sano's friends in the *bakufu.* "I don't know why."

"I can guess," Sano said. "The minister, who has recently joined Chamberlain Yanagisawa's faction, came to ask me to do the same. The captain, who has sworn allegiance to Lord Matsudaira, would like me to follow his example."

Both factions were eager to recruit Sano because he was close to the shogun and could use his influence to further their cause; they also wanted Sano and his detectives, all expert fighters, on their side in the event of war. The victor would rule Japan unopposed, via domination of the shogun. Sano could hardly believe that he, a former martial arts teacher and son of a *rōnin*—masterless samurai—had risen to a position where such important men courted his allegiance. But that position brought danger; both men would hasten to ruin any powerful official who opposed them.

"What are you going to tell your friends?" Reiko said.

"The same thing I've told everyone else who wants to lure me into one faction or the other," Sano said. "That I won't support either. My loyalty is to the shogun." Despite Tokugawa Tsunayoshi's shortcomings as a dictator, Sano felt bound by the samurai code of honor to stand by his lord. "I'll not join anyone who would usurp his authority."

Reiko bound a white cloth pad and bandage around Sano's wound. "Be careful," she said, patting his arm.

Sano perceived that her warning concerned more than his immediate injury; she feared for their future. He hated to worry her, especially since she was still suffering from the effects of being kidnapped along with the shogun's mother.

He didn't know exactly what had happened to Reiko while imprisoned by the man who'd called himself the Dragon King. But the normally adventurous Reiko had changed. During four years of marriage, she'd helped Sano with his investigations and developed quite a talent for detective work, but now she'd turned into a quiet recluse who hadn't left the estate since he'd brought her home. Sano wished for a little peace so she could recover, yet there was no prospect of peace anytime soon.

"This city is like a barrel of gunpowder," Sano said grimly. "The least incident could spark an explosion."

Footsteps creaked along the passage, and Hirata appeared at the door. "Excuse me, *Sōsakan-sama*." Although still free to enter Sano's private quarters, Hirata displayed the cautious deference with which he'd behaved since their breach. "You have a visitor."

"At this hour?" Sano glanced at the window. Gray daylight barely penetrated the paper panes. "Who is it?"

"His name is Juro. He's the valet of Senior Elder Makino. He says Makino sent him here with a message for you."

Sano raised his eyebrows in surprise. Makino Narisada was the longest-standing, dominant member of the Council of Elders, the shogun's primary advisers and Japan's highest governing body. He was also a crony of Chamberlain Yanagisawa and enemy of Sano. He had an ugly face like a skull, and a disposition to match.

"What is the message?" Sano said.

"I asked, but Juro wouldn't tell me," Hirata said. "He says his master ordered him to speak personally to you."

Sano couldn't refuse a communication from someone as important, quick to take offense, and dangerous as Makino. Besides, he was curious. "Very well."

He and Hirata walked to the reception room. Reiko followed. She watched from outside the door while they entered the cold, drafty room, where a man knelt. Thin and stooped, with a fringe of gray hair around his bald head, and clad in modest gray robes, Juro the valet appeared to be past sixty years of age. His bony features wore a sad expression. Two of Sano's detectives stood guard behind him. Although he looked harmless, they exercised caution toward strangers in the house, especially during these dangerous days.

"Here I am," Sano said. "Speak your message."

The valet bowed. "I'm sorry to impose on you, *Sōsakan-sama*, but I must tell you that the honorable Senior Elder Makino is dead."

"Dead?" Sano experienced three reactions in quick succession. The first was shock. "As of when?"

"Today," said Juro.

"How did it happen?" Sano asked.

"My master passed away in his sleep."

Sano's second reaction was puzzlement. "You told my chief retainer that Makino-*san* sent you. How could he, if he's dead?"

"Some time ago, he told me that if I should die, I must inform you at once. I'm honoring his order."

Sano looked at Hirata, who shrugged, equally perplexed.

"My condolences to you on the loss of your master," Sano said to the valet. "I'll go pay my respects to his family today."

As he spoke, a deep consternation beset him. Makino must have been almost eighty years old—he'd lived longer than he deserved—but his death, at this particular time, had the potential to aggravate the tensions within the Tokugawa regime.

"Why did Makino-*san* care that I should immediately know of his death?" Sano asked Juro.

"He wanted you to read this letter." The valet offered a folded paper to Sano.

Still mystified, Sano accepted the letter. Juro bowed with the air of a man who has discharged an important duty, and the detectives escorted him out of the house. Reiko entered the room. She and Hirata waited expectantly while Sano unfolded the letter and scanned the words written in gnarled black calligraphy. He read aloud, in surprise:

> *"To Sano Ichirō, sōsakan-sama to the shogun:*
>
> *"If you are reading this, I am dead. I am leaving you this letter to beg an important favor of you.*
> *"As you know, I have many enemies who want me gone. Assassination is a constant threat for a man in my position. Please investigate my death and determine whether it was murder. If it was, I ask that you identify the culprit, deliver him to justice, and avenge my death.*
> *"I regret to impose on you, but there is no one else I trust enough to ask this favor. I apologize for any inconvenience that my request causes you.*
>
> > *Senior Elder Makino Narisada."*

Reiko burst out, "The gall of that man, asking you for anything! After he accused you of treason last year and tried to get you executed!"

"Even in death he plagues me," Sano said, disturbed by the request that posed a serious dilemma for himself.

"But the valet said Makino died in his sleep," Hirata pointed out.

"Could his death have really been murder?" Reiko wondered. "The letter would have come to you even if Makino died of old age, as he seems to have done."

"Perhaps his death isn't what it seems." Sano narrowed his eyes in recollection. "There have been attempts on his life. His fear that he would die by foul play was justified. And he was extremely vindictive. If he was assassinated, he would want the culprit punished even though he wouldn't be around to see it."

"And lately, with the *bakufu* in turmoil, there's been all the more reason for his enemies to want him gone," Reiko said.

"But you don't have to grant his request to investigate his death," Hirata told Sano.

"You owe him nothing," Reiko agreed.

Yet Sano couldn't ignore the letter. "Since there's a chance that Makino was murdered, his death should be investigated. How I felt about him doesn't matter. A victim of a crime deserves justice."

"An inquiry into his death could create serious trouble for you that I think you should avoid." Hirata spoke with the authority of a chief retainer duty bound to divert his master from a risky path, yet a slight hesitation in his voice bespoke his awareness that Sano might doubt the value of his counsel.

"Hirata-*san* is right," Reiko told Sano. "If Makino was murdered, there's a killer at large who won't welcome you prying into his death."

"Makino's enemies include powerful, unscrupulous men," Hirata said. "Any one of them would rather kill you than be exposed and executed as a murderer."

"Investigating crimes against high-ranking citizens is my job," Sano said. "Danger comes with the responsibility. And in this case, the possible victim—who was my superior— asked me to look into his death."

"I can guess why Makino asked you," Reiko said in disgust at the senior elder. "Makino knew that your sense of honor wouldn't let you overlook a possible crime."

"He understood that justice matters more to you than your own safety," Hirata interjected.

"So he saddled you with a job that he knew no one else would bother to do for him. He tried to destroy you while he was alive. Now he's trying to manipulate you from the grave." Outrage sparked in Reiko's eyes. "Please don't let him!"

Even though Sano shared many of the concerns of his wife and chief retainer, he felt a duty toward Makino that superseded reason. "A posthumous request from a fellow samurai is a serious obligation," he said. "Refusing to honor it would be a breach of protocol."

"No one would fault you for refusing a favor to a man who treated you the way Makino did," Hirata said.

"You ignore protocol often enough," Reiko said, wryly alluding to Sano's independent streak.

But Sano had more reason to grant the request, no matter the consequences. "If Makino was murdered, the fact may come to light regardless of what I do. Even if he wasn't, rumors could arise that say he was." Rumors, true and false, abounded in Edo Castle during this political crisis. "Suspicion will fall on all his enemies—including me. By that time, evidence of how Makino died, and who killed him, will be lost, along with my chance to prove my innocence if I'm accused."

Understanding dawned on Reiko's and Hirata's faces. "Your enemies have tried to frame you for crimes in the past," Hirata recalled. "They would welcome this opportunity to destroy you."

"Most of your friends now belong to Chamberlain Yanagisawa or Lord Matsudaira," Reiko said. "Since you won't join either faction, you have the protection of neither. And if you're accused of murder, you can't count on the shogun to defend you."

Because the shogun's favor was as inconstant as the weather, Sano thought. He'd known that by resisting pressure to choose sides, he stood alone and vulnerable, but now the high price of neutrality had come due. "So I either investigate Makino's death, or jeopardize all of us," Sano said, for his family and retainers would share any punishment that came his way.

Reiko and Hirata nodded in resigned agreement. "I'll do everything in my power to help you," Hirata said.

"Where shall we begin?" Reiko said.

Their support gladdened Sano, yet misgivings disturbed him. Was Reiko ready to brave the hazards of this investigation so soon after her kidnapping? Sano also wondered how far he could trust Hirata, after Hirata had placed personal concerns above duty to his master during the kidnapping investigation. But Sano was in no position to turn away help.

"As soon as I've washed and dressed, we'll go to Makino's estate and inspect the scene of his death," Sano told Hirata.

Hirata bowed. He said, "I'll fetch some detectives to accompany us," then left the room.

"You must eat first and restore your strength," Reiko said to Sano. "I'll bring your breakfast." She paused in the doorway. "Is there anything else you need me to do?"

Sano read anxiety in her manner, instead of the eager excitement with which she usually greeted a new investigation. He said, "I won't know until I've determined whether Makino was indeed murdered. Maybe Hirata and I will discover that he died of natural causes. Maybe I can dispel suspicion of foul play, and everything will be all right."

2

Senior Elder Makino's estate was located on the main street of the Edo Castle official quarter. In accordance with his high rank, the estate was the largest of the compounds, surrounded by stone walls and retainers' barracks, that lined the road. The gate boasted a double-tiered roof; sentries occupied guard booths outside its double portals.

As Sano walked up to the gate with Hirata and four detectives, they passed officials hurrying about on business. A shrill pitch of anxiety rang from conversations Sano overheard between these men swirling at the periphery of the political maelstrom. The whole *bakufu* feared the consequences of the struggle between Chamberlain Yanagisawa and Lord Matsudaira. But Sano detected no sign of commotion around Makino's estate. He surmised that the news of Makino's death hadn't yet been made public.

After introducing himself to the guards in the booth, Sano told them, "I'm here to see the honorable Senior Elder Makino."

The guards exchanged uneasy glances. One man said, "I beg you to wait a moment," and went inside the compound. Evidently, the guards knew their master was dead but had orders not to tell anyone. Sano and his comrades waited in the chill gray morning until the guard reemerged, accompanied by a man whom Sano recognized as Makino's secretary.

The secretary, a pale, sleek man with a deferential air, bowed to Sano. "Will you please come with me?"

He led Sano, Hirata, and the detectives through the gate, between the barracks, through another gate to the inner compound, and up the stone steps to the mansion. Inside the entryway Sano and his comrades exchanged their shoes for guest slippers, then hung their swords on racks, according to custom when entering a private home. The secretary seated Sano, Hirata, and the detectives in a reception chamber and knelt opposite them.

"I regret to tell you that the honorable Senior Elder Makino just died," he said in the hushed tone reserved for such an announcement. "If you had business with him, perhaps I may assist you on his behalf?"

Sano said, "I already know about Makino-*san*. I would like to speak with whoever is now in charge here."

The secretary's face reflected startled confusion. He said, "I'll fetch Senior Elder Makino's chief retainer," then rose and edged out the door.

Soon, a man dressed in austere gray robes strode into the room. He knelt and bowed to Sano. "Greetings, *Sōsakan-sama*."

"Good morning, Tamura-*san*," replied Sano.

They were casual acquaintances, with a mutual wariness that stemmed from Sano and Makino's antagonism. Sano knew Tamura to be an old-fashioned samurai who considered himself as much a warrior as a bureaucrat; unlike many *bakufu* officials, he kept up his martial arts training. Although past fifty years of age, he had a hardy, muscular physique. His hands bore calluses and scars from combat. His features always reminded Sano of the carved wooden masks worn by villains in Nō plays: hard, shiny, prominent cheeks; a long nose with its sharp tip flattened downward; slanted eyebrows that gave him a severe expression.

"I am responsible for Senior Elder Makino's household and affairs," Tamura's voice—deep, raspy, and loud—befitted his appearance. "There are no male clan members in town, and until they can be summoned, it's my duty to handle any business concerning my master."

Sano recalled hearing that Makino had feuded with his four sons and numerous relatives, whom he'd suspected of plotting to oust him from power, and had banished them to remote provinces.

"I was just about to notify the shogun of Senior Elder Makino's death," Tamura said. "May I ask how you learned about it?"

"His valet came and told me," Sano said.

Disapproval drew together Tamura's slanted brows. "Everyone in the household was forbidden to spread the news until after the official announcement."

"Juro had permission, from his master," Sano said, then explained. Tamura stared, obviously disconcerted; Hirata and the detectives watched him and Sano in alert silence. Sano handed Makino's letter to Tamura. "The senior elder has requested that I investigate his death."

As Tamura read the letter, he shook his head in amazement. "I had no knowledge of this."

Was Tamura shocked, Sano wondered, because he'd prided himself on enjoying his superior's confidence, only to learn of secrets kept from him? Or were there other reasons for discomfiture?

Quickly regaining his poise, Tamura said, "I did know that the senior elder feared assassination. However, he died peacefully in his sleep." Tamura gave the letter back to Sano. "Many thanks for honoring my master's wish. You have no further obligation to him." He bowed and rose, concluding Sano's visit.

Sano thought Tamura seemed a bit too hasty to get rid of him. Perhaps Makino had had good cause not to tell his chief retainer about the letter. Sano, Hirata, and the detectives stood, but held their ground.

"I'd like to see for myself that Senior Elder Makino wasn't a victim of murder," Sano told Tamura. "Please take me to him."

Resistance swelled Tamura to his full height. "With all

due respect, *Sōsakan-sama*, but I must decline. An official examination of my master would be a disgrace to him."

"The senior elder knew what my inquiries would entail. He cared less about disgrace than that I should discover the truth about what happened." Sano observed the angry crimson flush spreading across Tamura's shiny cheeks. He conjectured that Tamura might prove to be his first suspect in a murder investigation. "Now, if you'll show me to Senior Elder Makino?" Sano paused. "Or do you want me to think you have something to hide?"

Calculation flickered in Tamura's eyes as he measured the threat posed by Sano against whatever was his actual motive for barring examination of the death scene.

"Come this way," he said at last. His courteous bow and gesture toward the door smacked of disdain.

As they all trooped down the corridor, Sano experienced a growing sense that Makino's death wasn't as natural as it seemed. He anticipated that Tamura's unwillingness to cooperate was only the first obstacle his inquiries would meet.

Senior Elder Makino's mansion had the same layout as other samurai estates, with family living quarters at the center. A separate building, with half-timbered plaster walls, heavy wooden shutters over the windows, a broad veranda, and surrounding gardens, housed his private chambers. Tamura, Sano, Hirata, and the detectives crossed a covered walkway built above raked white sand studded with low shrubs and mossy rocks. Two guards stood outside the building. Inside, a corridor encircled the chambers. Tamura slid open a panel in the lattice-and-paper wall, admitting Sano and his men into a spacious room heated by sunken charcoal braziers. Across an expanse of *tatami* floor, a platform extended below a mural that depicted treetops and clouds. On a bed on the platform lay Senior Elder Makino, covered by a quilt. But Sano's immediate attention focused on the people in the room.

Two women knelt, one on either side of Makino's head. A man crouched at his feet. All turned toward Sano, Hirata, and the detectives. Sano had a sudden impression of vultures feeding on a corpse, interrupted by a predator.

"This is Makino-*san*'s widow," Tamura said, introducing the older of the women.

Although Sano estimated her age at forty-five years, her face's elegant bone structure testified to the beauty she must have once possessed. A rich burgundy silk dressing gown embossed with medallions clothed her slim figure. Her hair fell in a long plait over her shoulder. She bowed to Sano, her features set in rigid lines of grief.

"That's his concubine." Tamura indicated the other woman.

She was small and very young—no more than fifteen, Sano guessed—yet voluptuous of body. Her scarlet kimono, gaily patterned with winter landscapes, looked out of place at a deathbed. But her round, pretty face was tear-streaked, her eyes red and swollen. As she bobbed a clumsy bow at Sano, she pressed a white kerchief to her nose.

"And that's the senior elder's houseguest." Tamura nodded at the man by the foot of the bed.

The houseguest rearranged his tall, agile figure in a kneeling position and bowed. He was in his twenties, clad in a plain brown robe, and stunningly handsome. His bold, lustrous eyes appraised Sano. Lively spirits flashed behind the somber expression on his strong, clean features. He wore his oiled black hair in a topknot above his shaved crown. Recognition jarred Sano, but he couldn't think where he'd seen the man before. He had a notion that the man wasn't a samurai, despite his hairstyle.

"Leave this building," Tamura ordered the three.

The concubine glanced at the houseguest. He jerked his chin at her, then rose and stepped off the platform. The concubine scrambled up, and together they hastened from the room. The widow glided after them. While Tamura stood by the door and the detectives waited at the end of the room, Sano and Hirata mounted the platform and gazed down at Makino.

He lay on his back with his legs straight and hands atop his chest under the quilt. A jade neck rest supported his head, which wore a white nightcap. His withered, sallow

skin spread across his ugly face, delineating the skull beneath. Wrinkles wattled his scrawny neck above the collar of
a beige silk robe; purplish shadows tinged his closed eyelids.
He looked much the same as when alive, Sano thought. Except that Makino had never shut his eyes in the presence of
other people because he was always on the lookout for
threats, or for advantages to seize. And he'd had too much
pride to let his mouth drop open like that. Sano experienced
a mixture of sadness at the spectacle of human mortality and
relief that his enemy was really dead.

"Who found him?" Sano asked Tamura.

"I did. I came to wake him, as usual, and there he was."
Arms folded, Tamura spoke in tone of resigned forbearance.

Sano noted the quilt draped smoothly over Makino, his
head balanced on the neck rest, his body in serene repose.
"Was he in this exact position? Or did anyone move his
body?"

"He was just as you see him," Tamura said.

Sano and Hirata exchanged glances, sharing the thought
that Makino looked too neat and composed even if he'd died
naturally, and that the person who discovers the body is often the killer. Now that he had more reason to doubt
Tamura's word, Sano felt his heart beat faster with the excitement that a new investigation always brought him along
with qualms about his next step.

In order to determine how Makino had died, an examination of the body was imperative. But Sano couldn't just strip
Makino naked and look for wounds, as that would transgress
Tokugawa law forbidding practices associated with foreign
science, including the examination of corpses. Sano had
broken the law often enough, but he couldn't do it here, in
the presence of Tamura, a hostile witness. He needed to get
Makino away from the estate. Besides, even if Sano examined the body, he might not be able to tell what had caused
the death. He needed expert advice. His mind raced, formu-
lating a ploy.

"Are you done?" Tamura asked impatiently.

"I'm not yet satisfied as to how Senior Elder Makino

died," Sano said. "I must order you to delay reporting his death. No one will leave here." Sano sent one detective to begin securing the estate and another to fetch more troops to help. He didn't want the news to spread and visitors over-running the premises before he could examine them. As Tamura gaped in outrage, Sano added, "And I must confis-cate Makino-*san*'s body."

"What?" Tamura's outrage turned to incredulity. He stalked across the room to the platform and stared at Sano. "Why?"

"The funeral rites must be postponed until my investiga-tion is done and the pronouncement of the cause of Makino-*san*'s death is official," Sano improvised. "Therefore, I shall take him into safekeeping."

Tamura's expression said he thought Sano had gone mad. "I've never heard of such a thing. What law allows you to do this?"

"Bring me a trunk large enough to carry the body," Sano said, eager to end the argument before it revealed his expla-nation as completely spurious.

Fists balled on his hips, Tamura said, "If you take my master, you'll displease many people."

Sano wondered whether Tamura was afraid of what he might see on the body. "If you stand in my way, you'll suf-fer," Sano said. "Get the trunk."

They were at an impasse. Sano knew that Makino's family and powerful friends—including Chamberlain Yanagisawa—could punish him for confiscating the body, especially if they guessed why he wanted it. But Tamura knew that Sano could have him stripped of his samurai status for disobeying orders. Hirata and the detectives moved closer to Sano, aligning themselves against Tamura. Evidently recognizing that the threat to him was more immediate than the one to Sano, the man visibly deflated. Surliness replaced his ire.

"As you wish," he said to Sano, then slunk out of the room.

Sano expelled his breath. The investigation had barely begun, and already the difficulties were mounting. He beckoned his two remaining detectives, Marume and Fukida, and whispered to them, "Take Senior Elder Makino to Edo Morgue."

The young, slight, serious detective and the jovial, brawny one nodded. They understood from past cases what Sano intended. They also knew the dangers involved and the caution necessary.

Tamura returned with two servants hauling a long wooden trunk. Marume and Fukida peeled the quilt off Makino, lifted his stiff body, placed it inside the trunk, and carried it away. Sano offered a silent prayer for its safe, secret arrival at Edo Morgue. Then he ordered Tamura, "Wait outside while I examine the senior elder's chambers."

As soon as Tamura was gone, the search for evidence of murder began.

"There's no sign of a struggle," Hirata said, walking around the chamber. "In fact, the room seems too neat. Just as Makino's body did."

Sano, pacing the platform, nodded. "Teapot, bowl, and lamp arranged in a precise triangle on the table near the bed," he said, pointing. His finger moved to indicate the room below the platform. "Cushions, lacquer chests, and kimono stand pushed against the walls. Not a thing out of place."

Hirata felt the tension between him and Sano, like a turbulence running under the smooth flow of their words and actions. Ever since Sano had reprimanded him for disobedience, he'd felt maimed and diminished, as though part of him had died.

He said, "And not an obvious mark anywhere on the *tatami*. If someone rearranged Makino's body after he died, whoever it was could also have cleaned up signs of what really happened in here last night."

"But maybe not all the signs," Sano said.

He crouched by the bed where Makino had lain. Hirata began opening drawers of the cabinets along the wall. Misery weighed upon him as his mind wandered to the circumstances that had caused his troubles.

While pursuing the man who'd kidnapped their women and the shogun's mother, he'd placed the safety of his pregnant wife Midori above his duty to Sano. Thus, he'd violated Bushido, the samurai code of loyalty. He'd not only lost the trust Sano had once placed in him, but his reputation had suffered too. Colleagues aware of his misdeed ostracized him. Half of Sano's detectives sympathized with Hirata; the rest thought Sano should have thrown him out. The controversy had undermined Hirata's authority and the harmony within the corps. Now, lifting folded robes from a drawer, Hirata covertly eyed Sano, who was inspecting the puffy silver-green satin quilt. Although Hirata deeply regretted the rift between them, and his lost honor, a part of him believed that his disobedience had been justified.

Surely there was an exception to every rule of Bushido. Surely his one lapse shouldn't cancel out years of faithful service. Hirata believed that Midori and his baby daughter Taeko would have died on that island, instead of coming home alive and well, if not for his disobedience. Furthermore, everything had turned out for the best. Yet Hirata couldn't fault Sano for reprimanding him, nor counter his detractors in good conscience.

A master had the right to expect absolute loyalty from a retainer, and Sano had more claim on Hirata than even Bushido granted him. By making Hirata his chief retainer, Sano had raised him far above his origins as a humble police officer, patrolling the streets in the job inherited from his father. If not for Sano, he wouldn't have Midori, Taeko, his post in the *bakufu*, his home at Edo Castle, or the generous stipend that supported his whole clan. Sano deserved to know that if his life were ever in Hirata's hands, Hirata wouldn't let him down again. Now Hirata lived with the consuming need to win back Sano's trust and esteem, through a heroic display of loyalty and duty.

"This bedding is so clean, fresh, and smooth that I doubt

Makino slept in it," Sano said. "But if he didn't, then where is the bedding he did use?"

Hirata opened a door in the cabinet. He saw, jammed inside a compartment, a large, wadded bundle of fabric. "In here."

He and Sano pulled out the bundle. They separated a crumpled gray-and-white floral quilt from the futon wrapped inside. From these wafted the odors of sweat, wintergreen hair oil, and the sour tinge of old age. Sano unrolled the futon, revealing yellowish stains on the middle.

"Why hide this?" Hirata asked. "There's no blood or other sign that Makino didn't die a natural death."

Sano shook the quilt. Out fell a long rectangle of shimmering ivory silk. Hirata picked it up. It was folded in half, seamed down both lengths, and sewn shut at one end. The other end had an opening at each seam—one hemmed, the other ragged. Rich, embroidered autumn grasses and wildflowers in metallic gold and silver thread encrusted the fabric.

"It's a sleeve." Hirata inserted his arm through the openings, held it horizontal, and let the long, flat wing droop.

"Torn from the kimono of an unmarried woman," Sano said, fingering the ragged armhole edge. The sleeve length and fabric design of a kimono indicated the owner's gender and marital status. Single women wore longer sleeves and gaudier fabric than did wives. Hirata and Sano contemplated the sleeve, a symbol of female genitals and soft, yielding nature, often featured in poetry. "I wonder how it got in Makino's bedding. Maybe he had company last night."

Hirata removed the sleeve from his arm and sniffed the fabric. "There's a sweet, smoky odor on this."

Sano lifted the other end of the sleeve to his nostrils. "It's incense. The woman who wore the kimono perfumed her sleeves." This was a practice among fashionable women. They burned incense and held their sleeves in the smoke so that the fabric absorbed it.

The odor nudged Hirata's memory. "My wife uses this type of incense. It's called Dawn to Dusk. It's very rare and expensive."

Examining the sleeve, Sano pointed out an irregularly shaped stain that darkened the pale fabric. "If I'm not mistaken, here's evidence that the woman was with Makino."

Hirata touched a fingertip to the stain. It was damp. When he lowered his face to the stain and inhaled, he recognized the fishy, animal scent of semen mixed with secretions from a woman's body. He nodded, confirming Sano's guess.

"The stain is fresh," he said. "Makino and the woman must have been together last night."

Sano and Hirata gazed toward the bed platform, visualizing the sex—and violence—that might have happened there. Hirata said, "Maybe Tamura isn't as guilty as he seemed."

"And maybe the murder is a case of romance gone bad, not the assassination that Makino feared," Sano said.

Although it would be less dangerous to investigate a crime of passion than a political assassination, Hirata did not welcome a quick, easy investigation that would afford him little opportunity to win back Sano's trust. But the selfishness of the thought immediately shamed him.

"Could Makino's concubine have been the woman with him last night?" he wondered, remembering the pretty, weeping girl. "Or was some other woman involved in his death?"

"We'll have to check into both possibilities," Sano said. "Meanwhile, let's continue searching for evidence."

They set aside the sleeve, then Sano slid open the partition that separated the bedchamber from the adjacent room. It was a study, furnished with a desk surrounded by shelves containing books and a collection of ceramic vases. Scrolls and writing brushes lay scattered everywhere. Dirty footprints marked the papers and floor. A jar of ink-tinged water had toppled on the desk; multicolored shards of broken vases littered books fallen from the shelves.

"No signs of a struggle in the bedchamber, but plenty here," Sano said thoughtfully.

Hirata stepped around trampled scrolls, to an area of floor that was bare amid the mess. There, large, reddish-brown stains soiled the *tatami*. "It's blood," Hirata said.

"And that area of bare floor is roughly the size of a human body," Sano said.

"Makino could have been murdered here and moved to his bed afterward," Hirata said eagerly. "If so, then maybe his death wasn't just a simple love crime."

Sano replied in a neutral tone, "Let's not jump to conclusions."

But hope sparked Hirata's detective instincts. He stepped over to the window near the desk and slid aside the wooden grid of paper panes. Behind it were plank shutters. An iron catch that had secured them dangled loose.

"This window has been forced." Hirata touched the splintered wood on the shutters, where a blade or other hard, flat object inserted between them had torn away the catch.

Sano joined him and inspected the window. "So it has."

He pushed open the shutters and revealed a small garden courtyard. A patch of grass, bordered by raked white sand, contained a flagstone path, a pond, and a stone lantern. Hirata and Sano peered at the evergreen shrub beneath the window.

"Trampled branches," Hirata said.

"And footprints in the sand," Sano said, pointing.

"It looks as though an intruder broke into the study and attacked Makino," Hirata said. "There was a violent struggle. The intruder killed Makino, then put him to bed as if he'd died there. Afterward, the intruder escaped." Hirata anticipated a hunt for the assassin, during which he triumphantly restored himself to Sano's good graces. "The evidence says so."

"The other evidence suggests a crime of passion," Sano countered. "Both theories can't be true."

Hirata could think of arguments in favor of the theory he preferred, but although he once would have felt free to debate with Sano, their bad blood now threatened to turn every discussion into a quarrel. "You're right," he said. "The evidence is too contradictory for us to be sure what happened."

"I'll see if Makino himself can tell us how he died," Sano said, and Hirata knew he meant he was going to Edo Morgue to examine the corpse. "While I'm gone, you interview everyone in the estate. Find out where they were last night. Also look for more signs that an assassin broke into the estate."

"Yes, *Sōsakan-sama*." Hirata had capably performed inquiries like this many times; but did Sano now doubt that he would do as told?

Sano said, "For now, we'll proceed under the assumption that Makino was murdered, and everyone inside the estate is a suspect. So are all of Makino's enemies outside."

Hirata recognized the wide scope of the case, but his spirit leaped at the challenge.

"The shogun must be informed about Makino's death and the investigation," Sano said. "I'll request an audience with him this evening."

As he and Sano parted, Hirata made a vow to learn as much as possible before they reported to the shogun. And by the end of the investigation, he would redeem himself as Sano's loyal chief retainer and an honorable samurai.

3

A bleak, sunless afternoon cast a pall over Kodemma-cho, the slum in the northeast sector of the Nihonbashi merchant district. Miserable shacks lined the twisting roads, along which filthy beggars warmed themselves at bonfires. Stray dogs and ragged, noisy children scavenged amid garbage heaps. Dispirited laborers, peddlers, and housewives plodded along open gutters streaming with foul water. They paid no attention to the samurai dressed in patched, threadbare garments who rode a decrepit horse through their midst.

Sano, disguised as a *rōnin,* kept his hat tipped low over his face as he headed toward Edo Jail, which raised its high walls and gabled roofs in the distance. Crossing the rickety bridge over the canal that fronted the prison, he paused, wary of spies. As his prominence in the *bakufu* had grown, so had his need for secrecy. No one must know that the shogun's *sōsakan-sama* frequented this place of death and defilement. And no one must associate this visit with his investigation into the murder of Senior Elder Makino.

The two guards stationed outside the jail opened the heavy, iron-banded gate for Sano. They knew who he was, but he paid them a salary to ignore his business and tell no tales. Once he'd ridden through the portals, Sano bypassed the fortified dungeon from which prisoners' howls emanated. He dismounted outside Edo Morgue, a low structure with scabrous plaster walls, a shaggy thatched roof, and barred windows.

Through the door emerged Dr. Ito Genboku, morgue custodian, followed by Detectives Marume and Fukida. The doctor wore a dark blue coat, the traditional garb of the medical profession; the wind ruffled his white hair. He and Sano had met five years ago, while Sano was a police commander investigating his first murder case, and had become friends.

"Good afternoon, Ito-*san*," Sano said, bowing. "I see that my detectives have arrived with the body I sent."

Dr. Ito returned the bow and greeting. "I was amazed when they told me who it was. I've never examined the corpse of such an important person." Concern deepened the lines in Dr. Ito's ascetic face. "You took a big risk sending it here."

"I know." If Sano's colleagues in the *bakufu* learned of his actions, there would be a scandal and he would be condemned for defiling Makino as well as for breaking the law against foreign science. Before him stood an example of what could happen.

Dr. Ito, once a prominent physician, had performed medical experiments and obtained scientific knowledge from Dutch traders. While the usual punishment for such offenses was exile, the *bakufu* had consigned Dr. Ito to a life sentence as custodian of Edo Morgue. Here he could continue his scientific studies in peace, but he'd lost his family, his status, and his freedom.

"We didn't bring Makino straight from his house to the jail," Detective Fukida said. "We brought him home first, removed him from the trunk, and put him in a palanquin, in a compartment under the floorboards."

"Then we rode out of Edo Castle in the palanquin," Detective Marume added. "The checkpoint guards never suspected there was anyone in it except us."

"No one followed me, either," Sano said.

Dr. Ito smiled wryly. "Your subterfuges are most ingenious. I recall that the last body you sent was hidden in a crate of vegetables. You've been lucky so far."

"Well, we'd better examine Makino while my luck holds," Sano said. "I have to get his body home before its absence raises any questions."

"I am ready to begin." Dr. Ito ushered Sano and the detectives into the morgue.

Its single large room was furnished with stone troughs used for washing the dead, cabinets containing tools, a podium stacked with papers, and three high tables. One table held a prone figure shrouded with a white drape. Beside it stood Dr. Ito's assistant, Mura. In his late fifties, Mura had hair gradually turning from gray to silver and a square face with a somber, intelligent aspect.

"Proceed, Mura-*san*," Dr. Ito said.

Everyone gathered around the table, and Mura folded back the drape. He was an *eta*—a member of Japan's outcast class, whose hereditary link with death-related occupations such as butchering and tanning rendered them spiritually contaminated. Other citizens shunned them. They served Edo Jail as wardens, corpse handlers, torturers, and executioners. Mura, befriended and educated by Dr. Ito in defiance of class customs, performed all the physical work associated with his master's studies. Now Mura and everyone else beheld Senior Elder Makino. He lay clothed in his nightcap and beige robe, his hands still on his chest, his thin ankles protruding. His knobby feet, shod in white socks, pointed at the ceiling. Permanent slumber shadowed his skull-like face.

"Death spares no one, not even the most rich and powerful," Dr. Ito murmured.

Nor the most cunning and spiteful, Sano thought. He could imagine Makino's outrage had he known he would end up in this place reviled by society. But Makino had asked Sano to investigate his death and left the methods up to Sano.

"Where did he die?" asked Dr. Ito.

Sano described the scene at Makino's mansion, then said, "I have to return him in the same condition as when I confiscated him. Can you determine the cause of his death without dissection or other procedures that will show on his body?"

"I'll do my best," Dr. Ito said. "Mura-*san*, please undress him."

Sano saw a problem. "How can we get his clothes off him and put them back on again when his body is stiffened into position? We can't cut or tear them."

"He isn't entirely stiff," Detective Marume said. "Fukida-*san* and I discovered that when we moved him to the palanquin."

Mura straightened Makino's arms at his sides. The wrists and fingers stayed rigid, but the elbows moved easily.

"The elbow joints were broken after the stiffness had set in to the upper extremities," Dr. Ito explained.

Enlightenment struck Sano. "They were broken so that his body could lie neatly in bed. Even if that doesn't mean Makino was murdered, it proves my suspicion that someone tampered with the death scene before I got there."

Mura untied Makino's sash and parted his robe, exposing the emaciated corpse with its visible ribs and shriveled genitals. He gently worked the sleeves off Makino's arms.

"Here is more proof of your suspicion." Dr. Ito pointed to a reddish-purple discoloration that ran along the left side of the corpse. "Blood pools beneath the skin on the parts of a dead body that lie nearest the ground. That means Makino lay on this side at some point after he died."

"And before being placed flat in bed," Sano said.

Dr. Ito told Mura to turn over the body. As Mura flopped the corpse onto its stomach, Sano's attention was riveted on Makino's back. Red and purple bruises marked the shoulder blades and rib cage.

"It looks as though he was beaten," Sano said.

"And with violent force," said Dr. Ito. "Observe the raw tissue where the blows broke the skin." He wrapped a clean cloth around his hand, then palpated Makino's ribs. "Some of the ribs are broken."

"Did the beating kill Makino?" said Sano.

"Certainly the blows could have caused fatal internal injuries," Dr. Ito said. "I've seen beatings less severe than this kill men much hardier than Makino was." He turned to Mura. "Please remove the cap."

Mura bared Makino's bony, age-speckled scalp and thin gray topknot. Sano saw another bruise that had dented Makino's skull and split open the skin behind his right ear.

"If I must hazard a guess as to which injury killed him, this will be my choice." Dr. Ito contemplated the damaged skull, then added, "It probably bled much, as head wounds do. But there's no blood on Makino. He appears to have been washed, then dressed in clean clothing."

"The head injury would account for the blood on the floor of Makino's study," Sano said. "The beating supports the theory that he died there, of an attack by an intruder." Sano perused a mental picture of the study. "But I didn't find a weapon. And the theory doesn't explain why his body was moved, cleaned, and put to bed, while the evidence of an assassination was allowed to remain." Sano had more reason for his reluctance to accept the scenario. Reporting that Makino had been assassinated would throw the *bakufu* into even greater turmoil.

"Maybe the killer didn't have time to restore order in the study," Dr. Ito said. "Maybe he needed to escape before he was caught, and he fled with the weapon."

Sano nodded, as unable to discount these ideas as prove them. "But there's still the sleeve to consider. I can't help thinking it's an important clue. I also have a hunch that sex, not necessarily politics, was involved in the murder."

Dr. Ito walked with his slow, stiff gait around the table, scrutinizing Makino's corpse. He suddenly halted and said, "You may be right."

"What do you see?" Sano said.

"A different sort of injury. Mura-*san*, please spread the buttocks."

The *eta* pried them apart with his fingers. The crack between the cheeks stretched open. Raw, abraded flesh circled Makino's anus and extended into the orifice.

"When I was a physician, I saw this symptom in men who

had been penetrated by other men during sex," Dr. Ito said. "It's most common in boys and young men." Good looks, and relatively low status, made them fair game for older, wealthier, more powerful men who practiced manly love. "However, it does occur in older males."

Accepted custom for manly love dictated that an elder partner should always penetrate a younger one. Ideally, the one penetrated should also be of inferior social status. When a man reached age nineteen, he should assume the role of the elder and never again experience penetration himself. But some men so enjoyed penetration that they continued receiving it as long as they lived. This was the case with the previous shogun, often criticized for his unseemly violation of custom.

"But Makino's preference for women was well-known," Sano said. "Besides, he would never have abased himself to anyone."

"Men have been known to hide practices that would compromise their reputations," Dr. Ito said. "However, there is an alternative explanation."

"Makino was forced to submit?"

"Yes—by an attacker who overpowered and penetrated him."

Shaking his head, Sano blew out his breath. "This case gets stranger with each new clue. The sleeve suggests that a woman killed Makino in the bedchamber. But the disorder and the blood in his study say he was beaten to death there. And the broken window latch suggests that an assassin entered his estate and killed him. Sometime during whatever happened, he was penetrated by a lover, or an attacker. The motive was sexual, or political." Sano counted off possibilities on his fingers, then upturned his empty palm.

"But the evidence is misleading, or perhaps false. Maybe the vital clues were destroyed by whoever tried to make Makino's death look natural in spite of all the signs to the contrary. Maybe none of those stories is true."

"Or maybe each contains part of the truth," Dr. Ito said.

Sano nodded, his mind sorting and recombining the evidence into ever more baffling patterns. "Can you look for other clues on Makino that might resolve the contradictions?"

But although Dr. Ito spent the next hour poring over the corpse with a magnifying glass, he found nothing more. "I am sorry I couldn't be of more help," he said. "What will you do now?"

"I'll continue investigating." Sano had a disturbing sense that he'd embarked on a journey to an unknown destination, from which there would be no return.

He liked a challenge, and his desire for the truth had strengthened with the first intimation of foul play against Makino. Yet now that he was sure Makino had been murdered, the matter involved more than a favor to a dead man or a personal quest for justice. For the next step in his journey, he must carry his investigation into the public realm, an arena fraught with hazards.

4

In the private chambers of Sano's estate, Reiko and her friend Midori, the wife of Sano's chief retainer Hirata, sat with their children at the *kotatsu* in the nursery. Coals burned inside the square wooden frame of the *kotatsu*. Its flat top formed a table, over which was spread a quilt that contained the heat from the coals, covered everyone's legs, and kept them warm. Lanterns brightened the gloom of the day. Maids placed a meal of soup, rice, roasted fish, and pickled vegetables on the table. While Reiko's son Masahiro hungrily gobbled food, Taeko, five months old, nursed at Midori's breast.

Reiko watched the cozy scene as if from a distance. Ever since she'd arrived home from the island where the Dragon King had held her, Midori, the shogun's mother, and Chamberlain Yanagisawa's wife captive, she'd inhabited a dimension separate from everyone else. What had happened during the abduction, and on that island, enclosed her in a private shadow that nothing could dispel.

"This morning, I found that Taeko had crept up beyond the head of her bed while she slept," Midori said. Her pretty face was still plump from the weight she'd gained during pregnancy. She lovingly stroked her daughter's glossy black hair. "That's a sign that she'll rise high in the world."

Superstitions connected with infants abounded, and Midori took them seriously. "Hirata-*san* hung a picture of a devil beating a prayer gong in Taeko's room. Now she doesn't cry at night. Hirata-*san* is such a good papa." Her tone bespoke her love for her husband.

"Mama, why do ladies shave their eyebrows?" Masahiro said, his mouth full of food. Almost three years old, he had a lively curiosity about the world. "When is it going to snow?"

Reiko automatically smiled, conversed, and ate. But the distance between herself and her companions worried her, as did the other ill effect wrought by the kidnapping.

After her rescue and a quiet month at home, she'd thought herself recovered from the horrors she'd experienced. But the first time she'd ventured outside the estate after her homecoming had proved her wrong. She'd gone to visit her father, and she'd been enjoying the trip, until her palanquin, bearers, and mounted escorts reached the official district outside Edo Castle. Suddenly, as if by evil magic, Reiko was transported back to the highway where the kidnappers had ambushed her and her friends. Memories of the attack came, terrifyingly real. Her heart hammered in panic; vertigo assailed her.

The spell lasted only an instant. Reiko decided that it had been a mental fluke that wouldn't recur.

But it did, several days later, when she went out again. Panic struck the moment Reiko cleared the Edo Castle gate. The next time, the spell started before her palanquin left her own courtyard, and it affected her so badly that she ran back into the house. Soon the mere thought of leaving home triggered the pounding heart, vertigo, and panic. Fear of the spells triggered more of them. Reiko tried to cure herself with meditation and martial arts practice. She took medicine composed of dragon bones and sweet flag root to combat nervous hysteria. Nothing worked. Reiko hadn't left home since that third episode.

Confined to the estate, she'd pondered the baffling spells. Why did she have them, when the other women seemed unaffected? It was true her experiences had been worse than theirs. She also believed that the terror she'd stifled, while they gave free rein to theirs, had become trapped inside her and demanded release. Yet understanding didn't cure the spells, nor did berating herself. Now she felt as much a prisoner as when locked in the Dragon King's palace. She realized that unless she forced herself to go outside despite the spells, she would remain always a prisoner. Unless she could brave the world's hazards, she must forever cease helping Sano with his investigations, abandon the detective work she loved, and shirk her duty to further her family's welfare.

Like it or not, the time to act was now. Reiko flung the quilt off her legs and rose from the *kotatsu*.

"Mama, where are you going?" Masahiro said.

Already Reiko felt her heartbeat speed up as the panic encroached. "Out," she said.

"Where, Mama?" said Masahiro.

"Someplace," Reiko said, fighting to control the tremor in her voice. "Anyplace."

"But the weather is so cold," Midori said. "Why not stay home, where it's warm and we can all be cozy together?"

Reiko saw that Midori was just as afraid to leave the security of the estate as she was. Midori hadn't even tried to go out since they'd come home. But while Midori was content to stay, happily occupied by new motherhood, Reiko was not. Although gripped by the fear that if she went she might never return, she hastened from the room.

She ordered a manservant to assemble an escort for her. As she donned her cloak and shoes, her mind recalled women screaming during the ambush. As she climbed into her palanquin, she envisioned fallen bodies and blood everywhere. While her palanquin and escorts bore her downhill through the winding passages of Edo Castle, shudders wracked her body. Her frantic gasps and thudding heartbeat sounded loud above the remembered voice of the man who'd almost killed her. But she held firm, like a lone, courageous warrior facing an enemy legion.

By the time her procession left Edo Castle, the spell receded. Reiko felt triumphant even though shaky. She was outside the castle, and she'd survived. Next time would be easier. Eventually she would conquer the evil magic and the spells wouldn't trouble her again. Now Reiko looked out the window of her palanquin at the city she'd not seen in five months. Her procession was moving down the wide boulevard through the district south of Edo Castle where the *daimyo* lived. Huge estates lined the boulevard, each surrounded by barracks, their white plaster walls decorated with black tiles set in geometric patterns. Multitudes of samurai rode along the street.

Suddenly a procession overtook Reiko's, and she saw the crest of the Yanagisawa clan on the riders' garments. A black palanquin pulled up alongside hers; its window opened, revealing a woman dressed in dark gray kimono and cloak. She was in her thirties, with a plain, flat face devoid of makeup. Her dour, narrow-eyed gaze brightened as she beheld Reiko, and a hint of a smile curved her broad lips. Now Reiko remembered that there were dangers that weren't just the product of her imagination and threats not dispelled when Sano had rescued her from the Dragon King.

"Hello, Reiko-*san*," murmured Lady Yanagisawa, wife of the chamberlain.

Beside her appeared a beautiful little girl with a happy smile, and a vacant expression in her eyes: Lady Yanagisawa's feebleminded nine-year-old daughter.

"Hello, Lady Yanagisawa," Reiko said. "And hello to you, Kikuko."

What a misfortune that she should encounter them, of all people! Yet Reiko knew this meeting was no coincidence as surely as she knew Lady Yanagisawa was capable of great harm.

Lady Yanagisawa, ignored by the husband she loved with a passion, and mother of a child who would never grow up, was so jealous of Reiko's beauty, adoring husband, and normal child that hatred infused her affection for Reiko. The affection drove the shy, reclusive Lady Yanagisawa to cling to Reiko, her only friend. The hatred drove her to mad acts of violence against Reiko.

"What a surprise that we should run into each other," Lady Yanagisawa said in her soft, gruff voice as their processions moved sedately in parallel.

"Indeed," Reiko said.

She knew that Lady Yanagisawa spied on her, bribing Reiko's servants to tell her everything Reiko did. Reiko had been forced to employ her own spies in her own household to catch the informants, whom she dismissed. But Lady Yanagisawa's money bought her more spies among the new servants. Reiko supposed they'd told Lady Yanagisawa she was going out, and Lady Yanagisawa had rushed to follow her.

"It's been so long since we've met," Lady Yanagisawa said. Her intense gaze flickered over Reiko, as if hungry for every detail she saw. Her jealous hatred shimmered like heat waves from a volcano. "How glad I am to see you again."

How glad you must be for a chance to attach yourself to me and attack me again, Reiko thought. The bad spells weren't the only reason for her reluctance to leave home. Her five months' hiding had protected her from Lady Yanagisawa.

"I'm glad to see you, too," Reiko lied. She didn't dare offend the wife of the chamberlain, who would punish any offense against a member of his family, even one for whom he cared nothing. "And you, Kikuko."

The child giggled. Reiko stifled the aversion she felt toward Kikuko. Kikuko was sweet and innocent, and Reiko pitied her, but she was her mother's obedient tool of destruction.

"I've called on you many times, but your servants said you were ill." A hint of slyness in Lady Yanagisawa's eyes said her spies had told her differently. "Are you feeling better?"

"Yes, thank you," said Reiko. She would feel even better if Lady Yanagisawa would leave her alone. Anger at the woman's machinations filled her.

Lady Yanagisawa lowered her head and gave Reiko a hooded, indirect glance. "I wouldn't like to think you've been avoiding me?" Accusation laced the humble query.

"Of course not. I've thought about you often and wished to know what you were doing." Indeed, Lady Yanagisawa haunted Reiko's thoughts like an evil spirit, and she'd wondered what new demented impulses bred inside the woman. "That we're face-to-face eases my mind."

Face-to-face, she could watch Lady Yanagisawa. It was when Reiko turned her back that disaster happened.

Lady Yanagisawa nodded, pacified, but her expression turned anxious. "You're not angry at me for . . ." She paused, then whispered, "For that . . . incident?"

"I don't know which incident you're talking about," Reiko said truthfully. Did Lady Yanagisawa mean the one that had involved Kikuko and Masahiro last winter? Or the one between herself and Reiko on the Dragon King's island?

A sigh of relief eased from Lady Yanagisawa. "I was worried that you hadn't forgiven me. Now I'm so glad to know you've forgotten what happened."

Reiko could never forget the first incident, when a scheme contrived by Lady Yanagisawa had almost killed Masahiro, or the second, when Lady Yanagisawa had tried to kill her. Since these attacks had occurred despite Reiko's friendship with Lady Yanagisawa, Reiko dreaded to think what unholy destruction Lady Yanagisawa would wreak should they become foes. Hence, she'd forgiven the unforgivable and endured Lady Yanagisawa's murderous friendship.

Their processions moved together into the Nihonbashi merchant district. Commoners thronged the streets; shops overflowed with furniture, baskets, ceramic dishware, shoes, and clothing, while proprietors and itinerant peddlers hawked their goods to the crowds. The road narrowed, requiring that Reiko's and Lady Yanagisawa's processions either go single file or separate.

"I have an idea," Lady Yanagisawa said, her plain face alight with eagerness. "Let's go to your house, and Kikuko can play with Masahiro." She addressed her daughter: "You'd enjoy that, wouldn't you?"

Kikuko nodded and smiled. Reiko shuddered inside, wishing she could bar the deadly pair from her home. A feeling of helplessness combined with her anger and hatred toward Lady Yanagisawa and her fear of what the woman might do next.

"Then it's all settled." Love and envy smoldered in the gaze Lady Yanagisawa turned on Reiko. Oblivious to the wrongs of her actions, her own motives, and Reiko's dislike, she said with perfunctory courtesy, "Unless you have other plans?"

"None," Reiko said.

Yet she did have plans that she forbore to mention. First she must overcome the spells. She would need all her courage, wits, and strength to carry out her second plan: ridding herself of Lady Yanagisawa once and for all, before Lady Yanagisawa killed her or someone dear to her.

5

Sano and Hirata ate dinner in Sano's office before reporting for their audience with the shogun. Sano described Dr. Ito's examination of Makino, then said, "Detectives Marume and Fukida are taking the body back to the estate." He sipped hot tea, warming his hands on the bowl. "What have you accomplished?"

"I questioned everyone at Makino's estate," Hirata answered nervously. Every time since Sano had reprimanded him, Hirata feared falling short of Sano's expectations. "There are a hundred fifty-nine retainers and servants. They all claim they never saw Makino after he retired to his quarters, soon after dark. Most of them spent last night in their barracks. I think they're telling the truth."

"Why do you think so?"

Sano spoke in a tone devoid of criticism, yet Hirata hastened to justify his opinion: "Makino had a strict security system. He had guards patrolling constantly, checking on everybody. The men on duty last night vouched for the rest of his staff."

"What about the guards themselves?" Sano said. He thought Hirata was trying too hard to atone for his misdeed. Sano had already expressed forgiveness to Hirata and wished he would stop torturing himself. Having transgressed Bushido in his own time, Sano felt that one infraction, committed during extreme circumstances, needn't ruin a samurai. "Did they have any contact with Makino?"

"They say not." Hirata explained, "The guards patrol in pairs. Each man had his partner to verify his story. Partners are changed every shift. Makino made sure to prevent his guards conspiring against him."

Chewing a rice cake, Sano nodded, convinced.

"Furthermore," Hirata said, "Makino had guards watching his private quarters. They say no one was there last night except the four people who shared them with Makino."

"And those are . . .?"

"His wife Agemaki. His concubine Okitsu. His houseguest, whose name is Koheiji. And Tamura, his chief retainer."

"The people we met this morning," Sano observed.

"Makino's security system didn't extend inside his own quarters," Hirata said. "His staff told me that he liked privacy. There was nobody checking on those four people. I recommend interviewing them."

"We will," Sano said. "In the meantime, did you find any other signs left by an intruder?"

"No luck. The footprints outside Makino's study ended at the edge of the garden. There was nothing to show how an intruder got into the estate—or got out afterward."

"You asked the guards if they saw or heard anything unusual last night?"

Hirata swallowed tea and nodded. "They say they didn't. But it's possible that someone who knew their patrol routine climbed over the wall when they weren't looking, then sneaked across the roofs to Makino's private quarters."

"Did you examine the roofs?" Sano said.

"Yes," Hirata said. "The tiles were clean and unbroken. If someone did cross them, he was careful."

Sano pondered as they finished their soup. "There's another possibility."

Hirata nodded in comprehension.

"We'd better go, or we'll be late for our meeting with the shogun." As Sano rose, he added, "Good work, Hirata-*san*."

But his praise didn't clear the anxiety from Hirata's face.

They both understood that Hirata needed to do much more to regain Sano's complete trust and their close friendship.

The shogun's palace occupied the innermost precinct of Edo Castle, at the top of the hill. Sano and Hirata walked through the dusk toward the palace, along paths that crossed formal gardens. Autumn had stripped most of the leaves from the oaks and maples; only the pines flourished green. Guards patrolled outside interconnected buildings with many-gabled tile roofs, white plaster walls, and dark cypress beams, shutters, and doors. Inside, sentries admitted Sano and Hirata to the audience hall. They crossed the long room, where guards stood and attendants knelt along the walls. From the far end of the room, six men watched Sano and Hirata.

The shogun sat upon the dais, in front of a mural of a snowy landscape. He wore the cylindrical black cap of his rank and a quilt wrapped around him despite the profusion of charcoal braziers that overheated the room. The six other men sat below the dais, on the upper of the floor's two levels.

"I hope you, ahh, have a good reason for requesting this audience, Sano-*san*," the shogun said. His frail body, mild, aristocratic features, and hesitant manner compromised the authority expected of Japan's supreme dictator. At age forty-eight, he seemed elderly. "I feel a cold coming on."

Sano and Hirata knelt on the lower floor level and bowed. "A million apologies, Your Excellency," Sano said, "but I have an important announcement to make."

On the upper level, Chamberlain Yanagisawa sat in the place of honor at the shogun's right. Tall, proud, and slender of figure, he wore lavish, multicolored silk robes. His handsome face was serene, his luminous eyes watchful.

"And what is this important announcement?" he said in his suave voice.

"Do tell us, *Sōsakan-sama*." Lord Matsudaira, rival of Chamberlain Yanagisawa and leader of the opposing faction, knelt at the shogun's left. He was the same age as his cousin the shogun, with similar features, but his physique was robust, his expression intelligent. Formally dressed in black robes adorned with gold crests, Lord Matsudaira projected the authority that the shogun lacked. In recent months, he'd insinuated himself into court business. "You have our undivided attention."

He and Yanagisawa ignored each other, but Sano sensed their antagonism, like war drums throbbing. Also on the upper floor level sat four members of the Council of Elders, in two rows facing one another. Nearest Yanagisawa sat the pair of elders loyal to him. Opposite them, and nearest Lord Matsudaira, were his two cronies on the council. Senior Elder Makino's place closest to the dais was conspicuously empty. His colleagues, all men in their sixties, regarded Sano with wary anticipation.

Sano felt like a warrior setting off a bomb that he hoped wouldn't blow up in his face. He said, "I regret to inform you that Senior Elder Makino is dead."

The bomb exploded in perfect silence. No one moved, but Sano sensed shock waves reverberating and saw consternation on the elders' faces. Chamberlain Yanagisawa stared at the place once occupied by Makino. He couldn't control the dismay that registered in his eyes as he comprehended that he'd lost a major ally and the Council of Elders was now evenly divided between his faction and his rival's. Lord Matsudaira watched Yanagisawa with the gaze of a falcon ready to swoop down on its prey.

A sob burst from the shogun. "Ahh, my dear old friend Makino-*san* is gone!" Tears welled in his eyes.

Sano knew that Tokugawa Tsunayoshi was oblivious of the battle for power that raged under his nose. Since he rarely left the palace, he hadn't noticed the troops massing. He didn't know the two factions existed, because no one wanted to tell him. Now, Sano observed, the shogun didn't realize that the balance of power had just tipped.

"When did Makino die?" Chamberlain Yanagisawa asked Sano in a voice that sounded dazed, as though he couldn't believe the misfortune that had befallen him.

"Sometime last night," Sano said.

"That long ago? Why wasn't I notified at once?" Yanagisawa demanded. His face darkened with anger; he seemed ready to punish Sano for his bad luck.

"How did you come to learn the news first?" Lord Matsudaira said, enjoying Yanagisawa's discomfiture even while his tone chastised Sano for delaying the announcement. "Why have you kept it to yourself all day?"

"I needed time to honor a posthumous request from Senior Elder Makino," said Sano. "Before he died, he ordered his valet to deliver this letter to me in the event of his death."

Frowns of confusion marked the faces turned to Sano as he passed Makino's letter up the line of elders to the shogun.

Tokugawa Tsunayoshi read the letter, silently mouthing the words, then looked up from the page. "Makino-*san* feared that he would be, ahh, assassinated. Therefore, he asked that the *sōsakan-sama* investigate his death."

Chamberlain Yanagisawa snatched the letter from the shogun's hand. While he read, Sano saw his face acquire the glow of a man who has found light amid darkness.

"Let me see the letter," commanded Lord Matsudaira. He looked as though he'd just stepped from high, solid ground into quicksand.

With mock courtesy, Yanagisawa handed over the letter. Lord Matsudaira read, his expression deliberately blank. Sano sensed his mind racing to chart a safe path through the dangers that the letter posed for him.

"Have you begun investigating Makino-*san*'s death as he wished?" Yanagisawa asked Sano.

"Yes," Sano said.

"And what has your investigation revealed?"

Sano gave a carefully edited summary: "At first it appeared that Makino died in his sleep. But I discovered that his elbow joints had been broken so he could lie flat. And there were bruises on him from a savage beating."

Sano didn't mention the anal injury, which wouldn't have been noticeable from casual observation. He hoped no one would ask exactly how—or where—the broken joints and bruises had been discovered. To his relief, no one did.

"Aah, my poor, dear friend," moaned the shogun.

Yanagisawa greeted the news with an air of satisfaction. The discomposure on Lord Matsudaira's face deepened. The elders watched the pair, more concerned about present developments than interested in what had happened to their colleague.

"Did you conclude that Makino was a victim of foul play?" Yanagisawa asked Sano.

"Yes, Honorable Chamberlain."

"And who murdered him?"

"That remains to be discovered." Sano saw Yanagisawa's thin smile, and his heart sank because he realized that the chamberlain intended to use him as a tool in a scheme against Lord Matsudaira.

Tears and puzzlement blurred the shogun's features. "But everyone respected and loved Makino-*san*." Everyone else in the room looked at the floor. "Who would want to kill him?"

"Someone who stood to gain by his death," Yanagisawa said—and looked straight at Lord Matsudaira.

Lord Matsudaira stared back at Yanagisawa, clearly appalled by the implicit accusation, though not surprised: He'd expected suspicion to fall on him the moment he'd heard murder mentioned in connection with Makino's death.

The two elders allied with Lord Matsudaira sat still as stones. Yanagisawa's cronies visibly swelled with the advantage they'd gained. Hirata stifled a sharp inhalation. The shogun gazed around in befuddlement. Everyone except him knew that the chamberlain meant to pin Makino's murder on his rival. And if he succeeded, he and his faction would dominate the shogun and rule Japan unopposed. Sano's heart beat fast with alarm.

"Before we decide who killed Makino, we need evidence," Lord Matsudaira said, hastening to parry Yanagisawa's strike against him. "*Sōsakan-sama,* what else did you find at the scene of the crime?"

Now Sano found himself Lord Matsudaira's tool, and he

liked it no better than serving Yanagisawa. That each man wanted his support disturbed Sano.

The corrupt chamberlain had parlayed his longtime sexual liaison with the shogun into his current high position and kept himself on top by purging or assassinating rivals. He'd enriched himself by channeling money from the Tokugawa treasury into his own. Yanagisawa had treated Sano as a rival until they'd established a truce some three years ago. But Sano knew their truce would continue only as long as it was convenient for the chamberlain.

Lord Matsudaira was the nobler character of the two rivals, a wise, humane ruler of the citizens in the Tokugawa province he controlled and a crusader against corruption in the *bakufu*. He had more claim to power than Yanagisawa because he was a Tokugawa clan member. But he lacked the birthright to head the regime, even though he was smarter and stronger than his cousin. And Sano knew that Lord Matsudaira was as ruthlessly ambitious as Yanagisawa. Power wouldn't improve his nature. Sano hated the thought of bloodshed for nothing more than another corrupt man ruling Japan from behind the scenes.

At the moment, however, honesty compelled Sano to play into Lord Matsudaira's hands. "I found a woman's torn sleeve tangled in the senior elder's bedding."

"A woman?" Lord Matsudaira's alert posture bespoke his urgent wish to implicate someone else in the murder. "She was with Makino last night?"

"It would appear that way," Sano said, though reluctant to cooperate with Lord Matsudaira. "A stain on the sleeve indicated that sex had recently occurred."

The shogun squinted with his effort to understand the conversation. Chamberlain Yanagisawa scowled at the evidence that diverted suspicion from his rival. Lord Matsudaira relaxed. He said, "Then the woman could have killed Makino."

"She could have had the opportunity," Sano clarified.

Questions about Lord Matsudaira surfaced in his mind. Could Lord Matsudaira have been involved in the murder, even if there wasn't yet any evidence that pointed to him? Perhaps he wasn't an innocent man defending himself from political attack but a killer trying to escape punishment.

"So this woman is a suspect in the murder." Chamberlain Yanagisawa addressed Sano, but his glare at Lord Matsudaira presaged another attack. "Can you tell us who she is?"

"I'm sorry to say my inquiries haven't progressed that far," Sano replied.

Satisfaction gleamed in Yanagisawa's eyes. "Then you haven't determined whether she did kill Makino."

"That's correct." Sano felt the reply detach him from Lord Matsudaira's camp and place him in Yanagisawa's. Hirata watched the rivals in fascination, as if he perceived their invisible lines reeling Sano back and forth.

Lord Matsudaira forced a chuckle as he saw the advantage move toward his enemy. "But the *sōsakan-sama* hasn't proved that the woman didn't kill Makino." Or that I did, said his gaze, which encompassed everyone in the room.

Yanagisawa acknowledged his rival's parry with a faint sneer. "What else did you find at the death scene, *Sōsakan* Sano?" he said, intent on wringing every last piece of ammunition out of Sano.

Much as Sano loathed to help the chamberlain, he couldn't withhold important facts. "There were signs that someone broke into the study adjacent to Makino's bedchamber."

While he described the scene in the study, he saw Yanagisawa's sneer turn to gloating exultation and Lord Matsudaira try in vain to hide distress.

"The woman had nothing to do with the murder," Yanagisawa said, stating opinion as fact. "It's obvious that Makino was killed by an assassin who sneaked into his estate, then attacked and beat him, on orders from one of his enemies."

His hostile gaze at Lord Matsudaira conveyed the accusation that he verged on speaking. A thrill of horror shot through Sano. Would his personal quest for truth and honor ignite the war he dreaded? The elders loyal to Yanagisawa shot vindictive glances at their counterparts, who looked anxiously toward Lord Matsudaira. Sweat glistened on his face. He knew, as Sano did, that if the shogun were made to believe he'd had Makino assassinated, and done it to gain power, his status as a Tokugawa branch clan leader wouldn't protect him from the law. The shogun would execute him to crush the threat to his own supremacy.

But Lord Matsudaira rallied without hesitation. "Have you identified the assassin?" he asked Sano.

"I'm sorry to say I haven't."

"What? Do you mean he didn't leave his name at the murder scene? He didn't drop a letter ordering him to kill Makino, signed by his employer?" Lord Matsudaira feigned surprise; the sharp blade of his sarcasm lashed out at Yanagisawa. When Sano gave a negative reply, he said, "Then there's no proof of who the assassin is or who hired him. Is that true?"

"Yes," Sano said as the invisible line hauled him back toward Lord Matsudaira's side.

"In fact," Lord Matsudaira said, "there's no proof that an assassin did break into the study and kill Makino. Someone already in the house could have killed him. Someone could have planted evidence that an outsider assassinated Makino."

This was the alternative possibility that Sano had hinted at to Hirata before the meeting.

"Your Excellency, I suggest that the evidence was planted to frame an innocent man who is your own blood kin," Lord Matsudaira concluded.

His eyes glinted at Yanagisawa. Now came Yanagisawa's turn to sweat, Sano thought as the chamberlain rolled his tongue in his mouth. If the shogun became convinced that Yanagisawa had framed his cousin for murder, he would execute Yanagisawa for treason against the Tokugawa clan. Their liaison wouldn't protect Yanagisawa. He and Lord Matsudaira had aimed insinuations like deadly guns at each other. Who would fire the first shot?

"Would somebody please, ahh, tell me what you are, ahh, trying to say?" the shogun burst out. He flapped his hands at Lord Matsudaira and Chamberlain Yanagisawa. "I order you both to, ahh, talk sense instead of riddles!"

Dread and excitement rose within Sano. He sensed Hirata and the elders breathing in shallow, careful inhalations. Suspense froze even the guards and attendants. Would Yanagisawa explain to the shogun that he accused Lord Matsudaira of political assassination, or Lord Matsudaira explain that he accused Yanagisawa of treason? Would the shogun finally realize that they were fighting for control of his regime?

Would the two rivals escalate their covert maneuvering into full-blown warfare that would determine who ruled Japan?

"We're discussing the murder, Your Excellency," Yanagisawa said in a semblance of his usual calm, suave tone.

"We're trying to determine who committed it and how." Lord Matsudaira matched his foe's deliberate nonchalance.

"Ahh," the shogun said doubtfully.

Yanagisawa said, "Perhaps the *sōsakan-sama* has something else to report that could shed light on the matter."

He and Lord Matsudaira leaned toward Sano and focused expectant gazes, replete with menace, on him. Sano realized that they were too smart and cautious to proceed against each other without hearing all the facts. Each wanted Sano to say something that benefited him and hurt his enemy—or else. Now Sano saw fate hinging on his answer.

But the only possible answer was the truth. "I have nothing else to report at this time, Your Excellency," he said.

Lord Matsudaira and Chamberlain Yanagisawa sat back: Neither wanted to voice a blatant accusation that later discoveries could disprove. Sano saw Hirata's and the elders' chests inflate with breaths of relief. His own breath eased from him as he envisioned two armies retreating from the battlefield. But the clash between the rivals had fueled the impetus toward war.

"You must, ahh, fulfill Makino-*san*'s request to avenge his death," the shogun told Sano.

"With your permission, I will continue my inquiries," Sano said.

"Permission granted," the shogun said. "Proceed without delay."

"Your Excellency," Chamberlain Yanagisawa said, "this is a very important investigation. Therefore, I shall supervise it and make sure that *Sōsakan* Sano does everything right."

"As you wish," the shogun said, always ready to go along with his lover.

Dismay struck Sano. He knew from experience that Yanagisawa was capable of manipulating an investigation to suit himself. With Yanagisawa at the helm, the investigation would become less a search for the truth than a weapon to incriminate and destroy Lord Matsudaira.

Awareness of this certainty flashed in Lord Matsudaira's eyes. "The murder of a high Tokugawa official requires that a Tokugawa clan member lead the investigation. Therefore, I shall be the one to supervise, not the honorable chamberlain."

"Very well." The shogun yielded to the cousin that Sano knew he feared as well as admired.

Yanagisawa's face reflected consternation. Sano himself didn't welcome Lord Matsudaira's oversight any more than he did Yanagisawa's. A fight for survival could compromise the principles of the most honorable man. Goaded and threatened, Lord Matsudaira was just as capable as Yanagisawa of forsaking justice and using the investigation to persecute his enemy.

"The honorable Lord Matsudaira has no experience with investigations," said Yanagisawa, "whereas I solved the murder case of the imperial minister three years ago." He and Sano had solved the case together, but Yanagisawa had stolen all the credit. "Amateurs should stand aside and let professionals do the job."

"Perhaps you're right," the shogun said, wavering.

Lord Matsudaira glowered at Yanagisawa's slight against him. "Tokugawa interests are at stake," he said. "Only a Tokugawa is qualified to protect them."

"Indeed," the shogun said meekly.

"Excuse me, Honorable Lord Matsudaira, but I've been protecting Tokugawa interests very well for years," Yanagisawa retorted. "And my friendship with Senior Elder

Makino qualifies me to ensure that his wish is fulfilled. You, on the other hand, have no reason to care about avenging his death."

"Your emotions toward Makino will interfere with your judgment," Lord Matsudaira argued, his voice harsh and his complexion red with anger. "You can't supervise the investigation in a fair, objective manner. I can."

Torn between his chamberlain and cousin, loath to offend either, the shogun flung up his hands and turned to Sano. "You decide who will supervise you!"

Sano was appalled that the shogun had passed the decision to him. Chamberlain Yanagisawa and Lord Matsudaira wore expressions of displeasure that they'd failed to coax the shogun and he'd put their fate in the hands of an inferior. They fixed ominous glares upon Sano.

Once more, Sano sensed their antagonism rising toward the danger point. He pictured armies poised to charge. Again he saw the moment depending on himself.

He said, "Your Excellency, I would be honored to have both Chamberlain Yanagisawa and Lord Matsudaira supervise my investigation."

"You asked for them both?" Reiko spoke as if she thought Sano had lost his mind.

"My only alternative would have been to choose one of them," Sano said, "and provoke the wrath of the other."

He and Reiko lay in bed in their chamber. He'd told her about his meeting with the shogun, as well as what he'd discovered about the death of Senior Elder Makino. A lantern on the table illuminated their somber faces as they listened to Edo Castle's nighttime sounds of mounted troops and foot soldiers patrolling the streets and grounds, horses neighing and stomping in stables, and dogs barking somewhere on the hill. Sano ached with exhaustion from his busy day and previous night without sleep, but the meeting had left him tense and wakeful.

"I see," Reiko said. "Choosing one would have forced you to join his faction. I think you were wise to avoid that.

And whichever you didn't choose would have interfered with your investigation nonetheless."

"This way, perhaps they'll counteract each other's interference," Sano said without much hope.

"But now you'll have both Chamberlain Yanagisawa and Lord Matsudaira on your back, each demanding that you implicate the other in Makino's murder and each certain to punish you if you don't."

"Refusing to serve either one exclusively is my only hope of conducting a thorough, impartial investigation," Sano said, though he feared the consequences as much as Reiko did.

She turned to Sano. He took her in his arms and drew comfort from their closeness. "What happens next?" Reiko asked.

"Lord Matsudaira and Chamberlain Yanagisawa have both assigned men to observe and report to them on my investigation," Sano said.

Reiko lay stiff in his arms, and Sano perceived that she had other worries besides the murder case. "Is something else wrong?" he said.

She emitted a tense sigh. "I went for a ride today."

"That's good." Sano was glad that she'd recovered enough spirit to go outside.

"I ran into Lady Yanagisawa. Or, I should say, she ran into me."

Sano was alarmed. The last thing they needed was that madwoman plotting more mischief against Reiko.

"Please don't worry," Reiko said, clearly anxious to spare Sano more problems. "I can handle Lady Yanagisawa." She changed the subject: "What are your plans for tomorrow?"

"I'll go back to Senior Elder Makino's estate and start looking for suspects. His wife, concubine, chief retainer, and houseguest are likely possibilities."

"Is there anything I can do?" Reiko asked.

"You can make inquiries about the wife and concubine," Sano said. Reiko moved in social circles that were closed to Sano, and she often brought him inside information about

the women in a case. "And you can pray that the killer is un-
connected with either Lord Matsudaira or Chamberlain
Yanagisawa, and the final result of my investigation will
please them both."

6

Shortly after daybreak the next morning, Sano and Hirata arrived at Senior Elder Makino's estate with a team of detectives and two men sent by Lord Matsudaira and Chamberlain Yanagisawa to observe the investigation. A chill rain puddled the pavements, dripped from eaves, and soaked the black mourning drapery that hung over the portals. A sign posted on the gate announced the funeral procession tomorrow. In spite of the early hour, news of Makino's death had spread; despite the bad weather, numerous officials converged on the estate to pay their respects to Makino—or gloat over his death. Servants ushered them and Sano's party through the courtyard, which was rapidly filling with sodden umbrellas, and into an entryway crammed with swords and wet shoes. As Sano and his party followed the crowd along the corridor, they passed a banquet room, where maids bustled, setting out food and drink for the guests.

"Detectives Marume-*san* and Fukida-*san,* you'll cover the banquet room," Sano said. From a reception hall down the corridor came the hum of chanting and subdued conversation. "Inoue-*san,* you and Arai-*san* take the reception hall. The rest of you, patrol the rest of the house."

As the detectives went off to obey, Lord Matsudaira's man said, "Wait." He halted in the corridor, forcing Sano and

Hirata to stop. He was a heavyset samurai named Otani, in his late thirties, with a puffy face. His shrewd eyes regarded Sano with suspicion. "What are your men going to do?"

"They're going to spy on the funeral guests," Sano said in a low voice that passersby wouldn't hear.

"Why?" demanded Chamberlain Yanagisawa's man, Ibe. He was a slight, nervous fellow whose nostrils twitched frequently, as if scenting trouble.

Sano realized that his two watchdogs knew nothing about investigating crimes. He said, "Senior Elder Makino's enemies as well as his friends will be here. My men will be on the alert for any behavior or conversations that implicate anyone in the murder."

"But I'm supposed to watch your investigation," Ibe said, his nasal voice rising to a whine. "You can't send your men off to do things for you in different places, because I can't see what they're up to and stay with you at the same time."

"He's right." Otani gave his grudging support to Ibe, whom he obviously detested as a member of the enemy faction. "Lord Matsudaira said nothing should happen in this investigation without my knowledge. Call back your men."

Sano realized with dismay that not only did Chamberlain Yanagisawa and Lord Matsudaira each want him to incriminate the other, but their representatives might keep him from accomplishing anything.

"I need my detectives to split up because I can't be everywhere and do everything at once," Sano explained patiently. "If we stick together, just so you can keep an eye on us, we may miss important clues."

"Is that what your masters want?" Hirata challenged Otani and Ibe.

They exchanged uneasy glances, then shook their heads.

"Then let me conduct this investigation as I see fit," Sano said. "When my men report their discoveries to me, you can listen. I promise we won't hide anything from you."

Otani and Ibe nodded in disgruntled approval. They followed Sano and Hirata into the reception hall, where guests lined up in front of the dais, upon which lay the oblong wooden coffin. Below the dais, a kneeling priest with a shaved head, dressed in saffron robe and brocade stole, chanted prayers. Near him, Senior Elder Makino's widow and chief retainer knelt by a table that held a wooden tablet inked with Makino's name, a branch of Chinese anise in a vase, a smoking incense burner, oil lamp, offerings of water and food, and a sword to avert evil spirits. Tamura wore formal black robes. The widow was dressed in muted violet, her face pale with white rice powder, her hair rolled neatly atop her head. One by one, the guests approached the coffin, knelt, and bowed. Each lit an incense stick at the lamp and spoke ritual condolences to the senior elder's chief retainer and wife: "Congratulations on the long, prosperous life that Makino-*san* lived. I hope we all enjoy similar good fortune."

Sano, Hirata, and their watchdogs joined the line. When Sano reached the dais, he was startled to discover that the coffin was open, not closed according to custom. Inside reposed Makino, his head shaved bald. He wore a white silk kimono. A pouch hung around his neck contained a coin to pay his toll on the road to the netherworld. His sandals faced backward to signify that he would never return to the world of the living. Beside him lay a Buddhist rosary and a bamboo staff, almost buried in the powdered incense that lined the coffin and sweetened the smell of the corpse. Sano supposed that the open coffin gave Makino's friends a chance to say good-bye and his enemies a chance to see that he was really dead.

When Sano reached the front of the line, the widow received him with the same wordless courtesy she'd shown everyone else, but Tamura grimaced in annoyance.

"*Sōsakan-sama.* I've been expecting you." Obviously, Tamura had heard that Sano had pronounced Makino a victim of murder and the shogun had ordered the investigation to continue. "But I hoped you would choose a better time to come looking for the murderer."

Hirata, Ibe, and Otani prayed briefly over the coffin and lit incense. Tamura bowed to Ibe, representative of Chamberlain Yanagisawa, who'd been his master's master. He ignored Lord Matsudaira's man Otani.

"I'm sorry to intrude on the funeral rites, but His Excellency has ordered me to proceed without delay," Sano said. "I need to speak to the wife of Senior Elder Makino."

Tamura's slanted eyebrows bunched together in a scowl. "Surely you wouldn't ask a widow to desert her duty to receive her dead husband's colleagues."

The widow murmured, "It's all right . . . I must do the *sōsakan-sama*'s bidding." Her hesitant voice was so quiet that it seemed to drift toward Sano from far away. She rose so gracefully that her body seemed made of pliant flesh without bone. She flowed up to Sano as if her feet under her trailing robes skimmed upon air above the floor.

Sano addressed Tamura: "I'll want a word with you later. In the meantime, where are Senior Elder Makino's houseguest and concubine?"

"I don't know," Tamura said with controlled calm. "Somewhere around the estate." Mustering his dignity, he turned away to greet other guests.

"Find the concubine and houseguest and interview them," Sano told Hirata. Then he said to the widow, "Is there a place where we can talk privately?"

She nodded, eyes modestly downcast. "I'll show you, if you'll come with me."

Hirata moved toward the door. Ibe and Otani blocked his way, their expressions obstinate.

"This divide-and-conquer approach has gone too far," Otani told Sano.

"You're trying to avoid our observation by running too many inquiries at once." Ibe's suspicion of Sano allied him with his enemy counterpart.

"You must conduct the interviews one at a time," Otani said, "so we can be present."

Ibe nodded. Hirata looked to Sano, who realized that if he did as his watchdogs said, they would continue to dictate his every move. It was bad enough to have Chamberlain Yanagisawa and Lord Matsudaira trying to control the investigation, and Sano refused to bow to their lackeys.

"We'll conduct the interviews simultaneously," Sano said. "That's final."

Otani and Ibe glared. Ibe said, "I'll tell the honorable chamberlain that you're resisting his supervision."

"Go ahead," Sano said. "I'll tell him—and Lord Matsudaira—that the two of you are hindering my progress."

Indecision, and fear of their masters, blinked the men's eyes. "I'll accompany you," Otani said to Sano.

"I'll go with Hirata-*san*," Ibe said.

"At the end of the day, I want a full report on the discoveries that I didn't witness," Otani said.

"Same here," Ibe said. "And you'd better not leave anything out."

Hirata and Ibe departed together. As Sano and Otani followed the widow down the corridor, Sano felt glad he'd established authority over his watchdogs, but his head had begun to ache. The widow led him and Otani to a smaller, vacant reception chamber. She gestured for them to sit in the place of honor before the alcove, which contained a verse on a scroll and bare branches in a black vase. She knelt and waited meekly.

Sano and Otani seated themselves. "My apologies for interrupting your husband's funeral rites and intruding on you, Lady Agemaki," Sano said. He recognized the name of a princess in *The Tale of Genji*, the famous novel of the Imperial Court, written some six centuries ago. Makino's widow had a certain regal, refined air that suited the name to her. "But the circumstances give me no choice. I'm sorry to say that your husband was murdered." Sano explained about Makino's letter. "The shogun has ordered me to honor your husband's wish that I bring his killer to justice and avenge his death. Now I need your help."

Agemaki nodded, glancing at Sano from beneath lowered eyelids. "For the sake of my beloved husband . . . I will gladly help you."

"Then I must ask you to answer some questions," Sano said.

"Very well."

"I understand that you live in Makino-*san*'s private quarters. Is that correct?"

"That is correct," Agemaki whispered. Her speech had a prim, formal quality.

"Were you there the night he died?"

"Yes . . . I was there."

"When was the last time you saw him alive?" Sano asked.

Agemaki hesitated. Sano had a feeling, based only on instinct, that she was deciding whether to tell the truth—or how much of it. "I believe I last saw my husband soon after the temple bells rang the hour of the dog," she said. "That was his usual bedtime."

"What happened?" Sano said.

"We bid each other good night," Agemaki said. "I retired to my chamber."

"You didn't sleep in his?"

An indefinable emotion fluttered the woman's eyelashes. "No."

If she was telling the truth, then she wasn't the woman who'd had sex with Makino that night, Sano thought. The fabric and style of the torn kimono sleeve didn't match her age or marital status. He had no reason to doubt her word, except an unfounded hunch.

"Did you speak to your husband after you left him?" Sano asked Agemaki.

"No . . . I did not."

"What did you do next?"

"I went to bed."

"Did you hear any sounds from your husband's chamber?"

Agemaki slowly inhaled, then exhaled, before she answered, "I heard nothing."

"Would you please show me your chamber?" Sano said.

"Certainly."

She led Sano out of the mansion, across the walkway and garden to the building that housed Makino's private quarters. Otani shadowed them, frowning as he tried to discern Sano's purpose. Inside the quarters they followed the corridor past Makino's chamber and turned a corner. As Sano had noted yesterday, the building was roughly square, with the rooms arranged around the courtyard. Agemaki opened the door to a room adjacent to Makino's. Upon entering, Sano saw furnishings appropriate for an aristocratic lady—a dressing table with mirror and jars of makeup, an expensive brocade kimono on a stand, a screen decorated with gilded birds, lacquer chests and silk floor cushions. Sano noted the lattice-and-paper partition that separated the chamber from Makino's.

"Are you sure you didn't hear anything that night?" Sano asked Agemaki.

She stood by the door, hands folded in her sleeves. "I am quite sure."

Sano wondered how she could not have heard Makino having sex on the other side of the flimsy partition or being beaten to death one room away. Agemaki murmured, "I took a sleeping potion. I slept very soundly."

A reasonable explanation, Sano thought; but he pictured her sliding open the partition and stealing into Makino's room in the dark of that night.

Her face suddenly contorted; tears flooded her eyes. She dabbed them with her sleeve. "I wish I had heard something," she said, her voice broken by a sob. "Maybe I could have saved my husband."

Sano pitied her even as he wondered if her grief was an act. "Have you any idea who killed him?"

She shook her head. "If only I did."

"May I look around your room?" Sano said.

Agemaki gestured, granting him permission. He opened cabinets and chests, surveyed neatly folded garments and paired shoes. Otani stuck close by him, peering over his shoulder. While Sano searched for a murder weapon and bloodstained clothes, Agemaki watched mutely, indifferent. He found neither. Maybe she was the blameless, grieving widow she seemed.

"How long had you and Senior Elder Makino been married?" Sano asked her.

"Six years," she said sadly.

Sano had known she wasn't a first, longtime wife to Makino, whose sons were in their forties. She was too young to have borne them, and at least three decades younger than Makino.

"Were there any problems between you and your husband?" Sano said.

". . . None whatsoever."

"Had you quarreled recently?" Sano prodded.

"We never quarreled," Agemaki said with pride. A fresh spate of weeping seized her. "We were devoted to each other."

But they hadn't shared a bed. And Makino had had a young, beautiful concubine, as did many rich husbands. Marital troubles often arose from such a situation. Sano wondered if Agemaki knew he was seeking a motive for her husband's murder. If so, she would also know to deny any reason for killing him, as well as protect herself by appearing to cooperate with Sano's inquiries.

"Who is your family?" Sano asked, curious about her.

"The Senge. They're retainers to Lord Torii."

Sano recognized the clan as a large, venerable one, and Lord Torii as *daimyo* of Iwaki Province in northern Japan. "Have you any children by Senior Elder Makino?"

Agemaki sighed. "I regret to say that I have none."

"What will you do now that your husband is dead?" Sano doubted that Makino's clan, which was notoriously venal and exclusive, would support a widow from a brief marriage who had no strong political connections to it. "Will you go back to your family?"

"No. My parents are dead, and I haven't any close relatives. I will stay here until my official period of mourning is done. After that, I will live in a villa that my husband owned in the hills outside Edo. He left me the villa, along with an income to provide for me."

Sano's detective instincts roused. "How much is the income?"

"Five hundred *koku* a year."

She spoke as if mentioning a trivial sum. Perhaps she didn't realize that it equaled the annual cost of the rice necessary to feed five hundred men, a fortune large enough to maintain her in affluence for the rest of her life. But Sano had seen Makino's villa, an opulent mansion with beautiful woodland surroundings and a breathtaking view. Even a gentlewoman, ignorant of finance, would recognize the value of such an inheritance.

"When did you learn that your husband had left you the property and income?" Sano asked.

"He showed me the document the day after we married."

So she'd known before Makino died. The legacy hadn't been an unexpected windfall. Agemaki might have decided long ago that she preferred freedom and inheritance over marriage to a decrepit husband. And perhaps she'd gained them by killing Makino the night before last. Yet there was no proof, and Sano still had other suspects to investigate.

"That will be all for now," he told Agemaki.

As he and Otani crossed the walkway from the private quarters toward the main house, Otani said, "That woman doesn't look capable of murder. She seems genuinely upset about Makino's death. And if she's responsible, she wouldn't have told you about her legacy. Even an ignorant female must know that would direct suspicion toward her."

"True," Sano said, although he supposed that a clever one might volunteer the information, which he would have discovered sooner or later anyway. Her openness might be a ploy to make him think her innocent.

"What's next?" Otani said.

"It's time for a talk with Makino's chief retainer," Sano said.

"You'd better learn more from Tamura than you did from the widow." Otani's tone hinted at the wrath that Lord Matsudaira would inflict upon Sano if he didn't prove someone else guilty of the murder and do it fast. "You were so easy on her that even if she's guilty, you wouldn't have gotten a confession. Talking to her was a waste of time."

But Sano thought perhaps not, because of something that

Otani didn't appear to realize. Agemaki hadn't seemed the least bit curious about how her husband had died. Maybe she was too shy and reticent to ask. Maybe she already knew because the information had filtered from the palace to her household. Or had she not needed to ask, because she knew firsthand what had happened to Senior Elder Makino?

7

After a lengthy search of Makino's estate, Hirata located the concubine and houseguest in a room designed as a Kabuki theater. A raised walkway extended along one wall to the stage, a platform flanked by pillars supporting an arched roof. Striped curtains hung open from the roof and framed a backdrop painted with blue waves to represent the ocean. When Hirata and Ibe—Chamberlain Yanagisawa's representative—entered the room, they found the handsome young houseguest and pretty girl standing below the stage, at opposite ends. Hirata sensed that they'd quickly moved to these positions from elsewhere when they heard him and Ibe coming. A furtive air surrounded them.

"Koheiji-*san*?" Hirata said.

The young man bowed. Today he wore robes in somber shades of blue, appropriate for funeral rites. "That's me," he said with a nervous smile that flashed strong white teeth.

Hirata looked toward the girl. "Okitsu?"

She bowed silently, with eyes downcast. Her hands fidgeted with her purple-gray sash that bound a kimono of lighter tint.

Hirata introduced himself, then said, "I'm assisting the *sōsakan-sama* with his investigation into Senior Elder Makino's death. I must ask you both to cooperate in my inquiries."

"We're at your service." Koheiji made an expansive gesture that indicated his willingness to fall all over himself to help Hirata, if necessary. "Aren't we?" he asked Okitsu.

The concubine bent at the knees, as if she would rather sink into the floor. Her lovely eyes were wide and fearful.

"Hey, I heard that Senior Elder Makino was murdered," Koheiji said to Hirata. "Is it true?"

"Yes," Hirata said, wondering if the man had reason to know already. But Koheiji's nervousness didn't necessarily mean he'd been involved in the murder. Anyone, whether guilty or not, would be nervous when chosen for questioning in connection with a crime punishable by death.

"Oh." Koheiji hesitated, digesting the news. "May I ask how Senior Elder Makino died?"

Hirata thought Koheiji was a little too eager to learn how much he knew. "By violence," he said, deliberately vague.

Koheiji seemed about to press for an explanation, then changed his mind. "Have you any idea who killed Senior Elder Makino?"

"I'll ask the questions," Hirata said. "First, who are you?"

"I am a Kabuki actor and star of the Nakamura-za Theater," Koheiji said. He struck a brief pose, lifting and turning his head at an angle that flattered his profile. "Don't you recognize me?"

Okitsu gazed at him in admiration. Ibe leaned against the walkway and looked bored. Hirata said, "Sorry, I don't see many plays." Kabuki was popular among people from all classes of society, but Hirata had little time for entertainment. "What was your relationship with Senior Elder Makino?"

"He was my patron," Koheiji said.

Wealthy Kabuki enthusiasts often gave money and gifts to their favorite actors, Hirata knew. "What were you doing in this estate on the night Senior Elder Makino died?"

"He hired me to give private performances to his household. I've been living here for, oh, about a year."

What a cozy, lucrative situation, Hirata thought. Makino had been generous to his protégé, despite a reputation for stinginess. But Hirata wondered why Makino, a man so concerned about security, had moved Koheiji into his home, when actors were renowned as unscrupulous ruffians.

"What did you do to deserve the honor of sleeping in Senior Elder Makino's quarters?" Hirata said.

Caution veiled Koheiji's brash countenance. "I was his friend."

Hirata eyed the actor skeptically, because friendship wasn't the usual reason that a man wanted a handsome youth nearby at night. "Were you also his lover?" Hirata said, recalling Makino's injured anus.

"Oh, no," Koheiji said. Then, as Hirata looked askance at him, he added, "Makino didn't practice manly love. Neither do I. There was never any sex between us."

As Hirata counted more denials than necessary, he heard a squeak from Okitsu. She clapped her hands over her mouth. Her eyes bulged with alarm at the involuntary sound she'd made. Did it mean she knew the actor was lying?

Koheiji must have read Hirata's thought, because he spoke with defensive haste: "Hey, maybe I don't seem like the kind of person that Senior Elder Makino would have for a friend, but sometimes he got tired of the other people he knew. He liked to drink with me and talk about the theater instead of government business." Koheiji moved, blocking Hirata's view of Okitsu. "It was a nice change for him."

This explanation didn't convince Hirata. Had Koheiji penetrated Makino during sex that night and caused the anal injury? Had a quarrel later arisen between them and led to Makino's death? If Koheiji should turn out to be the killer, what a letdown! The actor was a nobody and an unworthy opponent, in Hirata's estimation.

Yet Hirata must conduct as thorough an investigation of Koheiji as Sano would expect. He must obey Sano's slightest wish, or mire himself deeper in disgrace. "When did you last see Senior Elder Makino alive?" he asked Koheiji.

"The evening of the day before he was found dead," Koheiji answered, too readily. "At dinner, I performed for him and some of his retainers."

"You didn't have any contact with him after the performance?" Hirata said.

"None whatsoever." Koheiji spread empty hands. "I haven't the faintest idea what happened to him later."

Hirata peered around Koheiji. He saw Okitsu's queasy expression. "You didn't speak to Senior Elder Makino, or go into his chamber that night?" Hirata pressed Koheiji.

"No, I didn't," Koheiji said. "If you're hinting that I killed him, you're wrong. With all due respect," he added, giving Hirata a courteous bow and another dazzling smile. "I had no reason to murder my own patron."

Ibe, who'd been listening in silence, now said, "That's a good point." He sauntered over to Koheiji. His nose twitched, testing the actor's air. "Now that the senior elder is dead, you won't get any more money or gifts from him, will you?"

"Sad but true." Koheiji sighed.

"And you'll have to move out of Edo Castle," Ibe said.

"Yes," Koheiji said.

Consternation filled Hirata. "Excuse me, Ibe-*san,* but I'm conducting this interview."

Undaunted, Ibe said to Koheiji, "I've seen you in plays. Your acting is good but nothing special." Koheiji drew back from Ibe, miffed at the slight. "Without Makino's patronage, you'd never have gotten your starring roles."

"You're just supposed to observe," Hirata said, angry even though his own direction of thought paralleled Ibe's. "Stay out of this."

"In fact, Makino was worth more to you alive than dead, wasn't he?" Ibe asked the actor. When Koheiji nodded, Ibe turned to Hirata. "Therefore, this man didn't kill Makino."

"He's right." Koheiji's surly expression said he hadn't forgiven Ibe, but he moved closer to him, glad of any ally under the circumstances. "I'm innocent."

"That's for me to determine," Hirata said. Ibe was undercutting his authority as well as intruding on his business. "Stop interfering, or I'll—"

"Throw me out?" Ibe smirked. "You can't, because I'm here under orders from Chamberlain Yanagisawa."

Hirata gritted his teeth.

"Besides, I'm just trying to keep you from wasting your time on an innocent man," Ibe said.

"Listen to him," Koheiji eagerly urged Hirata. "He's doing you a favor."

Hirata eyed Ibe with contempt, for he knew that Ibe had other, less altruistic reasons to steer suspicion away from the actor. He asked Koheiji, "What did you do after you performed that evening?"

"I went to take off my costume and makeup."

"Show me where."

Ibe rolled his eyes, signaling that he thought Hirata was wasting more time. As the actor led him and Hirata out of the theater, the concubine lingered.

"You come, too," Hirata told her.

She reluctantly trailed them into the private quarters. There, Koheiji showed Hirata the room he occupied on the opposite end of the building from Makino's. The actor had furnished his lair as a theatrical dressing room. A table under a lantern held brushes and jars of face paint. On wooden stands hung kimonos assembled with cloaks, surcoats, trousers, and a suit of armor. Wooden heads on shelves wore helmets.

"I specialize in samurai roles," Koheiji said.

That explained his hairstyle—the topknot and shaved crown usually reserved for the warrior class. While Ibe examined the armor and Okitsu hovered at the door, Hirata looked inside a trunk. It contained swords, daggers, and clubs.

"Those are my props," Koheiji said.

Hirata lifted out a sword. Its blade was made of wood, as were the other weapons, so they wouldn't cut anyone during simulated fights onstage.

"There's no blood on those," Koheiji said.

"How do you know what I'm looking for?" Hirata said.

The actor shrugged and smiled. "It was just a guess."

Hirata sensed that Koheiji enjoyed matching wits with him. He grew increasingly sure that Koheiji knew more about the murder than he would admit. But although a club from the trunk could have killed Senior Elder Makino, the actor seemed too smart to leave incriminating evidence in his room. Hirata opened the cabinet. He beheld compartments crammed with clothes, shoes, and wigs; stacks of handbills displayed Koheiji's portrait and advertised his plays.

"Please allow me," Koheiji said.

He carefully lifted out and displayed garments for Hirata's examination. Hirata supposed that if Koheiji had gotten blood on his clothes while beating Makino, he'd have destroyed them, but Hirata had to look anyway. He predicted that the clever actor would soon offer an alibi in an attempt to clear himself.

"You won't find any proof that I killed Senior Elder Makino," said Koheiji, "because I didn't. In fact, I couldn't have. I was here, in this room, all night. And I have a witness to prove it."

There he went, Hirata thought. "Who might that be?" He could already guess.

"Okitsu," the actor said, proving him right. "She can vouch for my innocence."

Hirata turned to the concubine, who huddled in the doorway. "Is that true?"

She gulped and nodded. Hirata beckoned her, and she crept toward him like a child expecting punishment.

"You were here, in this room, with Koheiji-*san*, the night Senior Elder Makino died?" Hirata said.

"Yes, she was," Koheiji said.

"Let her speak for herself," Hirata said.

Okitsu quailed under his scrutiny; she replied in a barely audible whisper, "I was here."

"All night?" Hirata said. If Koheiji needed to invent an alibi, he shouldn't have picked such an unconvincing partner. Perhaps he'd not had any other choice.

"She came while Senior Elder Makino and his men were still drinking after their dinner," Koheiji said. "She stayed until morning, when Tamura-*san* found the senior elder dead, and we heard all the commotion."

Hirata signaled the actor to shut up. "A murder investigation is a very serious matter," he sternly told Okitsu. "Anyone who lies will go to prison. Do you understand?"

Whimpering, Okitsu nodded. Her face was so pinched with fear that Hirata felt sorry for her. "Now tell me," he said, "where were you that night?"

Okitsu flashed an anxious glance at Koheiji. "I was here," she blurted. "Just like he said."

Perhaps she felt more loyalty toward him than fear of punishment for lying. "What were you doing?" Hirata asked her.

She glanced again at Koheiji, and panic shone in her eyes.

"Never mind him." Hirata gave the actor a glare that warned him to keep quiet, or else. "Just answer me."

"I . . . I don't remember," Okitsu said, looking everywhere except at Hirata.

"It wasn't very long ago," Hirata said. Koheiji must not have prepared her with a story to explain how they'd spent that night. "You can't have forgotten." Or maybe she'd just forgotten what he'd told her to say.

"I don't remember," Okitsu repeated in a timorous voice.

Hirata stood directly in front of her so she couldn't look to Koheiji for cues. "Well, then, did you leave the room at any time?"

". . . I don't think so."

"Then you might have left?"

"No! I didn't!" Fresh panic filled Okitsu's eyes.

"Was Koheiji-*san* ever out of your sight?"

She shook her head so hard that her plump cheeks quivered.

"Did he force you to lie for him?" Hirata said.

"No!" Okitsu wailed. "I wanted to." She hastened to correct herself: "I mean, I'm not lying!"

"Hey, stop it!" Koheiji burst out. "You're confusing her so much that she can't talk straight." He hurried to stand beside Okitsu and put his arm around her. She clung to him. "It doesn't matter what we were doing," Koheiji told Hirata. "The important thing is that we were together, and she'll swear I didn't kill Senior Elder Makino."

"I believe them," Ibe told Hirata. "We're finished here."

"Maybe you are, but I'm not," Hirata retorted. He would bet his yearly stipend that Ibe didn't believe the pair's alibi any more than he did. "And you don't dictate where this investigation should go."

"Chamberlain Yanagisawa does," Ibe said, "and he expects me to keep the investigation on the right path. So I'm telling you to stop bothering these people and move on to more likely suspects."

Suspects in Lord Matsudaira's camp, Hirata knew he meant. "If and when any more likely suspects turn up, then I'll investigate them," Hirata said. His patience toward Ibe snapped. "For now, just shut up."

Offense flared Ibe's nostrils. "Rudeness to me will do you no good," he said with a mean smile. "When the chamberlain hears that you're resisting supervision, he'll punish your master as well as you."

Now Hirata regretted speaking so bluntly. "My apologies," he muttered, although his spirit rebelled at having to placate his adversary, and in front of onlookers.

Ibe sneered, pleased that he'd subdued Hirata, yet not mollified. "Be a dog who barks up a tree while his quarry hides elsewhere, if you like," he said, "but be warned: Chamberlain Yanagisawa expects fast results from this investigation. If he doesn't get them, your head can say goodbye to your body."

But Hirata couldn't yield to Ibe's pressure to pin the murder on the Matsudaira faction. With great effort he pretended Ibe wasn't there. He contemplated Koheiji and Okitsu, who stood united opposite him. The alibi that Okitsu had given Koheiji didn't protect only him, but her as well. If the alibi was a fraud, as Hirata believed, then Koheiji could have had opportunity if not reason to kill Makino, but so could she.

"Let's have a look at your room," he said to her.

She glanced at Koheiji. The actor nodded, smiled in encouragement, then gave Hirata a smug look. He clearly thought Hirata would find nothing dangerous to Okitsu—or himself. Okitsu led the group to her room, which was on the same side of the building as Koheiji's. Movable partitions allowed passage from her room to his through a bath chamber located between them. Hirata wondered if they really had been together when Makino died and doing what many a handsome entertainer and pretty girl did on the sly. Maybe they didn't want to admit having a sexual affair that would cast a bad light on them, and that was why they refused to say what they'd been doing that night.

Inside Okitsu's room, the floor was strewn with clothes and shoes and boxes of sweets jumbled among dolls and other trinkets. But Hirata hardly noticed the mess. He inhaled a familiar sweet, musky odor.

"I smell incense," he said. On a table he saw, almost lost in a clutter of hair ornaments, a brass incense burner. He picked up the burner and sniffed the ash inside. "It's Dawn to Dusk, isn't it?" he asked Okitsu.

She nodded. Perplexity showed on her face and the actor's. Ibe twitched his nose, perturbed that Hirata seemed to be on to something. Hirata set down the burner, lifted a pink kimono from the floor, and sniffed the fabric.

"You perfume your sleeves with Dawn to Dusk," he said to the concubine.

"So what if she does?" Koheiji said.

"When the *sōsakan-sama* and I searched Senior Elder Makino's room yesterday, we found a torn sleeve perfumed with this same incense," Hirata said.

He watched the concubine and actor look at each other. Okitsu's expression was horrified; Koheiji's combined confusion with dismay. Hirata strode to the cabinet and ransacked through the clothing jumbled inside until he pulled out a pale silk kimono embroidered with gold and silver flowers. He shook out the robe and held it up. The long, flowing right sleeve dangled. The left was missing. Unraveled threads hung from the ripped armhole edges.

"Does this belong to you?" Hirata asked Okitsu.

She didn't speak, but her stricken eyes were answer enough.

"The sleeve we found came from this kimono," Hirata

said. "You were with Senior Elder Makino the night he was murdered."

Such stark terror branded Okitsu's face that Hirata knew he was right. "When you said you were with Koheiji, in his room, you lied," he said. "You were in the senior elder's bed-chamber. You'd better tell me what happened there."

Her mouth moved, uttering inarticulate sounds. She gave Koheiji a look that begged for help.

"She was with me. I swear," the actor said, but his face had turned pale and tense.

Grasping Okitsu by her shoulders, Hirata said, "Then how did your sleeve come to be in Senior Elder Makino's bedding?"

"It must have gotten there some other time." Panic trembled in Koheiji's insistent voice. "Let her go."

Hirata shook Okitsu. "What happened?" he demanded.

Her breathing escalated to rapid, erratic gasps. Stammers burst from her: "I—he—we—"

"Be quiet!" Koheiji shouted. "Don't let him scare you into saying what he wants you to say. Just keep calm. Everything will be all right."

Compelled by his own urgency to learn the truth, Hirata shook Okitsu harder. "Did you kill Senior Elder Makino?"

Okitsu's head fell sideways as her body sagged. Her weight slipped from Hirata's grasp. She crashed to the floor.

"Okitsu!" the actor exclaimed.

She lay inert, her long eyelashes resting motionless against her cheeks, her mouth slack. As Hirata stared in dismay, Koheiji knelt beside her and caught up her limp hand.

"Speak to me, Okitsu," he begged. When she didn't respond, he glared up at Hirata. "Look what you did! She needs a doctor. I must fetch one immediately." Koheiji ran from the room.

"Come back!" Hirata ordered.

The actor didn't. Hirata patted Okitsu's cheeks, trying to revive her. She was breathing, but she didn't rouse. "Go catch Koheiji," Hirata commanded Ibe.

Ibe just grinned. "That's not my job. Remember what you said: I'm just supposed to observe."

Hirata seethed inside.

"A lot you've accomplished here," Ibe said snidely. "I hope you're happy."

Hirata swallowed a retort that would get him in deeper trouble with Ibe. He wanted to groan in frustration.

He'd weakened Okitsu's alibi and connected her to the murder. But if, despite her lie, she hadn't killed Makino, then he'd hurt an innocent girl. Even if Okitsu was guilty, Hirata couldn't get any facts from her now. Hirata had also undermined Koheiji's alibi, but the actor had escaped him.

It was an inauspicious beginning for the quest upon which his worth to Sano, and his own honor, depended.

"Excuse me if I don't understand what we have to talk about that we didn't already discuss yesterday," Tamura said to Sano.

They stood outside Makino's mansion, on a veranda where Tamura had brought Sano when he'd requested a private interview. They leaned, facing each other, against the veranda railing that overlooked the garden. Mist and clouds obscured their view of the palace above the official quarter. Nearby, Otani loitered. Rain dripped from the overhanging eaves and wetted the floorboards. Sano suspected that Makino's chief retainer had chosen this cold, uncomfortable place in order to keep their talk short.

"There are a few matters I need to clarify," Sano said.

Tamura scowled as he intently watched Sano. "I told you that I found my master dead in his bed. What could be clearer than that?"

Your wish to limit your testimony to that one statement of fact, Sano thought. "Let's talk about the time leading up to when you found Senior Elder Makino. When did you last see him alive?"

"It was after dinner the previous night," Tamura said with a weary air of humoring Sano.

"What happened then?"

"I asked Senior Elder Makino if there was anything he

needed me to do. He said no and retired to his private quarters."

"What did you do after that?"

"I made my usual evening rounds of the estate. I checked that the guards were covering their territory and the gates were secure. My aide accompanied me. He can vouch for what I did."

"And then?" Sano prompted.

Tamura hesitated for an instant, just long enough that Sano perceived he'd chosen to omit or alter something in the sequence of events. "I retired to my own room."

After his talk with Makino's wife, Sano had privately inspected Tamura's quarters. These were two rooms—a bedchamber and adjoining office—located on the side of the building perpendicular to the one that contained Makino's chambers. Sano had noted the movable wall panel that separated Makino's bedchamber from Tamura's office. He was not surprised that the search revealed nothing of interest. Tamura was smart enough to guess that Sano would search his rooms and to destroy anything that incriminated him.

The office contained only records pertaining to the management of the estate. The bedchamber housed Tamura's few clothes, bedding, and other necessities, all stored with neat precision. A special cabinet held his armor and many weapons. Each sword, dagger, and club occupied its own rack. None of the racks were missing a weapon, Sano noted, and the weapons bore no traces of blood. If Tamura had used one of them on Makino, he'd cleaned and replaced it afterward.

"What did you do after you went to your room?" Sano asked.

"I worked in my office until midnight," Tamura said. "Then I went to bed."

"Did you hear any noises from Senior Elder Makino's chambers?"

Tamura glared into the rain. "Not a one."

"Senior Elder Makino was beaten to death in his chambers, which are right next to yours, and you didn't hear anything?" Sano said skeptically.

A dour expression curved Tamura's mouth downward. "I wish I had. Then I would have woken up and saved my master."

Still doubtful, Sano said, "Were you and Senior Elder Makino on good terms?"

"Very good." Pride rang in Tamura's voice. "I served him well for thirty years, and I was his chief retainer for twenty. Our clans have been linked for three centuries. My loyalty to him was absolute. If you won't take my word for it, just ask around."

Sano would. He planned to check the statements and backgrounds of all the suspects. "Had there been any problems between you and Makino-*san*?"

Flashing Sano a look of exasperation, Tamura said, "Of course. No two people can live and work together for thirty years in complete peace. I'll admit that he wasn't an easy man to serve, but I revered him, no matter that he got crankier as he aged. That's the Way of the Warrior."

Sano contemplated the nature of the bond between master and retainer. It was the closest, most important relationship in samurai society, akin to marriage, and fraught with tension. The master gave orders, which the retainer must always obey. Their unequal footing, and the constant need to efface himself, often grated on a samurai's pride. Sano thought of the trouble between himself and Hirata, and he could easily imagine that Senior Elder Makino had exceeded the limits of Tamura's endurance.

"Had you any recent quarrels with your master?" Sano said.

"I would call them disagreements, not quarrels," Tamura said. "When he did things that I thought were wrong, I advised him against doing them. That's a chief retainer's duty."

"What were those wrong things he did?" Sano said, hoping for reasons that Tamura might have wanted him dead.

"Nothing important." Tamura's tone said he didn't intend to elaborate.

"Did he reject your advice?"

A wry smile twisted Tamura's mouth. "Often. He liked making his own decisions. He was difficult to sway."

"Did you mind that he didn't listen to you?"

"Not at all. A master has the right to do whatever he wants, regardless of what his retainer might say."

Sano had the feeling that Makino had been a constant trial to Tamura, who didn't seem the kind of man to appreciate having his advice ignored. "How did he treat you?"

"Usually with respect," Tamura said. "But when he was in a bad temper, he shouted curses at me. I didn't mind. I was used to it."

Nor did Tamura seem a man to readily tolerate abuse. Sano said, "Did you ever want to punish Senior Elder Makino for mistreating you?"

"By murdering him, I suppose you mean." Hostility narrowed Tamura's eyes. "For a samurai to kill his master is the worst violation of Bushido. I would never have killed Senior Elder Makino for any reason." Anger clenched his hand so hard on the veranda railing that his knuckles whitened. "That you would even suggest I did is the worst insult to my honor. I should challenge you to a duel and make you apologize for your accusation."

Sano could tell that Tamura was serious, whether guilty of murder or not. The last thing Sano needed was to fight Tamura and either kill his suspect or lose his own life. "I'll apologize right now for making any accusation that's unjust," he said mildly. "But even you can see that the circumstances suggest you killed Senior Elder Makino. You were one of a few people in his private quarters with him. Your rooms adjoin his. And you found his body."

"That doesn't prove I killed him," Tamura scoffed.

"If indeed you are innocent, and you want to protect your honor—and your life—you'd best tell me everything you know about that night," Sano said.

An intense frown contracted Tamura's forehead, slanting his brows so sharply that they formed an inverted chevron over his eyes. Behind them, Sano saw thoughts churning.

Then Tamura relaxed his features and blew out a gust of resignation.

"All right," he said. "There was somebody else besides Senior Elder Makino's wife, concubine, houseguest, and myself in the private quarters."

Sano regarded Tamura with disbelief. None of Hirata's interviews with the residents had placed a fifth person near Makino. Had Tamura been holding this fact in reserve, like a wartime general hoarding ammunition in case the enemy got too close? Or was he inventing a new suspect to cover his own guilt?

"Who was it?" Sano said.

"It was Matsudaira Daiemon," said Tamura. "Lord Matsudaira's nephew."

The young man was the shogun's latest favorite paramour and rumored to be his intended heir to the regime. He was also a strong supporter of his uncle's bid for power and a vocal opponent of the Yanagisawa faction to which Makino had belonged.

Concern struck Sano as the investigation took a perilous turn. Dismay sharpened Otani's features because he understood that his master had just been connected to the murder.

"Why would Daiemon come here?" Sano said.

"He was visiting my master," said Tamura.

Sano couldn't imagine Makino allowing a member of the enemy camp into his estate, let alone his private quarters. "Why didn't you mention this earlier? Why didn't anyone?"

"Senior Elder Makino ordered us to keep the visit a secret," Tamura said. "We had to obey him, even after his death."

"So why are you telling me now?"

"Because I've decided that an occasion like this justifies disobedience." Tamura exuded self-righteousness. "Lord Matsudaira's nephew might have killed my master. I can't keep quiet about his visit any longer."

While Sano scrutinized him, trying to gauge his veracity, Tamura added, "The guards will confirm that Daiemon was here, as soon as I let them know they should."

Sano intended to talk to them, although he expected they would say whatever Tamura ordered them to say, whether it was true or not. "Suppose you tell me about this visit. When am I to believe it occurred?"

"Just after dinner ended," Tamura said, ignoring Sano's skeptical tone. "Everyone was leaving the banquet hall, when a servant came to tell me that Daiemon was at the gate, wanting to see Senior Elder Makino. I went outside and asked Daiemon why he'd come. He said Senior Elder Makino had sent him a message that invited him for a visit. I left him waiting and went to tell Senior Elder Makino. He said to bring Daiemon to his private chambers. I advised against letting in someone from the opposition." Tamura shot Otani a hostile look. "But it was one of those times when Senior Elder Makino chose to shun my advice. He ordered me to bring Daiemon. He said they had private business, and they were not to be disturbed. So I fetched Daiemon, delivered him to Senior Elder Makino's office, and left them alone."

"What happened then?" Sano said.

"I began my rounds. Later, the guards at the private quarters told me that Daiemon had just seen himself out." Tamura grimaced in disgust. "The fools let him go, even though we have a strict rule that no outsider goes unescorted. I immediately gathered the patrol guards and mounted a search for Daiemon. He was nowhere to be found. The guards at the gates never saw him. No one knows how he got out."

"So you're saying Lord Matsudaira's nephew had free run of the estate?" Sano perceived the implications.

"Yes. Maybe, while we were busy looking for Daiemon, he sneaked back to the private quarters." Insinuation echoed in Tamura's voice. "Maybe he finished his business with Senior Elder Makino."

"Or maybe your story is pure fabrication," Sano said. Not only did he distrust Tamura's motives for telling it, but there were too many unexplained details, including why Daiemon had come and how he'd vanished without a trace afterward.

"But you'll have to check into it, won't you? That should

keep you occupied for a while." Obviously aware and pleased that he'd given Sano a clue that pointed him straight toward peril, Tamura said, "Now if you'll exeuse me, I must get back to my master's funeral rites."

He bowed and went into the house. Sano turned to his watchdog. "What do you have to say about this?"

"Tamura was lying." Although Otani's brusque voice rang with conviction, fear gleamed in his shrewd eyes. "My master's nephew never visited Senior Elder Makino."

"Do you know that for a fact?" Sano said.

"No," Otani admitted. His puffy face was slick with sweat, despite the cold. Clearly he knew that if suspicion should taint the Matsudaira clan, all its associates would be in trouble. "But I think Tamura killed Makino himself, and he's trying to save his own skin by blaming Makino's enemies."

These notions had already occurred to Sano, but he couldn't swallow them without question any more than he could Tamura's story.

Hirata, accompanied by Ibe, joined Sano and Otani on the veranda. Hirata wore a chastened attitude; Ibe, a sardonic smile.

"What happened?" Sano asked.

Hirata told how he'd discovered that the torn sleeve had come from a kimono he'd found in the concubine Okitsu's room. He related the dubious alibi that she and Koheiji had given.

"That's why Koheiji seemed familiar," Sano interjected. "I saw him in a play."

Next, Hirata explained how Okitsu had fainted during his interrogation and Koheiji had absconded. "I've got detectives after him," Hirata said. "An Edo Castle physician is with Okitsu now. She hasn't revived yet."

Hirata's unhappy tone told Sano that he expected to be rebuked for the outcome of his inquiry. Sano did wonder if Hirata could have done better, but Hirata had found the origin of the sleeve and unearthed information that might yet prove valuable. And Sano wouldn't criticize Hirata in front of their watchdogs.

"The actor and concubine can wait," Sano told Hirata. "We have a new possible suspect."

He described how Tamura had implicated Lord Matsudaira's nephew. Interest cleared the unhappiness from Hirata's eyes.

Ibe jabbed Hirata with his elbow. "See? Didn't I tell you?" Ibe said. "The actor and girl may have been up to no good, but neither of them killed Senior Elder Makino. The murderer is exactly where I tried to steer you—in the Matsudaira camp."

"Don't listen to him, *Sōsakan-sama*," Otani said, glaring at Ibe. "He's just following his master's orders to attack Lord Matsudaira."

"Are you afraid your master is headed for a downfall and he'll take you with him?" Ibe gloated over his rival. "You should be."

Loud argument, rife with insults and threats, ensued between Otani and Ibe.

"That's enough from both of you," Sano said with such authority that the men subsided into glowering quiet.

"Something strange went on in this estate that night, but maybe Senior Elder Makino's wife, concubine, actor, and chief retainer weren't the only ones involved," Hirata said to Sano. "What's our next step?"

"We'll have the detectives check Tamura's story about Daiemon with everyone who was in the estate during the murder. In the meantime . . ." As much as Sano dreaded the consequences of what he must do, he said, "We'll have a talk with Lord Matsudaira's nephew."

Political unrest had transformed the enclave inside
Edo Castle where important Tokugawa clan members lived.
The once-serene landscaped grounds were crowded with
tents pitched to house troops that Lord Matsudaira had
brought in from his province. In this camp, hundreds of idle
soldiers drank, brawled, and played cards. Makeshift stables
sheltered their horses. Smoke from cooking fires blackened
the air. As Sano walked through the enclave with Hirata,
Otani, and Ibe, he smelled the stench of privies. The soldiers' restless presence filled Sano with apprehension. War
seemed inevitable unless the conflict between Lord Matsudaira and Chamberlain Yanagisawa was quickly resolved.

At Lord Matsudaira's estate, guards confiscated the
weapons from Sano and his companions and escorted them
into the armory. This was a courtyard surrounded by plaster-
walled, fireproof storehouses with iron shutters and doors.
Lord Matsudaira and a group of his men stood outside a
storehouse while porters carried in wooden crates. An attendant pried open one of the crates with a crowbar and lifted
out an arquebus. Lord Matsudaira examined the long-
barreled gun, then sighted down the barrel. The round black
muzzle pointed directly at Sano, who understood that Lord
Matsudaira was stocking his arsenal for the civil war. Lord
Matsudaira lowered the weapon.

"Ah, *Sōsakan-sama*," he said with a genial, expectant smile. "Have you come to bring me news about your investigation?"

Sano bowed. "Yes, Lord Matsudaira," he said, uncomfortably aware that his news was bound to displease.

Then Lord Matsudaira noticed Ibe. Anger darkened his expression. "Why is he here? How dare you bring in a member of my enemy's faction?"

"I'm honoring the agreement that requires my investigation to be observed by agents of both you and Chamberlain Yanagisawa," Sano said.

Comprehension and rancor dawned on Lord Matsudaira's face. "And your investigation has brought you here. Have you cast your lot with Chamberlain Yanagisawa? Did he send you to pin Senior Elder Makino's murder on me?"

"No," said Sano. "I serve only the shogun. I'm sorry to say that I'm here because I've found evidence that implicates a member of your clan in the murder."

"Which member?" Lord Matsudaira demanded suspiciously. "What evidence?"

"Your nephew Daiemon," Sano said. "He visited Senior Elder Makino in his estate the night of the murder."

The guards at the estate had confirmed that Daiemon had visited Makino, and they'd seemed to be telling the truth. They'd also said they'd heard the two men arguing. Although Lord Matsudaira's expression turned stony and impenetrable, Sano sensed his dismay that his nephew had become a murder suspect. Ibe watched Lord Matsudaira with an unpleasant smile that said he enjoyed watching his master's rival in jeopardy.

"I smell Chamberlain Yanagisawa in this," said Lord Matsudaira. "All of Senior Elder Makino's men are his lackeys. He put them up to incriminating my nephew."

"Perhaps," Sano said. He did wonder if Tamura had acted on his own when telling the story, or on orders from Yanagisawa. "But I'm duty bound to investigate every possible clue. Therefore, I must ask to speak with Daiemon."

"Certainly not." Lord Matsudaira's tone was defensive as well as adamant. "Daiemon didn't kill Senior Elder Makino. I won't have you treat him like a criminal."

"If Daiemon is innocent, it would benefit him to tell his side of the story," Sano said.

Lord Matsudaira dismissed this idea with a savage cutting motion of his hand. "There's one side to the story: My enemies are attacking me through Daiemon. You'll not interrogate him."

"For you to forbid me to question him will only make me think you both have something to hide." Sano knew his words verged on an accusation. He read danger in the look that Lord Matsudaira gave him.

"I don't care what you think." Lord Matsudaira's steely voice emerged from between lips compressed with rage. "I won't let you persecute my clan."

"Very well," Sano said. "Then I must tell the shogun that your nephew was at the scene of the crime and you're shielding him from my investigation. His Excellency can draw his own conclusions about Daiemon."

Lord Matsudaira glared in outrage and alarm at Sano. They both knew the shogun rarely drew his own conclusions. In this case, Chamberlain Yanagisawa would hasten to draw them for him. Yanagisawa would do his best to convince the shogun that Daiemon's presence at the crime scene, and his uncle's unwillingness to bring him forth, proved he was guilty.

"You won't tell the shogun about my nephew," Lord Matsudaira said. His tone threatened bloody retaliation unless Sano cooperated.

"If he doesn't, I will," Ibe said.

Lord Matsudaira gave him a contemptuous look, and Sano and Hirata a regretful one. He signaled his attendants. "Persuade them that it's in their best interest to honor my wishes."

The attendants drew their swords on Sano, Hirata, and Ibe. Sano realized that the fight for power had already corrupted Lord Matsudaira. The fair, humane, honorable man he had once been would never have resorted to violence to bend others to his will. As Lord Matsudaira's men advanced, Sano, Hirata, and Ibe backed away. They instinctively reached for their swords, which the guards had confiscated.

A youthful male voice said, "Call off your dogs, Honorable Uncle."

Sano saw a samurai entering the courtyard. He was in his twenties, with a ruggedly handsome face, a strong, athletic build, and a swaggering gait. He wore his two swords at his waist and an armor tunic and leg guards over his robes. Two attendants followed him, carrying his lance and helmet. Sano recognized him as Daiemon.

"I've been expecting the *sōsakan-sama*," Daiemon told Lord Matsudaira, then bowed gallantly to Sano. "I came as soon as I heard you were here. I overheard your conversation with my uncle, and I understand you want to see me. I'll be happy to speak with you."

Surprised by Daiemon's attitude, Sano looked to Lord Matsudaira. The man said in a warning tone, "Don't be foolish, Nephew. Go about your business. Let me handle this."

"Sometimes a little cooperation works better than threats." Daiemon's manner verged on disdain toward Lord Matsudaira's heavy-handed treatment of Sano. "For me to be open and honest with the *sōsakan-sama* is the best way to make him believe I'm not the murderer he's hunting."

"I'm trying to protect you," Lord Matsudaira said, clearly flustered by Daiemon's willfulness. Sano predicted that if Daiemon did become the next shogun, Lord Matsudaira would find him difficult to control. Sano also wondered how strong Daiemon's loyalty was to Lord Matsudaira. "Either do as I say, or risk consequences that you'll regret."

"Relax, Uncle." Daiemon patted the air in a soothing gesture. "I know what I'm doing." He turned to Sano. "Ask me whatever you like."

Lord Matsudaira glowered at them both. Much as Sano hated to offend the uncle, he couldn't pass up a chance to question the nephew. "Did you visit Senior Elder Makino at his estate the night he was murdered?"

"Yes, I did," Daiemon said.

Sano was disconcerted; he'd expected Daiemon to deny visiting Makino and offer an alibi for that night. "Why did you visit him?"

"To settle some unfinished business we had," said Daiemon. "A few months ago, I decided that Senior Elder Makino would be a valuable ally. So I began trying to win him over. He always resisted. But that evening, he sent me an invitation to visit him. When I got there, he told me that he'd made up his mind to join our faction."

Amazement struck Sano. He saw shock on Hirata's and Ibe's faces. "Are you saying that Senior Elder Makino meant to defect from Chamberlain Yanagisawa?" Sano said.

"That's exactly what I'm saying," Daiemon said.

Yet it seemed impossible. Makino and Yanagisawa had been cronies for the entire fourteen years of the shogun's reign. Not a hint of a rupture between them had Sano ever heard.

"Makino would never have betrayed my master," Ibe burst out. "His loyalty was absolute. He wouldn't have deserted the chamberlain, especially at a time like this!"

"I regret to disappoint you, but he did." Daiemon's callous tone said he wasn't at all sorry.

"Why would Makino defect?" Sano said, still disbelieving.

"I persuaded him that our faction was likely to be the victor in a war against Chamberlain Yanagisawa," said Daiemon, "and he wanted to be on the winning side."

Ibe started to protest, then fell silent. He looked as though his perception of the whole world had changed. Sano realized that Daiemon's story could also change the course of the murder investigation.

"So you can see that I had no reason to kill Makino," said Daiemon. "He wasn't the enemy any longer. With him on our side, we had a majority on the Council of Elders. He could influence the shogun in our favor. It was in my interest for him to stay alive."

If the story were true, Sano thought. "Who besides you was aware that Makino planned to switch sides?"

"My uncle was," Daiemon said.

Sano glanced at Lord Matsudaira, who nodded. Sano realized that he'd known all along that his nephew had been at the crime scene. He'd never denied it.

"Did anybody else know about the defection?" Sano said.

Daiemon shook his head. "We meant to keep it a secret."

"Why?"

A sly smile curved Daiemon's mouth. "It was better that Chamberlain Yanagisawa didn't know Makino had turned traitor. We wanted to use Makino as a spy in the enemy camp."

"Then I have only your word, and your uncle's, that Makino did betray Chamberlain Yanagisawa and join you," Sano said.

Daiemon shrugged, unperturbed by Sano's hint that he and his uncle had concocted the story. "It's the truth."

"Is it also true that you and Makino had an argument that night?" Sano said, recalling what the guards had told him.

"Yes," Daiemon said promptly. "Makino demanded a bribe in exchange for his allegiance. It was more than I wanted to pay. We haggled over the price. Finally we struck a deal."

But Sano conjectured that Daiemon could have invented this explanation because he knew about Makino's obsession with security and had anticipated that a spy in the house would overhear the argument. Maybe Makino had intended to defect, but when Daiemon balked at paying a bribe, Makino had changed his mind. Daiemon wouldn't have taken kindly the loss of a potential major ally, and he'd have seen the advantage of eliminating Makino. With Makino gone, and Chamberlain Yanagisawa's influence over the shogun weakened, Daiemon had an even better chance at the succession. The murder of one frail, helpless old man could have ensured his place at the head of the next regime.

"Then what happened?" Sano asked.

"We said good night," Daiemon replied. "I went home."

"Did you leave the estate right away?" Sano asked. When Daiemon nodded, he said, "No one there saw you leave."

Daiemon chuckled. "I played a little joke on the guards

and took a shortcut. There's a gate in the back wall. It's small, overgrown with ivy, and barred shut. I doubt if it's ever used. Probably the guards don't know it exists. They weren't watching it that night. I slipped out the gate, with them none the wiser."

Sano planned to look for the gate, which he didn't doubt he would find. He said, "If the guards don't know about the gate, then how do you?"

"I grew up in Edo Castle. When I was a boy, I explored every part of it. I amused myself by sneaking into places where I didn't belong." Daiemon smiled at his youthful daring. "I've been inside most of the estates, including the one you live in now. By the way, you'd better seal up that trapdoor outside the kitchen that leads to the cellar, if you haven't already." He laughed at Sano's disconcerted expression, adding, "I must know Edo Castle better than anyone else does."

His knowledge, and talent for stealth, might have come in handy years later. Sano imagined Daiemon sneaking back to the private quarters while Tamura and the guards searched for him, beating Makino to death, then fleeing out his secret escape hatch.

"There's evidence that someone broke into Makino's quarters," Sano said. If Daiemon had returned to kill Makino, he couldn't have entered through a door because the guards would have seen him.

"It wasn't me," Daiemon said with brazen nonchalance. "And I didn't kill Makino. He was alive when I left his estate."

"Can anyone vouch for your innocence?" Sano said.

"No, but you have my word. And my word carries a lot of weight these days."

Daiemon's smug smile alluded to his relationship with the shogun. Sano knew he was no meek sexual slave to his lord but a man who used his body and charm as weapons to get what he wanted.

"To accuse my nephew of murder would be a big mistake," Lord Matsudaira said, clearly hinting that the shogun would protect Daiemon and punish Sano for maligning his lover.

"I may have no choice," Sano said.

Honor required him to pursue the investigation no matter what. He'd reached a fork in the path of his inquiries. One branch led to Daiemon and Lord Matsudaira, and a perilous clash with them should his findings implicate them in Makino's murder. The other branch pointed the way to a new suspect who could be just as dangerous.

Daiemon grinned. "You've got a choice between sticking your neck in front of the executioner's blade or walking into fire, *Sōsakan-sama*. Because you and I both know there's someone besides me who bears investigation. Someone who'd have done anything to keep an ally from defecting— or to punish a traitor."

"Betrayal by Makino would give Chamberlain Yanagisawa a motive for murder," Sano said.

"It would have put him at a serious disadvantage against the Matsudaira clan," said Hirata.

They were walking through the army camp in the Tokugawa enclave, away from Lord Matsudaira's estate. Otani dogged their heels, while Ibe trailed behind them. Dark gray clouds still blanketed the sky, threatening more rain. Mutters and laughter emanated from soldiers huddled around fires and in tents.

"Makino's defection might have cost the chamberlain control of the regime," Otani hastened to add, removing aspersion from his master by shoveling it upon the enemy.

"And here I thought that for once Yanagisawa was above suspicion," Hirata said.

"My master wasn't responsible for the murder," Ibe said, but he spoke with much less conviction than before.

Glancing backward, Sano noted how shriveled and sick Ibe looked. He must be dreading how his master would react to Daiemon's insinuations. Yet Sano understood that although things looked bad for Chamberlain Yanagisawa, his role in the murder was debatable.

"The question of Yanagisawa's guilt or innocence hinges

on two issues," Sano said. "The first is whether Senior Elder Makino really was going to defect. The second is whether Yanagisawa knew."

"If he didn't know—or if Daiemon lied—then he had no reason to assassinate Makino." Hope brightened Ibe's voice. "As far as he knew, Makino was still his ally."

"Even if Daiemon told the truth about the defection, he claims it was a secret," recalled Hirata. "According to him, Yanagisawa couldn't have known. Yet he wants us to believe that Yanagisawa killed Makino for betraying him."

"Daiemon was telling us that although only he, his uncle, and Makino were supposed to be in on the secret, no secrets are safe from Yanagisawa," said Otani. "But let's not waste time debating the issue. There's one way to settle it: Accuse Yanagisawa publicly and hear what he has to say for himself." Eagerness to ruin the chamberlain blazed in Otani's eyes.

"Not yet," Sano said firmly. "Before I confront Yanagisawa, the theory that Makino planned to defect needs further investigation. Daiemon can't be trusted, because he's still a suspect himself. Neither can Lord Matsudaira, because he and his nephew are on the same side. I'll not have them use me as a cannon to shoot down their rival who may be innocent."

Sano reflected that "innocent" was an unapt term to describe Yanagisawa, who was guilty of so much. Still, it would be dishonorable to punish him for a crime he might not have committed. And if Sano was going to take on the powerful Yanagisawa, and break their truce, which had protected him for three years, he should prepare himself for a fight to the death.

"I want to be armed with evidence against Yanagisawa before I walk into fire," Sano said.

10

A separate compound within Edo Castle enclosed Chamberlain Yanagisawa's estate. Guards in watchtowers, and high stone walls topped by sharp spikes, kept out trespassers. The mansion was a labyrinth of interconnected wings surrounded by retainers' barracks. Deep within its protected center was the private domain of the chamberlain. In his office, where a painted map of Japan covered an entire wall, Yanagisawa sat at his desk on a raised platform. Below the platform knelt two men. One was Kato Kinhide—the shogun's adviser on national finance, a member of the Council of Elders, and Yanagisawa's principal crony. The other man was Yanagisawa's chief retainer, Mori Eigoro.

"What's the report on my war treasury?" Yanagisawa said.

Kato unfurled a scroll on the desk. He had a broad, bland face, with eyes and a mouth like slits in a worn leather mask. "Here is the balance as of today." He pointed at characters inked on the scroll. "And here are the tributes we expect to receive from our allies."

Chin in hand, Yanagisawa frowned at the sums. Lord Matsudaira surely had much more in his war treasury. Yanagisawa battled his doubts about the wisdom of challenging Lord Matsudaira. Yet it was too late for misgivings.

And determination had won many a battle against over-whelming odds.

"How many troops do we have?" Yanagisawa asked.

"Five thousand currently in Edo," said Mori. His lithe, fit physique contrasted with his pitted complexion, puffy eyes, and air of dissipation. "Two thousand more are on their way from the provinces."

But Lord Matsudaira had the entire Tokugawa army. Yanagisawa inhaled on his silver tobacco pipe, trying to calm his nerves. The air in the room was already hazy and acrid with smoke. Perhaps his downfall had begun.

"How goes our campaign to purge our opponents from the *bakufu*?" Yanagisawa said.

Kato presented another scroll that bore a list of detractors. He pointed to three names. "These men are gone," he said. "I convinced them to accept posts in the far north. They decided not to gamble that joining Lord Matsudaira would protect their families from you." Kato's finger touched a name near the top of the list. "After I tell him I've discovered he's been stealing and selling rice from the Tokugawa estates, he'll never lift a hand against you."

Satisfaction abated Yanagisawa's fears. "Very good," he said. "Where do we stand on allies?"

Mori opened a third scroll. Pointing to four names at the bottom of a list, he said, "Yesterday these men swore allegiance to you."

"It's a pity they don't have more troops or wealth," said Kato.

"Most of the men who do chose sides a long time ago," Yanagisawa said. "Not many of them are still available. Though there's one notable exception."

"Sano Ichirō?" said Kato.

Yanagisawa nodded.

"But Sano has resisted all our attempts to win him over," Mori said. "I think he's a lost cause."

Yanagisawa said, "We'll see about that." He and Kato and Mori smoked their pipes while they contemplated the scroll.

"There's one person we can cross off the list." Yanagisawa picked up a writing brush from his desk, dipped it in ink, and drew a line through Senior Elder Makino's name.

"How fortunate for us that he died at this particular time," Kato said.

"Indeed," Mori said. "After he decided to join Lord Matsudaira's faction, he was a mortal danger to us."

"You've never told me how you found out he planned to defect," Kato said to Yanagisawa.

"Makino started hinting that he wanted me to give him more money and authority in exchange for his support," Yanagisawa said. "I ignored his hints because he already had as much as he should, but I knew he would try to satisfy his greed elsewhere."

"So we had him watched," Mori said. "Our spies saw him talking with Lord Matsudaira's nephew Daiemon several times."

"Lately Makino had seemed afraid that our side would lose," Yanagisawa said. "When we added up his greed, his fear, and his relations with the enemy, we concluded that he would soon turn traitor."

Admiration for Yanagisawa's perspicacity glinted in Kato's eyes. "Makino could have done us much harm by spying for Lord Matsudaira while pretending he was still loyal to us. It's a good thing you caught on to him."

"We can be thankful that someone eliminated him and saved us the trouble," Mori said.

Yanagisawa watched his companions avoid his gaze. The atmosphere seethed with their suspicion that he was responsible for their stroke of luck. That he'd known about Makino's betrayal had given him ample cause to want his former crony dead. That he'd had a spy planted in Makino's estate implied opportunity to commit the murder. But Yanagisawa didn't answer their unspoken question of whether he was guilty or innocent. He wouldn't admit to the crime, not even to his most trusted comrades, for he knew they could betray his trust as Makino had done. Nor would he claim innocence, for he wanted them to believe him capable of assassinating whoever crossed him. Intimidation was his strongest hold over his subordinates.

Fear for his own future was his primary concern.

"Makino's death isn't an unmitigated blessing," Yanagisawa said. "The murder investigation is as serious a threat to us as he ever was."

Above Chamberlain Yanagisawa's office, a hole the diameter of a coin pierced the elaborate woodwork of the ceiling and overlooked the desk. In the attic above, Lady Yanagisawa lay on a *tatami* mat on the floor, an eye to the hole, peering through it at the chamberlain, Kato, and Mori. Their voices drifted up to her. Beside her lay her daughter Kikuko. A quilt shielded them from the damp winter cold. Daylight from grilles set in the peaked gables dimly illuminated their faces. Nearby, rodents scrabbled, their pungent odor fouling the musty air. But Lady Yanagisawa didn't notice the discomforts of this place from which she habitually spied on the chamberlain. All her attention focused on him, the beautiful, clever, and powerful husband she adored.

Throughout their ten-year marriage, she'd hoped for him to love her in return, despite overwhelming odds. Theirs had been a union of political and economic convenience. She came from an affluent clan related to the Tokugawa, and the chamberlain had wed her for her dowry and connections. Why else would he choose a woman so ugly, so devoid of charm? He'd engaged in sexual relations with her during the few months after their wedding, then stopped when she'd become pregnant with Kikuko. After he discovered that their child was feebleminded, he'd never touched Lady Yanagisawa again. For years he had ignored her and Kikuko. But although his indifference tormented Lady Yanagisawa, she still dreamed of winning his love.

To her joy, recent events had given her fresh hope.

Her abduction by the Dragon King, and her brush with death, had taught Lady Yanagisawa that life was short, and those who waited for what they wanted might die before ever getting it. The revelations had overcome her innate shyness. Instead of just spying on her husband from a distance, she'd dared approach so close within his view that he couldn't help noticing her. At first she'd lacked the nerve to speak, but one day, upon encountering him in the garden, she murmured, "Good morning, my lord." And miracle of miracles, he answered!

More emboldened than ever, Lady Yanagisawa insinuated herself into his life. On the rare evenings when he didn't go out, she served him his dinner. He talked of politics, vented ire at his enemies, celebrated triumphs over them. Lady Yanagisawa cherished those evenings and the privilege of his company. Yet he never said anything personal to her; he treated her as he would a faithful servant. His gaze never lingered on her, never reflected the need that burned within her.

Then one night she told her husband how she'd almost killed Reiko on the Dragon King's island. For once he looked at her with genuine interest. That drove her to even greater audacity. She began to frequent his bedchamber, where he'd slept alone since Police Commissioner Hoshina left him. In the mornings she brought him tea and helped him dress. At night, during his bath, she scrubbed and rinsed him before he soaked in the tub. The sight of his naked body filled her with such desire! But he never showed the least sign of wanting her. Why he allowed her this intimacy with him, she didn't understand. Perhaps he enjoyed her frustration; perhaps he was lonely now that Hoshina was gone.

Now, as Lady Yanagisawa listened to her husband talking with Kato and Mori, she realized that the chamberlain was in trouble. His problems created a fresh opportunity for her. In her mind coalesced vague plans for endearing herself to her husband and reaching her heart's desire.

"Surely Sano doesn't suspect that Senior Elder Makino was killed by someone in your faction," Kato said to Chamberlain Yanagisawa. "When he announced that Makino had been murdered, you did a superb job of pretending you were upset. You almost fooled me. Surely you fooled Sano as well as the shogun."

Yanagisawa prided himself on his performance, but he said, "I accomplished no more than to gain us time to protect ourselves. Should Sano learn about Makino's defection, he'll realize that Makino was worth more to me dead than alive."

"He won't learn it from us," Mori said.

"But Daiemon and Lord Matsudaira will tell him, if they haven't already," Yanagisawa said. "They'll jump to save their own necks by incriminating me. I'll become his primary suspect." Yanagisawa felt a grudging admiration for Sano. "He's like a dog who won't let go of a bone even if it bites him back."

"What shall we do?" Apprehension creased Kato's leathery face.

"The obvious course of action is to get Sano on our side," Yanagisawa said. "But in case we can't recruit him, we need an alternate plan to divert his suspicion and, at the same time, weaken the Matsudaira."

Just then, Yanagisawa heard footsteps in the corridor, approaching along the nightingale floor, which was specially designed to emit loud chirps when trod upon. Few persons were allowed in his private domain, and Yanagisawa recognized this one from his step. He dismissed Kato and Mori. After they'd departed, he called through the open door: "Enter."

In walked his son Yoritomo, seventeen years old, a youthful image of Yanagisawa. He had the same slender build and striking beauty. But his gait was hesitant, his expression perpetually shadowed by self-doubt. He had a sweet, vulnerable air of innocence, inherited from his mother, who was a Tokugawa relative and former palace lady-in-waiting, with whom Yanagisawa had enjoyed a brief love affair.

As he knelt cautiously before Yanagisawa and bowed, Yanagisawa felt a possessive affection toward him. The boy touched a tender, hidden spot in his heart. The blood they shared bound them together. And Yoritomo was not just the fruit of his loins, but his means to supremacy.

"My apologies for interrupting your business, Honorable Father." Yoritomo's voice was a faint, immature echo of Yanagisawa's. "But I thought I should tell you that the shogun has just sent for me."

"Excellent," Yanagisawa said. "That's the fifth time this month. The shogun's fondness for you is growing."

And every moment the shogun spent with Yoritomo was one he didn't spend with Daiemon, the rumored heir apparent. When the shogun named an official successor, Yanagisawa wanted it to be his son, not Lord Matsudaira's nephew.

"You've done a brilliant job attaching yourself to our lord," Yanagisawa said.

Yoritomo blushed with pleasure at the compliment. Yanagisawa recalled visits he'd made to the isolated country villa where he'd kept the boy and his mother. Yoritomo wasn't the only child that Yanagisawa maintained in this fashion—he had five sons, all by different women, living in separate households. He regularly visited them all, establishing himself as a figure of authority and watching them for signs of usefulness. But Yoritomo was not only the one most likely to attract the shogun; he was, from his infancy, the one most attached to his father.

Whenever Yanagisawa had come to call, the little boy had toddled to Yanagisawa and flung out his arms. Later, Yoritomo had recited his school lessons and demonstrated his martial arts skills for his father. He'd always excelled at both, but afterward he stood tense with fear, awaiting Yanagisawa's judgment. If Yanagisawa criticized his performance, he fought tears; if Yanagisawa praised him, he shone as though blessed by a god. His eagerness to please Yanagisawa continued to this very day. It moved Yanagisawa, as well as confirmed Yoritomo as his best chance of placing a son at the head of the next regime and ruling Japan through him.

Now Yoritomo said humbly, "I'm grateful for your praise,

Honorable Father, but I don't deserve it. Your teaching is responsible for any success I've had with the shogun."

Several years ago, Yanagisawa had hired one of Edo's best male prostitutes to instruct Yoritomo in the art of manly love. Although Yoritomo had no inherent taste for it, he'd dutifully cooperated and learned the techniques the shogun most enjoyed. When Yanagisawa had introduced Yoritomo to the shogun last year and secretly watched them together in the bedchamber, Yoritomo had performed with an expertise that ravished the shogun.

"We mustn't keep His Excellency waiting," Yanagisawa said now. "You'd better hurry to him."

"Yes, Honorable Father." Yoritomo obediently rose.

But Yanagisawa perceived a hint of reluctance in Yoritomo's manner. He felt the qualm that had struck a repeated, dissonant chord in him since he'd first pandered his own son to his lord. He knew from experience that the shogun's weak, aging body afforded little pleasure even to a partner who enjoyed manly love. Sex with the shogun could give only disgust to Yoritomo. Recalling too well that his own father had used him in similar fashion with the aim of advancing the family fortunes, Yanagisawa felt guilt, shame, and pity toward his son.

He hastened to intercept Yoritomo at the door, then put his hands on his son's shoulders and looked into the clear, guileless eyes that gazed back at him.

"You do understand why it's necessary that you please the shogun?" Yanagisawa asked.

"Yes, Honorable Father," Yoritomo said. "I must supplant Lord Matsudaira's nephew as the heir apparent. When the shogun dies, I must succeed him as dictator of the next regime."

Yanagisawa had drilled this lesson into Yoritomo during the five years since he'd chosen the boy as the best candidate to fulfill his political ambitions. "And why must you?" Yanagisawa said, anxious to make sure Yoritomo remembered the whole lesson.

"So that I can rule Japan with your help, Honorable Father," Yoritomo said dutifully. "So that together we will command supreme power over everyone else."

"What will happen if the shogun dies and you don't succeed him?" Yanagisawa said.

"We'll lose His Excellency's protection and your control over the *bakufu*," Yoritomo said. "We'll be vulnerable to our enemies. For me to become the next dictator is the only way to ensure that we survive a change in regime."

Conviction rang in his voice. He stood tall with his determination to achieve the goal Yanagisawa had set. Yanagisawa told himself that survival justified schooling Yoritomo to be a whore. Lord Matsudaira would have done the same with Daiemon, except Daiemon willingly prostituted himself. Daiemon, a rake experienced with both men and women, had no need of lessons on how to pleasure the shogun. Still, Yanagisawa's guilt toward Yoritomo persisted.

"Do you understand that what we're doing pains me as much as you?" he said urgently. "Do you understand that if there were any other way, I wouldn't ask so much of you?"

"Yes, Honorable Father, I understand," Yoritomo said with perfect, ardent sincerity. "I'll gladly do whatever you ask, because you know what's best for us both."

"I thank you, Son. I hope that someday you'll thank me." Humbled by Yoritomo's attitude, overcome by love, Yanagisawa squeezed his shoulders, then released him.

Yoritomo spread his arms, as if to embrace his father. Yanagisawa had a sudden memory of a little boy running to greet him. Then Yoritomo apparently recalled that he was no longer a child. He dropped his arms, bowed, and exited the room. Anguish and doubts plagued Yanagisawa. If he should be implicated in Senior Elder Makino's murder, and if he should lose the battle against Lord Matsudaira, then his sole hope for the future rested upon Yoritomo.

Lady Yanagisawa and Kikuko peered in through the door of the chamberlain's office. Inside, he'd seated himself at his desk. His hand plied a writing brush, inking a page with his elegant script. Lady Yanagisawa's heart beat fast with the excitement she always felt when near him.

Without looking up, the chamberlain said to her, "Don't just stand out there, come in."

Lady Yanagisawa crept into the room. Its air was charged with the erotic energy that her husband radiated. He glanced up and saw Kikuko trailing her. His face darkened.

"How many times do I have to tell you that I don't want to see her?" he said.

Lady Yanagisawa knew he didn't like to be reminded that he'd sired an idiot, even though he blamed his wife for Kikuko's defects. But Lady Yanagisawa hoped he'd come to appreciate how pretty and sweet Kikuko was. His treatment of their daughter caused Lady Yanagisawa terrible anguish, but not even this could diminish her love or need for him.

"I'm sorry," she said humbly, and turned to Kikuko. "Go to your room, dearest."

Kikuko, normally docile and obedient, clutched Lady Yanagisawa's sleeve. Her sunny expression turned plaintive. "Me stay with you."

Lady Yanagisawa realized that her daughter was jealous of her new relationship with the chamberlain. Kikuko had grown tired of being shunted aside in favor of a man who was a hostile stranger to her; she didn't understand why she must share her mother with him. But although Lady Yanagisawa hated to hurt Kikuko, she couldn't let her daughter come between her husband and herself.

"You must go," she said, pushing Kikuko toward the door.

"Me no want go!" Kikuko cried. She burst into sobs. She fell to the floor, pounding her fists, kicking, and shrieking.

"Get her out of here!" the chamberlain shouted, enraged.

Desperate to preserve her foothold in his life, Lady Yanagisawa carried the hysterical Kikuko out of the office and thrust her into the arms of a maid passing along the corridor.

"Take Kikuko-*chan* to her room," she ordered.

As the maid bore her away, Kikuko screamed, "Mama, Mama!"

Fighting the urge to rush after her beloved daughter, Lady Yanagisawa returned to her husband. He was pacing the room in swift, restless strides, as he always did when agitated. "If that ever happens again, I'll send the brat away," he said.

Lady Yanagisawa clasped a hand against her throat. That he might banish his own child and separate her from Kikuko! Stabbed by his cruelty, she suddenly thought of the reports from her spies in Reiko's house, who'd described Sano romping and laughing with Masahiro. Sano adored his child. Sano would never treat Reiko the way the chamberlain did Lady Yanagisawa. According to her spies, Sano made passionate love to Reiko almost every night. Reiko didn't have to act like a dog begging for crumbs of affection. Lady Yanagisawa seethed with anger and hatred toward Reiko, who had more than her share of good luck.

"Forgive me," she said as she knelt and humbly bowed to her husband. "I'll see that Kikuko behaves herself in the future."

"See that you do," the chamberlain said, pacing. "I don't need any more annoyance at a time like this."

"No, my lord," Lady Yanagisawa murmured. "I know you've been troubled recently."

He halted, and his gaze pierced her. "How do you know?"

Lady Yanagisawa didn't want to anger him further by confessing that she spied on him. "I—I've heard talk about you and Lord Matsudaira."

The chamberlain's sneer mocked her clumsy fib. She was mortified to realize that he knew all about her spying. Probably he thought her obsession a harmless joke. Why else would he allow her to intrude on his privacy? Blinking away tears of humiliation, she thought enviously once more of Reiko, who was Sano's confidante.

"It's true that Lord Matsudaira poses a major problem to me," the chamberlain said. "Unless I defeat him, I'll be ousted from the *bakufu* and run out of Edo—or put to death."

A gasp of horror rose in Lady Yanagisawa. Despite all her eavesdropping, she'd not guessed how bad things were. The idea of her beloved husband gone forever was too terrible to contemplate. Instead, Lady Yanagisawa was determined to change misfortune to triumph for them both.

"My lord—" The presumptuousness of what she planned to say caused her to hesitate.

The chamberlain gave her an impatient, quizzical frown.

She blurted, "My lord, I beg you to let me help you."

Surprise arched the chamberlain's eyebrows. "My troubles concern politics and war. Those are hardly the business of women. What could you do against my enemies?"

Lady Yanagisawa knew how small, weak, and useless she must appear to him and the whole world of men. She hadn't the slightest notion of how she might serve his purposes. But an unfamiliar, physical sensation of power flooded her like a magic spell born of her desires and his peril. She rose and stood directly facing the chamberlain. For the first time ever, she looked straight into his eyes.

"You'd be surprised at what I can do," she said.

The chamberlain stared, disconcerted, as if he, too, felt the magic. Then he bestowed upon her a smile so replete with approval and insinuation that a sexual thrill rushed through her. "I may give you a chance to surprise me," he said.

Just then, his principal secretary appeared at the door. "Excuse me, Honorable Chamberlain, but here are the latest reports on Lord Matsudaira's army."

The chamberlain flicked his fingers at Lady Yanagisawa, dismissing her. For once she didn't mind. She hastened from the room, filled with such gleeful anticipation that she ran outside to the cold, wet garden, where she spun around in an exuberant dance.

She would help her husband defeat Lord Matsudaira and gain supreme, permanent control over the *bakufu*. His love would be her reward. When he ruled Japan with her by his side, she need never be jealous of Reiko again.

11

Late at night, Reiko sat in her chamber, drying her freshly washed hair at the charcoal brazier. Her old nurse, O-sugi, came to the door and said, "Your honorable husband has arrived."

"Good." Reiko eagerly looked forward to hearing news of his investigation and telling him what she'd discovered.

When Sano didn't appear at once, she went looking for him. She found him outside the kitchen, a low building near the back of the estate, where cooks prepared the vast quantities of food required to feed everyone in the household. He and two servants stood in the yard that contained a well, outdoor hearths, and cooking paraphernalia. Sano held a lantern, while the servants moved a huge wooden tub.

"There it is." Sano pointed to a trapdoor in the ground where the tub had sat. "Seal it up right away."

"Yes, master," chorused the servants.

Icy wind chilled Reiko as she watched them from the veranda. "What are you doing?" she called to Sano.

"I'm plugging a hole in our defenses. Anyone who managed to climb the wall could sneak through this trapdoor, into the cellar, and then into the rest of the house."

Reiko beheld the trapdoor with surprise. "I never knew it was there."

"I only learned about it today," Sano said.

"How?" Reiko said.

"From Lord Matsudaira's nephew Daiemon. But it's a long story. Let's go inside, and I'll tell you."

In their chamber, a maid brought them sake, which Reiko heated and poured into cups. They drank, and Sano described the events of his day.

"So now Daiemon and Chamberlain Yanagisawa are both definitely suspects in the murder," Reiko said, alarmed by the dangerous turn the investigation had taken. "Whichever you pursue, you'll be in trouble."

Sano nodded. "And it's looking as though Yanagisawa is the likelier culprit."

"You've proved that Makino was going to defect and the chamberlain had reason to assassinate him?" Reiko said.

"Not exactly proved," Sano said. "I did find the hidden gate that Daiemon claims he used to sneak out of Makino's estate. That suggests there's some truth in what he said. And I've talked to my informants in the *bakufu*. They say they've heard rumors that Makino and Yanagisawa had a falling-out."

"Could the rumors have been spread by the Matsudaira clan to mislead you?"

"Possibly. That would explain why they've surfaced only now, after Daiemon became a suspect and needed corroboration for his story. But I can't ignore them just because I don't want to believe them."

Coals hissed in the brazier and the wind buffeted the mansion as they contemplated Chamberlain Yanagisawa as a primary suspect. Although Lord Matsudaira was just as ruthless, Reiko would rather have Sano pitted against him, because she feared Yanagisawa more. Yanagisawa, not Lord Matsudaira, had conspired to destroy Sano in the past. If Sano accused Yanagisawa of the murder, their truce would end.

"The fact that Yanagisawa has been implicated doesn't clear the members of Makino's household," said Reiko. "According to what you've just told me, they had the most obvious opportunity to kill Makino. And their stories about that night leave plenty of room for doubt. Can you apply more force to get the facts from them?"

"I will," Sano said, "but too much force can produce false confessions. I want the truth about this crime."

Reiko carefully chose her next words. "If one of them should prove to be guilty, that would solve many problems."

Sano nodded as he understood her hint that he could benefit by fixing the blame for the murder within Makino's household. "Even though Yanagisawa and Lord Matsudaira would each prefer that I pronounce the other guilty, each would be less angry at me if I persecuted somebody else than if I went after him. But I'll not risk punishing an innocent person for the murder." His tone was adamant. "Not even to serve my own interests."

"Nor would I want you to," said Reiko. "But will you at least continue investigating the suspects in Makino's own household?"

"Of course," Sano said. "While they're in his funeral procession tomorrow, I can search their pasts for clues to their guilt or innocence."

"I've learned some things that might help you with that," Reiko said. "Today I called on some friends. They say that Makino's wife was once an attendant at Asakusa Jinja Shrine. And his concubine once lived with a merchant named Rakuami."

Sano raised his eyebrows, signifying interest and approval. "That gives me a place to start investigating the women."

"I just wish I'd been able to learn what went on in Makino's house that might have led up to the murder," Reiko said. "But the folk there keep to themselves. Nobody could tell me anything about the relations between Makino and the people closest to him."

"Nor could my informants tell me," Sano said. "Only the people in his estate were privy to their own business with Makino. And since they're all suspects or potential suspects, I can't rely on anything they say."

Sano compressed his lips in frustration. "I had considered planting one of my detectives among the servants as a spy. But the residents aren't likely to trust a strange man who suddenly appears while they're under suspicion of murder."

A sudden idea occurred to Reiko. Her heartbeat quickened with excitement, daring, and trepidation. "What if you had a spy who was practically invisible?"

"If I did, I could solve the mystery in no time." Sano laughed, taking her suggestion as a joke.

"I'm serious," Reiko said. "You do have such a spy."

Sano regarded her with puzzlement. "Who is it you're talking about?"

"Myself," said Reiko.

"You?" Surprise inflected Sano's voice.

"Yes. I could disguise myself as a ladies' maid and wait on the women." Animated by enthusiasm, Reiko ignored the shocked look Sano gave her. "Maids are hardly noticed by their employers. People say and do the most private things in front of them. If you could arrange a post for me in Makino's house, I could spy to my heart's content and no one would suspect me of working for you. No one would even take a second look at me."

"I notice the maids," Sano protested. "A samurai is always aware of who's near him."

"Which of our maids brought us our sake?" Reiko challenged.

Sano pondered. Confusion clouded his eyes.

"It was O-aki," Reiko said, vindicated. "You don't remember because you didn't notice her."

"You did," Sano pointed out.

"I'm different from other people. I have Lady Yanagisawa to thank for that." Only by closely observing her maids, and weeding out those who showed too much interest in her, could Reiko rid herself of Lady Yanagisawa's spies.

"But I never talk about anything confidential when the maids are around," Sano said.

"That's because your life has accustomed you to being discreet," Reiko said. "But I think Makino's wife and concubine are probably just as careless as most people."

"All right, you win that argument," Sano conceded reluctantly. "But for an official like me to disguise his wife and send her out spying—" A gesture of his hand negated the very idea.

Reiko gave Sano a glance that reminded him how often they did things that weren't done by other people. "I could call on the wife and concubine, and ask them outright questions, but even a fool would know better than to admit anything to the wife of the *sōsakan-sama*. And if one of those women killed Makino, she was smart enough to alter the scene of his death and hide what happened to him."

"If someone in that house is the murderer, then it's too dangerous for you to go spying there," Sano said. "Someone who dared kill a man as important as Makino would certainly kill you to avoid exposure if you were to get caught spying."

"I would be careful not to get caught," Reiko insisted. "Besides, I'm trained in the martial arts. Makino's wife and concubine aren't. I can handle those women."

"Don't forget that two of the suspects in the house are men," Sano said. "One of them could be the killer."

"I've fought men before, and won," Reiko reminded him.

A sudden memory flared in her mind. For an instant she was on the mountain highway, fighting the Dragon King's men. The abduction had taught her the limitations of her strength. Now Reiko felt a bad spell encroaching. This time, the panic spawned by her ordeal bred new fear of what could happen to her in Makino's house. She'd survived one encounter with a killer, but she might not be so lucky again.

She gulped sake to quell the panic and hoped Sano wouldn't notice her agitation. She'd hidden the spells from him because she didn't want him to worry about her. And if he knew she had them, he would not only never let her spy, he might never let her help him again.

Sano was watching her hands tremble around the sake cup. "Why are you shaking?" he said. "What's wrong?"

"Nothing," Reiko said in a tone that denied any problems and implied that he was imagining them.

To her relief, the spell faded; yet Sano eyed her with wary

concern. He said, "I won't allow you to risk yourself. The investigation is my responsibility, not yours."

Although Reiko dreaded to leave home, and expose herself to terrors possibly worse than in the Dragon King's palace, spying on Makino's household now became a test she needed to pass. "It's my duty to help you," she said.

Sano shook his head regretfully and clasped her hands in his. "I almost lost you to the Dragon King. I can't bear to chance losing you again."

"But I believe that the danger to our whole family is greater if I don't go." Reiko withdrew her hands from Sano's restraining grasp. "If you can't prove that somebody in Makino's house is guilty, you'll have to go after Chamberlain Yanagisawa or Lord Matsudaira. Neither one wants to be punished for killing the shogun's dear friend. Either one would kill you to prevent you from naming him as the murderer. Maybe you don't mind sacrificing yourself for the sake of honor, but what about Masahiro and me?"

Sano's features clouded at the thought of his wife a widow, his son fatherless, at the mercy of a cruel world. But he said, "You might not be able to find evidence against Makino's wife or concubine even if you do spy on them."

Reiko nodded, acknowledging his logic, yet her resolve held firm. "What if you can't solve the mystery? The shogun will execute you, as well as all your family and retainers." A samurai who disobeyed orders from the shogun was considered a criminal, and the law decreed that the kin and close associates of a criminal share his punishment.

"Let's not assume I'm going to fail," Sano said, clearly affronted by the suggestion. "I've always succeeded in the past. I'll succeed this time—without involving you."

"I might actually be safer in Makino's estate than at home," Reiko said.

"How can that be?" Sano said, perplexed.

"Lady Yanagisawa is still after me," Reiko said. "I need a place to hide from her while I think what to do about her."

"In Senior Elder Makino's house?" Sano gave Reiko a

look of sheer disbelief. "You're seeking haven from one danger in a place filled with other dangers?"

"Lady Yanagisawa and her spies might wonder where I'd gone, but they'd never think to look for me there," Reiko said. "I'd be safe from her, while helping you."

Sano lifted his gaze toward the ceiling. His chest heaved as he blew out his breath. Reiko could feel him weighing the threats posed by Lady Yanagisawa, the factions, the murder suspects, and the investigation. She waited anxiously while he debated the arguments she'd presented.

He said, "I can't just take you to Makino's estate and order his people to hire you as a maid. They would guess why I wanted you there, if not who you are."

Reiko smiled. The fact that Sano was raising practical concerns meant he'd decided in favor of her plan. Apprehension filled her because the prospect of leaving home, in search of a killer, was now a terrifying reality.

"We'll think of a way around the problem," she said.

"I can't send you into that estate by yourself," Sano hedged.

"There are ways around that, too."

Sano remained silent for a long, suspenseful moment. At last he nodded. Feeling as much doomed as victorious, Reiko put her arms around Sano; he held her close.

"I'll go tomorrow," Reiko said. "I promise I'll discover things that will make you glad you agreed."

"I promise that no harm will come to you," Sano said.

With her face pressed against his chest, neither could see the other's expression.

12

The morning of Senior Elder Makino's funeral dawned clear, bright, and cold. Through the Edo Castle official district moved the procession led by black-clad samurai bearing white lanterns on poles. Wind ruffled the gold paper lotuses carried by more samurai. Priests followed, tinkling bells, beating drums, scattering rose petals on the ground, waving incense burners whose drifting smoke scented the wintry air. Tamura rode on horseback, carrying the funeral tablet, ahead of Makino's coffin. More priests, chanting sutras, preceded three palanquins that transported Makino's wife, concubine, and actor.

Sano stood outside his gate with Hirata and some of his detectives. They held the reins of their horses as they watched the procession pass, destined for the riverside cremation ground. Hirata said, "I see that Okitsu has recovered."

He sounded glad that his interrogation had done her no permanent harm. Sano nodded, preoccupied with worries that stemmed from the plans that he and Reiko had devised last night.

Last in the funeral procession came the household attendants, the men wearing black, the women in white. A few samurai officials trailed them.

"Not much of a crowd to escort Makino on his last journey," said Detective Marume.

"Everybody's afraid to leave the castle," said Detective Fukida. "They don't want to miss any political developments."

In the wake of the procession arrived another, which consisted of mounted samurai—Ibe and Otani, each accompanied by a team of comrades to help him observe Sano at work.

"What is the plan for today?" Ibe asked Sano.

"We're going to look into the histories of the suspects from Senior Elder Makino's house," Sano said. "I'll take the chief retainer and the actor. Hirata will take the wife and the concubine."

Hirata flashed a glance that thanked Sano for giving him an opportunity to make up for yesterday's fiasco, but Ibe and Otani burst into protests. "We should be hunting for more evidence against Lord Matsudaira's nephew Daiemon instead of those other people," Ibe said.

"I say we should look for more clues that Chamberlain Yanagisawa is the murderer," Otani hastened to object.

Sano lost all patience with his watchdogs. He was regretting that he'd let Reiko convince him to let her spy on Makino's household. Tense and edgy, he couldn't tolerate any more trouble from Otani or Ibe.

"We'll do as I say," Sano curtly told them.

He didn't mention that he would investigate Chamberlain Yanagisawa and Daiemon when necessary. He also forbore to tell them of Reiko's plan. Only Hirata and a few of his most trusted detectives knew he'd called in a favor and arranged her employment at Makino's estate.

Now he said to Otani and Ibe, "If you want to see anything to report to your masters, come with us."

He and five detectives mounted their horses and started up the street. Hirata and the other five rode in the opposite direction. Otani and Ibe exchanged indignant glances. Then Ibe sent half his men to follow Hirata, while he and the others hurried to catch up with Sano. Otani also divided his party, then he chased after Hirata.

"Where are we going?" Ibe asked Sano as they and their

men cleared a checkpoint in the winding, walled passage between the official district and the palace.

"To *metsuke* headquarters," Sano said.

The *metsuke* was the Tokugawa intelligence service that
guarded the regime's power over Japan. Its agents collated
and interpreted information gathered by a widespread net-
work of spies and informers. Sano now hoped to tap the *metsuke's* treasure trove of facts about citizens.

He and his entourage left their horses outside the palace
compound. They walked through the palace's labyrinth of
corridors, government offices, and reception rooms to a
chamber divided by paper-and-wood screens. Here, men
rushed back and forth between desks that overflowed with
scrolls, message containers, and writing implements. They
smoked tobacco pipes while they pored together over maps
hung on the walls; they conversed in urgent mutters. Sano
observed that the political unrest had the *metsuke* agents
working hard to keep abreast of developments and anxious
about their own fate.

As he hesitated near the door, the agents noticed him and
his fellow intruders. Talk gradually ceased. Sano scanned
the faces turned toward him but didn't find the one he
sought.

"I'm looking for Toda Ikkyu," he finally announced.

A samurai dressed in gray stepped out from a group of
agents. He bowed to Sano. "Greetings, *Sōsakan-sama.*"

Sano returned the bow. "Greetings, Toda-*san.*"

Toda, a senior intelligence agent, had such an indistinct
appearance that Sano always forgot what he looked like,
even after consulting him often during past investigations.
He was neither short nor tall, fat nor thin, old nor young. He
had a face that no one would remember—an advantage in
his profession.

"Let me guess," Toda said. "You've come to get my help
in investigating Senior Elder Makino's murder." Now his
world-weary voice and manner jibed with Sano's vague
memory. Toda's gaze took in the men ranged behind Sano.

"And you've brought the observers assigned to you by Chamberlain Yanagisawa and Lord Matsudaira."

As usual, he demonstrated his knowledge about what went on in the *bakufu*. He moved partitions, enlarging the space around his desk. "Please make yourselves comfortable," he said.

"Thank you," Sano said.

He and his detectives knelt on the floor; Ibe and his men, and Lord Matsudaira's, crowded around them. Sano knew that despite the ready welcome, Toda wasn't eager to part with information: The *metsuke* jealously hoarded knowledge, the basis of its unique power. But Toda dared not refuse to help apprehend the killer of the shogun's friend and high official.

"I have Makino's dossier right here." Toda sat behind his desk and placed his hands atop a ledger. "Which of your murder suspects among his associates do you wish me to tell you about?"

"Start with Makino's wife and concubine," Sano said.

Toda paged through the ledger. "I've nothing listed on them except the dates that Makino married Agemaki and brought Okitsu into his house. There was no reason to think they merited our attention, until now."

Sano reflected that the entire *bakufu* considered most women too unimportant to notice. Reiko had proved more helpful in this instance. "What about the actor?"

"Here he is," Toda said, pointing to a column of text. "Born Yuichi, son of a teahouse owner, twenty-five years ago. Present stage name Koheiji; employed at the Nakamura-za Theater; specializes in samurai roles. Formerly known as Kozakura and employed at the Owari Theater. There's no record that he's ever been in any trouble. He was considered harmless company for Senior Elder Makino."

Sano memorized the information for later use. "What do you have on Tamura?"

Toda scanned several pages, then summarized, "Tamura Banzan, age forty-seven. Hereditary vassal to Makino. He's renowned as a sword fighter, but his combat experience has been confined to the training grounds." Toda met Sano's eyes and added, "A samurai with his taste for the martial arts has usually blooded his sword at least once by his age. But there's no record that Tamura has ever killed."

"A record free of killings doesn't exonerate him," Sano said, "nor does it prove he's incapable of murder." A bureaucrat like Tamura had few occasions to fight to the death. "What can you tell me about Tamura's relations with Senior Elder Makino?"

"Sources within Makino's retinue have reported frequent altercations between him and Tamura."

"Altercations about what?"

"Makino had a habit of demanding money from lesser *bakufu* officials," Toda said. "Since he had the power to ruin them if they didn't pay, they seldom resisted him. Tamura disapproved of this habit. He also disapproved of Makino's profligate relations with women. Tamura told Makino that his extreme greed for money and sex was a transgression against Bushido."

The warrior code of honor decreed that money was dirty and beneath the notice of a samurai, who should rise above material concerns. He should also abstain from over-indulging in the pleasures of the flesh, which distracted him from duty. Sano observed that the conflict between Tamura and Makino had run far deeper than Tamura had suggested.

"How did Makino react when Tamura accused him of dishonor?" Sano asked.

"Makino was understandably insulted," Toda answered. "He said his personal affairs were none of Tamura's business, he would do as he pleased, and if Tamura didn't keep his mouth shut, he would lose his post."

To be dismissed from the servitude that gave him a livelihood, a respectable place in society, and meaning to his existence was a catastrophe for a samurai.

"Tamura should have humbly accepted Makino's judgment and never raised the subject again," Toda said. This was the custom when a samurai exercised his duty to criticize his master and the master spurned the criticism. "But Tamura considered Makino's faults a personal insult to himself. He kept after Makino to change his habits. His objections, and Makino's threats, grew louder and more violent over the years. They came to despise each other. But Tamura was a competent, valuable chief retainer. Makino needed him."

"Makino died before their problems could result in Tamura's dismissal," Sano said thoughtfully. "And now that Makino is gone, one of his sons will take his place as head of the clan."

Toda nodded, giving credence to this suggestion that Tamura had killed Makino to keep his post and gain a new master more worthy of him.

"But Tamura prizes his own honor," Ibe broke in, obviously displeased to see suspicion gathering around the chief retainer instead of Lord Matsudaira. "He wouldn't have committed the ultimate sin of murdering his master."

"Allow me to remind you that there's one instance when murdering one's master is justified," Toda said.

"That's when the master is such an incorrigible disgrace that only his death can redeem his honor," Sano said. "If Tamura believed this to be the case, he'd have considered it his duty to kill Makino."

"But Tamura wouldn't have killed a favored friend of the shogun," Ibe protested. "He wouldn't have wanted to offend our lord—or risk the punishment."

"Whoever killed Makino tried to cover up the murder," Sano said. "Maybe Tamura did it in order to escape the consequences."

"Here's some news that might interest you," Toda said. "Late yesterday, Tamura swore out a vendetta."

Vendetta was the means by which a citizen could exact personal revenge for a serious offense, usually the murder of a relative. The law required the avenger to follow a strict procedure. He must first present to the authorities a letter of complaint that described the offense and named his enemy. The authorities would grant him permission to slay his foe. The avenger would locate his enemy, declare his aim to kill him, and specify the reason. The two would then fight a duel to the death. If the avenger won, he presented the head of his foe to the officials who had authorized the vendetta. The advantage of this system was that as long as the avenger followed the rules, he could murder his foe and walk away a free man. The disadvantage was that the procedure allowed his target to hear about the vendetta and run, hide, or otherwise protect himself.

"Against whom did Tamura swear this vendetta?" Sano said, puzzled.

"The murderer of Senior Elder Makino," said Toda. "Tamura wrote in his complaint that he can't specify the name of his target because he doesn't yet know who killed his master."

"But his vendetta was sanctioned anyway?" Sano had thought that any deviation from the rules would cause the authorities to reject a vendetta.

"The magistrate apparently decided that the circumstances justified bending the rules," Toda said.

A samurai owed his master an even greater loyalty after death than in life. Should his master die by foul play, a samurai had the right and solemn duty to avenge him. This explained why the magistrate had made an exception for Tamura. Now Sano perceived the implications that Tamura's vendetta had for his investigation.

"Well, now there's all the more reason to believe that Tamura isn't the killer," Ibe said, voicing Sano's thoughts. "He wouldn't swear out a vendetta on himself."

"He might, to make himself appear innocent," Sano said.

"That's mere, unfounded supposition," Ibe scoffed. "You know as well as I that the killer is most likely someone outside Makino's circle."

He cut a hostile glance at Lord Matsudaira's men. They'd been listening in attentive quiet, but now one of them rose to Ibe's bait: "I agree that we're seeking the killer in the wrong place." A young samurai with a hungry look of ambition, he said to Toda, "What information do you have about Chamberlain Yanagisawa that might indicate he's behind the murder?"

Caution hooded the *metsuke* agent's eyes. "I've nothing to say on the subject of the chamberlain."

"How prudent you are," Ibe said. His smirk expressed condescension toward Toda and triumph over the man who'd asked about Yanagisawa. "Remember that the chamberlain controls the *metsuke*," he told the Matsudaira contingent. "Don't expect it to serve your master." He said to Toda, "What I want to know is, can you connect Lord Matsudaira to the murder?"

"I've nothing to say about him, either," Toda said.

"Remember that your master's position is subject to change," the young samurai told Ibe. His gaze challenged Toda. "When the dust settles, you may find that the *metsuke* has lost the chamberlain's protection and you need new friends. So you'd better answer my question."

Toda's face was perfectly still and calm; yet Sano sensed him trying to navigate a safe path between the two factions. At last he spoke: "Chamberlain Yanagisawa had a spy in Senior Elder Makino's retinue." Ibe exclaimed in angry protest, while the Matsudaira man grinned, triumphant. Toda continued smoothly, "So did Lord Matsudaira." The Matsudaira man frowned; Ibe's protests subsided. "Yanagisawa's spy is a guard named Eiichi," Toda said to Sano. "Lord Matsudaira's is a guard named Sayama. You may want to ask them what they were doing the night Senior Elder Makino died."

Ibe and the Matsudaira man looked nonplussed; neither spoke. Each was obviously glad to have the opposition incriminated yet at the same time fearful that Toda would further compromise his master. Although perturbed that Toda had handed him new evidence connected to the warring factions, Sano felt a reluctant admiration for Toda's finesse at placating both sides but favoring neither.

"What I've told you should be enough to occupy you for a while." Toda gave Sano a rueful smile that recognized him as a comrade in the same battle for survival. "If you need any more help, by all means ask me again."

As Sano thanked Toda and rose to leave, the tension in him wound tighter; his misgivings about the investigation burgeoned. By this afternoon, Reiko would take her position in Makino's estate, among four murder suspects.

13

Hirata and his comrades from Sano's detective
corps rode through the Nihonbashi merchant district. The
shops that lined the narrow, winding streets crowded them
together, and housewives, porters, and laborers on foot hin-
dered their progress. After them hastened Otani, accompanied by Lord Matsudaira's and Chamberlain Yanagisawa's
other men. As their horses trampled wares set outside for
sale, shopkeepers cried out and mothers rushed to yank children out of their path. Hirata felt irritably conspicuous and
hampered by his watchdogs in his efforts to solve the crime.

At least he didn't have Ibe to rile him. And he did have an
advantage that would help him investigate Makino's concubine. The merchant named Rakuami, with whom Okitsu had
previously lived, was an old acquaintance of Hirata's.

Now Hirata arrived in a lane bordered on one side by a
dignified row of substantial houses with heavy tile roofs, low
earthen walls, and roofed gates—the abodes of prosperous
merchants. Opposite stood a lone mansion. Its walls enclosed a spacious garden, and its eaves sported gay red
lanterns. The gate was open, revealing a gravel path that led
to the door. Samisen music and raucous laughter emanated
from within the premises. As the detectives and watchdogs
grouped around Hirata, a party of dandyish samurai strolled
in through the gate.

"What kind of place is this?" Otani said.

"You'll see," Hirata said.

They secured their mounts to posts near the gate, then went inside the mansion. Beyond the entryway, which was filled with shoes and swords left by guests, men lolled on cushions in a parlor. Pretty young women dressed in colorful robes served the men drinks, flirted and played cards with them, or sat on their laps. A comely youth plinked the samisen, while maids circulated with trays of food. As Hirata and his companions paused at the threshold, a samurai and a girl walked together to a man who stood by a doorway. The samurai dropped coins into the man's hand. The girl led the samurai through the doorway and down a corridor, from which came giggles, grunts, and moans.

"This is an illegal brothel," Otani said.

"Good guess," Hirata said.

Although prostitution in Edo was officially confined to the licensed Yoshiwara pleasure quarter, it flourished throughout the city. Private establishments served men who couldn't afford the high prices in Yoshiwara or didn't want to travel so far. This exclusive establishment catered to the wealthiest, most prominent clientele.

A man rose from amid the revelry. "Greetings, Hirata-*san*," he called. His face was round, his head bald, his age nearing sixty, his manner genial. He wore a red-and-black-patterned dressing gown that exposed his bare chest, legs, and feet. "It's been a long time since I've seen you hereabouts."

"Greetings, Rakuami-*san*," Hirata said. "Business is still thriving, I see."

"Yes, yes." Rakuami's skin had an oily sheen, and his smiling lips glistened moistly, as if he ate so many rich meals that grease oozed from him. He added slyly, "Despite the police's occasional attempts to arrest me and close down my operation."

As a young, inexperienced patrol officer, Hirata had once raided the house and tried to enforce the law against prostitution outside Yoshiwara. He hadn't realized that Rakuami had clients in high places who protected him from the law.

Hirata's mistake had earned him a reprimand from his superior and a cantankerous sort of friendship with Rakuami.

"To what do I owe the honor of a visit from you?" Rakuami said. "And aren't you going to introduce me to your friends?"

Otani elbowed Hirata aside. "My name is Otani," he said with authoritative pomp. "I'm a retainer to Lord Matsudaira. I'm conducting an inquiry into the murder of Senior Elder Makino."

"_I'm_ conducting the inquiry," Hirata said. Offended that his watchdog would try to seize control of the interview, he jostled Otani and reclaimed his position. "And I've come to ask for your assistance," he told Rakuami.

Rakuami appraised Hirata and Otani with his shrewd, bright eyes. Then he smiled at Otani. "I'll be delighted to give you all the help that I possibly can."

Hirata saw, to his chagrin, that Rakuami was more concerned about pleasing an envoy from the powerful Lord Matsudaira than a retainer to the shogun's detective. "Is there someplace quiet we can talk?" Hirata said, asserting his own authority.

"How about a drink?" Rakuami asked Otani.

"No, thank you," Hirata said loudly.

"That would be most appreciated," said Otani.

"Right this way."

Rakuami ushered Otani to a corner of the parlor. Otani's men followed, as did those sent by the chamberlain. Rakuami seated everyone and beckoned the maids, who poured the men cups of sake. The festivities continued noisily around them. The detectives looked at Hirata.

"Come on," he told them. Resentment simmered inside him as he squeezed in beside Rakuami and the detectives sat at the edge of the group.

"Was a girl named Okitsu ever one of your courtesans?" Otani was saying to Rakuami.

"Yes," Rakuami said. Eager to please Otani, he added, "I bought her from a broker who was selling farm girls."

Brokers traveled the country, buying daughters from impoverished peasant families to sell to pleasure houses in the city. The prettiest girls went to Yoshiwara for high prices. The others ended up in places such as Rakuami's, or worse.

"Okitsu was a sweet little thing." Rakuami's lewd smile suggested that he'd partaken of her favors himself. "I hope she's not in any trouble?"

"She's a suspect in the crime," Hirata said.

"You don't say!" Rakuami glanced at Hirata, then turned back to Otani. "I can't believe little Okitsu had anything to do with the murder."

"She never caused problems here?" Otani said.

"None at all," Rakuami said. "She was pleasant-natured and obedient. Everybody liked her. She was very popular with my guests."

"That should be enough to settle whatever doubts you have about her character and clear her of suspicion," Otani said, condescending to address Hirata.

"But of course Rakuami would speak well of her," Hirata said angrily. "He wouldn't want to get a reputation for employing troublesome girls."

Otani and Rakuami exchanged a glance that deplored Hirata's temper. Rakuami said, "Hirata-san, you take life too seriously. You need to relax." He called to a saucy girl in a bright pink kimono: "Come entertain my young friend."

The girl knelt behind Hirata and began massaging his shoulders. "Go away," Hirata ordered. "Leave me alone!"

The other men chuckled at his discomfiture. Even the detectives hid smiles as the girl continued her attentions and giggled. That Rakuami was making a fool of him in front of everyone increased Hirata's anger. His onetime friend was paying him back for that long-ago raid. Hirata put the girl firmly aside. He said to Rakuami, "Did Senior Elder Makino meet Okitsu here?"

"Yes. Makino was a regular guest here. And Okitsu was one of his favorite girls."

Although Rakuami still twinkled with mirth at Hirata's expense, a cautious note in his voice suggested that he would rather not discuss the relations between Makino and Okitsu.

Scenting a clue, Hirata said, "Was Makino one of Okitsu's favorite clients?"

"Yes, indeed," Rakuami said.

Hirata looked askance at him. "Okitsu was a pretty young girl. Makino was a mean, ugly old man. But she liked him anyway?"

"Very much." Rakuami was no longer smiling; his manner turned defensive. Otani frowned.

"He paid for her favors, so she was forced to serve him, but she enjoyed it because she liked him," Hirata said with disdainful skepticism.

"All right, she wasn't fond of him. But that didn't matter. She behaved very nicely toward him." Rakuami's face now glistened with sweat as well as grease. "All my girls do toward their clients."

"Can your girls and your servants confirm what you've told me?" Hirata said. "Go ask them," he ordered the detectives.

"Wait." Rakuami raised his hand, loath to disrupt the party. Hirata motioned the detectives to stay. Rakuami said reluctantly, "The first time Makino asked for Okitsu's company, she begged me not to make her serve him. She said he frightened her. The very sight of him made her sick. She said she hated him. But I told her she'd better make him happy because he was an important client."

"And she made him so happy that he wanted her all to himself," Hirata deduced, glad that he'd finally gotten the upper hand. "Did he buy her from you?" When Rakuami nodded, Hirata said, "How did Okitsu like the idea of being concubine to a man who frightened and revolted her?"

Rakuami's gaze roved the room, avoiding Hirata. "It was an advantageous opportunity for Okitsu. When my girls get too old to attract clients, I have to let them go. I can't afford to keep them if they're not earning money. A lot of them end up begging on the streets." He spoke with casual indifference to their fate. "For Okitsu to latch onto a rich, powerful man like Makino would secure her future."

"But she didn't want to live with him," Hirata said, perceiving the truth that Rakuami wanted to deny.

"She's young and foolish," Rakuami scoffed. "She didn't know what was best for her. I told her that Makino would give her a good home. She would have to serve only one man instead of many."

"What happened when Okitsu found out you were selling her to Makino?"

Rakuami hesitated, licking his moist lips.

"I'm sure there's someone else here who will tell me." Hirata started to rise; the detectives followed suit.

Rakuami grimaced in annoyed resignation. "Okitsu tried to commit suicide," he said in a flat, low voice that his guests wouldn't hear.

"How?" Hirata said as he and the detectives resettled themselves.

"She jumped into the canal behind the house and tried to drown herself," Rakuami said. "But some boatmen rescued her. I sent her to Makino's house the next day."

Otani broke into the conversation: "This is irrelevant. The girl tried to hurt herself, not Makino. We've heard nothing to suggest that she murdered him."

"Maybe Makino treated her badly while they lived together," Hirata said. "Maybe Okitsu was desperate to be rid of him, and she decided she would rather kill Makino than herself."

"Maybe you're making up stories that you want to believe," Otani mocked Hirata. Then he said to Rakuami, "Thank you for your assistance. We won't trouble you any longer."

He and his men stood, as did Chamberlain Yanagisawa's watchdogs. Rakuami jumped to his feet, bowed, and smiled, relieved to end Hirata's interrogation. "To serve you is my pleasure," he told Otani. "Perhaps you'll do me the honor of visiting me again some other time?" His expansive gesture offered Otani his girls, food, drink, and music.

"I will," Otani said.

Hirata and his detectives also rose, but Hirata said, "We're not leaving yet. First, we'll see what everyone else here has to say about Okitsu."

He began separating girls and servants from the clients, who hastily absconded rather than get involved. Rakuami watched in helpless outrage. Hirata took a malicious, shameful pleasure in causing Rakuami trouble while forcing Otani and the other watchdogs to observe a tedious round of interviews. And although the interviews produced nothing more than Rakuami had told him, Hirata felt relieved that despite Otani's hindrance, he'd discovered that Okitsu had a motive for the murder. He would have something to report to Sano.

At last, he and his party left the house. When they went outside to reclaim their horses, Otani drew Hirata aside and spoke in a confidential tone: "There's something I must tell you, for your own good."

Hirata eyed him warily.

"The *sōsakan-sama* is making a big mistake by conducting the investigation in this way," Otani said. "If you follow his lead, you'll go down with him. Do yourself a favor. Cooperate with me. Protect your own future."

"Are you saying I should defy my master's wish for the truth about the murder and conspire with you to incriminate the chamberlain so that Lord Matsudaira will reward me?" Hirata stared in disbelief at Otani's puffy face.

"You needn't put it so bluntly," Otani said.

That Otani should try to suborn his loyalty to Sano! Enraged, Hirata wanted to lash out at Otani for insulting him and criticizing Sano's judgment. But he mustn't offend Otani and risk bringing Sano more trouble.

"Thank you for your offer, but I must decline," he said with all the control he could manage.

Otani shrugged. "The offer stands, in case you come to your senses."

Hirata was suddenly overwhelmed by fear that unless he could be free to carry out his inquiries without constant pressure, he would ultimately fail. Turning his back on Otani, he climbed on his horse and joined the detectives, who already sat astride their mounts, and whispered orders to them. As everybody rode away from Rakuami's house, one detective suddenly bolted ahead. Another cantered his horse in the opposite direction. Another turned left at the intersection, while the last turned right.

"Where are they going?" demanded Otani.

"To follow some leads for me," Hirata said.

Otani shouted at his men to go after the detectives. Chamberlain Yanagisawa's men joined the pursuit. In the general confusion, Hirata slapped the reins and galloped away.

"Hey! Come back here!" Otani yelled.

As Hirata rode, he heard hooves pounding behind him as Otani gave chase. But he knew Nihonbashi better than Otani did. He veered down alleys, cut across marketplaces, and soon lost his watchdog. An exhilarating sense of freedom filled him as he raced alone through the wind and sunshine, bound for Asakusa Jinja Shrine, to investigate Senior Elder Makino's wife.

14

Reiko alit from her palanquin in the Hibiya administrative district south of Edo Castle, in front of a mansion that belonged to her father, one of two magistrates who maintained law and order in Edo. She sent home the palanquin and her escorts, then carried a cloth-wrapped bundle to the gate. The sentries opened it for her, and she hurried through the courtyard, where police officers guarded shackled prisoners awaiting trial by the magistrate. Inside the mansion, she bypassed the public chambers that housed the Court of Justice. She went to the private quarters and closed herself inside the room that had been hers during her childhood. Ensconced amid the familiar teak cabinets, lacquer furniture, raised study niche, and painted murals of blossoming plum trees, she knelt on the *tatami* floor and opened her bundle.

It contained two plain indigo cotton kimonos with matching sashes, two white cotton under-robes, coarse white socks, a padded cotton cloak, and straw sandals—typical clothing for servants. Wrapped inside the clothing were a rice bowl and chopsticks, a comb, hairpins, a head kerchief, a Buddhist rosary, and a few copper coins. The only item not normally owned by a maid was a dagger in a leather sheath. Reiko changed her silk robes for the rough cotton clothes, then sat at the dressing table and studied her reflection in the mirror.

She picked up a cloth and wiped the rouge and white powder from her face and mouth. Her teeth, dyed gleaming black in the fashionable custom for married women, betrayed her rank. Reiko scrubbed them with a brush until they faded to a drab gray. She hoped no one would notice her shaved eyebrows—another mark of class and fashion. She unpinned her shiny, black waist-length hair, then opened a charcoal brazier and scooped out a handful of ash, which she worked into her hair until it was streaked a dull, sooty gray. Then she pinned her hair into a simple knot and smiled at her reflection. The gray streaks dimmed her natural beauty and aged her twenty years. Satisfaction with her disguise almost eclipsed her fear of leaving safe territory.

Reiko strapped the dagger to her thigh under her skirts, put on the cloak, and repacked her bundle, which she carried as she left the room. She hunched down the passage, imitating an old woman. When she turned a corner, she saw her father walking toward her, clad in his black judicial robes. Alarm jolted Reiko. She'd hoped not to see him because she didn't want him to know what she was doing. But she couldn't avoid him—he'd seen her. Reiko cringed as he approached . . .

. . . and passed her without a second glance. He hadn't recognized her! He'd thought she was one of his maids. Reiko suppressed a giggle of delight that her disguise had passed the first test, then hastened from the mansion.

In the street she spied two peasant men carrying an empty *kago*—a basketlike chair for hire. She waved them down, climbed into the *kago,* and told them to take her to Edo Castle. As they trotted her past the walled estates, she felt vulnerable without her usual attendants. She shivered in the cold wind, missing the enclosed security of her palanquin. Mounted samurai towered over her. Stripped of the trappings of rank, she attracted little notice from the men, but invisibility was a mixed blessing. If one of Edo's many thieves or marauders should attack her, no one would come to her aid. Now Reiko's doubts returned in full force. She had the strange, disturbing sense that she'd lost her talents as well as her identity. How would she ever learn anything useful about Senior Elder Makino's wife or concubine? How would she protect herself, even with the dagger she carried?

Reiko fought the insidious panic that waited to ensnare her. She prayed that a bad spell wouldn't overtake her now, as the *kago* bore her onto the promenade outside Edo Castle. Its walls, towers, and roofs, looming on the hill above her, no longer represented home or safety. Instead, the castle proclaimed the might of the Tokugawa regime and signaled danger to outsiders—such as herself. Now the *kago* men stopped near the gate.

"Get out!" they ordered her. "Pay up!"

She reluctantly climbed out of the chair amid the soldiers and officials who thronged the promenade. As she paid the *kago* men, she saw a florid, thickset samurai standing outside the castle gate, scanning the crowds. Reiko recognized him as Nomura, a palace guard captain and the friend whom Sano had asked to meet her here and get her inside Senior Elder Makino's estate. He saw her and approached.

"Are you Emi?" he said, calling her by the alias that Sano had given her.

"Yes, honorable master."

Reiko bowed, noting that he didn't recognize her, although he'd seen her when she'd accompanied the palace ladies on outings and he'd escorted them. Sano had told Nomura that Emi was his cast-off mistress who needed work. Nomura owed Sano a favor because Sano had recommended him for a promotion, and he'd willingly agreed to help her, even if he didn't understand why she must work in Senior Elder Makino's house. Honor demanded that he fulfill his obligation without asking questions.

"Let's go, then," Nomura said.

He walked to the castle gate. Reiko trailed behind him. Sentries let her in the gate because Nomura vouched for her. His authority got her past the guards at the checkpoints along the passages. Reiko's heart thudded as they walked the

familiar streets of the official quarter. Soon they arrived at
Senior Elder Makino's estate. Black mourning drapery
sagged from the portals. The mansion looked as ominous as
a dungeon.

Nomura said his name and rank to the sentries in the
guard booth. "I want to see the estate manager," he told
them.

They sent word inside, and presently a samurai appeared.
He bore a strong resemblance to Nomura. "Greetings, Honorable Cousin," he said. "What brings you here?"

"I'm seeking employment for this woman." Nomura indicated Reiko. "Her name is Emi. I want you to hire her as a
ladies' maid."

"Very well," the estate manager said, automatically granting the favor that his high-ranking cousin asked. "Come with
me," he ordered Reiko.

She followed him through the gate. The guards closed it behind them. An awful sense of imprisonment undermined
Reiko's triumph at gaining entry to the estate. She recalled
visits she'd made to friends at similar places, when she'd been
shown every courtesy due the wife of the shogun's *sōsakan-
sama*. But now the estate manager led her around the mansion to the servants' quarters, a plain, two-story wooden
building. Here he turned her over to the housekeeper, whom
he introduced as Yasue. She was an old woman with white
hair, sallow skin, and a hunched back. She carried a thick,
blunt stick under the sash of her gray kimono.

"This is Emi, a new maid I've just hired for the ladies," he
said to Yasue. "Put her to work."

He departed, and Reiko felt as though she'd lost her last
link with her ordinary world. She knew she wasn't alone, because Sano had stationed two detectives inside the estate in
case she needed help, but she had no idea where they were.
She belatedly realized how little she knew about the lives of
maids. The recollection that not all employers treated their
servants as well as she and Sano did increased her terror.

"Don't look so frightened," Yasue said. Amusement glittered in her sharp eyes, which had yellowish whites. Her

mouth, filled with large, protruding yellow teeth, grinned at Reiko. "I won't bite you."

She took Reiko to a cold, dank room in the servants' quarters. On the bare earth floor lay rows of wooden pallets topped by straw-filled mattresses. Yasue opened a cupboard and said, "Leave your things here."

Reiko stowed her bundle and cloak in one of many compartments that held clothes and other personal items belonging to the maids. She smelled the pungent reek of urine and feces from privies outside. The thought of sleeping in such crowded, squalid conditions made her physically ill.

Yasue led her through various buildings, named their functions, and laid out the household rules: "Maids should be as invisible and quiet as possible. Don't go near Senior Elder Makino's family, retainers, or guests unless you're ordered to serve them. Don't speak to them unless they speak to you."

There went her hope of initiating conversations with the suspects and attempting to establish their guilt or innocence, Reiko thought. She and Yasue followed a path to a garden of rocks, white sand, and shrubs. In it stood a half-timbered building with wooden shutters and a broad veranda.

"Those are the private chambers," Yasue said.

As Reiko gazed with interest at the scene of the murder, a woman glided across a covered walkway toward the building. Slim, elegant, and in her forties, she fit Sano's description of Agemaki, widow of Senior Elder Makino. Then came a young, pretty girl accompanied by a strikingly handsome young man. Reiko surmised that they must be the concubine Okitsu and the actor Koheiji. She craned her neck, avid for a closer look at the murder suspects she'd come to observe. But they quickly disappeared into the private chambers.

"You're not to go in there without permission," Yasue said. "Come along now."

Reiko had no choice but to let the woman hurry her away. They went to the kitchen, a vast den where hearths blazed and smoke and steam filled the air. Male cooks labored over boiling pots and sliced raw fish. They shouted orders to boys who stoked the fires, and maids who flung dishes onto trays and ladled food into the dishes.

"There's a banquet for the important people in Senior Elder Makino's funeral procession," Yasue said. "You can help out."

She sat Reiko at a table where maids furiously chopped vegetables. She handed Reiko a knife, then left. Reiko was dismayed, for she'd not expected to do kitchen labor. A manservant hurled a bunch of huge white radishes at her. Never having learned much about cooking, she clumsily sliced a radish. The knife slipped and cut her finger; her blood stained the radish. The maids working beside Reiko ignored her. They were both older women, their faces hardened by toil.

"I heard that the master of this house was murdered," Reiko said. "Did you see or hear anything?"

They frowned, skillfully wielding their knives. One woman said, "We've been ordered not to talk about that. Don't mention it again—you'll get somebody in trouble."

More rules to thwart her aims! Reiko sighed in frustration. She wiped sweat off her face and grimly hacked the radishes. After what seemed like hours, Yasue reappeared.

"The ladies have ordered meals," she told Reiko. "You can help serve them."

Reiko was delighted to leave the kitchen with two other maids also assigned to the task. Carrying trays laden with covered dishes, they filed across the walkway to the private chambers. The guards let them inside. Excitement tingled through Reiko. Here she might discover the truth about Senior Elder Makino's death.

"You go to Lady Agemaki," one of the other maids told Reiko. "Her room is that way."

They turned a corner, vanishing from sight. Reiko carried her tray along the corridor and came to an open door. Through it she saw the widow sitting alone. Reiko started to walk in, but suddenly a hand seized her arm in a fierce, startling grip.

"Kneel when you enter a room!" Yasue hissed in her ear.

She cuffed Reiko's head, then withdrew. Reiko stood, her ears ringing from the blow, shaken because she'd forgotten the protocol for maids and she'd not known Yasue had followed her. The old woman moved as stealthily as a cat. Reiko knelt and hobbled across the threshold of the chamber. Agemaki stared into space, absorbed in her own musings. Thrilled to get close to the object of her interest, Reiko rose, crept toward Agemaki, and set the tray beside her.

Agemaki remained silent; she didn't look at Reiko or the food. Reiko wondered if she should dare initiate an acquaintance. Was Yasue loitering about, watching to make sure she obeyed the rules? Reiko began removing the covers from the dishes on the tray while she awaited some cue from Agemaki.

"You can go now," Agemaki said in a remote voice.

Reiko's hands faltered.

"Didn't you hear me?" Agemaki said. "Get out."

Although Reiko hated losing a chance to spy, she meekly obeyed. She hesitated outside the door, reluctant to leave without accomplishing anything. From somewhere came the sound of samisen music, a man's voice singing, and women giggling. Reiko crept down the corridor and peeked into a room where the actor Koheiji was entertaining the concubine Okitsu and the maids. Reiko told herself that no one would miss her if she took a moment to examine the scene of the murder. Maybe she would find something that Sano and his detectives had overlooked.

She hurried down the corridor to the room she identified as Senior Elder Makino's. She eased open the door, slipped inside, then slid the door shut and appraised her surroundings. Cold and bare of furniture, they had the eerie atmosphere of a place in which death has recently occurred. A shiver passed over Reiko as she gazed at the platform where Makino's body had lain. She opened the cabinets along the wall only to find empty compartments: Someone had cleared out the dead man's possessions. Then she noticed a narrow, vertical gap between two sections of shelves.

Alerted by quickening instinct, Reiko inserted her finger

into the gap. She found an indentation on the side of one
section of shelves. She pressed, and the section pivoted, one
half swinging outward, the other into a dim space beyond
the room. She'd found a secret chamber! Eagerly she peered
inside.

Human figures stared back at her. Reiko stifled a scream.
But the figures didn't move or make a sound. A second look
showed her that their heads lolled at unnatural angles, and
their limbs dangled inside their robes. They were life-sized
dolls, suspended from hooks. Puzzled, Reiko ventured into
the chamber, which smelled of sweat and stale breath. Now
she counted ten dolls, all female. They had beautiful faces
made of skillfully carved and painted wood; they all wore
elaborate wigs and expensive patterned silk kimonos. Reiko
noticed characters written on the wall above each figure. She
read, "Takao of the Great Miura," "Otowa of the Matsuba" . . .
They represented courtesans from the Yoshiwara pleasure
quarter.

Comprehension banished Reiko's puzzlement. She'd
heard stories about men who owned "shapes"—effigies of
women with whom they'd enjoyed sexual relations. They re-
lived their pleasures by making love to the shapes. A rolled
futon in the corner, and a look under the robes of one doll,
confirmed Reiko's belief that Senior Elder Makino had practiced this strange habit. The doll's body, fashioned from
stuffed leather, had an opening at the crotch that was filled
with boiled, mashed radish used to simulate the texture of
female genitalia.

Reiko wrinkled her nose at the sour smell of the radish as
she imagined Makino coupling with a shape on the futon.
She noticed a shelf filled with numerous scrolls. Opening
some, she found that they were pictures of couples engaged
in erotic acts. Stains discolored the pictures.

Below the shelf stood two lacquer chests. Reiko looked
inside them. One contained wooden clubs padded with
leather, atop coiled ropes. Makino's habits must have included ritual violence during sex. The other chest contained
nine phalluses of different sizes, each realistically carved

from jade and resting in a slot in the chest's padded lining. A tenth, empty slot had once contained a huge phallus. Reiko recalled what Sano had told her about the examination of Senior Elder Makino's corpse. Could the missing phallus have inflicted the anal injury—and the fatal beating? If so, then somebody who'd known about this chamber had killed Makino.

Perhaps that somebody was one of the women upon whom Reiko had come to spy.

Suddenly Reiko heard stealthy footsteps approaching along the corridor. She froze in alarm. The door of Makino's room slid open. She mustn't let anyone find her here! She yanked on the shelves, closing the entrance to the secret chamber, sealing herself inside. The footsteps padded across the floor. Reiko saw a finger protrude between the shelves and press the indentation. Her heart lurched as the secret door swung open. Quickly she stepped behind it.

A samurai strode into the chamber, carrying a long bundle. Reiko held her breath, peered cautiously around the door, and watched him kneel before the chest that contained the jade phalluses. He lifted the lid, then unwrapped his bundle. It was a quilt folded around a cylindrical object. This he set inside the empty slot in the chest. Then he shut the lid and rose. Leaving the room, he passed very near Reiko. She recognized him from Sano's description of Tamura, chief retainer to Senior Elder Makino. The shelves pivoted shut. Reiko breathed a sigh of fervent relief as she listened to Tamura leave the room.

On her first day here, she'd already discovered evidence that pointed away from the warring factions and toward the suspects in Makino's inner circle. If the phallus was the weapon used on Makino, then Tamura's behavior suggested that he was the killer. He could have hidden the weapon after his crime and thought that now was a good time to replace it. Reiko couldn't wait to tell Sano.

But now she noticed that the music had stopped. She could no longer hear the maids giggling—they must have gone. She mustn't linger.

She slipped out of the secret room and pivoted the shelf back into position. When she left the private chambers, the guards eyed her suspiciously. She hurried along paths, between buildings, in the direction of the kitchen, so elated that the prospect of more toil barely fazed her. But as she crossed a garden, Yasue appeared so suddenly that she seemed to materialize out of thin air. She scowled at Reiko, grasped her arm, and demanded, "Where have you been?"

"I got lost," Reiko lied.

Yasue snorted in disbelief. "Snooping around, I'd say."

She yanked the stick from under her sash and smote Reiko three hard blows across the back. Reiko fell on hands and knees, crying out in pain and angry protest.

"I'll be watching you," Yasue said. She grabbed Reiko's collar and hauled her to her feet. "Remember that when you get the urge to snoop again." Her stick prodded Reiko along the paths. "Now I'll give you enough work to keep you too busy to cause trouble."

She'd already made an enemy, Reiko realized unhappily. She hoped she could last long enough here to discover the truth about Senior Elder Makino's death.

15

"If you must investigate that actor, shouldn't you start at the place where he performs?" Ibe asked Sano as they and their entourage rode through the Saru-waka-cho theater district. "We just passed the Nakamura-za, in case you hadn't noticed."

He gestured toward a theater on the avenue. Signs on its façade pictured Koheiji and proclaimed the title of the play: *Amorous Adventures of an Edo Samurai*. Men and women lined up at ticket booths there and at the other theaters. Song, laughter, and applause issued from upper-story windows.

"We'll start at the place where Koheiji started his career," Sano said.

He had an intuition that he would learn more there, but he didn't bother trying to explain this to Ibe or Lord Matsu-daira's men, who wouldn't want him chasing hunches instead of pursuing the suspects they wanted him to incriminate. He led the group into Kobiki-cho, a lesser theatrical quarter. Here, the theaters were small and shabby, the audiences exclusively male. Men crowded the teahouses, drinking sake, playing cards, and wagering on cockfights. Drummers led more men through the streets in search of amusement. Teahouse proprietors rushed out to greet Sano and his entourage.

"Would you like a companion for the night?"

"I can set you up with the handsomest actors!"

"One piece of gold, and he's yours from the final curtain until daybreak of the morning after!"

The Kobiki-cho district was famous as a gathering place for devotees of manly love, Sano knew. It generated more revenue from male prostitution than from ticket sales. Boys in their teens swarmed the street, offering free tickets, luring men to their plays. Men called propositions to youths who leaned out second-story windows. Sano politely declined all offers, although a few of his companions eyed the boys with interest. Maybe some actors enjoyed manly sex as much as did their suitors, but Sano knew that young, unknown performers earned so little that if they wanted to eat, they must sell themselves. Hence, Kobiki-cho was a carnal paradise for wealthy men who craved boys.

At the Owari Theater, Sano and his party dismounted; stableboys took charge of their horses. Police officers loitered outside the dingy wooden building, ready to quell the riots that often occurred when men quarreled over their favorite actors. Entering the theater, Sano found a play in progress. On a raised stage lit by skylights and decorated with a painted backdrop of a forest scene, an actor in peasant garb sang a soulful duet with an *onnagata*—female impersonator—dressed as a courtesan. Musicians played an off-key accompaniment. Men filled the seats along the walls and compartments in front of the stage. Raucous cheers burst from the audience. Smoke from tobacco pipes fouled the air.

As the actors sang, a samurai in the audience rose. "Ebisuya-*san*!" he called. "Here's a token of my love for you!"

He drew his dagger, hacked off his little finger, and hurled it at the *onnagata*. He tried to leap onto the stage, but the police hauled him away. No one seemed much bothered by the incident, which was not uncommon in Kobiki-cho. The performance continued without pause. Afterward, the audience straggled out of the theater. Sano led his watchdogs and detectives to an elderly man who stood below the stage.

"Are you the proprietor?" Sano asked him.

"Yes, master." The man had shoulders drawn up to his ears; white tufts of hair circled his bald pate. He yelled at the actors lounging and smoking on the stage: "Don't just stand there—change the set for the next performance!"

The actors, who apparently doubled as stagehands, moved the backdrop. Ebisuya, the female impersonator, clenched his tobacco pipe between his rouged lips as he worked. The proprietor said to Sano, "What can I do for you?" He spoke courteously, but his expression was sour.

Sano introduced himself. "I'm investigating the affairs of the actor Koheiji. I want your help."

"I'm sorry, but I don't know any actor by that name."

"Yes, he does," Ebisuya told Sano. He'd dropped his ladylike falsetto voice, and his deep, male tone contrasted bizarrely with his female costume. He jerked his chin toward the proprietor. "His memory's gone to rot. Koheiji worked here before he moved to the Nakamura-za and switched from girl roles to samurai roles."

Sano was interested to learn that Koheiji had once been an *onnagata.* Did he still impersonate women, perhaps in private if not onstage? The torn sleeve at the murder scene had come from a kimono belonging to Okitsu, but who had worn it the night Makino died?

"My memory is just fine," the proprietor said angrily. Pointing at Ebisuya, he said, "You watch your mouth, or I'll throw your lazy behind out in the street."

Ebisuya shot Sano a glance that said his employer was daft, but he wanted to keep his job.

"I know who you're talking about now," the proprietor said to Sano. "I must have hired Koheiji ten or eleven years ago. I gave him his start in the theater, but he moved on to bigger and better things. What's he done wrong?"

"Why do you think he's done anything wrong?" Sano said.

"The shogun's detective wouldn't come asking about him otherwise." Senile he might be, but the proprietor knew the ways of the world. "And all these actors are troublemakers."

"Koheiji is a suspect in a murder," Ibe cut in, impatient.

Another blank stare came from the proprietor. "Who was murdered?"

"His patron. Senior Elder Makino." Ibe spoke in the emphatic, disdainful tone reserved for addressing idiots.

"Oh," the proprietor said.

"Did Koheiji meet Senior Elder Makino here?" Sano said.

The proprietor's expression turned vague. "Maybe. If not here, then in one of the teahouses. That's the usual thing."

Sano began to doubt that the man had a true recollection of who Koheiji was, let alone anything else about him. What he said about Koheiji probably applied to many actors.

"This is getting us nowhere," Ibe said in exasperation.

Lord Matsudaira's men voiced their agreement that Sano should end the interview. On stage, Ebisuya adjusted a new backdrop. He caught Sano's eye and tilted his head toward the back door.

"We can go now," Sano said, earning nods of approval from the Matsudaira contingent and a suspicious look from Ibe.

Outside the theater, Sano told his detectives, "Go talk to people around the district and find out what they know about Koheiji." The detectives split up and headed down the street; Ibe's and Lord Matsudaira's men dogged their heels. Sano said to Ibe, "Please excuse me a moment."

As if intending to use the privy, he strode down the alley between the theater and the neighboring teahouse. A young boy stood pressed against the wall, his kimono raised above his waist. A groaning, panting samurai thrust himself against the boy's naked buttocks. Sano squeezed past the pair and turned the corner. Behind the theater were reeking privies in open wooden stalls. Near them slouched the *onnagata*. At first Sano didn't recognize him—he'd removed his wig, female garb, and makeup. Ebisuya now sported black robes and cropped hair. Smoke rose from the pipe dangling in his fingers.

"You have something to tell me about Koheiji?" Sano said.

"I'll help you if you help me," Ebisuya said.

He was in his thirties—getting too old to have much hope of stardom. He held out his hand for money, and Sano saw scars on his arm—from self-inflicted cuts, meant to convince patrons of his love for them. Probably he, like many actors, had thereby sought to coax men into ransoming him from his contract with the theater that owned actors the way that brothels owned courtesans. He was also getting too old to attract patrons much longer. His features were pretty but hard with the desperation that drove him to bargain with a Tokugawa official.

"Talk," Sano said. "If your information is worthwhile, I'll pay."

Nodding sullenly, Ebisuya withdrew his hand. "I don't like to tell tales on a fellow actor," he said, "but I owe Koheiji a bad turn. I was an apprentice at the Owari when he was hired. Before he came, I had the best roles. Afterward, Koheiji played the lead parts that should have been mine." Ebisuya's eyes flashed resentment at his rival's good luck. "He's not more talented than I am—just better at sucking up to people."

"People like Senior Elder Makino?"

"Him among others. Koheiji was a favorite with audiences, and not just for his performances onstage. He wanted to hook a patron who would buy his way into leading roles at a top theater."

So Koheiji engaged in manly love in the past, thought Sano. Perhaps he'd lied when he said he hadn't had sexual relations with Senior Elder Makino. If so, he could also have lied when he'd claimed he hadn't been with Makino the night of the murder.

"He knew how to please men, even though he prefers women," Ebisuya continued. "He gave his clients good *sumata*."

In *sumata*—the "secret thigh technique"—one man thrust his organ between another's thighs, simulating anal intercourse. Thus had Koheiji satisfied his clients with minimal discomfort to himself.

"Did his *sumata* win him the patronage of Senior Elder Makino?" Sano said.

Ebisuya gave Sano a look that scorned the idea. "Senior Elder Makino didn't practice manly love. That's not why he paid the Nakamura-za to hire Koheiji and make him a star."

"Then why did he?"

"Koheiji found a way to attract men who didn't want sex with him." The *onnagata*'s tone conveyed reluctant admiration for his clever rival. "Makino was one of them. He liked the special performances that Koheiji put on after the theaters closed at night."

"What sort of performances?" Sano said, intrigued.

"Koheiji would hire a female prostitute and make love to her in front of his clients. They were all rich, impotent old men who couldn't make love to a woman themselves. Instead, they watched Koheiji do it."

Sano imagined Koheiji and the woman naked and coupling while the elderly men looked on, their lined faces avid with their need for vicarious sexual gratification. "Did Senior Elder Makino become Koheiji's patron after watching his act?"

"Yes," Ebisuya said, "but he didn't just watch. For an extra charge, Koheiji would give shows for only one client at a time. The client could join in the fun—if he got excited enough."

"Makino paid for private shows?" Sano said.

"So I've heard. And he must have enjoyed them a lot, because not only did he become Koheiji's patron, he also took him into his home. He probably wanted to save himself the trouble of a trip to Kobiki-cho every time he wanted a show."

On the night of the murder, had Koheiji performed a sex show for his host? Sano envisioned the skull-faced Makino with Koheiji, both fondling a nude woman pressed between them. If this revolting scene had indeed occurred that night, who had she been? The torn sleeve pointed to the concubine Okitsu. But Makino's wife had also shared his chambers, and perhaps his sexual proclivities. And Sano wondered whether a three-way encounter had any connection with Makino's death. Ebisuya had portrayed Koheiji as a greedy, ambitious user of men, but no worse. Sano had heard nothing to suggest that he'd killed the patron on whom his career depended.

"But Makino wasn't aware that he was risking his life every time Koheiji put on a show for him." Ebisuya's portentous tone announced that he'd come to the part of his story he most wanted to tell. "There were rumors that Koheiji played rough during those private shows. Some men liked it that way. But he went too far at least once." Ebisuya inhaled on his pipe, blew out smoke, and continued: "It happened late at night about five years ago. I woke up to hear someone calling my name and knocking on the window beside my bed. I looked outside and saw Koheiji standing there.

"He said, 'I need your help.' When I asked him what was wrong, he wouldn't tell me. He was all upset. He begged me to come with him. I was curious, so I went. He took me to a room at an inn. There was an old samurai lying naked inside. He was covered with bruises and blood. At first I thought he was dead, but then I heard him groan."

A tingle of anticipation coursed through Sano.

"I asked Koheiji what happened," Ebisuya said. "He said, 'It was a private show. Things got out of control. I just sort of lost my mind. The next thing I knew, I'd beaten him up.'"

Sano's pulse accelerated as he transposed the scene to Senior Elder Makino's estate. He pictured Koheiji beating Makino in a frenzy, mounting him, and violating him. Perhaps Koheiji harbored a secret hatred for the men that his ambitions forced him to please. Had he lost control that night and killed Makino in a fit of rage?

Ebisuya said, "I asked Koheiji, 'Where's the girl?' He said, 'Gone. She must have run away.' I said, 'Why did you come to me?' He said, 'Because I know you'll do anything for the right price.' I asked him what he wanted from me. He said, 'That man is an important official. If word of this gets out, I'll be ruined.'" Ebisuya panted and wrung his hands, reenacting Koheiji's fright. "'People know I rented this room. I can't let him be found here. You have to help me move him out.'"

"Did you?" Sano said as Ebisuya paused to prolong the suspense.

"Yes," Ebisuya said. "He paid me to help him and keep quiet about what had happened. We dressed the old man. We carried him to the highway and left him on the side of the road."

Makino's murder had elements in common with the other crime—the age and gender of the victim, his injuries. That Koheiji had covered up a crime in the past implicated him even more strongly in the death of Senior Elder Makino and the alteration of the murder scene.

"What happened to the old man?" Sano asked.

"I later heard that the highway patrol found him and took him home," Ebisuya said. "I still see him hanging around the theaters."

"Who is he?"

"Oyama Banzan."

Sano recognized the name of a judicial councilor. "And the girl?" he said, in case he needed another witness to the incident.

"I don't know. Koheiji didn't tell me."

"They didn't report him to the police?"

Ebisuya shook his head in pitying contempt. "Oyama must have been too ashamed to admit he'd been beaten up during a sex game. The girl must have been too scared to talk." A malicious grin curved Ebisuya's mouth. "And I waited until now."

When Koheiji was a suspect in a serious crime, and Ebisuya could do him the most harm, thought Sano.

"Was my story worth your while?" Ebisuya held out his hand and wiggled the fingers.

"Time will tell," Sano said, but he opened the pouch he wore at his waist and handed over a gold coin from the stash he carried for occasions like this.

Ebisuya tossed the coin up in the air, then closed it in his fist. "A thousand thanks. Good luck with your investigation. May Koheiji get his just reward."

He dumped ash from his pipe and ground out the sparks with his foot. He opened the theater's back door and slipped inside. Sano walked down the alley to the street and found Ibe waiting for him in front of the theater.

"I was beginning to think you'd run out on me," Ibe said.

"My apologies for taking so long," Sano said.

He decided not to tell his watchdog what he'd learned from Ebisuya. Woe to him if Chamberlain Yanagisawa found out he'd withheld information! Yet Sano also feared what Yanagisawa might do to an informant who could vindicate Lord Matsudaira. Sano could find himself discovering who had killed Makino yet unable to prove his case because witnesses had mysteriously vanished.

"We'll go to the Nakamura-za Theater and see what the people there have to say about Koheiji, while my detectives finish up here," he said.

As he and Ibe mounted their horses, Sano looked up at the sky above the tawdry theater signs. The bright afternoon sun was still high but had begun its descent toward the west. Reiko should be employed in Senior Elder Makino's house by now. Sano wondered what she was doing. He'd been trying to concentrate on his work and block out fears about Reiko, but now he couldn't force them from his mind. Ebisuya's story incriminated a man situated dangerously close to her. Even though she was supposed to spy on the women, she would cross paths with Koheiji, whose savage impulses had seriously harmed at least one person. And if Koheiji was the murderer, chances were he'd had a female partner during the crime and cover-up—an accomplice just as eager as he to hide the truth about Makino's death.

Yesterday, Sano would have rejoiced at finding evidence that pointed away from Lord Matsudaira and Chamberlain Yanagisawa. Now he must hope, for Reiko's sake, that the killer was someone within the warring factions instead.

16

Chamberlain Yanagisawa and Lord Matsudaira knelt facing each other in the great audience hall of the palace. Beside the chamberlain sat his chief retainer, Mori; beside Lord Matsudaira sat his nephew, Daiemon. Behind each pair stood attendants and armed guards. Yanagisawa read menace in the somber faces of Lord Matsudaira and Daiemon; he breathed the fiery scent of battle fever in the atmosphere. Neither his high rank nor his bodyguards guaranteed his safety. The law against drawing weapons inside Edo Castle seemed a flimsy barrier to violence. And he saw, among Lord Matsudaira's minions, one face that reduced the others to a blur.

Police Commissioner Hoshina stood in the first row behind his master. He regarded Yanagisawa with fierce, belligerent defiance. Yanagisawa averted his gaze from the onetime paramour he still loved with a passion and missed every moment.

"Why did you call this meeting?" he asked Lord Matsudaira in a deliberately calm voice.

"I decided that it's time for a talk about the future," Lord Matsudaira said, matching his tone.

Was this a hint that Lord Matsudaira wished to negotiate a truce? Although Yanagisawa had serious doubts that they could peaceably settle their differences, he was willing to try. Just today, his spies had sent him word of new enemy troops arriving in Edo. His own position grew more precarious, and Lord Matsudaira's stronger, as time went on.

"Very well," he told Lord Matsudaira. "Let's talk."

Lord Matsudaira nodded, then said, "If things continue in this direction, a war is inevitable."

"True." Yanagisawa felt Hoshina's gaze piercing him. He realized that Lord Matsudaira knew about their bad blood and had brought Hoshina along to rattle his nerves.

"No man is invincible," said Daiemon. Cunning and ambition shone on his youthful face; he ignored his uncle's frown of displeasure that he'd interrupted the conversation. "Do you really want to risk dying in battle, Honorable Chamberlain?"

His sneer mocked Yanagisawa as a coward who feared death more than he wanted supreme power. Yanagisawa glared at Daiemon. Lord Matsudaira raised a hand to silence his nephew.

"Let us presume that neither of us wishes to die," Lord Matsudaira said. "But let us not presume that the survivor will have an easy time. History has shown us that the result of a civil war is widespread poverty, famine, and disorder. To rule over a land in such condition would be a poor prize for the victor."

Yanagisawa narrowed his eyes. Surely Lord Matsudaira didn't expect to persuade him to back down because a war-torn kingdom wasn't worth having.

"And the victor won't rule unopposed," Daiemon said, undaunted by his uncle's authority. "What makes you think that you could keep our allies—or your own—under your thumb forever?" He grinned, belittling Yanagisawa's chances of maintaining control over Japan even if he beat Lord Matsudaira.

"What makes you think you could do any better than I?" Yanagisawa forced himself to stay calm. The rude young upstart plagued him worse than did Lord Matsudaira. "You have quite a gift for offending people."

"My nephew meant no offense, Honorable Chamberlain.

Please excuse him." Lord Matsudaira shot a warning glance at Daiemon, then addressed Yanagisawa in a conciliatory manner: "I didn't bring you here to bait you. I'd hoped we could find a way to avoid a war that neither of us really wants."

Yanagisawa would fight Lord Matsudaira to the death if necessary; but his fear for his life inclined him toward negotiation. And although he knew he shouldn't let affairs of the heart influence his political decisions, he couldn't help hoping that if they declared a truce, he and Hoshina might somehow reconcile.

"Suppose I do agree that peace is preferable to war," he said cautiously. "What terms would you propose?"

A glance between Lord Matsudaira and Daiemon conveyed their mutual satisfaction that they'd lured him into bargaining. "I propose that we both disband our armies," Lord Matsudaira said. "Afterward, we would undertake a reorganization of the government."

"What sort of reorganization?" Yanagisawa said. He smelled an unfavorable deal, like a bad wind approaching.

"Uemori Yoichi will be promoted to Senior Elder Makino's position," said Lord Matsudaira. "The vacant seat on the council will be filled by Goto Kaemon."

Yanagisawa stared in amazed disbelief. He'd expected Lord Matsudaira to offer him at least some concessions, but he was proposing to overload the nation's highest governing body with men loyal to himself!

"In addition," Lord Matsudaira said, "my nephew Daiemon will be appointed premier of the regime. He will oversee the relations between the shogun and his officials."

Daiemon preened with self-importance. Outrage stunned Yanagisawa. This arrangement would give Lord Matsudaira and Daiemon complete control of the *bakufu!*

"That's a very one-sided proposal," he said sardonically. "What would I get in exchange for agreeing?"

"You would get to keep your position as chamberlain, your residence, and your personal wealth."

Although Lord Matsudaira spoke as though bestowing a

generous gift, Yanagisawa was not prepared to agree to terms that would reduce him to a feeble shadow of himself.

"Your terms are unacceptable," he spat furiously. "That you would even think I'd consider your proposal is a gross insult to me."

He surged to his feet. Swords clanked and armor creaked as his entourage stirred behind him. "This discussion is finished," Yanagisawa announced.

Lord Matsudaira and Daiemon also rose. "Don't be in such a hurry to reject our deal," Lord Matsudaira said. All his pretense at conciliation vanished; his manner turned dictatorial. "It's the best you're going to get."

"I'll take my chances." Yanagisawa headed for the door.

"You can't win a war against us," Daiemon said. Now that his sly barbs had failed to intimidate Yanagisawa, he resorted to outright bluster. "We'll crush you like an insect."

Yanagisawa feared that Daiemon was right. He'd never commanded a full-scale war, and his talent for politics didn't compensate for a lack of military experience. Yet his foes' eagerness for a truce gave him heart. They'd never fought a war either.

He said, "If you were so sure you can beat me, you wouldn't have called this meeting." He locked stares with Daiemon. "And a man in a position as vulnerable as yours should know better than to threaten the man who controls the intelligence service."

Lord Matsudaira looked puzzled by this remark, but wariness sharpened Daiemon's features. Yanagisawa smiled as he watched Daiemon recalling that he had dangerous secrets and wondering how much Yanagisawa knew. But instead of showing his hand, Yanagisawa chose to hoard his knowledge for a time when he had even greater need—or better use—for a weapon against Daiemon.

"Now if you'll excuse me," Yanagisawa said, "I've more important things to do than listen to nonsense."

"You won't get another opportunity to save your neck," Lord Matsudaira said, his fists clenched and his face dark with anger. "I'll show no more mercy toward you!"

"Nor will I toward you, when we meet on the battlefield," Yanagisawa retorted. He now realized that there had never been a possibility that he and Lord Matsudaira could reach a truce on terms acceptable to them both. "May the better man win."

As he strode from the audience hall, his entourage in tow, Yanagisawa glimpsed Hoshina. The hatred in Hoshina's eyes told him there had never been any chance that they would reconcile. Yanagisawa experienced an awful sense of embarking on a path toward a fatal destiny.

But he projected regal self-confidence as he walked through the castle grounds to his estate. Inside, he secluded himself in his office and sat at the desk. A mere moment passed before his poise shattered. Tremors wracked his muscles; his lungs expelled harsh gasps as he released pent-up tension. His head throbbed painfully from the pressure of the blood inside his skull. With jittering fingers he massaged his temples. Eventually, his body calmed, but his spirit remained troubled by other problems besides Lord Matsudaira.

The murder investigation could destroy him even before a war began. If Sano were to discover that Yanagisawa had known about Senior Elder Makino's defection, Yanagisawa could find himself the primary suspect in the crime. Lord Matsudaira would leap to influence the shogun and the entire *bakufu* against him. He could bid farewell to his plans to bring Japan under his control, place his son Yoritomo in line for the succession, and rule the nation through him.

The very thought raised a tide of nausea in Yanagisawa. How could he protect himself against the evil forces closing in on him? As he pondered, he suddenly noticed his wife standing in the doorway.

"What do you want?" he lashed out at her. She was always hanging around him, always spying on him through peepholes that she thought he didn't know about. He let her spy because he didn't care. He tolerated her presence because her adoration had been a balm to his pride after Police Commissioner Hoshina had left him. But now she was a convenient target for his frustrations. "Can't you just leave me alone?"

Her homely face blanched; she shrank from his anger. "I—I'm sorry," she whispered. "If you don't want me, I'll go." She backed away, her gaze lingering on him, as if wanting to keep him in sight for as long as possible.

Inspiration struck Yanagisawa with a stunning, radiant force. His needs suddenly meshed with the circumstances surrounding him. His scowl relaxed into a smile.

"Wait," he told her. "Don't leave. I want you to stay."

She hesitated, distrusting his change in mood.

"I'm sorry I spoke harshly to you." Yanagisawa had never before thought to use his charm on his wife, but now he must. "Please forgive me." Even a devoted slave would balk at what he wanted her to do. To secure her cooperation would require all his persuasive powers. He hastened to her and put his arm around her.

"Come," he said, leading her into an adjacent chamber comfortably furnished with floor cushions and seascape murals.

He felt her shiver with delight at his touch, and her breathing quickened. As he seated her, she looked up at him, her face dazed, as if unable to believe she was receiving the rare, wonderful gift of his attention. He settled himself opposite her, so close that their knees touched. He poured two cups of wine and placed one in her trembling hands.

"My lord . . . This is a tremendous honor . . ." Gasps of awe unsteadied her speech. Her cheeks were flushed.

"It's no more than you deserve in exchange for your devotion to me," Yanagisawa said. "And I'm glad we have a chance to talk together."

She hung on his words, her expression rapt. He drank his wine, and she gulped hers.

"I'm afraid I haven't been a very good husband," Yanagisawa said. "I know I've neglected you. That was wrong, especially since you've been a faithful wife to me."

As he spoke, her shining gaze told him that he was saying what she'd always longed to hear. She moved her lips, silently repeating his words to herself, committing them to memory.

"And you have so many wonderful qualities." Yanagisawa hadn't realized what his wife was capable of until she'd told him about her attacks on Sano's wife Reiko. "I want to make up for the way I've treated you." He lowered his voice to a husky, pleading tone: "Will you let me?"

"Yes!" Her hands dropped her empty cup. She clasped them to her bosom, so agitated by glee that he thought she would swoon. "Oh, yes!"

"A million thanks," he said, feigning humbleness. "Your generosity is one of the traits I value most in you." And he meant to take full advantage of it. "From now on, I'll try to be a better husband. I'll also try to be a better father. I'll pay more attention to Kikuko as well as you."

She glowed with joyous, complete faith in him. People tended to believe what they wanted to believe, and Yanagisawa had fooled many a wiser person. "You're being so good to me," she murmured. "How can I ever repay your kindness?"

Yanagisawa smiled in sly satisfaction. "There is a small favor you can do for me." He leaned close to her, put his lips to her ear, and whispered.

Lady Yanagisawa recoiled in shock from the chamberlain. He raised his eyebrows, prompting a reply. What he'd asked of her was so horrifying that her mind spurned his very words, although she was desperately eager to please him.

"I . . . I can't do it," she said. She averted her eyes from him, afraid to see anger on his face, terrified that he would revert to his usual, cold self. "I couldn't."

"Why not?" he said in such a gentle voice that she risked a glance at him. His handsome face showed only concern for her and a wish to understand her objection.

"It's—it's wrong."

Vague suspicion kindled in Lady Yanagisawa. That her

husband had suddenly begun to treat her as she'd always hoped now seemed as disturbing as marvelous. Was he putting on an act designed to manipulate her into doing his terrible bidding? Her heart repelled the idea.

"I know it sounds bad," the chamberlain said, "and I hate asking you to do it, but there's no one else I can trust. I'm surrounded by enemies and traitors. You're the only person who's loyal to me." His gaze compelled her. "I need you."

Lady Yanagisawa yearned to fill his need. To commit treachery seemed worthwhile if she could win his approval, yet the ingrained morals of society prohibited her. "I've never done anything like that," she said. "I—I don't think I'm capable."

"I know you are," said the chamberlain.

They both knew she'd done things not so far removed from what he wanted, but she'd excused them as impulses provoked by circumstances beyond her control. If she carried out his wishes, she must act deliberately, with full knowledge of what she did and the possible consequences of her actions.

"I'll tell you exactly what to say and do," he said.

"But I couldn't do that to a friend, or an enemy," Lady Yanagisawa said.

The chamberlain eyed her with reproach. "Does the welfare of friends and enemies matter more to you than I do?"

"Of course not, my lord!" Lady Yanagisawa hastened to say. "You are the person most important to me." She huddled, arms wrapped around herself, and shook her head. "But I'm afraid."

"Afraid of getting in trouble?" When she nodded, the chamberlain said, "Don't be." His personality and beauty exerted a powerful force upon her. "I won't let anything bad happen to you."

Lady Yanagisawa stiffened her crumbling will. "I just can't do it." Her voice wobbled; tears smarted her eyes. She realized that her fondest wishes hinged on obeying him. This dreadful favor was the price of his affection toward Kikuko as well as herself. "Couldn't I do something else for you instead?" she pleaded.

The chamberlain regarded her with a grave compassion that stirred her ever-present desire for him. "Let me explain why you must do me this favor and none other."

He took her hand in his. Lady Yanagisawa's breath caught as the warm press of his flesh sent a thrill of excitation through her.

"I need to weaken my enemies," he said. "Together we can strike their very heart."

His fingers fondled and kneaded hers. She sat immobile, her eyelids lowered, savoring his touch and her arousal.

"But if you don't help me, I'll lose my fight against Lord Matsudaira. He'll have my head as his war trophy. You and I will be separated." Sadness tinged the chamberlain's voice. "You wouldn't want that to happen . . . would you?"

He eased himself so close beside her that she could hear him breathing, smell his masculine scent of tobacco smoke and wintergreen hair oil. The nearness of him raised a hot, tumultuous fever in her blood. He stroked her cheek.

A groan escaped Lady Yanagisawa as her skin burned under the caress that wandered over her lips, trailed down her throat. He loosened her robes. His intense, luminous gaze and smile transfixed her as he caressed her breasts. Her nipples hardened and tingled. She cried out with a pleasure and a keenness of desire she'd never known before. Now the chamberlain lowered her to the floor and reclined at her side. His hand moved under her skirts, up her thigh, sending shivers through her. His fingers caressed her moist, slick womanhood. She heard herself moaning while her pleasure mounted toward heights she'd never scaled. And he alone could send her to those heights.

"If you love me, you'll help me," the chamberlain murmured, his breath like fire upon her ear.

Lady Yanagisawa heard his meaning that he would never love her unless she gave in. "Please," she whimpered, begging him to love her without conditions attached. Ravenous for him, she clutched at his surcoat and pulled him toward her.

The chamberlain pried her fingers off him, sat back on his heels. "Not until you've done what I've asked."

Beautiful and adamant, alluring and cruel, he loomed over Lady Yanagisawa. Her desperate need for him shattered the remains of her will. If she wanted him to fulfill her lusts and dreams, she had no choice but to capitulate. Sobs of terror and surrender convulsed Lady Yanagisawa.

"Yes," she cried, "I'll do it."

17

An hour's brisk ride out of Edo brought Hirata to Asakusa Kannon Temple. Located near the Sumida River and on a main highway, the Buddhist temple was a popular attraction surrounded by inns, shops, and teahouses. The famous pagoda raised its five scarlet tiers and golden spire into the frigid blue afternoon sky. Bells pealed as Hirata dismounted and left his horse outside the temple grounds. He joined the crowds streaming through the main gate. By the time he entered the precinct, the joy of escaping his watchdogs had completely dissipated.

They would be furious. If only he'd just put up with them instead of running away like a bad boy playing a game! This murder case was no child's play. Hirata didn't want to think what might happen to him on account of his rash impulses. He decided that it was too late for regrets, and he would face the consequences when necessary. For now, he must concentrate on investigating Senior Elder Makino's widow, Agemaki.

Inside the temple precinct, Buddhist and Shinto religion coexisted with commerce. Market stalls decorated with colorful lanterns and banners lined the main avenue. Vendors sold food, plants, medicines, umbrellas, toys, and rosaries. People haggled over prices; money changed hands. Roving entertainers performed puppet shows and acrobatics; monks begged alms. Fragrant incense smoke drifted over the crowds.

Hirata walked past the main hall to Asakusa Jinja Shrine, dedicated to the men whose discovery of a statue of Kannon, Buddhist goddess of mercy, had led to the founding of the temple. Painted woodwork and sculpture embellished the building. Sacred doves cooed from the eaves. Shinto shrine attendants dressed in white, and gray-robed Buddhist nuns with their heads shaved bald, flocked outside the shrine, accosting male pilgrims. Their shrill voices besieged the men with offers of their favors. At Asakusa Kannon, religion also coexisted with sex. Many nuns and shrine attendants lived by selling themselves as well as by begging alms, Hirata knew. Although the law forbade prostitution outside the Yoshiwara pleasure quarter, enforcement was lax in the temple districts.

A young nun, gawky and plain, rushed up to Hirata, caught hold of his arm, and said, "Do you want some company, master?"

A shrine attendant grabbed Hirata by his other arm. "Come with me," she wheedled. "We can have fun together." She was pretty, with long, streaming hair and a winsome smile.

"I saw him first," the nun said, scowling at her rival. "Go away."

The women began squabbling over Hirata, tugging him back and forth, cursing each other. An elderly, bald priest dressed in a gray cloak over his saffron robes, leaning on a cane, hobbled up to them.

"Are these girls bothering you, master?" he asked Hirata. He spoke in a loud voice that indicated he was deaf. Cloudy eyes denoted failing vision. The women let go of Hirata; they stood demure and respectful in their superior's presence.

"Not at all," Hirata said, then introduced himself. "I'm seeking information on a woman named Agemaki. She was once a shrine attendant here. She was the wife of Senior Elder Makino, whose murder I'm investigating."

"I knew her. I can tell you all about her," the pretty shrine attendant said with a sly, knowing look.

"Me, too," the plain nun hurried to say.

The priest appeared not to hear them. "I am the caretaker of Asakusa Jinja Shrine," he told Hirata. "I knew Agemaki quite well. Perhaps you'd like to come in from the cold and have some refreshment while we talk?"

"Yes, I would, thank you."

Hirata, who also wanted to hear what the women had to say, was about to ask them to wait for him, when the priest said to the shrine attendant, "Come along, Yuriko-*san,* and help me serve our guest."

Yuriko flashed a triumphant look at the disappointed nun. She trailed Hirata and the priest to the clergy residence, a rustic plaster and timber building secluded in a garden. The priest seated Hirata and himself in an austere chamber whose alcove held a vase of winter branches and a religious poem written on a scroll. Yuriko heated an urn of water on a hearth sunk in the floor. The tranquil atmosphere muted the bustle of the temple grounds outside.

"Agemaki was born and raised at Asakusa Kannon," the priest said. "Her mother was a shrine attendant, too. She died many years ago. She was a very dedicated religious woman."

Yuriko, kneeling at the hearth, spoke to Hirata in a low, covert tone. "Don't believe it. Agemaki's mother was a beggar and a whore, just like most of us. She came to Asakusa Kannon because the temple gives us a place to live and food to eat, and the law doesn't bother us here."

There were two different versions of the history of Senior Elder Makino's wife, Hirata realized. Thanks to the priest's deafness, he was going to hear both. "Who is Agemaki's father?" Hirata asked the priest.

"He was a wealthy samurai official. He died in a fire the year she was born. His death left her and her mother to fend for themselves."

"That's what Agemaki told everyone," Yuriko muttered.

"She liked to put on airs. But everyone here knows her father was a *rōnin* who spent a few months with her mother, then left town, never to be seen again." Casting a fond, apologetic glance at the priest, Yuriko added, "He always thinks the best of people."

"Agemaki grew up to be as beautiful as her mother," the priest continued, oblivious. "She followed in her footsteps."

"Indeed she did," Yuriko said while measuring powdered green tea into porcelain bowls. "She was popular with the men. Sometimes she had seven or eight customers a day."

Hirata reflected that Senior Elder Makino had displayed a low taste in women for a man of his high rank. First his concubine had proved to be a former prostitute; now, his wife. Had his low taste—and dubious choice of female companions—led to his death?

"Agemaki had a rare, genuine spiritual calling," the priest said. "She seemed not quite of this world."

Yuriko snorted as she poured hot water into the tea bowls. "That holy, mysterious manner was just an act. Some men like that. It excites them. But we girls knew the real Agemaki. She was crude and selfish. She loved money and the things it bought."

Hirata remembered the widow he'd seen. Had her refined dignity, her grief for her murdered husband, and her desire to help apprehend his killer also been an act? "Agemaki left the temple to marry Senior Elder Makino," Hirata reminded the priest. "That doesn't suggest a very strong religious faith."

The priest smiled gently and spread his hands. "When a man as important as the senior elder wanted her, Agemaki was powerless to say no."

"Ha! She had no intention of resisting him." In her vehemence Yuriko spoke too loudly. The priest squinted at her. Ducking her head, she stirred the tea with a wooden whisk. She murmured to Hirata: "Agemaki wanted a rich patron. When Makino came here looking for girls, she was eager to latch onto him."

"Senior Elder Makino was captivated by Agemaki's virtue," said the priest.

Hirata raised his eyebrows at Yuriko.

"It wasn't her virtue that he liked best about her," Yuriko said with a sneer. "He was weak. He'd lost his manhood. I know because he once hired me to entertain him, and no matter what we did—" Yuriko's finger pantomimed a limp penis. "But Agemaki knew ways to excite men. She knew potions for curing their weakness. Her mother taught her. She made Makino feel young and strong again. That's why he wanted her. But she wouldn't let him have her unless he took her away from here, to Edo Castle."

"So he married Agemaki," the priest said. "She went to live in his house as his wife."

"Not quite so," Yuriko said, handing bowls of tea to Hirata and the priest. While they drank, she said, "Makino was still married to his first wife when he took Agemaki from the temple. Agemaki was the senior elder's concubine at the beginning. They married later on."

"What happened to Makino's first wife?" Hirata said.

"I heard she died of a fever," said the priest.

"Don't be too quick to believe it," Yuriko said. "Agemaki set her heart on becoming the wife of an important official. She wasn't satisfied to be a concubine. She begged Makino to divorce his old wife and marry her, but he refused. I know because I overheard them arguing. But her mother also taught Agemaki about poisons. There were rumors that Agemaki poisoned Makino's first wife so that she could take her place."

Hirata glanced sharply at Yuriko, whose expression said that she believed the rumors. If they were true, then a woman who'd bloodied her hands in the past might have the inclination to kill again. Yet Hirata couldn't take the word of a jealous, spiteful gossip. And even if Agemaki had killed her predecessor, why would she later kill the man she'd wanted so badly to wed?

"Agemaki is a suspect in the murder of her husband," Hirata told Yuriko and the priest. "Can you think of any reason why she might have wanted Makino dead?"

"None," the priest said. "Perhaps she had little affection for her husband, but she was dependent on him."

"He's right about that," Yuriko said. "Old Makino gave Agemaki food, clothes, servants, and a fine place to live."

"But he granted her a fortune," Hirata said.

"I know," said Yuriko. "After he married her, she came back here to show off. She bragged about the money she would get when he died."

"I'm glad to hear that she wasn't left destitute," the priest said, still unaware of the two conversations taking place simultaneously.

"Maybe Agemaki killed Makino for the money," Hirata suggested.

As the priest protested, Yuriko said, "Now that Makino is dead, Agemaki will have to move out of his house because his family won't want a common whore around. She won't be a high-ranking lady any longer. She would have hated to come down in the world." Yuriko made a moue of distaste, as though hating to speak in favor of Agemaki's innocence. "If money is the only thing she would get by killing him, then I don't think she did."

The priest regarded Hirata and Yuriko with his cloudy gaze. A mild frown puckered his face, as though he'd finally noticed the communication between them and wondered what he'd missed. "Have I told you what you wanted to know?" he asked Hirata.

"Yes," Hirata said. "A thousand thanks."

"I'm glad to be of assistance," said the priest.

Hirata bid him farewell, then walked outside and across the temple precinct with Yuriko. Pilgrims strolled and doves swooped around them. The sunlight had dimmed, casting a bronze glow on the tile rooftops; the air had turned colder with the declining afternoon.

"I'm glad to be of assistance, too," Yuriko said with a saucy smile. "Have I told you what you really wanted to know about Agemaki?"

Reserving judgment, Hirata said, "I'll have to talk to other people who know her."

"Let me go with you," Yuriko said. "I can introduce you to people. Afterward, we can have some fun together." She took Hirata's arm. Her eyes shone with her need to attach herself to a man who could rescue her from poverty and degradation.

"Introductions would be appreciated. I'll pay you for your trouble, but I can't accept your other kind offer." Happily married, Hirata had no desire for women other than Midori. "I must get back to town as soon as my work here is finished." And he was eager to find out what Sano had discovered today, if not to face Sano's reaction to his escaping his watchdogs.

Yuriko accepted the rebuff with the nonchalance of someone who'd survived many disappointments in life. "Maybe next time."

As she led him toward the nuns and shrine attendants who still flocked outside Asakusa Jinja Shrine, Hirata reflected that he'd unearthed compromising evidence against both Agemaki and Okitsu. It might justify his misbehavior and please Sano, if not solve the murder case. There remained suspects in Senior Elder Makino's household who were still unknown quantities to Hirata. He would give much to know what was going on inside that estate now.

Reiko carried a tray laden with food and drink down the corridor of Senior Elder Makino's private chambers. After hours of washing laundry under the housekeeper Yasue's strict supervision, she was more exhausted than from the most strenuous martial arts practice. Her clothes were damp, grimy, and sweaty. A bump had sprouted on her head where Yasue had hit her again, and her cut finger burned from the lye soap used in the laundry. Never did she want to touch another piece of soiled bedding or underwear! When Yasue had ordered her to serve dinner to the actor and concubine, Reiko had rejoiced at the chance to escape drudgery and spy on them.

She knelt at the open door of Koheiji's room and staggered across the threshold, awkwardly balancing the tray. The room was bright and warm from glowing lanterns and numerous charcoal braziers. Inside, surrounded by theatrical costumes on wooden stands, Koheiji and Okitsu lolled on floor cushions, laughing together at some joke. They both wore colorful silk dressing gowns. His head lay in her lap. As Reiko set the tray near them, she reflected that she'd learned something today besides that Senior Elder Makino had had bizarre sexual habits and his chief retainer had behaved suspiciously.

There could be no doubt that his concubine and house-guest were lovers.

"Oh, good, our meal is here!" Okitsu said. "I'm starving!"

She ignored Reiko; the lavish spread of sashimi, grilled prawns, sweet cakes, and other delicacies commanded all her attention. Koheiji gave Reiko an appraising glance that she thought he probably gave all women who happened into his view. She saw his eyes register her plain looks and dismiss her as unworthy of his interest. He said to Okitsu, "Feed me."

Okitsu popped morsels into his mouth and her own. Reiko set the sake decanter on a brazier to warm. She was glad that her disguise worked and Koheiji and Okitsu considered her beneath their notice, but she felt an unexpected sting of wounded pride. Though admired for her beauty and respected for her high social status all her life, she was nothing to these people.

"Isn't it nice that we can be together without sneaking around?" Okitsu said, feeding a prawn to Koheiji.

He chewed and swallowed. "Yes, it certainly is. Making love in the garden at night was a bit uncomfortable. But the sneaking added excitement." He leered up at Okitsu and tickled her ribs.

Okitsu giggled. "Naughty boy!" she said, slapping Koheiji. "I was always afraid that Makino would find out what we were up to. If he'd known, he would have been very angry."

Koheiji snorted. "That's an understatement. Makino was a jealous old dog. He would have thrown us both out of the house. You'd have had to go back to the brothel. And Makino would have ordered the theaters to ban me from their stages."

Reiko felt a thrill of excitement. Had Makino indeed found out about Okitsu and Koheiji's love affair? If so, one of them might have killed him to protect themselves.

"But now we don't have to worry about old Makino anymore. Everything is wonderful." Okitsu exuded a sigh of bliss. She fed Koheiji raw tuna and stroked his cheek. "You're so clever!"

"Yes, I am," Koheiji said, basking in her admiration.

Did Okitsu mean he'd been clever to rid them of the man who stood between them? Reiko pictured the actor beating Makino to death, then tucking his corpse into bed.

"I adore you," Okitsu said, gazing raptly at Koheiji.

"I know," Koheiji said with a conceited smile.

He pointed at the sake decanter and gestured at Reiko. She obediently poured liquor for the couple. They continued ignoring her. She felt as invisible as she'd told Sano she would be. Anticipation eclipsed hurt pride. Might the couple be foolish enough to reveal the truth about the murder while never suspecting that she was a spy?

Okitsu sipped her sake and looked coyly at Koheiji over the rim of her cup. "Koheiji-*san* . . . ?"

The actor downed his drink and crammed more sashimi into his mouth. "Hmm?"

"Do you remember what you promised me?" Okitsu's voice took on a teasing, wheedling tone.

"What did I promise?" Koheiji said, his face blank with confusion.

Okitsu playfully swatted his shoulder. "Silly!" she cried. "You know. You promised we would marry someday."

"Oh. Right," Koheiji said with a notable lack of enthusiasm. "I guess I did."

"Well, now that Makino is gone, we can marry." Okitsu appeared not to notice her lover's reaction. Eagerness sparkled in her eyes. "Let's do it tomorrow!"

Here Reiko perceived another possible motive for the murder. Maybe the concubine and actor had wanted Makino dead so that they could wed. But although she seemed besotted with him, Reiko saw that he cared less for her. Intuition told Reiko that this man could have killed Makino to protect his career but not to marry Okitsu.

"We shouldn't rush into marriage," Koheiji said. His gaze avoided Okitsu's. He edged away from her.

Surprise and disappointment showed on Okitsu's face. "Why not?" she said. "Why should we wait?"

"Because our future is uncertain. We don't even have a place to live." Koheiji spoke as if concerned with practical matters, but Reiko thought he was grasping at excuses. "You know we can't stay here forever."

"But Makino gave me some money," Okitsu said. "He gave some to you, too, didn't he? Between us we should have enough to get a house of our own."

"Yes . . ." Koheiji pondered; his hands toyed nervously with dishes on the tray. "But there's a more serious reason why we should wait at least until the fuss about Makino's murder blows over. If we marry too soon, everybody will know we were lovers before he died and we were cheating on him. Everybody will believe I killed him."

"But you didn't!" Okitsu exclaimed, widening her eyes in horror. "We—"

"Whether I'm innocent doesn't matter," Koheiji interrupted. "It's what people think that counts."

Reiko longed to know what Okitsu had meant to say when Koheiji cut her off. Did Okitsu know the truth about the murder? Was Koheiji innocent or not? The trouble with spying was that even if Reiko could see and hear people as plain as day, she could only guess at what was in their minds.

"The *sōsakan-sama* and his men are already snooping around, asking questions, making accusations," Koheiji said. "You and I were two of the four people in these chambers the night Makino died. I'm afraid the *sōsakan-sama* will pick me to blame for the murder. Actors have a bad reputation, and nobody who matters to him cares what happens to me. It will be his word against mine, and which of us do you think his superiors will believe?"

Koheiji shook his head. "Not me. I'll be convicted and executed." Okitsu gaped at him in alarm. He clasped her hand and gazed earnestly into her face. "So you see, we must be cautious. To marry now would be a dangerous mistake."

Okitsu sighed. "Yes. You're right." Doubt puckered her brow; she regarded Koheiji as though she feared deceit. "But sometimes I wonder if maybe you don't want to marry me at all."

"Of course I do," Koheiji said with an ardent sincerity that didn't convince Reiko. "How can you doubt my word?"

"If you really loved me and wanted to marry me, you would be willing to take a few risks to be together." Okitsu pouted, her lower lip thrust out. "You wouldn't let a little danger stand between us."

Koheiji laughed, amused by her childish naïveté. "You're getting me mixed up with the heroes I play in the theater. The danger is only make-believe for them. After the play is over, they can walk offstage unharmed. But if I run afoul of the law, I'll die for real."

"Don't laugh at me!" Okitsu flared, yanking her hands out of his. Her cheeks flushed; she eyed Koheiji with sharp suspicion. "Is there someone else?" she said, her voice accusing yet querulous. "Is that why you're putting me off?"

"There's nobody but you," Koheiji said. His masculine dislike of emotional scenes and his desire to forestall this one were obvious to Reiko. "You're the only one I love."

He reached toward Okitsu, but she angrily batted his hands away. "What about all those girls who hang around you at the theater?" she demanded. "Those girls who go to all your performances, follow you in the streets, and send you gifts and love letters? Is she one of them?"

"Those girls mean nothing to me," Koheiji said, loud in his vehement denial.

"But I know you accept their gifts. You answer their letters. I've seen you flirting with them when you don't think I'm looking." Tears quavered Okitsu's voice.

"They're my audience," Koheiji defended himself. "I have to keep them happy."

"And you care more about their happiness than mine." Having whipped herself into a fit of hysteria, Okitsu began to sob. "I can't bear for you to have anyone else. I can't bear to lose you. Especially after what happened with Senior Elder Makino. Especially after everything I've done for you!"

Reiko stared at Okitsu, forgetting to pretend she had no

interest in the conversation. Did Okitsu mean *she* had killed
Makino for the sake of her lover? Reiko cautioned herself
against reading too much into Okitsu's words; yet perhaps
Okitsu had more motive for the murder than did Koheiji. His
concern for his career and dependence on his patron could
have outweighed his feelings toward Okitsu and inhibited
him from harming Makino. She, on the other hand, seemed
fixated on Koheiji, reckless in her love for him. Perhaps
she'd beaten Makino to death and eliminated the obstacle to
the marriage she so desired.

"There's no other woman," Koheiji insisted.

Reiko heard panic in his voice. Did he know that Okitsu
had killed Makino for him and fear that if she couldn't keep
it a secret, they would both be punished? Reiko waited
breathless, gazing at the floor, hoping Okitsu would incriminate herself.

"I love you and only you," Koheiji told Okitsu. His hand
cupped her face; his manner turned seductive. "Let me show
you how much."

To Reiko's disappointment, Okitsu said no more about
Senior Elder Makino. She clamped her mouth shut, swallowed sobs, and cringed from Koheiji. He murmured endear-
ments and stroked her cheek. A reluctant smile twitched her
lips; her tongue licked his fingers. Obviously relieved that
he'd placated her, Koheiji put his arm around Okitsu and
squeezed her waist. She giggled, undulating provocatively,
shrugging her robe off her bare shoulders. Koheiji caressed
them, while she fondled the bulge that swelled at his crotch
beneath his robe.

Reiko decided that they wouldn't want her around while
they made love, and she wouldn't hear anything else worth
her spying. She moved quietly toward the door.

"Don't go," Koheiji said. "I haven't dismissed you yet."

She paused, surprised that he had noticed her after ignoring her until now and apparently didn't want her to leave. As
Okitsu fondled him, he gave Reiko a lazy, sensuous smile.
"We'll need you to serve us drinks later," he said. "Sit down
and enjoy yourself."

His gaze condescended to her. Reiko realized that he thought he was doing her a favor by inviting her to experience vicarious carnal pleasure. She was so flabbergasted that words failed her.

"I always perform best in front of an audience," Koheiji said.

Okitsu gave Reiko a sly, superior glance that said she didn't mind an audience because she liked being the object of another woman's envy. Then she turned her attention back to her lover. Reiko wanted to bolt from the room rather than watch the pair, but if she did, she might be thrown out of the house for disobeying an order. And she'd not learned enough that she could give up future chances for spying. She knelt as far from Koheiji and Okitsu as possible.

They giggled and nuzzled each other, shedding their clothes. Naked, they entwined their legs. Koheiji's manhood curved upward, long and thick; Okitsu's sleek, plump body and rosy nipples gleamed in the lantern light. Reiko had never before watched other people engage in intimacies. Her face burned with embarrassment, but she couldn't look away. Horrified fascination kept her gaze fixed on the lovers.

Koheiji picked up a sweet cake from the tray of food. He blew powdered pink sugar from the cake onto Okitsu's chest. He licked the sugar off her while she cooed and tittered.

"Oh, look, there's some on you," she said, pointing to his erection.

She bent over him and sucked on his member; he held her head, groaning dramatically. Reiko felt her body respond against her will. Arousal increased her embarrassment.

Okitsu flopped onto her back and reached for Koheiji. "Wait," he said, "I need a little aphrodisiac."

He plucked a hard-boiled quail egg from the tray and discarded the shell. Okitsu spread her legs. He inserted the peeled egg into her womanhood, then crouched between her legs and sucked out the egg. As he chewed, smacked his lips, and uttered sounds of relish, Okitsu laughed uproariously. Reiko cringed, mortified by a different sort of humiliation

than the housekeeper Yasue had inflicted on her. What other
trials must she endure while spying? She beheld the lovers,
now coupling with noisy, energetic abandon. If one of them
was the murderer she sought, was it Koheiji or Okitsu?

19

The sky above Edo Castle's official quarter glowed with the cold red fire of sunset. Moon and stars glittered like ice shards in the darkening heavens. Smoke drifted from inside the mansions and lanterns burning at the gates; sentries stamped their feet and rubbed their arms to keep themselves warm. Hirata rode along the empty street, dawdling as he neared Sano's estate. Soon would come his moment of reckoning. He prayed that he wasn't in too much trouble.

"The *sōsakan-sama* is waiting for you," said the guard who opened the gate for Hirata.

The guard's tone said Hirata was in very much trouble. Hirata's heart began a slow, sickening descent. When he entered the mansion, he found Sano, Otani, and Ibe kneeling in the reception room.

"Hirata-*san*. Please join us," Sano said.

His manner was unusually formal. Ibe and Otani regarded Hirata with open animosity. Hirata's heart pounded as he knelt, greeted Sano and his guests, and bowed to them.

"I understand that you ran out on the men assigned to observe your inquiries today," Sano said. "Is that true?"

"Yes, *Sōsakan-sama*," Hirata said in a monotone that he hoped would conceal his nervousness.

"Where did you go?"

"To investigate Senior Elder Makino's wife at Asakusa Jinja Shrine."

"See? I told you." Otani shot a look at Sano. "He went off investigating on his own. He broke the rule that all inquiries pertaining to Senior Elder Makino's murder should be overseen by representatives of Lord Matsudaira."

"And Chamberlain Yanagisawa," added Ibe. "He also left my men breathing his dust."

The disappointment in Sano's eyes pained Hirata. "I can explain," he said, anxious to defend himself although his only, poor excuse was that he'd snapped under pressure.

Otani's hand sliced a cutting gesture at Hirata. "It doesn't matter why you did it."

"What's important is that you never cause us trouble again," said Ibe.

"As of this moment, you are removed from the investigation," Otani said.

Shock and horror combined with humiliation as Hirata realized that his watchdogs thought him such a trivial person that they wouldn't bother inflicting a more severe punishment on him. They were just cutting him out of the investigation as if he were a rotten spot on an apple.

"That's fair," Sano said, his tone as stoic as his expression.

And Sano was going along with them! Hirata stared in dismay at the master who'd just sacrificed him to appease Chamberlain Yanagisawa and Lord Matsudaira. A sense of injustice filled Hirata even though he knew he'd earned his fate. He couldn't let the watchdogs take away his chance to solve the murder case and regain Sano's esteem.

"A thousand apologies for my bad behavior," he said, reluctantly abasing himself to Otani and Ibe. "Please allow me to make amends to you and continue in the investigation."

"Save your breath," Otani said. "The decision is final."

Otani and Ibe rose. As Sano accompanied them to the door, Otani paused and said to Hirata, "By the way, what did you learn at Asakusa Jinja Shrine?"

Hirata rebelled against sharing the results of his clandestine inquiries with the men who'd exacted painful retribution for them. "Nothing," he lied.

Ibe chuckled. "Then your escapade wasn't worth the consequences, was it?"

Hirata sat alone, furious and miserable, while Sano escorted the watchdogs out of the estate. Presently, Sano returned and knelt facing Hirata.

"Things could be worse," Sano said. "Otani and Ibe could have ordered you put to death for insubordination. If either of us had objected to your punishment, they'd have done it out of spite."

That Sano had good reason for not objecting gave Hirata little solace. "Do you want me out of the investigation, too?" he said.

Conflicting emotions battled in Sano's eyes. He exhaled and said, "You've shown poor judgment. This murder case is difficult enough without my own men causing problems."

Hirata bowed his head, aware that Sano was right and he'd made himself a liability to Sano. When he'd disobeyed orders during the hunt for their wives and the kidnapper, he'd lowered himself into a hole of disgrace. Now, after only three days on the murder case that he'd hoped would restore him to honor, he'd dug the hole deeper.

Forlorn, he said, "How can I make up for what I did today?"

"You might start by telling me what you discovered about Senior Elder Makino's widow," said Sano. "Maybe you fooled Otani and Ibe, but I doubt that you came away from Asakusa Jinja Shrine empty-handed."

At least he could prove himself a competent detective as well as a fool and liar, Hirata thought glumly. He told Sano the rumors that Agemaki had murdered Makino's first wife. "Before I came home, I questioned the Edo Castle physician who attended Makino's first wife when she took ill." Hirata mentioned some interesting facts gleaned from the doctor. "He's always suspected she was poisoned. And Agemaki certainly benefited from her death."

Sano nodded, absorbing the news, delaying judgment.

"Otani told me about your trip to Rakuami's pleasure house. He says you learned nothing worthwhile about the concubine."

"I beg to disagree," Hirata said, irked that the man who'd expelled him from the investigation had also demeaned his hard-won evidence. "We learned that Okitsu hated Makino enough that she tried to drown herself rather than be sold to him."

"Whether or not that means either woman killed Makino, it appears that his household was no model of peace and harmony," Sano said. "He and his chief retainer had their differences." He described Tamura's disapproval of his master's greed for money and sex. "His vendetta against the murderer could mean he's innocent, or that he's covering his guilt. And that actor is a shady character." Sano told how Koheiji had staged sex shows and once beaten up an elderly client.

"We've discovered evidence against all the people who were in Makino's private chambers that night," Hirata said, "but none that proves any of them is guilty."

"Maybe Reiko will find some," Sano said.

Hirata belatedly noticed the haggard, careworn look that shadowed Sano's face. He must be worrying about Reiko. "Has there been any news of her?" Hirata hated that he'd caused Sano additional worries.

"None," Sano said. "The detectives I put in Makino's house to report on her have said they can't find her. I don't know what's happened to her."

Neither he nor Hirata speculated aloud on the mishaps that might have befallen Reiko by now.

"What's the next step in the investigation?" Hirata said, wondering if he even dared ask, now that it was none of his business.

Sano breathed, slowly and deliberately, as though to gird himself for an unpleasant task. "Much as I would like to avoid the factions, I can't. I've already skirmished with Lord Matsudaira and his nephew." Sano described what he'd discovered about Daiemon. "It's time for a talk with Chamberlain Yanagisawa."

And Hirata would be left out of it. More than ever he regretted his mistake. As Sano rose, Hirata said, "What shall I do?"

"Attend to your other duties as my chief retainer," Sano said. "You can handle the business we've neglected since Makino's murder."

To occupy himself with mundane, everyday matters while the investigation went on without him seemed a sentence of doom to Hirata. "Yes, *Sōsakan-sama*," he said, bowing humbly.

Sano hesitated. The concern in his eyes worsened Hirata's anguish. "I'll see you tomorrow," Sano said.

With bitter despair, Hirata watched Sano walk out of the room.

Sano, accompanied by Detectives Marume and Fukida, met Chamberlain Yanagisawa in the passage that led to the heart of Edo Castle. Yanagisawa walked amid his entourage. Lights from torches in the guard turrets and carried by soldiers patrolling atop the stone walls flickered in the black night. Dogs howled somewhere on the hill.

"Good evening, *Sōsakan-sama*," the chamberlain said with cool courtesy as their two parties met.

Sano bowed, returned the greeting, then said, "May I have a word with you, Honorable Chamberlain?"

Yanagisawa nodded. Sano fell into step with Yanagisawa; their escorts trailed them. Yanagisawa said, "Don't tell me— let me guess: Your investigation into Senior Elder Makino's murder has led you to me."

"I suppose Ibe-*san* has reported to you what we discovered today," Sano said.

"I haven't yet heard from Ibe-*san*. Why don't you tell me what happened?"

Sano described his talk with Lord Matsudaira and Daiemon, and their allegation that Makino had defected. "They claim that they therefore had no reason to want him dead, and you did," Sano said.

"That's a good one." Yanagisawa gave Sano a sidelong, amused glance. "Was it Daiemon who introduced the idea that Makino had turned on me?" When Sano nodded, Yanagisawa chuckled. "I underestimated his talent for fabricating lies."

"Then it's untrue that Makino defected?" Sano's skepticism extended to Yanagisawa as well as the Matsudaira.

"Makino and I were longtime allies. There wasn't a chance that he would betray me at this stage," Yanagisawa said. "What proof do my enemies offer that he did?"

"None," Sano admitted. "That's why I came to hear your side of the story."

"Before accusing me of murdering Makino, based on their story?" Yanagisawa interpreted Sano's silence as assent. "That was wise of you." Respect tinged his tone. "Five years in the *bakufu* have refined your judgment. I scarcely recognize you as the raw amateur who used to rush headlong into every dangerous situation. Tell me: Under what circumstances did Daiemon announce that Makino had joined the Matsudaira faction?"

"I was questioning him about a visit he paid to Makino the night of the murder."

A cloud of vapor issued from Yanagisawa's nostrils as he snorted. "How unsurprising. You placed Daiemon at the scene of the crime. He knew he was in a dangerous position. What better way for him to cast off your suspicion than by foisting it onto me? That was quick thinking on his part."

"The same logic applies to you," Sano said. "What better way for you to reflect my suspicion back at Daiemon than by pointing out that he had reason to mislead me?"

Yanagisawa shrugged. "It's up to you to decide which of us is telling the truth."

And unless Sano found evidence to support Daiemon's story, he must give Yanagisawa the benefit of the doubt. Sometimes he could discern Yanagisawa's thoughts, but not tonight. Sano couldn't tell if Yanagisawa felt threatened by Daiemon's accusation or as unworried as he appeared. Yet Sano guessed that Yanagisawa had some scheme underway. He always did.

"But I must warn you against jumping to the conclusion that I'm the liar and not Daiemon," Yanagisawa said. "The fact remains that Daiemon was in Makino's house the night of the murder. I was at a banquet in my own house, with officials who can attest to my presence there."

Here was the alibi that Sano had expected Yanagisawa to offer. At least the chamberlain had spared him the trouble of asking his whereabouts the night of the murder.

"How am I supposed to have killed Makino while entertaining my guests?" Yanagisawa gave Sano a sly glance as they walked. "I presume you've investigated my spy whose name was given you by our mutual friend in the *metsuke*?"

Sano had stopped by Makino's estate before returning home tonight and questioned the guard Yanagisawa had employed to spy on Makino. The interview had negated the theory that the spy had assassinated Makino on orders from Yanagisawa. "Luckily for you, your spy was locked in the barracks that night," Sano said, "and the patrol guards confirmed that he was in his bed. He couldn't have killed Makino."

"What about Lord Matsudaira's spy?" Yanagisawa said in a tone of mild curiosity.

"He was stationed outside the front gate," said Sano. "According to his partner, he never left until their shift ended at dawn."

Torches in a guard turret above Sano and Yanagisawa briefly illuminated a smug expression on the chamberlain's face. "Then your only evidence that the murder was committed by either faction is Daiemon's presence at the scene of the crime. Daiemon is therefore your best suspect among us."

"Not necessarily," Sano said. "If Makino did defect, you could have hired someone else in his estate to kill him. And your elite troops are known for their skill at stealth." Those troops were assassins whom Yanagisawa employed to keep himself in power. "They'd have had no problem invading Makino's house—or killing him under his guards' noses."

"*If* I had sent them to kill Makino. But I didn't," said Yanagisawa.

They'd reached his compound. As they halted outside the high stone wall, their escorts stopped behind them.

"Trace the movements of my troops that night if you like," he told Sano, "but it will be a waste of your time. Any evidence you find that implicates them in the murder will have been planted by my enemies. You'll exhaust yourself trying to separate fact from fraud." Yanagisawa shunned the notion with a flick of his hand. "There's a better solution to your problems. Go along with the evidence that says Daiemon is guilty. It's enough to convict him in the Court of Justice. Lodge an official accusation against him. Consider your investigation finished."

"And join your campaign against his uncle?" Sano said.

"Would that be such a bad idea?" Yanagisawa responded to Sano's lack of enthusiasm. "Remember that you've prospered during my time as chamberlain. I promise that if you ruin Daiemon and help me defeat Lord Matsudaira, you'll enjoy a larger income and more authority when my power is secure."

"I remember what my life was like before you agreed to a truce," Sano said, alluding to Yanagisawa's attacks on his person and reputation. "I also remember that you can call off our truce anytime you choose. And with all due respect, I would be a fool to believe a promise from you."

"You would be a fool to think that Lord Matsudaira can give you better terms than I can," Yanagisawa said. "Lord Matsudaira is more vulnerable than he seems. He's going to lose our battle. Join me and be on the winning side."

Sano felt the potent combination of will, menace, and charm by which Yanagisawa won allies and compelled their obedience. The vast, fortified bulk of his estate silently proclaimed his power. But despite his intelligence and his skill at manipulating people, Yanagisawa had never understood what motivated Sano. He couldn't offer Sano anything that would atone for years of torment or induce him to compromise his principles.

"Winning isn't as important to me as honor," Sano said, although Yanagisawa would never believe him. "And I'll serve honor by standing by the shogun, not conniving behind his back for control of the regime. Not with you, or with Lord Matsudaira."

"You'll be answering to one of us eventually." A cunning smile hovered around Yanagisawa's mouth. "At least you and I are old colleagues. You're hardly acquainted with Lord Matsudaira at all."

"And the familiar is better than the unknown?" Sano laughed at this argument that he recognized as a last resort. "Many thanks for your advice, Honorable Chamberlain, but I must go the way I've chosen."

Yanagisawa laughed, too, but his laughter had a mirthless, steely ring. "You're walking a dangerous path," he said. "Sooner or later you'll fall off on one side or the other. For your sake, it had better be my side. Because if you think you've already experienced the worst I can do to someone who opposes me, you're sadly mistaken."

Late that night, Sano lay wide awake in bed. He shut his eyes tight and willed sleep to come and replenish his strength for whatever challenges that tomorrow would bring. But images, conversations, and disturbing thoughts from the day seethed in his head. He turned under the heavy quilts, trying and failing to find a comfortable position. The bed felt cold and empty without Reiko. Wondering if she was safe increased his anxiety. His mind reprised the tense scene with Hirata and his doubts that things would ever again be right between them. He endlessly sorted through the results of his inquiries and tried to decide which of the suspects had most likely killed Makino, but all the facts he'd gleaned led him nowhere so far. The investigation seemed at an impasse.

When he heard footsteps in the corridor outside his room and Detective Marume call his name, he welcomed the distraction, even though he knew that a summons late at night usually meant trouble.

"Come in," he said, throwing off the quilt. "What is it?"

The door slid open, revealing the bulky figure of Marume,

lit by the flame of a lamp he carried. "I'm sorry to wake you, *Sōsakan-sama,* but there's a message from one of your informants in town. Lord Matsudaira's nephew Daiemon has just been murdered."

20

The building was a commonplace two-story wooden structure, located in the Nihonbashi merchant district, on a street that paralleled the nearby rice warehouses along the Sumida River. Bamboo shades screened the balcony; shutters covered the windows. A short blue curtain hung over the recessed doorway, where two soldiers whose armor bore the crest of the Matsudaira clan stood guard. Opposite were rundown shops and teahouses, the doors closed over their storefronts. A crowd of townspeople had gathered outside the building. In the sky, a faint ruddy glow in the east presaged dawn. Lanterns shone at neighborhood gates at either end of the street. As Sano rode through a gate with Marume, Fukida, and three other detectives, the crowd parted to let them pass. They dismounted outside the building.

"What is this place?" Marume said.

"It's a house of assignation," Sano said. He remembered the house from his days as a police commander of this district. "Lovers come here to engage in illicit affairs. It's called the Sign of Bedazzlement."

Here, in this seedy, disreputable place, had died Daiemon, the ambitious upstart of the Matsudaira faction and heir apparent to the shogun.

Sano, Marume, and Fukida climbed the steps and went into the house. The sounds of men muttering and women

crying greeted them. The house's proprietor, a frightened
old man, huddled in the entryway. Beyond this, more Matsudaira troops stood along a lamp-lit passage. Police Commissioner Hoshina came striding down the passage toward Sano
and the detectives.

"*Sōsakan-sama.* What are you doing here?" Hoshina said
in a tone that branded Sano as a trespasser.

"I heard that Daiemon was murdered," Sano said. "I've
come to investigate."

Hoshina spread his arms, planted his hands on the walls
of the passage, and blocked Sano's way. "There's no need.
My officers have already begun inquiries. This is police
business." And none of yours, said his hostile expression.

"Daiemon was a suspect in a crime that the shogun ordered me to investigate," Sano said. Hoshina never ceased
his petty squabbling over what crimes comprised whose territory. He grasped every chance to enlarge his sphere of authority and diminish Sano's. The war between the factions
had only aggravated his sense of rivalry. "That makes his
murder my business."

Indecision broke Hoshina's gaze; he seemed to recall that
Lord Matsudaira, his master, needed as many allies as possible and particularly wanted Sano. "Very well," he said
grudgingly.

He let Sano and the detectives pass, but he dogged their
heels as they moved down the corridor, which was lined with
dim chambers enclosed by wooden partitions. Through the
open doors of several chambers Sano saw couples, shame-
faced and disheveled, guarded by Lord Matsudaira's troops.
Sano recognized an army official and a prominent banker.
Although Hoshina was more interested in politics than in
police practice, at least he'd trapped the potential witnesses.

"He's in the last room on the left," Hoshina said.

Sano preceded Marume and Fukida into the room. More
troops loitered against walls painted with crude, gaudy landscape murals. A cold draft wavered the flame inside a torn
paper lantern suspended from the ceiling. Furniture consisted of a charcoal brazier, a washbasin behind a cheap

wooden screen, and a lacquer table that held a sake decanter and cups. On the *tatami* floor Daiemon lay, covered by a striped quilt, upon the futon. Only his face showed; his eyes were closed and his handsome features blank as if in sleep. Beside him knelt his uncle, clad in an opulent padded satin cloak and an armor helmet studded with gold. Lord Matsudaira looked up at Sano.

"Honorable Lord Matsudaira," Sano said, bowing, "please accept my condolences on the death of your nephew."

The man's eyes blazed with rage and grief. Tears streaked glistening trails down his cheeks. He seemed mute and stunned, like a warrior who'd taken a severe blow during battle. Sano felt an eerie echo of the past. A year ago he'd investigated the murder of Lord Matsudaira's son, a former favorite of the shogun. Being heir apparent brought bad luck, Sano reflected. Now Lord Matsudaira had lost another important kinsman.

"Can you tell me what happened?" Sano said.

"See for yourself," Lord Matsudaira said in a tight, bitter voice. He flung back the quilt that covered Daiemon.

Air saturated with the metallic smell of blood billowed up at Sano. Nausea clenched his stomach. Daiemon's torso was twisted and his limbs bent as if he'd crumpled onto the bed where he lay. Wet, gleaming blood stained the front of his silk kimono and the white cotton cover of the futon. The hilt of a dagger, bound in plain black cord in a crisscross pattern, protruded from his chest. Sano observed that the blade had been driven under his breastbone at an upward angle, beneath the rib cage, and into his heart.

Turning away from the gory sight, Sano said, "Was Daiemon here with a woman?"

Lord Matsudaira regarded Sano as if he thought the question idiotic. "That's what this place is for."

"Who was she?" Sano said.

"I have no idea."

"Where is she?"

Police Commissioner Hoshina said, "There was no sign of her when we arrived. Daiemon was alone."

More echoes from the past resonated through Sano. The murder of Lord Matsudaira's son had also involved a missing woman. "Go question the other people in the house," Sano told Marume and Fukida. "Bring me anyone who knows anything about the woman, or saw or heard anything."

The detectives bowed and went. Sano had brought them because Hirata was in bad odor with the factions, and Sano couldn't risk employing him in anything that involved them. Now Sano missed his chief retainer. He hoped Marume and Fukida would do as good a job as Hirata had always done. Inspecting the room, Sano found Daiemon's shoes and swords on the floor by the door, where he'd apparently left them. There was no trace of anyone else's presence. Examining the window shutters, Sano found the latches intact and no sign that the killer had forced his way into the room from outside.

"Is the room just as you found it?" Sano asked Lord Matsudaira.

Lord Matsudaira stared in bitter silence at his dead nephew. Hoshina said, "We didn't change anything, except to cover the body."

Sano crouched and peered at Daiemon's hands. They were smeared with blood, as though from clutching his wound before he'd fallen, but uninjured. Daiemon apparently had not tried to defend himself against the dagger. As Sano rose, Detectives Marume and Fukida returned, bringing the proprietor of the house.

"None of the couples saw Daiemon or his lady," said Fukida. "They were too busy to notice anything going on in this room."

Marume pushed the proprietor toward Sano and said, "He's the only witness. He rented the room to Daiemon and the woman. He discovered the body."

"Who was the woman?" Sano asked the proprietor.

The proprietor had bulging eyes that bulged wider as he shrank fearfully from Sano. "I don't know her name."

"What does she look like?" Sano said.

"I don't know. She's been here many times, but she always hides her face."

"Does anyone come with her?"

"No, master. She always comes by herself."

"By palanquin?"

"On foot."

Sano gave up the notion of identifying the woman through her vehicle or escorts. If she'd had them, she'd left them where they wouldn't be seen. "What time did she come?"

"At half past the hour of the boar," said the proprietor.

Late evening, the time preferred for secret assignations. Sano said, "What happened when she arrived?"

"She knocked on the door, as usual," the proprietor said. "I showed her to the room. It was reserved and paid for in advance, as usual."

"Was Daiemon already here when she arrived?" Sano said.

"No," said the proprietor. "He always came later."

"Tell me what happened when he came."

"I let him in the door, but I didn't show him to the room. He went by himself. He knew where it was—they always used the same one. That was the last time I saw him alive."

"Were there any noises from this room after he went in?"

The proprietor hunched his shoulders. "Maybe some whispering or cries. But that's normal here. And they could have come from my other customers."

The sounds of lovemaking had obscured whatever sounds Daiemon or his killer had uttered during the stabbing, Sano observed. "How did you happen to discover the murder?"

"I was passing by the door and I looked through the peephole." A guilty, sheepish look came over the proprietor's face. "All the doors have peepholes. I like to check the rooms once in a while, to make sure everything is all right."

And he probably enjoyed watching the lovers. Sano said, "So you looked inside this room. What happened next?"

"I saw him like that." The proprietor glanced at the corpse, gulped, and averted his gaze.

"You fetched the police?"

"No." The proprietor hastened to add, "Of course I was going to fetch them, but I didn't have a chance. First I thought I should tell my customers what had happened and give them time to leave."

Sano knew that the illicit lovers wouldn't have wanted to be caught here, by the police, at the scene of a crime; nor would the proprietor have wanted to expose them to scandal and lose their business.

"But just then, I heard banging on the door," the proprietor said, "and voices shouting, 'Police! Let us in!' When I opened the door, they ran straight to this room—they seemed to already know about the murder."

Sano cut his gaze to Police Commissioner Hoshina, loitering nearby. "How did they?"

"The local patrol officer was patrolling his territory with his civilian assistants, when they heard someone shouting, 'The Honorable Lord Matsudaira Daiemon has been murdered at the Sign of Bedazzlement!'" Hoshina said. "They didn't see who shouted. Whoever it was ran away. They came here and found Daiemon. They notified me. I notified Lord Matsudaira. We came immediately."

This strange story of an anonymous herald sounded unlikely to Sano. He hesitated to believe anything Hoshina said, but perhaps the killer had wanted the murder discovered and thus had told the police.

"The woman was gone when you found Daiemon?" Sano asked the proprietor.

"Yes, master."

"Did you see her go?"

"No, master. She must have left through the secret passage." The proprietor slid aside a partition camouflaged by the mural on a wall, revealing a closet. From a square black hole in the floor issued a cold draft that smelled of earth and drains. "It leads to the alley behind the house."

Sano turned to his detectives. "Marume-*san,* tell our men outside to search the neighborhood for the woman," he said, although he knew she could have gotten far away during the time that had elapsed since the murder. "Fukida-*san*, examine the secret passage and the alley for clues she might have left."

Marume departed. Fukida borrowed a lamp from the proprietor and jumped into the passage that the illicit lovers used to escape when necessary. Lord Matsudaira got to his feet like a pile of rubble coalescing into a mountain. His stunned expression vanished; anger focused his eyes as his combative spirit returned.

"Why must you bother hunting for the woman?" he asked Sano.

"She may have witnessed the murder," Sano said, "or she may have committed it."

"Who cares about witnesses?" Lord Matsudaira said, his fists clenched and nostrils flared. "We don't need anyone to tell us what happened here tonight. And we both know my nephew wasn't killed by his lady."

"She was with him," Sano pointed out. "That she's gone now suggests she's guilty. Daiemon appears to have been killed by someone he knew and trusted. His murder could be a case of romance gone bad."

Yet Sano doubted the crime was that simple. Daiemon's murder, so soon after Makino's, was unlikely to be a coincidence.

"This was no lovers' quarrel. This was political assassination," Lord Matsudaira said, voicing Sano's thoughts.

"And it's obvious who's responsible," Hoshina said.

"Chamberlain Yanagisawa." Lord Matsudaira spat the name as though expelling poison from his mouth.

The grin on Hoshina's face expressed his pleasure at the implication of his onetime lover in the murder of the shogun's heir apparent. Sano felt his heart sink as he foresaw a rise in the strife between the factions, no matter how or why Daiemon had actually died.

"Bring my nephew home to be prepared for his funeral," Lord Matsudaira told his troops. Then he addressed Sano

and Hoshina: "I must inform the shogun about the murder."
Vindictive intent glittered in Lord Matsudaira's eyes. "And
I will make Chamberlain Yanagisawa pay with his own
blood."

21

"No!" the shogun cried. "It can't be! First my old friend Makino dies of, ahh, foul play, and now my dearest, beloved Daiemon. Why are these terrible things happening to me?" He flung himself face-down on his dais and sobbed.

Below him, to his right on the upper floor level of the reception hall, knelt Lord Matsudaira, who had just broken the news of Daiemon's murder. He wore a somber air appropriate for the occasion. Sano knelt opposite the shogun. Police Commissioner Hoshina sat near Sano. Suppressed excitement animated Hoshina's dignified pose. On the lower level of the floor sat a crowd of Matsudaira troops, Sano's detectives, and Hoshina's police officers. Along the walls stood the shogun's bodyguards. A tense, waiting silence gripped the assembly. The sunrise tinted the windows red as if with blood.

"Tell me," the shogun entreated Lord Matsudaira as he sat up and wiped his tear-drenched face, "what villain has, ahh, cut Daiemon down in the prime of his life?"

Lord Matsudaira leaned toward the shogun like a general riding into a decisive battle. "My nephew had an enemy who was envious of your affection for him. That enemy has been plotting to destroy Daiemon and strike at you by killing him."

He didn't come right out and name Yanagisawa because

he first wanted to lay groundwork for his accusation, Sano understood. And he couldn't name Yanagisawa's real motive for the murder—to weaken the Matsudaira clan and clear his son's way to inherit the dictatorship—because the shogun wasn't supposed to know about the factions' struggle for power. The whole *bakufu* had an unspoken agreement to keep him in the dark.

"Last night his enemy stabbed Daiemon to death," Lord Matsudaira said.

Confusion wrinkled the shogun's forehead. "And who is this enemy?"

"I regret to say that he is none other than your chamberlain." Lord Matsudaira spoke with grave sincerity that hid his enjoyment of openly attacking his rival at last.

Sano braced himself for the reaction. Police Commissioner Hoshina kneaded his hands, while everyone else sat frozen. The shogun gasped in wide-eyed shock.

"Chamberlain Yanagisawa? But that's, ahh, impossible. He would never hurt anyone who matters to me . . . would he?" Sudden doubt colored the shogun's features. Ever open to influence by people more forceful than himself, he looked from Lord Matsudaira to Sano to Hoshina. "What makes you think he, ahh, killed Daiemon?"

"The evidence points to him," Lord Matsudaira said.

Hoshina nodded in staunch affirmation. And Sano couldn't say that Lord Matsudaira had no real evidence to justify an accusation against the chamberlain. Before the meeting, Lord Matsudaira had told Sano to keep quiet or he would be expelled.

Sputtering with fury, the shogun said, "Well, ahh, I shall have Yanagisawa-*san* come and, ahh, answer for what he has done."

"A good idea." Lord Matsudaira's tone hinted at how much he welcomed a face-to-face clash with his rival.

Tokugawa Tsunayoshi ordered his attendants, "Bring the chamberlain here."

The attendants hastened to obey. Soon the door to the reception hall opened to reveal Yanagisawa standing at the threshold. Apprehension glimmered in his eyes as he saw Lord Matsudaira. His gaze bypassed Sano and skittered over Hoshina.

"You wished to see me, Your Excellency?" he said.

Glaring at him, the shogun said, "Don't just, ahh, stand there, you scoundrel—come in."

The apprehension in Yanagisawa's eyes deepened, but he strode toward the dais. After him walked his son Yoritomo. Sano was surprised to see the boy, for Yanagisawa had never before included him in official business. Why did he now? Lord Matsudaira's and Hoshina's faces also showed surprise as the handsome, shy Yoritomo neared them. The chamberlain noted Lord Matsudaira seated in his own usual place by the shogun. He paused, tacitly ordering Lord Matsudaira to move. When Lord Matsudaira didn't, Yanagisawa knelt in the lesser position to the shogun's left. He motioned for his son to kneel between them. As Yoritomo complied, Sano watched the shogun's attention fix upon the boy.

"May I inquire what this is about?" Yanagisawa asked the shogun.

"Ahh . . ." Distracted by Yoritomo, the shogun faltered, then said, "I have just heard some terrible news. Daiemon was murdered last night."

His admiration for the son had depleted some of his ire toward the father as well as his grief over the death of his favorite. Lord Matsudaira and Hoshina stared in dismay. Sano marveled at whatever prescience or genius had inspired Yanagisawa to bring his son as a weapon to protect himself.

Yanagisawa's face expressed shock, apparently genuine, at the news of the murder. If he realized that Daiemon's death had benefited him and the Matsudaira faction had lost ground, he didn't show it. "What happened?"

"He was stabbed to death while in a house of assignation," Hoshina said. His manner toward the chamberlain reflected the bitterness that had accompanied the demise of their affair. "Except you didn't really need to ask, did you?"

"What is that supposed to mean?" Yanagisawa's perplexity seemed as honest as his shock.

"He means that you knew how and where Daiemon died, because you killed him," Lord Matsudaira declared.

The shogun reluctantly detached his gaze from Yoritomo and eyed Yanagisawa with renewed suspicion.

"Your Excellency, that's ridiculous." Amazement and outrage visibly jolted Yanagisawa. His breath exploded from him in a loud huff. "I did not kill Daiemon."

"Not with your own hands," Lord Matsudaira said. "You'd have kept them free of blood by sending one of your minions to do your dirty work."

"I was nowhere near any house of assignation," Yanagisawa continued, raising his voice over Lord Matsudaira's and directing his vehemence at the shogun. "My guards will verify that I didn't leave my compound last night."

"See how careful he is to arrange himself an alibi." Hoshina sneered. "A man of his wealth and power can easily bribe or force other men to lie for him."

Yanagisawa shifted position, blocking the shogun's view of Hoshina. "I had no need to kill Daiemon." He flashed Lord Matsudaira a glance that Sano interpreted to mean he could win their fight without resorting to assassination. "Their accusations are false, Your Excellency. Don't listen to them. Trust me." The gaze he fixed on Tokugawa Tsunayoshi alluded to their longtime companionship. His voice took on a husky, fervent tone: "I swear I'm innocent."

But Sano remembered their conversation last night and his suspicion that Yanagisawa was up to something. Had the chamberlain been plotting Daiemon's murder? Was that why he'd felt confident enough to claim that Lord Matsudaira was vulnerable and promise Sano rewards for joining his side?

Vacillation played across the shogun's weak features as Yanagisawa held his gaze captive. "Don't believe him," Lord Matsudaira said, enraged that Yanagisawa was foiling him. "He's guilty. He's lying to save his disgraceful neck. And he's brought his bastard to soften your feelings toward him and make you forget my nephew."

Lord Matsudaira shot a contemptuous look at Yoritomo,

who blushed and bowed his head. If Yanagisawa had killed Daiemon, he would have expected to be accused of the crime and come prepared to defend himself, Sano realized. Yoritomo was his weapon against Lord Matsudaira as well as his shield against the shogun's wrath.

"He's playing you for the fool he thinks you are, Honorable Cousin," said Lord Matsudaira.

The shogun goggled at Yanagisawa. "Are you?" he said, hovering between fear and anger.

"Of course not," Yanagisawa said. "Lord Matsudaira and Police Commissioner Hoshina are the ones trying to deceive you. Let us ask ourselves why they're so eager to convince you that I murdered Daiemon. I suggest that they killed him, and they want to frame me."

Lord Matsudaira and Hoshina looked flabbergasted by the counterattack, although Sano thought they should have known that Yanagisawa considered a good offense as the best defense. The shogun turned his suspicion, fear, and anger on them. "Is that why you, ahh, accused Yanagisawa-*san*?" he demanded.

"The very idea is blasphemy!" Lord Matsudaira's complexion turned so red that Sano thought he would burst a vein. "Why would I kill my own nephew?"

Tokugawa Tsunayoshi shrank from his cousin's anger. The chamberlain sat calm and smug, in control of the situation now. He said, "Everyone knows Daiemon was ambitious for power within your clan. Many a high-ranking samurai has protected his position by killing off young challengers among his kin."

That Daiemon was ambitious, and Lord Matsudaira hard-pressed to restrain him, Sano had seen for himself. Sano now wondered if Lord Matsudaira was indeed responsible for his nephew's death.

Lord Matsudaira, reduced to blustering indignation, shouted, "I would never shed the blood of my own clan!" The strain of waging political warfare during many months had undermined his self-discipline. Fear shone through his rage, because now the shogun beheld him with distrust.

"Oh, I doubt that you stabbed Daiemon yourself," Yanagisawa said. "You'd have had other hands wield the dagger."
Now his accusing gaze swung to Hoshina. "The hands of
your lackey the police commissioner."

Hoshina stiffened as though Yanagisawa had tossed a
bomb into his lap. Sano saw that Yanagisawa wasn't content
to attack Lord Matsudaira; he sought to harm his onetime
lover who'd joined forces with his rival. Hoshina went very
still, as though afraid the bomb would explode if he moved.

"That's absurd," he said. His matter-of-fact tone didn't
hide his panic. "I had nothing to do with the murder."

"Your officers were surely familiar with the house of
assignation," Yanagisawa said. "They must have known that
Daiemon was a patron, and they passed the gossip to you. It
served you well when you needed to rid your master of his
unruly nephew." The chamberlain swelled with vengeful
pleasure at paying back Hoshina for hurts and insults inflicted on him. "You found out when Daiemon was due to
visit the house. You lay in wait for him there. You took him
by surprise and stabbed him."

"I didn't!" As Hoshina's panic broke through his self-
control, sweat glistened on his face. "I'm innocent!" He
looked to Lord Matsudaira, who frowned severely at him.

Sano longed for the power to divine their thoughts. Was
Hoshina afraid because he and Lord Matsudaira really had
conspired to murder the shogun's heir apparent? Or was
there no conspiracy, and did Hoshina fear only that Yanagisawa would drive a wedge between him and Lord Matsudaira by implicating him in the murder? The accusation
against Hoshina could hurt him either way. Sano had to ad-
mire Yanagisawa's cleverness.

Desperate, Hoshina addressed the shogun. "Chamberlain
Yanagisawa is just flinging mud at me in the hope that you
won't notice the stains of guilt on him!"

The shogun put his arms over his head to shield himself
from the storm of conflicting ideas. The distrust in his eyes
encompassed all three combatants.

"Chamberlain Yanagisawa killed Daiemon, and I'll tell

you exactly why," Hoshina said, brazen in his need to save himself. "Daiemon knew that Yanagisawa killed Senior Elder Makino. He was going to use his knowledge to destroy Yanagisawa. Therefore, Yanagisawa had Daiemon assassinated."

"Daiemon knew nothing of the sort," Yanagisawa said with a gesture that disdained Hoshina's attempt to pin both crimes on him. "I didn't kill Makino. I didn't kill Daiemon, either. But you needn't take my word against Lord Matsudaira's or the police commissioner's for it, Your Excellency. Let's consult an impartial source." Yanagisawa turned to Sano. "Tell us how your investigation has exonerated me of both crimes."

His intent gaze reminded Sano of the rewards he'd promised in exchange for Sano's cooperation. Sano felt a stab of dismay. So far, his investigation hadn't proved Yanagisawa guilty of either murder, but it hadn't cleared him, and honor forbade Sano to twist the truth to benefit Yanagisawa. Yet Sano realized that the chamberlain was giving him one last chance to accept his offer. If he refused now . . .

"*Sōsakan* Sano has nothing to say in defense of the chamberlain," Lord Matsudaira said. His emphatic tone reminded Sano that he'd been ordered not to speak. "His findings show that the chamberlain is guilty of two murders, while I and my associates are innocent of any wrongdoing." He nodded to Sano, and an ominous smile thinned his lips. "You now have my permission to say so."

Although Sano was loath to lie for Yanagisawa, he couldn't compromise the facts to please Lord Matsudaira either. He sat tongue-tied while the path he'd been navigating between the two adversaries became a narrow, slippery ridge with deep chasms on either side.

"Have you lost your voice, *Sōsakan* Sano?" the shogun said, peeved by the argument whose undertones escaped him. "Tell me what to believe. Everyone else will, ahh, remain silent. All this shouting is, ahh, giving me a headache."

Damned no matter what he said, Sano opted for the truth. "Daiemon might have seen or heard or found out something that told him who killed Makino. Maybe the murderer did kill Daiemon to keep him quiet."

Hoshina looked vindicated and Lord Matsudaira appeased. But Yanagisawa's face darkened with the thought that Sano had chosen to side with his enemies.

"That's possible because Daiemon was at the scene of the murder that night," Sano continued. "He told me so. But his presence there also makes him a suspect. It's possible that he killed Makino himself."

Yanagisawa nodded, placated. Lord Matsudaira bristled because Sano had impugned his dead nephew.

Sano continued tiptoeing along the slippery ridge. "But there are other possible reasons for Daiemon's murder—such as bad blood between him and Chamberlain Yanagisawa." Sano forbore to say why and break the news of the faction wars to the shogun. As Yanagisawa glared at him, and gratification vied with caution on Lord Matsudaira's and Hoshina's faces, Sano said, "I've not even begun making inquiries regarding Daiemon. His family will have to be investigated because many murders are committed by someone close to the victim."

Loud gusts of breath issued from between Lord Matsudaira's clenched teeth as he tried to control his fury at Sano's agreeing that he might, as Yanagisawa had suggested, have killed his own nephew.

"The police are also suspects," Sano said, and watched Hoshina tense, ready to lunge at him in a rage. He described the strange tale of how they'd heard about the murder and how quickly they'd arrived on the scene. "And they're closely associated with Lord Matsudaira."

Fear, hostility, and foreboding thickened the atmosphere in the room. Sano knew he'd cast enough aspersion on Chamberlain Yanagisawa, Lord Matsudaira, and Police Commissioner Hoshina to land them all in deep trouble no matter who was guilty or not. But the shogun regarded Sano with an expression of utter, blank confusion.

"I ahh, did not quite follow everything you said," Tokugawa Tsunayoshi said. His timid voice conveyed his everpresent fear of seeming stupid. "What I want to know is, who killed Makino? Who killed Daiemon?"

Yanagisawa and Lord Matsudaira impaled Sano with sharp, steely gazes, each compelling him to name the other. This, Sano realized, was his last opportunity to choose sides, the end of negotiating the path between the two rivals. He felt angry as well as hounded by them. His natural stubbornness hardened his will. He would not bend to pressure, come what might.

"It's too early to know who the murderer is," Sano said. "There are still other suspects who must be investigated, such as the members of Senior Elder Makino's household and the woman who met Daiemon at the house of assignation and is now missing."

Disappointment sagged the shogun's posture. Lord Matsudaira and Chamberlain Yanagisawa glared at Sano. He saw that by refusing to bend to either, he'd outraged both. Then their gazes turned cold and distant; they looked away from him. Sano imagined himself standing at the edge of a river full of perilous rapids. He envisioned the tenuous security offered by Yanagisawa and Lord Matsudaira as fragile rope bridges, slashed by his own sword, falling into the water.

"Well, ahh, you had better get busy," the shogun told Sano. "I hold you responsible for, ahh, finding out who killed Daiemon as well as Senior Elder Makino."

In addition to all his other troubles, Sano must now solve two murder cases instead of one. Maybe they were related, and the killer was the same person in both instances, maybe not. But both cases promised him the same, dire penalties for failure—demotion, exile, or death.

"You'd better watch your step, *Sōsakan* Sano," Lord Matsudaira said in a tone replete with malevolence.

"A man who walks alone has no one to catch him if he falls," Yanagisawa said softly. "A warrior who throws away his shield during battle invites injury."

Menace, scorn for Sano's stubbornness, and pity mingled in his voice. His meaning was clear: If Sano failed to solve the crimes, he couldn't expect either faction to protect him from punishment as he could have if he'd allied himself with one or the other. And Yanagisawa had just revoked the truce that had shielded Sano against attacks from him.

"As for you . . ." The shogun pointed a trembling finger at Yanagisawa, Lord Matsudaira, and Hoshina. His eyes shone with the atavistic fear of a man confronted by evil spirits. "I don't want to see any of you again until, ahh, I am certain that you did not kill Daiemon or Senior Elder Makino."

Concern marked Yanagisawa's, Lord Matsudaira's, and Hoshina's faces. Sano saw that this meeting had worsened their situation, too. Their open attacks on each other had backfired, and they'd all lost the shogun's trust. Without it, one faction might crush the other but fail to reach the ultimate goal of dominating the present regime or the next. To what lengths would they go to recoup this critical ammunition that could determine the victor?

"You are dismissed," the shogun said, flapping his hand at Sano, Lord Matsudaira, Chamberlain Yanagisawa, and their men. As they rose, so did Yoritomo. The shogun reached toward him and caught the hem of his robe. "You may stay."

Sano saw the triumphant look that Yanagisawa flashed at Lord Matsudaira as they all led their men from the reception hall. Lord Matsudaira scowled in reply. Yanagisawa had entered the meeting as a man in extreme jeopardy and left it with a slim advantage: His potential successor to the dictatorship was alive, while Lord Matsudaira's was gone.

Outside the palace, a wintry wind rattled the bare, black branches of the trees. Gray clouds trapped the rising sun and darkened the sky. Lord Matsudaira and Chamberlain Yanagisawa ranged themselves and their troops against each other.

"I won't wait for *Sōsakan* Sano to deliver you to justice for killing my nephew," Lord Matsudaira told the chamberlain. An ugly smile bared his teeth; hatred, grief, and fury raged like wildfire in his eyes. "I'll avenge his death myself. My retribution will begin this very day."

"Then so will your demise," Chamberlain Yanagisawa said, equally hostile.

The two foes and their troops stalked away. Sano suddenly saw his personal concerns dwarfed by the perils that faced Japan. The murder of Daiemon had escalated political strife to the point of war.

22

Thousands of soldiers marched through Edo. Banner bearers waved flags; horses in battle caparison carried swordsmen, archers sporting bows and arrows, and gunners equipped with arquebuses. Foot soldiers held their spears high. Pale rays of morning sun glinted on armor. As the armies moved along the main street, commanders shouted orders; drummers conveyed signals to troops. War trumpets blared while townspeople exclaimed at the sight of such a great military force, unseen since the civil wars that had ended almost a century ago.

A short distance away, Reiko and three other maids walked behind a palanquin in which rode Senior Elder Makino's widow and concubine. Mounted guards and male servants on foot escorted the women. Reiko shivered with cold in her thin cloak and cotton robes, hungry after a meager breakfast of gruel and tea, fatigued from her first night in the servants' quarters of Makino's estate.

It had been almost midnight when the servants were finally excused from work. Reiko had endured a bath in a communal tub of scummy, lukewarm water, then retired to quarters so crowded that she could hardly move on her narrow pallet without bumping someone. Snores, coughs, mutters, and biting fleas kept her awake. Before dawn, the housekeeper Yasue had bustled through the room, beating wooden clappers and ordering everyone out of bed. She'd allowed them barely enough time to dash to the reeking privies outside and wash themselves with ice-cold water in buckets. Then Reiko had cleaned fish until sent out with Agemaki and Okitsu on a shopping expedition. At last she had another chance to spy on them.

Now a horde of troops galloped by, squeezing Reiko and her companions against a wall. Reiko was alarmed to see the Matsudaira and Yanagisawa clan crests on their armor. Excited cries arose from the other maids: "Where can all those soldiers be going? What's happening?"

Lord Matsudaira and Chamberlain Yanagisawa must have declared war, Reiko realized. What had finally ignited the war? Cut off from her husband, Reiko could only wonder. But she had a premonition that solving the murder case might be more important now than ever. As the procession began moving again, she hurried after Agemaki and Okitsu.

Lady Yanagisawa disembarked from her palanquin outside the *sōsakan-sama*'s estate. Her legs were so wobbly and her head so dizzy that she almost fell. Recent, momentous events in her life had caused her a turmoil never before experienced. Her body still burned with the memory of the chamberlain's caresses; she heard again his every tender word. But other, less pleasant memories intruded.

The conditions attached to his love were even more appalling than Lady Yanagisawa had at first thought. A black, noxious cesspool in her mind churned with thoughts she didn't want to think. Nausea born of guilt and revulsion spoiled her anticipation of the rewards to come. She wavered among exhilaration, horror, and the temptation to give up now and avoid further torment. But she'd come this far, and the gods hadn't struck her down as punishment for treachery committed or intended. She must go the rest of the way toward fulfilling her husband's wishes.

She stumbled up to the guards at the gate and said, "I want to see Lady Reiko."

"She isn't here," said a guard.

Lady Yanagisawa gasped and stared in surprise. She hadn't expected to be thwarted by the simple mishap of Reiko's absence. Her need to please her husband reinforced her need to be with her friend. Struck by her constant suspicion that Reiko wished to avoid her, she told the guard, "I don't believe you." Her voice shook as tremors rippled her muscles. "Take me to Lady Reiko at once!"

"I'm sorry, but that's impossible," the other guard said. "When she returns, I'll tell her you called."

Crazed by frustration, Lady Yanagisawa began screaming at the men. The commotion brought one of the *sōsakan-sama*'s detectives hurrying out the gate. He tried to calm her while she demanded to see Reiko.

"You can come back later," he said.

"I know she's here!" Lady Yanagisawa shrieked. "She has to receive me!"

After much argument, the detective said, "Very well— you can see for yourself that Lady Reiko isn't home."

Lady Yanagisawa ran in the gate, past the barracks, and across the courtyard; the detective hurried after her. She rushed through the mansion to the private quarters. Maids busy with their chores exclaimed in surprise. Lady Yanagisawa burst, panting and wild-eyed, into the nursery. There, the old nursemaid O-sugi sat playing with Reiko's little son Masahiro amid his toys. But Reiko was nowhere in sight.

"Where is your mistress?" Lady Yanagisawa demanded.

O-sugi regarded her with stern disapproval. "Not here. She left yesterday."

"Where did she go?" Hysteria rose in Lady Yanagisawa. "I don't know."

"When will she be back?"

The old nursemaid shook her head. The detective propelled Lady Yanagisawa from the house. Lady Yanagisawa uttered a groan of despair. Everyone was in league against her, conspiring to deny her access to Reiko and her chance to carry out her husband's wishes. But her determination strengthened, even as a voice inside her whispered that

Reiko's absence was a sign from fate that she could renege on her bargain with the chamberlain and lessen the measure of her sins. She must find Reiko. She must do whatever was necessary to win the love of her husband and satisfy the desires he'd awakened in her.

The palanquin that carried Makino's widow and concubine stopped at Yanagiya, a shop in the Nihonbashi merchant district. Lanterns painted with a willow-tree crest decorated the eaves of the shop. Women inspected goods displayed on stands outside its open storefront. Their gaily colored cloaks brightened the drab, gray morning. Male clerks proclaimed the virtues of their wares and urged the women to buy.

"How wonderful it is to get outside and see people!" Okitsu exclaimed as the bearers set down the palanquin. "This is such a nice change from staying home!"

"You've said that at least a hundred times," Agemaki said. "Do curb your tendency to repeat yourself. A little variety would improve your conversation."

As usual, Agemaki hid her dislike of Okitsu behind a false, affectionate smile. Okitsu, easily deceived as always, took no offense at the rebuke. "Thank you for your kind advice," she said with sincere affection. "And thank you for inviting me to go shopping with you."

While they climbed out of the palanquin, Agemaki resisted the urge to remind Okitsu that she hadn't been invited. Agemaki had meant this trip as an escape from the gloom of her dead husband's estate, as well as a distraction from the worrisome events that had followed the murder. She'd also wanted to escape the other inhabitants of the private chambers, who were a daily, sore vexation to her. But Okitsu had spotted her on her way out.

"Where are you going?" Okitsu had said. When told, she'd run after Agemaki. "I'm going with you."

Agemaki had let Okitsu come because she had to pretend she liked the stupid little hussy. She'd been pretending ever since Senior Elder Makino had bought Okitsu. And she must pretend awhile longer, for her own good.

They entered the Yanagiya. Their maids followed them into a large room crowded with chattering customers. Shelves on the walls held pretty ceramic jars of the face powder, rouge, and scented oil that had made the Yanagiya a favorite among the women of Edo. Clerks rushed about, serving their customers and calculating prices on the beads of their *soroban*. Jasmine, orange blossom, and ginger perfumed the air. The proprietor, a sleek man with a fawning smile, greeted and bowed to Agemaki.

"I want to see whatever you have that's new," Agemaki said.

"Of course, Honorable Lady Makino."

The proprietor whisked her and Okitsu into a small private room reserved for important customers and seated them at a dressing table and mirror. A curtain secluded them from the bustle in the shop. He and a clerk began wiping the makeup off Agemaki's and Okitsu's faces, preparing to demonstrate the new cosmetics. Agemaki watched in the mirror as their naked features emerged. Her skin was sallow and dry, faintly sunken beneath the cheekbones. But Okitsu's youthful complexion was fair, smooth, and perfect. Okitsu smiled at their reflections while Agemaki seethed with jealousy.

Throughout her marriage to Senior Elder Makino, she'd lived in fear that he would tire of her, for he'd been a man who needed novelty to satisfy his pride and keep him aroused. And he'd preferred his women young. Agemaki had never loved Makino, but she'd loved the status that marriage to him conferred upon her, and she'd loved the things his money bought. She'd labored to preserve the youth and beauty that had attracted her husband, but Makino had begun seeking amusement in the pleasure quarters instead of her bedchamber. Her attempts to entice him back all failed. On the day Okitsu became his concubine, Agemaki knew her days as his wife were numbered; she had no family or political connections to bind Makino to her. But she'd refused to give up her husband without a fight.

Now the proprietor daubed fresh makeup onto her face. "This is the finest, whitest rice powder, mixed with the best-quality camellia wax," he said.

Okitsu, receiving the same treatment from the clerk, said, "Look, Agemaki-*san,* it almost hides those terrible wrinkles around your eyes and mouth."

Offense at the careless insult stoked the jealous rage in Agemaki. She could almost see flames leaping in the eyes of her reflection. Not for the first time she wanted to smack Okitsu. But instead Agemaki smiled. "It's too bad that makeup can't hide rudeness or stupidity," she said in the sweetest voice she could manage.

Okitsu laughed in delight as if Agemaki had made a joke, unaware of the barb directed at her. Agemaki never permitted herself to vent her emotions toward Okitsu in any other way. Because she'd known that making ugly scenes would only disgust her husband, she'd graciously welcomed Okitsu into their home. She'd befriended the girl and suffered silently as she listened to her husband play sexual games with Okitsu and that despicable actor. Most important, she'd never given the slightest hint that she hated Makino for shunning her in favor of his new woman and feared he would cast her off. She'd bided her time, scheming how to take her revenge on him. Now her self-control was benefiting her in a way she'd not foreseen.

The shogun's *sōsakan-sama* had questioned her after the murder because he obviously thought she might have killed her husband. Yet she needn't fear him, even though she'd been in the private chambers that night and she was the wife supplanted by a younger rival. Her behavior testified that she didn't mind about Okitsu. Nobody could tell the *sōsakan-sama* otherwise. All she need do to prevent his suspicion was continue acting the demure, grieving widow.

The proprietor and clerk painted Agemaki's and Okitsu's cheeks and lips with rouge. "What do you think?" said the proprietor.

Okitsu viewed her reflection and gasped with delight. "I

look beautiful!" Glancing at Agemaki, she said with an un-flattering lack of enthusiasm, "You look better than usual."

Agemaki managed a grim smile.

"We have new potions for softening calluses," said the proprietor. "Would you like to try them?" When the women agreed, he immersed their hands and feet in basins of fragrant oil. Then he and the clerk left to attend other customers.

"I'm so worried about Koheiji and me," Okitsu said.

Agemaki prepared to endure another tiresome discussion about Okitsu's romantic affairs. She always marveled that the girl would talk about them to anyone willing to listen. She wasn't as discreet as Agemaki, who knew that she must not say anything that would put her in a bad light.

"I love Koheiji so much," Okitsu said. "Sometimes I think he loves me, and other times I'm not so sure." Her anxious gaze met Agemaki's eyes in the mirror. "Do you think he loves me?"

"I think he loves you as much as it's possible for him to love anyone." Besides himself, the conceited oaf, thought Agemaki. "You give him such pleasure." And that's the only reason he wants a whining, clinging nuisance like you. "Accept what he's capable of giving. Don't expect more." Because if you nag him, you'll lose him, and you'll cry while I laugh.

A breathy sigh issued from Okitsu. "I guess you're right," she said doubtfully. "But do you think he'll marry me?"

"If you make a special pilgrimage to Kannei Temple, maybe he will." And maybe monkeys will fly.

Reassured, Okitsu smiled. "I'm so glad I have you to talk to. You're so wise, even though it must be hard for you to understand what it's like to be young and in love."

Agemaki gritted her teeth while her hands curled into claws in the basin of oil. She envisioned bloody red scratches on Okitsu's face. "Someday you'll understand that you don't know as much as you thought you did when you were young. If you live long enough."

Blind to Agemaki's implicit threat, Okitsu said, "Oh, I

forgot—you have experienced love. You were in love with Senior Elder Makino. But I can't imagine how you could love that mean, ugly old man." Okitsu gave an exaggerated shudder of revulsion.

Agemaki wished the *sōsakan-sama* were here to see how much Okitsu had hated Makino. He would arrest Okitsu for the murder, which would delight Agemaki. "I loved my husband for his excellent qualities," Agemaki said. Money and power excused most evils in a man.

Okitsu looked unconvinced. "You didn't mind when I came along. You've always been so nice to me. If some woman had a man I wanted, I would hate her. I think I'd kill her."

Agemaki remembered slipping poisonous herbs into an old lady's tea. "A man can always get more women," she said. "One can't do away with all of one's competition." She knew there were people who suspected that she'd killed Makino's first wife. If not for fear that another mysterious death of a woman in his household would get her in trouble, Agemaki would have dispatched Okitsu to the netherworld a long time ago.

"But weren't you furious at Makino? I've never seen him pay you any attention. He didn't want you; he wanted me." Okitsu spoke as though it were an indisputable truth that any man in his right mind would prefer her to Agemaki. Completely insensitive to Agemaki's feelings, she said, "If a man treated me like that, I'd kill him."

Resentment stung Agemaki. "If Koheiji did, you would fall on your knees to welcome him back," she said.

Okitsu gazed at her in wounded surprise. "I wouldn't!"

Agemaki thought perhaps she'd gone too far and revealed too much of her true feelings to Okitsu. "I'm just teasing you," she said with a kindly smile. "But let us imagine that Koheiji did betray you. Then you would do better to kill him than kill all your rivals. You'd have a better chance of getting away with one murder than with many. And to punish him would be more satisfying than to waste your vengeance on people who don't matter as much."

The night Senior Elder Makino died, Agemaki had exulted in having him helpless at her mercy. Such savage joy of venting her rage at him for the humiliation he'd caused her! In some ways his death hadn't been as good as she'd hoped, but she'd decided that things had turned out for the best.

"No matter what Koheiji did to me or how badly I felt toward him, I would miss him if he died," said Okitsu.

"A woman does tend to miss a man," Agemaki said, "especially when he's given her everything she has in the world." She thought fondly of the big estate in Edo Castle, the servants, the expensive clothes. "But the company of a man is worth much less than what he leaves behind after he has gone to his grave." Agemaki cherished the money Makino had left her. "And when a woman has managed to secure her future, she has no need of any man—or fear of any rival. No one can take away what's rightfully hers."

Gone was her privileged status as the senior elder's wife, but luckily he'd died before he'd divorced Agemaki, remarried, and reneged on the inheritance he'd promised her. Agemaki was glad she'd behaved with shrewdness rather than follow her emotions. And as long as she continued thus, she wouldn't be punished for Makino's murder. Everything would be fine.

Reiko hovered outside the private room of the Yanagiya, peering through a gap in the curtains at Agemaki and Okitsu, astounded by what she'd heard.

None of the words Agemaki had spoken showed her to be anything but the decent, honorable widow that Sano had described, the wife who'd gladly tolerated her beloved husband's infidelity. But Reiko had perceived her subtle expressions and the undertones in her voice, even though Okitsu was apparently oblivious to them. They painted Agemaki as a jealous, deceitful woman who hated Okitsu for taking her place in Makino's affections and bedchamber.

They were tantamount to a confession that she'd not only

killed Makino to punish him and safeguard her inheritance, but previously killed his first wife so she could marry him in the first place.

Yet Agemaki hadn't actually admitted to the crimes. She hadn't said anything that couldn't be interpreted some other way than Reiko had, or that Sano would deem proof of her guilt. Reiko needed more evidence besides veiled remarks and her own intuition.

The proprietor brushed past Reiko and entered the private room. Reiko heard him selling Agemaki and Okitsu the merchandise they'd tried. Soon the two women left the shop and climbed into their palanquin. Reiko and the other maids followed them down the street, laden with packages tied in cloth bundles. As they wended through the *daimyo* district toward Edo Castle, Reiko saw soldiers pouring out from the walled estates and palanquins filled with women and children, escorted by mounted troops and followed by servants carrying baggage. The feudal lords were evacuating their families—a sure sign that war had begun.

A sudden thought distracted Reiko from her fear. Since beginning her employment as a maid and spy in Makino's house, she'd not had any bad spells. Had her mind been too occupied for the evil magic to penetrate? Maybe real dangers had exorcised the imaginary ones that haunted her. But there was no such ready cure for the evils that now threatened all of Japan.

23

"This morning we'll investigate Daiemon's murder," Sano told the detectives gathered in his office. "That crime is foremost in the shogun's mind. The Makino case will have to wait." Furthermore, Sano already had an array of suspects associated with the first crime, while the unexplored trail of the second was fast going cold. "We'll search the area around the Sign of Bedazzlement for witnesses. We'll try to find out who and where the woman is."

A manservant came to the door. "Excuse me, master, but Ibe-*san* and Otani-*san* have arrived. They're waiting for you."

Sano went to the reception room, where the watchdogs sat side by side. Ibe said, "Before we begin the day's business, we need to have a talk."

The men's sinister air put Sano on his guard. "About what?"

"Sit down, *Sōsakan-sama*," said Otani.

Sano warily knelt opposite the men.

"The events of last night require a change in your procedure," Ibe said.

"What kind of change?" Sano saw that the watchdogs knew he'd alienated Lord Matsudaira and Chamberlain Yanagisawa. Probably the whole *bakufu* would know before long. There would be no more visits from men courting him on behalf of either faction. Sano had hoped Ibe and Otani would stop trying to coerce him now that their superiors had realized that he was a lost cause, but they obviously had other ideas.

"You must conclude the investigation as soon as possible, with the minimum amount of fuss," Otani said.

"From now on, you will not investigate Chamberlain Yanagisawa in connection with the murders of Daiemon and Senior Elder Makino," said Ibe.

"Nor will you investigate Lord Matsudaira," said Otani.

"On whose orders?" Sano demanded, amazed at how far they meant to stretch their interference.

A glance between Ibe and Otani united them. "On ours," Ibe said.

Whatever obedience Sano owed Lord Matsudaira and Chamberlain Yanagisawa didn't extend to their lackeys, whose hindrance had vexed him enough already. "I'll not let you dictate whom I will or won't investigate," Sano said. "What makes you think you can command me?"

Otani gave Sano a condescending look. "You don't seem to understand that the rules of the game have been changed by Daiemon's murder and your own decision to cut yourself off from both Lord Matsudaira and Chamberlain Yanagisawa."

"And you don't seem to understand that following our orders will be to your advantage." Scorn inflected Ibe's voice. "Let me explain. Should you persist in investigating Lord Matsudaira or Chamberlain Yanagisawa, the outcome is sure to displease one of them. Steer clear of them both and save yourself a lot of trouble."

Sano began to perceive the reason behind his watchdogs' orders. "Somehow I don't think my welfare is what concerns you most," he said. "Do your superiors know about this?"

"Lord Matsudaira and Chamberlain Yanagisawa are very busy men," Otani said. "They don't bother themselves with everything their retainers do to serve their interests."

"I'm sure that if one of them is responsible for killing Daiemon or Senior Elder Makino, he would prefer that I didn't find out," Sano said. "But I don't think your superiors' interests are your main concern, either. What do you gain from colluding together behind their backs?"

An unpleasant smile compressed Ibe's mouth. "Let's just say that we, as well as our masters, will benefit if the murders are no longer a factor in the crisis at hand."

Enlightenment dawned. "What you mean is that you each fear that your superior is guilty of murder," Sano said, "and neither of you wishes to be punished as an associate. You want Chamberlain Yanagisawa and Lord Matsudaira to be free to settle their differences on the battlefield because you'd rather take your chances on the outcome of a war than gamble on the result of the murder investigation."

Silence was Ibe and Otani's assent. Sano realized that Daiemon's murder had left nothing unchanged and the repercussions continued. Although he had no intention of obeying his watchdogs, curiosity led him to ask, "What am I supposed to do while I'm not investigating Chamberlain Yanagisawa or Lord Matsudaira?"

"There are other suspects to occupy you," Otani said. "We recommend that you concentrate on Senior Elder Makino's women."

"Why them?"

"They were in the private chambers the night Makino died," Ibe said. "Chances are one is the murderer."

"The same logic applies to Makino's chief retainer and resident actor," Sano said. "Are you warning me off them, too?"

Otani inclined his head in an almost imperceptible nod, which Sano interpreted to mean that Tamura had friends in the Yanagisawa camp, and Koheiji had enthusiasts in both factions, who might object if they were incriminated.

"And you needn't investigate Daiemon's murder at all," Otani said. "It's most certainly connected to the murder of Senior Elder Makino. The same culprit will do for both."

"Then you expect me to pin the murder on Agemaki or Okitsu, and which one doesn't matter, because they're both nobodies as far as you're concerned. You don't care if they're innocent and the killer goes free. All you want is to

protect your own skins." Sano's voice rose with his mounting anger. "Well, I'm sorry to disappoint you, but I'll conduct this investigation as I see fit, according to my orders
from the shogun."

Otani and Ibe shared a glance that said they'd underestimated Sano's capacity for defiance. Ibe said, "His Excellency will like our solution to the crimes."

"If Lord Matsudaira comes out on top, I'll put in a good
word for you with him," Otani said.

"I'll put in a good word for you with Chamberlain Yanagisawa, should he win," Ibe said.

"Do as we advise, and everyone will be happy," Otani
said.

"Not I," Sano declared, furious now. "What you advise is
a travesty of justice. I'll take no part in it."

Otani and Ibe nodded to each other, as if resigned to a
course of action they'd predicted to be necessary but hoped
to avoid. "Our apologies, but you will," Ibe told Sano.

Armed troops barreled past the doorway, pursued by
Sano's detectives. Voices rose in loud argument as the detec-
tives tried to stop the intruders. Sano leaped to his feet.
"What's going on?" he demanded.

"Force often persuades when reason fails," Otani said,
smug as well as regretful.

Hirata, accompanied by Detectives Marume and Fukida,
rushed into the room. "Ibe's and Otani's troops got past the
gate sentries," Hirata said. "By the time we found out and
tried to stop them, they'd already overrun the estate."

"Get them out of my house!" Sano ordered. As Hirata,
Marume, and Fukida hastened off to obey, Sano turned to
Otani and Ibe. "Go call off your troops!"

The watchdogs remained seated, nervous yet steadfast.
Sano rushed toward the door, then stopped as two soldiers
walked into the room. Masahiro toddled between them, his
little hands clasped in their large, armor-gloved ones. He
smiled as though delighted to have two new friends. They
grinned as if they'd just captured a valuable prize. Horror
stabbed Sano.

"Let go of my son!" he shouted.

The soldiers held tight to Masahiro, whose face puckered in confusion at his father's outburst. Ibe addressed the soldiers: "Where is Lady Reiko?"

"We couldn't find her," replied a soldier.

"Never mind," Otani said. "The boy will serve our purpose well enough."

Incensed, Sano grabbed Otani by the front of his surcoat. "Tell me what's going on!"

Otani wrenched Sano's hands off him and stood. "Our men will keep your son company during the investigation."

"Which ought to ensure that you do as we say," Ibe added as he rose.

"You're holding my son hostage." Disbelief filled Sano even as he couldn't deny the obvious truth.

"Yes, if you must put it so bluntly," Ibe said.

"Papa?" Masahiro said.

His plaintive voice trembled with fright because he sensed that something was amiss even if he didn't understand what. Sano's horror escalated because he must choose between justice and his son's safety. For once he was glad that Reiko was gone. Perhaps she was safer in Senior Elder Makino's estate than here.

Hirata rushed into the room, followed by a horde of detectives, shouting, "Release my master's son!"

He and the detectives drew their swords. So did Ibe and Otani. Their troops crowded through the door, brandishing their weapons. The room went silent except for the sound of rapid, harsh breathing; antagonism permeated the air. Masahiro stared, wide-eyed, at everyone. His throat contracted as he bravely tried not to cry. Sano stood paralyzed, his hand on the hilt of his sword. Otani and Ibe faced him down. Sano realized that they were serious enough in their wish to subjugate him that they would risk a fight. He also realized that unless he wanted combat in his house—and Masahiro accidentally wounded or killed—he must submit.

"Everybody, put away your weapons," he said, dropping his hand from his own sword.

Metal rasped as blades slid into scabbards. Sano felt the tension in the air slacken but not dissipate, like a rope stretched between two men who have relaxed their grip without letting go. Triumph marked the faces of the aggressors. Sano saw his own defeat and humiliation reflected in his men's eyes. He also saw that while the scope of the investigation had widened to include two murders, his watchdogs had seriously impaired his ability to solve either.

"A wise decision, *Sōsakan-sama*," said Otani. "We really wouldn't like to harm you. And you don't want to find out what will happen to your son should you resist us."

"Are you really going to follow Otani and Ibe's orders?" Hirata asked, incredulous because he'd never seen Sano back down for anyone. Yet he knew from experience that a man can be driven beyond the bounds of honor by the need to protect his kin.

"As long as they're holding my son hostage, what else can I do?" Sano said with bitter resignation.

Hirata and Sano stood in the stable, where Sano had gone to fetch his horse while Otani and Ibe waited for him outside the gate. Sano had covertly signaled Hirata to follow him. After a short delay, Hirata had slipped past the troops now occupying the estate and joined Sano. Horses snorted and munched feed; stableboys shoveled manure out of the stalls, while a groom saddled a mount for Sano.

"Now I can better understand what you did at the Dragon King's island," Sano said.

Hirata derived no satisfaction from seeing his master put in the same position that had led himself to ruin. He didn't want Sano forced to compromise himself. He counted on Sano to uphold the honor of the samurai class.

"My hands are tied." But even as Sano admitted defeat, cunning inspiration gleamed in his eyes. "But yours aren't."

Hirata felt a sudden resurgence of the hope that he'd thought impossible.

"You're officially banned from the investigation," Sano

continued. "No one is watching you. You can go places and talk to people that I can't. I need you to reinvestigate Koheiji and Tamura in the light of what we've learned about them. I need to know if they have any connection to Daiemon's murder. But I can't do it with Otani and Ibe shadowing me and ready to harm my son if I step out of line. Therefore, I'm ordering you to act on my behalf."

Joy exhilarated Hirata. Here was a new chance to solve the case and atone for past mistakes. The murder of Daiemon had begotten good fortune as well as bad. Hirata stifled an urge to cheer. Bowing solemnly, he said, "I'll do my best."

"Keep your inquiries as discreet as possible," Sano warned. "Don't let Otani or Ibe get wise to you."

"Yes, *Sōsakan-sama.*" Hirata understood the responsibility that came with his new chance. Now it wasn't just his life or reputation at risk, but the welfare of his master's child. "But what if I discover evidence against Tamura or Koheiji—or someone in the factions? That would displease Otani and Ibe."

"Let's just solve the crimes and hope that everything somehow turns out all right."

Hirata saw that Sano didn't feel much optimism. Neither did Hirata. But he had his new chance. He swore to himself that he wouldn't blow it.

Business in the theater district was well under way by the time Hirata arrived. Clad in plain garments that obscured his rank and a wide wicker hat that hid his face, he rode down Saru-waka-cho. Drummers in the wooden framework towers called theatergoers to the plays. People laden with quilts to keep them warm filed into the buildings. Gay music and fluttering banners spangled the cold, gray morning. Vendors did a brisk trade in hot tea and roasted chestnuts. But Hirata observed that the crowds seemed thinner than usual, minus the samurai who'd been mobilized for the coming battle between Chamberlain Yanagisawa and Lord

Matsudaira. Distant war drums pulsed in counterrhythm to the drums in the towers. A dangerous energy in the air heightened the urgency of Hirata's own mission. He dismounted outside the Nakamura-za Theater, secured his horse, bought a ticket, and entered through the door beneath a huge poster of Koheiji.

Inside, the theater was sparsely peopled, the stage empty except for musicians tuning their instruments: The play was late in starting. So much the better, Hirata thought—he could snare Koheiji now instead of waiting out the play. The actor still didn't strike Hirata as the best suspect, but Sano wanted him reinvestigated, and Hirata and Koheiji had things to settle.

Hirata climbed onto the runway that extended from the stage, between rows of seating compartments, to a curtained door at the side of the room. He pushed through the curtain into a corridor, past actors lining up to go onstage. Walking down the corridor, Hirata peered into rooms where more actors fussed while attendants adjusted their costumes and makeup. Gaudy courtesans and strutting samurai abounded among the cast. Hirata came to the last door along the passage. A man's breathy grunts and a woman's moans issued from inside the room. Hirata lifted the curtain that screened the door.

Costumes on wooden stands, a dressing table and mirror, and theatrical props jammed the small space. On a futon in the corner, Koheiji lay, his kimono hiked above his bare buttocks, his trousers fallen around his knees, atop a woman who sprawled nude in a tangle of her long hair and brightly colored robes. He panted while thrusting into her; she bit on a cloth to stifle her moans. Hirata cleared his throat. The lovers' heads turned toward him, and the lust on their faces turned to dismay. The woman squealed.

"Who are you?" Koheiji demanded, springing to his feet and glaring at Hirata through a mask of white face powder, painted black eyebrows, and rouged cheeks and lips. "How dare you barge in here?"

The woman scrambled into her robes, then ran out the

door. Hirata tilted back his hat. "You remember me," he said. "I'm here for a little talk with you."

The actor's face showed alarm as he recognized Hirata. He seemed to decide against arguing with the chief retainer of the shogun's *sōsakan-sama*. Nodding sullenly, he straightened his clothes. "All right, but please be quick." He looked in the mirror, checking his makeup, then hung two wooden swords at his waist. "I have to go onstage in a few moments." Sudden anxiety colored his expression as he faced Hirata. "Hey—I hope you won't tell anyone what you just saw?"

"Why shouldn't I?" Hirata said.

"She's the wife of the theater owner," Koheiji said. "If he found out about us, he would fire me."

The explanation sounded credible, but Hirata heard a tinny, discordant note in Koheiji's voice. Instinct told Hirata who the actor was really afraid would learn about the affair, and the reason why. Hirata tucked the knowledge into the back of his mind for future use. "I might be persuaded to keep quiet," he said, "if you tell me what you were doing the night Senior Elder Makino died."

Koheiji's eyes gleamed, wary and sharp, from within the mask of theatrical makeup. He leaned against the wall near the door and folded his arms. "I already told you, when we talked the day before yesterday."

"You told me at least one lie then," said Hirata. "You said there was no sex between you and Makino. Did you forget to mention the sex shows that he hired you to perform for him? Or do you think they don't count?"

The actor cursed under his breath. "There's no privacy in this town. Everybody talks about everybody else. I should have known you'd find out about my little business."

"Then why did you try to hide it from me?"

"I thought it would make me look guilty."

"You look even guiltier because you lied."

"So what if I did?" Koheiji pushed himself away from the wall, defensive and belligerent now. "I told the truth when I said I didn't kill Makino. And so what if I put on sex shows for him? That's not a crime."

"What about when you almost beat a judicial councilor to death during one of your shows?" Hirata said. "That was a crime."

Alarm flashed in Koheiji's eyes, but he quickly blinked it away. He said, "That never happened," and slouched against the door with care-free nonchalance. But his nonchalance was obvious fakery. He was, as Hirata recalled the watchdog Ibe saying, not an especially good actor. "Who told you it did?"

Hirata didn't answer. He waited, knowing that people would often spill compromising facts just because they can't tolerate silence when under pressure. From the theater came the smack of wooden swords clashing and voices shouting in a duel scene.

"It must have been that pitiful, second-rate actor, Ebisuya. He was always jealous of me. He'll say anything to get me in trouble." The need to excuse himself superseded wisdom in Koheiji. He blurted, "Things got out of control. I didn't hurt the judicial councilor that much. He lived."

"Senior Elder Makino didn't," Hirata said. "Did things get out of control with him, too? Did you beat him to death during one of your sex shows?"

Efforts at nonchalance failed Koheiji. He stood rigid with anxiety, his back, hands, and heels pressed to the wall. "I didn't kill Makino. There was no show that night."

"Who was the woman?" Hirata said. "Was it Okitsu? Did her sleeve get torn when things got rough?"

"No!" Vehemence raised Koheiji's voice. "Makino brought in courtesans for me to use. But not that night." Again Hirata heard the tinny note in the actor's voice that signaled lies. "I didn't see Makino at all. Okitsu will tell you—she and I were together the whole night."

Frustration filled Hirata because Koheiji seemed determined to stick to his story. The actor had no reason to tell the truth when lying would protect him better. Under different circumstances, Hirata would have applied physical force to make Koheiji talk. But Sano didn't approve of forced confessions because even innocent people would incriminate themselves if hurt or frightened enough. Furthermore, he'd told Hirata to be discreet in his inquiries, and Hirata meant to do everything right this time.

"What about last night?" Hirata said, switching the interrogation to a different course. "Where were you and what were you doing then?"

Koheiji's painted face went blank with confusion. "I was here, at the theater," he said slowly, as if to give himself time to figure out where the conversation was heading. "We were rehearsing a new play."

"When did you begin and when did you finish?" Hirata said.

"The rehearsal started around the hour of the boar. We worked long past midnight. We slept in the dressing rooms until it was time to get ready to perform this morning."

"Were you with the rest of the cast during the whole rehearsal?"

Koheiji nodded. "I'm the star. I'm in every scene. I may have slipped outside between acts a few times, but . . ." His posture had gradually relaxed since Hirata had dropped the subject of Makino's murder, but he spoke with caution: "Why are you asking me all this? What's so important about last night?"

"Last night Lord Matsudaira's nephew Daiemon was murdered," Hirata said. He watched emotion contract the muscles of Koheiji's face under the garish makeup. But he couldn't tell whether the actor was surprised by the news or worried about why Hirata had brought it up.

"Hey, I'm sorry to hear that," Koheiji said in the tone appropriate when speaking of the death of a prominent citizen. "How did it happen?"

Either he didn't know or he thought it wise to feign ignorance, Hirata speculated. "Daiemon was stabbed."

"Oh," Koheiji said. Tilting his head, he regarded Hirata with a mixture of curiosity and apprehension. "What does his death have to do with me?"

"Did you know him?" Hirata said.

"Not very well. I met him at parties where actors were

hired to entertain the guests. But wait just a moment." Koheiji thrust his hands palms up toward Hirata and waggled them. "You don't think I had something to do with . . . ?" He chuckled nervously as he dropped his hands. "I haven't seen Daiemon in months. Not since a party at his uncle's house."

But here was a connection between Koheiji and Daiemon, and perhaps a link between the two murders. Hirata said, "Daiemon was in Senior Elder Makino's estate the night Makino died. You didn't see him then?"

Although Koheiji shook his head, his face acquired a queasy expression. "I had no idea he was there."

But even if Koheiji hadn't seen Daiemon, Daiemon might have seen him, Hirata conjectured.

"Besides," Koheiji said, "why would I kill him, when we barely knew each other?"

And what, Hirata wondered, might Daiemon have seen Koheiji doing? Beating Makino to death? Maybe the actor had later, somehow, found out that Daiemon had seen him, and killed Daiemon to keep him quiet. Yet if Daiemon had witnessed the murder, why hadn't he said so when Sano interrogated him? Hirata began to lose hope that solving one murder would solve both.

"Look," Koheiji said, "you've got the wrong man. I'm sure your boss would be happy to have you pin both murders on me, but I didn't kill Daiemon any more than I killed Makino. Okitsu will swear to it. So will the people at the theater."

Despite his adamant denial, he'd lost his cockiness. His samurai garb and makeup contrasted pathetically with his fear of ruin. Just then, the curtain over the door lifted. A scowl-faced man stuck his head inside the room.

"It's time for you to go onstage. Get out there right now!" the man told Koheiji, then vanished.

Koheiji breathed a glad sigh, as though reprieved at the brink of disaster. He scuttled past Hirata, who let him go, for the time being. Before darting out the door, he said, "If Daiemon really was in Makino's estate that night, maybe he killed Makino. Just because he's dead, it doesn't mean he's innocent. Why don't you look into his business?"

That was exactly what Hirata must do, after he'd talked to Tamura, the other suspect Sano had sent him to investigate.

24

The play was the longest Koheiji had ever performed. He sang and ranted; he strutted across the stage; he romanced beautiful women; he fought a thrilling sword battle. The audience wildly cheered and applauded him, but for once he didn't care. All he could think about was his visit from the *sōsakan-sama*'s chief retainer and how his situation had gone from bad to dire. He'd reached the height of success, and all he cared about was averting the demons of destruction, whose hot breath he could already feel on his neck.

As soon as the play ended, Koheiji rushed to his dressing room, hastily scrubbed off his makeup, and changed his costume for everyday clothes. He ran out to the street and spied a palanquin for hire.

"Take me to Edo Castle," he told the bearers as he leaped into the vehicle.

While it bounced and veered along the streets, he brooded upon how his life seemed an endless series of good and bad luck, as though he'd been born under a star that shone brightly then went dark in unpredictable phases. He'd had the good fortune to be born the son of a rich merchant, but then his father had died, leaving nothing but debts. Koheiji found himself out on the street at age nine, forced to beg, rob, and sell his body. He was always running from the police, fighting off bigger boys who tried to steal his money; he slept under bridges.

His luck had turned when the Owari Theater took him in. At first Koheiji had been overjoyed at having shelter, food, and a chance at a glamorous, lucrative career. But he'd soon become embroiled in the vicious gossip, dirty tricks, and bullying that the struggling actors used against one another. Koheiji had had no choice but to do worse to his competitors than they did to him. He'd pushed one especially talented rival down the stairs and broken his back, crippling him. He'd made a lot of enemies, but his reward was lead roles in the plays. His star brightened.

But new troubles developed. Even the lead roles at the Owari paid a pittance. Koheiji still had to sell himself for money to buy costumes and have fun. He'd spent too much in the teahouses and pleasure quarter. He'd begun borrowing from moneylenders, run up more debts, and borrowed more money to pay the creditors who hounded him. Then he made the fortuitous discovery that rich men would pay to see him having sex. His shows had paid his debts and increased his popularity. If only he'd never met Judicial Councilor Banzan!

The old coot had demanded that Koheiji beat him with a leather strap while the girl watched. When Koheiji began striking Banzan, a sudden, furious rage possessed him. Banzan seemed to personify everyone who'd ever done Koheiji wrong, everyone he'd been forced to please. Koheiji didn't stop until Banzan was bloody and unconscious. He'd had to pay his foe, Ebisuya, for help cleaning up the mess he'd made. A new cycle of debt and borrowing plunged him into despair, until Senior Elder Makino rescued him.

Makino had become his patron and raised him to fame and fortune. But the brightest phase of his star gave way to the darkest after Makino's death. Somehow Koheiji had always managed to blunder along until good fortune shone on him again, but now his adversaries weren't just jealous actors; they were the *sōsakan-sama* and his henchmen, backed by the might of the Tokugawa regime. Two murders doubled the likelihood that he would be the one punished. If he didn't act fast, his star would burn out for good.

Impatient, Koheiji looked out the window of his palanquin to gauge his progress toward Edo Castle. He saw, crossing an intersection ahead of him, a familiar palanquin and entourage. Koheiji called, "Let me off here!" He jumped from his vehicle, tossed coins to the bearers, ran after the palanquin, and banged on the window shutters.

They opened, and Okitsu and Agemaki peered at him from within the palanquin as he trotted alongside it. Okitsu smiled and cried, "Koheiji-san! I'm so glad to see you!"

"Get out," Koheiji said, barely looking at her.

"What?" Confusion wiped the smile off Okitsu's face.

Koheiji flung open the palanquin's door and yanked Okitsu out. As she squealed protests, he climbed in, took her seat opposite Agemaki, then shut the doors and window.

"I need to talk to you," he said. "There's bad news."

Agemaki sat, prim and quiet as usual, her tranquil face averted from him. She waited for him to speak.

"First, I must thank you for not telling the *sōsakan-sama* about me and the night Senior Elder Makino died," Koheiji said, his voice lowered to a loud whisper.

"I promised I would say nothing," Agemaki murmured. "And I kept my promise." She paused, then said, "Please allow me to thank you for not telling the *sōsakan-sama* about me."

The morning after Makino's murder, they'd agreed to protect each other. So far their bargain had held; their guilty secrets were safe from the *sōsakan-sama*, who hadn't arrested either of them. But Koheiji wanted to ensure that Agemaki didn't fail him now.

"It's more important than ever that we honor our bargain," Koheiji said. "Something has happened that puts us both in more danger than before."

Agemaki turned her head slightly toward Koheiji, signifying interest, although her tranquil expression didn't change.

"Daiemon was stabbed to death last night," Koheiji said.

"How do you know this?"

"The *sōsakan-sama*'s chief retainer told me," Koheiji said. "He came to see me at the theater this morning. I must warn you that he and his master aren't finished asking questions yet. Now that they have two crimes to solve, I'm guessing they're under twice as much pressure from their superiors. They seem to believe that whoever killed Makino also killed Daiemon. That makes you and me suspects in both murders."

He watched to see what effect the news had on Agemaki, but she hid her emotions so well that he never knew what she was thinking. Koheiji despised her cold, remote demeanor. He preferred women like Okitsu, who were as transparent as water. But circumstances had thrown him and Agemaki together in mutual dependency.

"The *sōsakan-sama* or his retainer will surely call on you again," Koheiji said. "And when they do, you must keep your silence about me."

Shrouded by her impenetrable thoughts, Agemaki sat unmoving, hands clasped and eyelids lowered, as the palanquin jounced along the street. The voices of beggars pleading for alms and the smell of decaying garbage filtered through the shutters. Koheiji squirmed, eager for reassurance from Agemaki.

Her gaze slid toward him, not quite meeting his. She murmured, "When the *sōsakan-sama* does call on me, I may be forced to tell him what you did."

For once Koheiji could read her mind. She thought that if the *sōsakan-sama* accused her of murdering Daiemon, she could save herself by breaking the bargain and revealing the knowledge that would condemn Koheiji instead. Koheiji had always sensed that Agemaki was smarter, crueler, and more self-serving than she appeared; now he was certain. But if she thought she could betray him, she wasn't as clever as she believed. Even while she held his fate in her hands, Koheiji held hers.

"If you tell the *sōsakan-sama* what I did," Koheiji said, "I'll have to tell him all about you."

She seemed unruffled by his counterthreat. A hint of a smile touched her lips. "Whose story do you think the *sōsakan-sama* would consider more important? Yours or mine?"

The tinge of superiority in her voice nettled Koheiji. The danger that her betrayal posed struck dread into him. He felt sweat dampening his armpits and smelled his sweet stench of nerves filling the palanquin. Maybe the *sōsakan-sama* would think that what Agemaki knew was indisputable evidence that Koheiji had killed Makino, while Koheiji's story didn't prove Agemaki had. Agemaki obviously believed so, and maybe she was right. Yet Koheiji mustn't let her intimidate him.

"If you think the *sōsakan-sama* would listen to a former shrine attendant and whore like you rather than a Kabuki star like me, I think you've got a lot to learn," he said. "But, hey, there's a way to settle the question. Let's go to the *sōsakan-sama*, together, right now. We'll each tell him our story and see which of us he arrests."

He was bluffing; he didn't dare take such a gamble. But Agemaki swiveled and raised her head until their gazes met. Koheiji saw fearful uncertainty, and hatred toward him, in her eyes. She looked away first.

"Perhaps it's best that we keep our bargain," she said.

Gladness and relief flooded Koheiji. He drew his first easy breath since Hirata had interrupted his tryst in the theater. "Oh, indeed it is best," he said. "That way, the *sōsakan-sama* will have to pick somebody else to blame for the murders instead of either of us."

And soon Koheiji's darkest season would end. His star would shine once more.

As Reiko trudged behind the palanquin bearers, along the avenue outside the wall and moat of Edo Castle, she saw Koheiji jump out of the vehicle. Okitsu, who'd been walking alongside the maids and pouting, ran to him.

"Koheiji-*san*!" she cried petulantly. "What's going on?"

"I'll explain later," he said, shaking her hand off his sleeve. "I have to get back to the theater."

He whispered in Okitsu's ear, then hurried away, cut between two squadrons of marching soldiers, and disappeared. Okitsu hesitated, obviously upset and wishing to go after him, then clambered into the palanquin. Reiko thought about the conversation that had just passed between Agemaki and Koheiji. Her keen ears had heard enough to know that the pair were engaging in a conspiracy of silence. Each appeared to have evidence that implicated the other in Makino's murder. Questions teemed in Reiko's mind. Was one of them the killer? The conversation she'd overheard in Yanagiya suggested that it was Agemaki. Or were the actor and widow conspirators in the crime as well as in subterfuge?

Reiko remembered the scene she'd witnessed between Koheiji and Okitsu last night, which had almost convinced her that the guilty party was one or both of them. She felt as though her suspicion were a ball that kept bouncing from one person to another. Upon whom would it finally land?

Rain spiked with ice stippled the courtyard of Senior Elder Makino's estate and clattered on the roofs of the surrounding barracks. In the courtyard, Sano greeted one of the detectives he'd assigned to watch the estate.

"Did Senior Elder Makino's widow or concubine leave the premises yesterday evening?" Sano asked.

"Yes," the detective said. "They went out separately, in palanquins, at around the hour of the boar."

Sano glanced at Ibe and Otani, who stood nearby with their troops and Detectives Marume and Fukida, the only men they'd allowed him to bring along. Otani said, "That's evidence that either woman had the opportunity to kill Daiemon."

"For your son's sake, you'd better find more evidence that they did," Ibe said, his thin features stiff with cold and bad will toward Sano.

"What about Makino's actor and chief retainer?" Sano asked his detective.

Otani said, "I'm warning you."

"They both went out before the women did," said the detective. "Koheiji hasn't yet returned. Tamura came back after midnight and went out again a little while ago."

"Forget you heard that," Ibe told Sano. "Concentrate on the women, or else."

Anger that the watchdogs had commandeered his investigation boiled up in Sano, but an image of Masahiro surrounded by their thugs stifled his retort. He longed to ask the detective for news of Reiko, but he couldn't in the presence of Otani and Ibe. With great effort he banished the thought of his wife and son both in jeopardy and focused on the business at hand. "Where are Agemaki and Okitsu?" he asked the detective.

"They went out together early this morning. They're not back yet."

"I'm sure you can find something to occupy you here until they return," Ibe said.

"Why don't you search their quarters again?" Otani said.

He and Ibe escorted Sano to the private chambers, thwarting Sano's hope of sneaking off to find Reiko or investigate the scene of Daiemon's murder. Their troops followed, guarding Detectives Marume and Fukida. Sano and the detectives first searched Okitsu's cluttered room. Otani and Ibe wandered off, but their troops stayed. If Okitsu had killed Daiemon, Sano found no sign of it. Sano moved on to Agemaki's pristine quarters. There he and his men had just finished another fruitless search, when Ibe and Otani burst into the room. Ibe dragged the concubine; Otani brought the widow. Okitsu whimpered in terror, while Agemaki remained tranquil.

"Here they are," said Ibe. "Pick one."

Sano's gaze flew to a group of maids who hovered fearfully outside the door. Reiko wasn't among them. Sano said, "Take Okitsu to her room." He thought her the weakest of the suspects, and giving her time to worry should goad her to reveal whatever secrets she might know about Makino's murder. "I'll question Agemaki first."

The watchdogs' troops took the concubine away. Ibe pushed the widow to her knees on the floor in front of the screen decorated with gilded birds. He and Otani stood on either side of her, their troops ranged around them. It was a situation designed to intimidate, Sano observed, but it wasn't working. Agemaki seemed completely indifferent to the display of power surrounding her. He wondered if she'd been expecting another interrogation. Either she was innocent and felt safe in her virtue, or her stoicism was worthy of a samurai.

"When we talked yesterday, you told me that you last saw your husband before he went to bed the night he died," Sano said. "You slept all that night in your own room. You were unaware of anything that happened because you'd taken a sleeping potion, and you don't know how your husband died or who killed him. Is that correct?"

"That is correct." A sigh accompanied Agemaki's response.

"My investigation has uncovered facts that cast doubt on your story," Sano said. "Is there anything that you forgot to mention—or that you'd like to change?"

He was certain that the murder hadn't gone unnoticed by everybody except the killer. The thin walls of the private chambers, and the proximity of Makino's room to the others, made it likely that someone else who'd been there that night had witnessed something. Someone, perhaps not just the killer, was withholding information, and it could be Agemaki.

"If so, now is the time to tell me," Sano said. "I'd be more inclined to excuse a mistake than I might be later."

Agemaki hesitated for an almost imperceptible instant before she murmured, "There is nothing else. I cannot alter the truth."

Her hesitation spoke more truth to Sano than did her words. Now he knew she was hiding something. Yet people had other reasons to keep secrets besides being guilty of a crime. Those reasons included the desire to protect someone else.

"What are your feelings toward your husband's concubine?" Sano said.

She gave him a sidelong glance from beneath lowered eyelashes. He thought he saw a glimmer of confusion cross her face. "Okitsu-*san* is like a little sister to me. We are the best of friends."

Sano wondered how often a wife felt kindly toward her husband's beautiful young concubine. "You didn't care that Okitsu had won Senior Elder Makino's affections?"

"Not at all."

She wisely kept her response brief; if she felt any compulsion to protest too much or explain herself, she resisted it. But Sano wondered if Agemaki was more likely to have killed to protect her future from Okitsu than to have lied to protect Okitsu from the law.

"What about the actor Koheiji and your husband's chief retainer?" said Sano. "Are you also friends with them?"

"No."

A single word could convey many shades of meaning, Sano observed. In Agemaki's reply he'd heard scorn for the idea that a lady of her rank would be friends with a hired entertainer or a family vassal. She wouldn't have lied to protect them, either. If she'd withheld compromising information about Makino's death, she aimed to protect herself.

The troops stirred, restless; Detectives Marume and Fukida watched Sano, ready to defend him if need be. Ibe and Otani gestured for Sano to speed up the interrogation.

"Yesterday you told me that your family is in service to Lord Torii," said Sano. "But in fact, your father was a wandering *rōnin*. Your mother was an attendant at Asakusa Jinja Shrine, and so were you. Isn't that true?"

He saw Agemaki's throat contract as she swallowed: He'd shaken her composure. But she said calmly, "My father was a samurai retainer to the Torii clan."

"Your friends at the shrine say not."

Her gaze briefly touched his; pride flashed like a torn banner in her eyes. "I know better than they do."

"Very well." Sano understood that her background was her vulnerable spot. That he'd exposed it might open her up to more revelations. He strode closer to her. "You were a prostitute, a woman of uncertain parentage and few prospects."

Agemaki flinched at the words as though he'd flung nightsoil on her expensive robes. Sano knew of other women in her position who liked to forget the past and pretend that their existences as wives of rich, powerful men were the only lives they'd ever known. He hoped he was tormenting a criminal, not an innocent victim.

"Senior Elder Makino brought you to his house . . . as his concubine. He was still married to his first wife then, wasn't he?" Sano said.

"Yes." Involuntary movement shifted Agemaki's body.

"What happened to his first wife?"

"She died," Agemaki whispered.

"How did she die?"

"From a fever."

"According to the Edo Castle physician, you nursed her when she took ill," Sano said, bringing into play the information Hirata had given him.

"She wanted me to take care of her." As self-defensiveness overrode her feminine reticence, Agemaki explained, "She wouldn't let anyone else. She trusted my healing skills."

"But she got worse instead of better," Sano said.

He watched Agemaki twist and rub her hands together, as if washing them. He was interested that she seemed more upset now than while discussing Makino's murder. She must have been prepared for questions about his death but not his first wife's or her own past. Maybe she'd not expected the subjects to come up. A person's ability to dissemble stretched only so far.

"I did my best to save her," Agemaki said, "but she was too ill."

"According to the Edo Castle physician, you were the one who mixed her medicines," Sano said. "You fed them to her. What did you put in them besides healing herbs?"

"Nothing!" Agemaki's head came up; her eyes glittered.

"Did you poison her?" Sano said.

"I didn't!" Panic crumbled Agemaki's sedate mien. The

guise of the demure, grieving widow deserted her. "It wasn't my fault that she died! Anyone who says otherwise is lying!"

Sano wished he could tell whether she'd killed Makino's first wife and feared due punishment, or if she was panicking because she was innocent and wrongfully accused. He'd seen similar reactions from guilty as well as innocent people.

"You gained by the death of Makino's first wife," Sano reminded Agemaki. "Makino married you. But then he took a new concubine. History repeats itself. You knew that Okitsu could replace you just as you'd replaced his first wife. Did you kill him to prevent him from divorcing you, marrying Okitsu, and cutting off your inheritance?"

Agemaki relaxed her body, stilled her hands, and spread a mask of false serenity across her features. "I did not."

"Lord Matsudaira's nephew, Daiemon, was in this estate the night your husband was murdered," Sano said. "Did you see him?"

"No. If he was here, he must have come while I was asleep."

"You're not investigating Daiemon," Otani said with a dark frown at Sano. "No more questions about him."

"While you were asleep, or while you were beating your husband to death?" Sano said, ignoring Otani. "Did he catch you in the act?"

"Careful, *Sōsakan-sama,*" said Ibe.

Agemaki repeated quietly, "I didn't see him. I did nothing for him to see."

"Last night Daiemon was stabbed to death in a house of assignation," Sano said even as the watchdogs glared at him. "What were you doing then?"

"I went out for a ride in my palanquin." Agemaki seemed indifferent to the news of Daiemon's death.

"Where did you go?" Sano said.

"Nowhere in particular. Just around town."

"Enough of this," Ibe told Sano.

Sano nodded. He'd learned what he'd wanted to know. Agemaki had been in the city last night. Perhaps she was Daiemon's missing paramour—and killer.

"I'm satisfied that she killed Makino's first wife," Ibe said.

"And Makino as well," Otani said. "Once a murderer, twice a murderer."

"Go ahead and arrest her," Ibe told Sano. "If you're so anxious to solve Daiemon's murder, let her take the blame for that, too."

Agemaki sat frozen between the watchdogs, like a cat who thinks that if she doesn't move, predators won't notice or attack her.

Sano said, "The evidence against her is indirect. It's not sufficient for me."

"It's sufficient to convict her in the Court of Justice," Ibe said.

Sano knew that for a fact, but he also knew that virtually all trials in the Tokugawa justice system resulted in conviction, even if the defendant was innocent. Agemaki might be guilty of multiple murders—or not. He was by no means certain which. Even while the watchdogs held his son hostage, Sano refused to let them rush him into a faulty decision.

"You gave me a choice of two suspects," he told them. "I'll interrogate Okitsu before arresting anyone."

A silent consultation ensued between Ibe and Otani. "Suit yourself," Ibe said at last. "But don't tax our patience."

As they and their troops ushered Sano and his detectives out of the room, Sano looked backward at Agemaki. She stayed kneeling and immobile, her head bowed, the bare nape of her neck white and vulnerable, as though waiting for the executioner's sword to descend.

25

Hirata knew better than to march into Makino's estate, accost Tamura, and start asking questions. He couldn't risk running into Ibe or Otani after they'd banned him from the murder investigation. After leaving the theater district, he went home and sent Detective Inoue to Makino's estate, with orders to find Tamura and lure him someplace that Hirata could talk to him. Detective Inoue returned with the news that Tamura was at the Edo Castle martial arts training ground. Hirata decided that was as good a place as any. The training ground was virtually deserted in winter, when most Tokugawa samurai would rather laze indoors than practice their combat skills.

But when Hirata entered the grounds, he found them crowded with squadrons of mounted soldiers roving the field. More soldiers dressed themselves and their horses in armor. Some sparred together, eager for combat. Weapons masters hauled cannon, guns, and ammunition through the sleety rain. Commanders roamed, trying to establish order. Everyone wore the crest of Lord Matsudaira. The training ground had become a staging area for his army. Hirata looked around in amazement. He wondered why Tamura, who belonged to the opposing faction, had come here. And where was he in all this commotion?

Hirata elbowed his way through the crowd. He caught

snatches of conversation: "Lord Matsudaira has summoned Chamberlain Yanagisawa to battle in the fields north of town." "The fighting has already started. We'll be on our way soon." Battle fever was contagious. Hirata felt his samurai blood roil with excitement. As he scanned the crowds, light and movement inside a building near the wall of the enclosure caught his attention.

The building was a barnlike hall used for sword practice. A lone figure threw fleeting shadows against paper windowpanes screened by wooden bars. Hirata slipped through the door, into a cavernous space that smelled of male sweat, urine, blood, and temper. Burning lanterns hung from the bare rafters; straw dummies stood along walls nicked by blades. Tamura, dressed in white trousers, darted and lunged across the hall, wielding his sword. As he slashed at an imaginary opponent, his bare feet stamped the dingy cypress floor. He took no notice of Hirata. Sweat gleamed on his naked torso and shaved crown; his severe face wore a look of intense concentration. His muscles were defined and tough, his movements fluid, his form impressive for a man nearing sixty.

Tamura ended with a series of flourishes so rapid that his sword was a silver blur. He halted, his chest heaving. His breath puffed white clouds into the chilly room. He lowered his weapon and bowed.

"Very good," Hirata said.

Tamura appeared not to hear. Hirata walked up to Tamura and clapped his hands loudly. Tamura turned at the sound, which echoed through the hall. Irritation slanted his eyebrows at a sharper angle as he became aware of Hirata.

"Did the *sōsakan-sama* send you to pester me with more questions?" Tamura said. "I thought I heard you'd been barred from investigating the murder."

"This is just a friendly, informal chance encounter," Hirata said.

Tamura's reply was a stare filled with distrust. He placed his sword on a rack, picked up a water jar, and drank deeply. He wiped his mouth on his arm and waited for Hirata to state the purpose of his visit. A thought occurred to Hirata. That Tamura hadn't at first heard him speak suggested that Tamura was deaf. Was that why he hadn't heard anything the night Senior Elder Makino died? He wouldn't have said so because a proud samurai like him never admitted to any physical defects. Rather, he would read lips and pretend he could hear. But deafness didn't equal innocence. There were other reasons why Tamura might withhold the truth.

"Why are you in here, fencing with your shadow, instead of riding off to war?" Hirata said. "Are you preparing to carry out the vendetta you swore yesterday?"

Tamura showed no surprise that Hirata knew about the vendetta. "Yes, although it's none of your business. My samurai duty to avenge the death of my master outweighs all other concerns."

"Even though you despised him?"

A scowl darkened Tamura's features, but instead of rising to Hirata's bait, he took up a cloth and rubbed sweat off himself.

"Your arguments with Makino are a matter of record," Hirata said. "You disapproved of his greed for money, the bribes he extorted, and his whoremongering. You called him dishonorable to his face. Yet you expect me to believe that you think his death is worth avenging?"

"Duty must be served regardless of the master's faults." Tamura sounded as if he were quoting some Bushido tract. "My personal feelings are irrelevant."

He threw down the cloth and hefted his sword. His kind of pompous, old-fashioned warrior virtue always irritated Hirata, who knew that it was often nothing but hypocrisy. "So who's the lucky target of your vendetta?" Hirata said.

"I don't know yet." Tamura crouched, holding his sword horizontal, sweeping it slowly across the room, and sighting along the blade. "But I'm not waiting for the *sōsakan-sama* to figure out who killed my master." His sneer said he didn't think much of Sano's chances.

"Are you conducting your own inquiries, then?" Hirata said, displeased by the tacit insult to his own master.

Tamura raked a disdainful glance across Hirata. "There's no need for inquiries. Meditation will reveal the truth to me."

If meditation could reveal a murderer's identity, it would save him and Sano a lot of trouble, Hirata thought skeptically. But of course it worked without fail when one already knew the truth.

"Maybe it's appropriate for you to be fencing against yourself," Hirata said. "Maybe your vendetta is nothing but a charade to hide your own guilt."

A contemptuous grin curled Tamura's lip as he carved a swath of air with his sword. "If the *sōsakan-sama* were sure of that, he would have already arrested me."

Hirata couldn't deny this. Maybe Tamura really was innocent and his vendetta genuine. The lack of witnesses and evidence argued in his favor. Yet Hirata had a strong hunch that Tamura would figure into the solution of the mystery.

"Supposing you didn't kill your master," Hirata said, "maybe you've already carried out your vendetta. One of the murder suspects was stabbed to death last night."

A slight, awkward fumble interrupted the motion of Tamura's blade. But Tamura said calmly, "So I've heard. The news about Lord Matsudaira's nephew is all over Edo Castle."

"Did you already know it?" Hirata said.

"Because I killed him?" Tamura snorted. "Don't make me laugh. I had nothing to do with Daiemon's death. You're just fishing and hoping for a bite."

"You went out yesterday evening."

"I was nowhere near that filthy place where Daiemon died." Pivoting, Tamura maneuvered his sword in a smooth arc.

"Where did you go?" Hirata circled Tamura, keeping his face in view.

"I inspected Chamberlain Yanagisawa's army camp outside town. Eight of my men were with me. You can ask them."

Hirata knew that men loyal to Tamura would say anything for him, but instead of challenging the man, he waited. Unlike the actor, Tamura didn't fill the silence with self-compromising blabber. But Hirata noticed that even while Tamura performed strenuous lunges, the puffs of vapor from his mouth ceased momentarily: Tamura was holding his breath, anxious for Hirata to believe his alibi . . . because it was false?

"Did meditation reveal to you that Daiemon killed your master and deserved to die?" Hirata said.

Tamura breathed again, apparently thinking that his alibi had stymied Hirata, who'd resorted to fishing again. "It's common knowledge that Daiemon was a poor excuse for a samurai," he said between whistling sword strokes. "He had too good an opinion of himself, too little respect for his elders, and too much appetite for women. He spread disgusting lies that my master had defected. Someone did the world a favor by getting rid of Daiemon. Bleeding to death in his whore's bed was a fitting end to him."

"Your attitude toward him sounds like a motive for murder," Hirata said.

The sword flashed close to him, and he leaped back just in time to avoid a cut across the throat. Tamura said; "I wouldn't dirty my blade on a rat like Daiemon."

"What if he knew something about you that you'd rather keep secret? When he was at Senior Elder Makino's estate, did he see you killing your master or covering up the murder?"

"Nonsense!" Tamura whacked at Hirata's shins; Hirata sprang above the blade. "Even if I'd wanted to kill Daiemon, I wouldn't have sneaked up on him in the dark, stabbed him, and run. That's a coward's way of killing."

"Instead you'd have marched up to Daiemon on the street in broad daylight and cut off his head?" said Hirata.

"As a true samurai would."

Hirata could picture Tamura doing such a thing. The murder of Daiemon did seem out of character for him—but perhaps that had been intentional. Hirata said, "Suppose you didn't want anyone to know you'd killed Daiemon. You might have done it in a way that you thought no one would think you would, to avoid punishment from Lord Matsudaira."

Tamura gave an abrasive chuckle as his sword sliced intricate, lightning-fast patterns in the air. "Deceit is dishonorable. A true samurai takes credit for his actions and accepts the consequences. When I carry out my vendetta, everyone will know what I've done. I'll go to my fate with my head held high."

His gaze deplored Hirata. "But I don't expect you to understand. After all, you're famous for your disloyalty to your master. Who are you to accuse me of disgrace?"

Hot shame and rage erupted in Hirata. Tamura stood still, his sword held motionless in both hands, the blade canted toward Hirata. With instinctive haste, Hirata drew his own weapon. Tamura grinned.

"Now we'll see who's the true samurai and who's the disgrace to Bushido," Tamura said.

The lantern light glinted on their blades. Hirata felt danger vibrating in the air between them, his heart drumming with a primitive urge for a battle to the death, his muscles tensed to lunge. But second thoughts gave him pause. He didn't fear losing; although Tamura was an expert swordsman, he was some thirty years older than Hirata, and he'd never fought real battles, as Hirata had. Instead, Hirata realized that killing one of the suspects would hurt the investigation. Rising to Tamura's challenge to defend his honor would only prove Hirata an incorrigible disgrace to Sano and condemn himself to death as a murderer.

Hirata stepped back from Tamura. He sheathed his sword and endured the contempt he saw on his adversary's face. It was one of the hardest things he'd ever done.

"Coward," Tamura said.

Swallowing humiliation, fighting his temper, Hirata forced himself to speak quietly: "You know something about Makino's murder that you haven't told. If you killed him— or Daiemon—I will personally deliver you to justice."

He left the building before Tamura could reply or his urge to fight could overrule his better judgment. Outside, he breathed in vigorous huffs, expelling evil thoughts. Learning self-restraint was painful. As Hirata walked through the troops milling on the martial arts training ground, he forced himself to concentrate on the investigation.

Logic and instinct convinced him that Tamura and Ko-heiji were both lying about the night Makino died. But while both men lacked definite alibis for Daiemon's murder, their connections to him were tenuous, and there was no evidence that Daiemon had witnessed either of them killing Makino, or anything at all, that night. The only news Hirata had for Sano was that he'd followed orders and kept out of trouble today.

He decided to try another tactic. Scanning the Matsudaira soldiers, he saw a heavyset samurai, clad in armor, galloping his horse across the field. The visor of his helmet was tipped back to reveal a youthful face with rosy cheeks and a square jaw. Hirata waved at him, calling, "Noro-*san*!"

Noro reined his mount to a stop beside Hirata and swung down from the saddle. "Hirata-*san*," he said with a quick bow and smile. "What brings you here? Are you joining our side?"

"I've come on other business," Hirata said. "By the way, my condolences on the death of your master."

Noro's expression saddened as he nodded in thanks. He had been a personal bodyguard to Daiemon.

Hirata steered Noro behind a range of archery targets, where they could talk unobserved. "I need a favor."

"Just name it," Noro said.

His willingness to oblige stemmed from an incident six years ago, when he and some friends had gotten into a brawl with a gang of peasant toughs. The gang had outnumbered and overpowered Noro and his friends. Noro had lost his sword in the scuffle, and one of the toughs had begun savagely beating him with an iron pole, when Hirata—a patrol officer at the time—had happened along. Hirata had broken up the fight and saved Noro's life. That initial acquaintance had grown into friendship when Hirata came to Edo Castle. Noro had sworn to thank Hirata by doing him any favor he wanted.

"Who was the woman Daiemon went to meet at the Sign of Bedazzlement?" Hirata asked.

Noro's eyes strayed. "I wish you'd asked me anything but that," he said. "I can't tell anybody, including you."

"Can't, or won't?"

"I made a promise to Daiemon."

Although a samurai's promise to his master overrode any other, Hirata persisted. "What does it matter if you tell, now that Daiemon is dead?"

"I can't tell you that, either," Noro said, obviously ashamed to disappoint the man to whom he owed his life. "But believe me, it matters."

"She may have killed Daiemon," Hirata pointed out. "If you don't tell me who she is, you could be protecting his murderer. And you're also standing in the way of my duty to help my master solve the crime."

Misery clouded Noro's honest gaze, but he shook his head, refusing to be drawn into an argument.

"Could you at least get me inside the Matsudaira estate so that I can look for clues in Daiemon's quarters?" Hirata said.

"Lord Matsudaira would kill me. I'm sorry," Noro said.

"All right." Hirata walked away, but slowly, giving Noro time to change his mind. Hirata felt his hopes hinging on Noro's sense of honor.

"Wait," Noro said.

Hirata turned expectantly.

"I can't say who the woman is, but I must help you somehow," Noro said. He rocked his weight from one armor-clad leg to the other. "I probably shouldn't tell you this, either, but . . . Daiemon had other quarters besides the ones in the Matsudaira estate. He kept a house in Kanda." Noro described the location. "But you didn't hear about it from me."

26

Sano arrived in Okitsu's room to find her kneeling amid scattered clothing, surrounded by Ibe and Otani's troops. Her eyes were round, wide pools of fright; audible gulps contracted her throat. When she saw Sano enter with his detectives, his watchdogs, and their men, she blurted, "I didn't tell everything I know about the night Senior Elder Makino died. Please allow me to tell you now."

"Go ahead," Sano said, surprised that Okitsu would volunteer information before he'd even asked.

Okitsu gulped, drew a deep breath, and picked at her cuticles, which were already red and raw. "That night, when it was very late, I—I went to the Place of Relief." This was the polite term for the privy. "On my way back, I—I saw him."

"Who?" Sano felt Ibe and Otani tense, alert, at his back. "Senior Elder Makino?"

"No!" Okitsu gasped. "It was Lord Matsudaira's nephew."

Now Sano sensed disapproval and concern in his watchdogs. Excitement flared in him, for here was the first evidence that anyone had seen Daiemon after his visit to Makino. "Where did you see him?"

"He was in the, uh, study. The door was open a little. I peeked in, and—and there he was."

Sano scrutinized Okitsu. "How did you recognize Daiemon?"

She wriggled under his gaze. After a lengthy pause, she said, "I—I'd seen him before—at parties?" Her voice rose at the end of the sentence, as if she was uncertain that this was the right answer and wanted reassurance.

"What was he doing?" Sano said.

"He—he was standing by the desk? There was a, uh, pole in his hands?" Again came that questioning lilt in Okitsu's voice. "He was looking down at something on the floor?"

"What was it?"

"I—I don't know. I couldn't see?"

Sano pictured Daiemon, the weapon in his hands, standing over Senior Elder Makino's battered corpse, and Okitsu peeking through the door, a witness to the aftermath of the crime.

"You'll stop this line of questioning right now," Otani ordered Sano.

Lord Matsudaira wouldn't want his nephew implicated in the crime, even now that Daiemon was dead, Sano understood, lest it harm his clan's standing with the shogun.

"What else did you see?" Sano asked Okitsu.

"Nothing?" Her tone implored Sano to accept her word and leave her in peace.

Threatening stares from his watchdogs told Sano that he was pushing their forbearance. He said, "Okitsu-*san*, why didn't you tell my chief retainer about this when he questioned you?"

"Because I was too afraid," Okitsu said. Her fingers worried at her cuticles.

"And why did you choose to tell me about him now?"

Okitsu risked a furtive glance at Sano. "Now that Lord Matsudaira's nephew is dead, he can't hurt me."

"How do you know he's dead?" Sano said.

The girl mumbled, "I heard people talking."

Perhaps she had seen Daiemon and feared what he would do to her if she incriminated him, Sano thought. But perhaps she had also feared to confess that she'd been wandering the private chambers that night and could have committed the murder herself instead of almost catching the killer in the act. What was the real reason for the alibi she'd given Hirata?

"What happened after you saw Daiemon?" Sano said.

"I went back to Koheiji. He was in his room."

"What did you do then?"

"I don't remember."

Okitsu ducked her head. Sano bent down to peer into her face. Her eyes were so wide with terror that rings of white showed around the pupils. Her story now suggested that she and the actor had been apart long enough for him, as well as her, to kill Makino—if Daiemon hadn't.

"There's something else you neglected to tell my chief retainer," said Sano. "Yesterday he visited Rakuami, your former master. Rakuami said you hated Senior Elder Makino so much that you tried to commit suicide rather than be his concubine. Is it true?"

A gulp that ended in a retch convulsed Okitsu; her arms wrapped tight around her stomach. "No."

"Then Rakuami was lying?"

"No!"

"Either he lied about you, or you hated Makino. Which is it?" Sano said.

"I didn't hate him. I mean, I did at first, but . . ." Okitsu babbled, "After I'd lived with him awhile, and he was so kind to me, I was grateful to him, and I didn't hate him anymore, I loved him very much . . ."

She'd told Sano what he needed to know about her feelings toward Makino. "You said you knew Daiemon from parties. Were they parties at Rakuami's club?"

"I don't remember," Okitsu said. She moaned while clutching her stomach.

"Was he a client that you entertained for Rakuami?"

"I don't remember."

Her favorite answer didn't convince Sano, for he observed the blush that reddened the back of her neck above her kimono: Even Okitsu, who must have served many men at the club, hadn't forgotten that she'd served Daiemon. "When was the last time you saw him?"

Okitsu moved her head from side to side, then up, then

down, as if trying to catch thoughts that sped and jumbled in her mind. "It was—it was the night Senior Elder Makino died."

"Think again," Sano said. "Was it yesterday evening instead?"

"No."

"Where were you last night?"

"I was . . . with Koheiji."

Her favorite alibi didn't convince Sano either. "He went out alone. You left here after he did."

"I was with him. I was!" Okitsu began sobbing.

"Did you meet Daiemon at the Sign of Bedazzlement?" Sano said. "Were you his mistress?"

"No!"

"Did you go to him there last night? Did you stab him to death?"

"I didn't meet him! I didn't kill anyone!"

A terrible stench of diarrhea arose: Okitsu's bowels had moved. Ibe grimaced in disgust. "Let's get out of here," he said. He and Otani and their troops herded Sano and his men outside, where they gathered on the veranda. Hemmed in by his watchdogs, Sano stood at the railing. In the garden, the sand was pocked by raindrops, the boulders dark and slick with moisture. Distant war drums throbbed; distant gunshots cracked the cold air.

"The girl lied about seeing Daiemon the night of Makino's death," Ibe said. "Her alibis for both murders stink like fish ten days old."

Sano agreed, but he said, "That doesn't mean she's guilty." And he didn't think she was. She seemed incapable of stabbing or beating a man to death—at least without help. Yet she could be the common factor in both murders, if indeed they were connected.

"Why else would she lie?" Otani said with disdain.

"To protect someone else," Sano suggested. "To hide secrets that have nothing to do with the murders."

"Well, as far as I'm concerned, she's as good as guilty," said Ibe, "and so is the widow."

"Arrest one or the other," said Otani.

"Choose now. Waste no more time," Ibe said.

Sano didn't budge, although he could feel the pressure of their wills against his and he envisioned Masahiro, tiny and helpless, surrounded by their thugs. "Not yet," he said. "Not based on such flimsy evidence."

Ibe expelled a curse. "You've got two women who hated Makino, had the opportunity to kill him, and gave unsatisfactory accounts of their actions on the nights of his murder and Daiemon's. What more do you want?"

Sano wanted to assure himself that he wasn't persecuting an innocent person, subverting justice, and compromising his honor, but he didn't expect his watchdogs to have any sympathy for that. "At the very least, I must prove what the women were up to during the time when Daiemon was killed. That means tracing their whereabouts last night. Until I've done that, I'll not arrest anyone."

Ibe and Otani leaned over the railing and looked at each other across Sano. He discerned their reluctance to use the threat they held over him. Cowards both, they were as afraid of hurting Masahiro and provoking Sano's wrath as Sano was of having his son harmed. A deadlock paralyzed everyone. In a lull of battle noises, Sano heard rain trickling down a drain spout.

Finally, the watchdogs exchanged nods, their expressions churlish. "All right," Ibe told Sano. "You can trace the women's whereabouts. But no dragging your feet."

Sano felt little relief. Could he keep stalling his watchdogs until he solved the crimes—and before impatience forced them to make good on their threat?

In the meantime, war might destroy them all.

On a fallow rice field outside Edo, the two armies clashed. Matsudaira horsemen charged at mounted troops from the Yanagisawa faction. Banners marked with their leaders' crests fluttered on poles worn on their backs. Hooves pounded the earth; lances skewered riders on both sides. Foot soldiers whirled and darted, their swords lashing their enemies. Gunners at the sidelines fired volleys of bullets. Arrows sizzled through clouds of gunpowder smoke. Men fell, amid howls of agony, in mud already strewn with corpses and darkened by bloodshed. From the combatants rose savage cries of exultation as they shattered the peace that had stifled the warrior spirit during almost a century of Tokugawa rule. Atop high terrain at either end of the field, generals on horseback surveyed the action. They called to the commanders, who conveyed their orders to the troops via braying conch trumpets and thundering war drums. Soldiers charged, attacked, retreated, regrouped, and counterattacked. Scouts scanned the battlefield through spyglasses, counting casualties.

The victor would be the man who had a large enough army left after the battle to maintain himself in power over the regime.

        At the Matsudaira estate, black mourning drapery festooned the portals. A notice of the clan's bereavement hung on the gate. Inside a wooden tub in a chamber in the private quarters, the naked corpse of Daiemon reposed. Matsudaira womenfolk dressed in white poured water out of dippers filled from ceramic urns into the tub. They wept as they bathed Daiemon, washing away blood from the wound in his chest, tenderly wiping his handsome, lifeless face.

Lord Matsudaira squatted nearby, his head propped on his clenched fists. He wore battle armor, but his golden-horned helmet lay on the floor beside him. As the women prepared his nephew for the journey to the netherworld, grief tortured his spirit.

Someone knelt beside him, and he looked around to see Uemori Yoichi, his crony on the Council of Elders. Uemori was a short, squat man in his fifties, with sagging jowls. He said, "Please pardon my intrusion, but I thought you would want to hear the latest news from the battlefield."

"Yes? What is it?" Lord Matsudaira said, momentarily distracted from his torment.

"Casualties are estimated at two hundred men," Uemori said, "with more than half of them on Chamberlain Yanagisawa's side."

Grim satisfaction filled Lord Matsudaira. He rose and walked to the corpse of his nephew. The women had lifted Daiemon from the tub and laid him on a wooden pallet. As they dried his body with cloths and sobbed bitterly, Lord Matsudaira gazed down at Daiemon.

"I'll win this war in your name," Lord Matsudaira promised. "You won't have lived or died for nothing. And when I rule Japan, I will expose Chamberlain Yanagisawa as the scoundrel and murderer that he is."

Chamberlain Yanagisawa and his son Yoritomo stood in a watchtower on the wall of his compound. They gazed through the barred windows, across Edo. Mist and smoke obscured the field where the battle raged. Distance muffled the blaring of conch trumpets. Yanagisawa inhaled deeply, his keen nose detecting the faint, sulfurous odor of gunpowder. He imagined he tasted blood in the air. Exultation pulsed alongside dread inside him.

"I've heard that some of our allies have defected to Lord Matsudaira," said Yoritomo. "That he has three troops for every two of ours, and more guns. Things are bad for us, aren't they, Honorable Father?"

Yanagisawa nodded, for he couldn't deny the truth. "But don't despair. We've other weapons against Lord Matsudaira besides troops and guns."

He looked out the open door, which led to an enclosed corridor that ran along the top of the wall. Some twenty paces down the corridor, in the dim light from its tiny windows, stood his wife. She watched Yanagisawa with such intensity that he could feel her gaze like flames licking his body. He smiled slyly to himself as he turned back to Yoritomo.

"There are other ways to destroy our enemy than fighting on a battlefield." Yanagisawa laid a reassuring hand on his son's shoulder. "When we're finished, we'll control the regime."

And he would be above the law, immune to evil consequences from the murder investigation.

27

A party that evening in the reception hall of Senior Elder Makino's estate mocked the threat posed by the war.

While Koheiji played the samisen and sang, male servants beat drums. Okitsu and two maids danced in a circle, singing along, tipsy and giggling. Other maids poured sake for samurai guards who lounged around the room, laughing, calling out encouragement to the dancers, and toasting one another. The widow and her ladies-in-waiting sat in a corner, drinking. Agemaki's eyes were glazed; she swayed back and forth. Lanterns glowed brightly. A desperate, uneasy gaiety infused the air.

Reiko, who'd sneaked away from the kitchen, peered in through a gap between the lattice-and-paper partitions. A door across the room from her scraped open. Into the party strode Tamura. His face wore an angry scowl.

"Stop this racket!" he shouted.

Koheiji plinked a few last, discordant notes on the samisen. As his singing trailed off, the drummers fell silent; Okitsu and the dancers stumbled to a halt, their giggles ending in nervous twitters. The guards put down their cups and sat upright; their cheer gave way to apprehension. All the revelers stared in surprise at Tamura.

"What do you think you're doing?" Tamura demanded, surveying the revelers with contempt.

Reiko was glad to witness something more than drunken merriment and glad to see Tamura, whom she'd not had a chance to observe since yesterday in Makino's chamber.

After a brief, uncomfortable silence, Koheiji said, "We're just having a little fun."

"Fun? With the Honorable Senior Elder Makino dead only four days?" Tamura said, incredulous. His hard, shiny complexion turned purplish-red with rage. "You ought to be ashamed of yourselves. Such disrespect toward your master! Such disregard for propriety!"

He pointed at the guards. "Get back to your posts." The men leaped to their feet and collided with one another in their haste to leave the room. Tamura dismissed the maids and ladies-in-waiting, then addressed Agemaki, Koheiji, and Okitsu: "As for you, there will be no more such entertainment."

His back was toward Reiko, so she couldn't see his expression, but she had a clear view of the other three people. She saw guilt on Okitsu's face, blankness on Agemaki's, and offense on Koheiji's.

"Hey, you can't order us around," Koheiji said. "You're not our master. We'll do as we please."

"I'm in charge here for the time being," Tamura said. "My master is gone, and I needn't put up with nonsense from you three for his sake anymore. You'll behave properly from now on. Now go to your rooms at once."

Reiko saw anger focus Agemaki's blank gaze. Okitsu gasped in offense. "Can he make us?" she asked Koheiji.

"Of course he can't." Koheiji's chest swelled with outrage as he glared at Tamura. "I'm not going anywhere."

"Nor am I," Agemaki said, her voice slurred by drink.

"We'll see about that," Tamura said. He stalked over to Agemaki, seized her arm, and hauled her to her feet.

"Let me go!" she cried. "How dare you treat your master's widow like this!"

"You're nothing but a whore who took advantage of an old man," Tamura said. "I've seen you fawn over Senior Elder Makino, then gag behind his back. I warned him that you were a selfish, greedy witch and up to no good, but did he listen? No—the fool married you anyway. Well, you've wrung your last bit of gold from him. Your days here are numbered."

Agemaki shouted protests, clawing at his arm, but he dragged her toward the door. On the way, he grabbed Okitsu.

"No!" shrieked Okitsu. "Help me, Koheiji-*san*!"

She flung out her hand toward the actor. As he and Tamura tugged her in opposite directions, she reeled between them.

"Let go of her," Koheiji shouted.

"You two are the scum of the earth," Tamura said, struggling with Agemaki. "I've seen you playing your filthy sex games with my master, distracting him from duty, sinking him into degradation. None of you respected or cared for him. You're all nothing but parasites who fed on his wealth!"

"Hey! What about you? Do you think you're so much better than us?" Koheiji said. He and Tamura yanked on Okitsu, who squealed. "You lived off Makino, too. You'd be nothing if not for him. And everybody knows you hated him because he wasn't the virtuous samurai you wanted him to be."

"You'll regret that you dared speak to me with such disrespect," Tamura said, his eyes black with fury. "Especially if I find out that one of you killed my master." Tamura moved toward the door, dragging Agemaki. With brutal strength, he hauled Koheiji as well as Okitsu along after him. "I'll carry out my vendetta and make you pay with your own life for his death."

"Oh, I'm sure you'd love to have the murder pinned on one of us," Koheiji said, bracing his feet on the floor and clinging to the squealing, sobbing Okitsu. "That would get you off the hook, wouldn't it? But do you know what I say? I say *you* murdered old Makino." Brazen with anger and fear, he jabbed his index finger at Tamura. "You wanted to get rid of him, and us, as well. You killed four birds with one arrow."

Reiko wondered if Tamura had indeed killed Makino, for those very reasons. She recalled watching Tamura's suspicious behavior in the hidden chamber. Perhaps he'd sought to purge the house, the clan, and himself of evil influences by killing Makino and banishing his hangers-on. But Reiko also recalled her suspicions regarding the other three.

A sudden, fierce grip on her shoulder halted Reiko's thoughts. She snapped her head around to find herself looking into the ugly, triumphant face of Yasue.

"Hah! Caught you!" Yasue said.

Her voice was so loud that the people in the room turned at the sound. Dismay filled Reiko as they ceased their tussling and peered in her direction.

"What's going on out there?" Tamura demanded.

Reiko tore free of Yasue. She bolted, but the old woman caught her sleeve. They wrestled together, crashed against the partition. As the flimsy lattice and paper ripped and splintered, Reiko and Yasue stumbled, through the jagged hole they'd made, into the room. Tamura, Koheiji, Agemaki, and Okitsu stared in amazement.

"Hey, hey," the actor said.

He let go of Okitsu and walked toward Reiko and Yasue. A mischievous grin lit up his face. Reiko understood that he was happy for a distraction that prevented Tamura from further mistreating him. Her heart sank as she also understood that his good luck was to be her downfall.

"You're the new maid, aren't you?" Koheiji said to her. "What have you been up to?"

"She's been snooping," Yasue said, her hand locked around Reiko's wrist. "This is the second time I've caught her."

"Get her out of here," Tamura ordered Yasue. "Don't bother me with domestic problems."

Then he leaned toward Reiko for a closer look. As she shrank away from him, he frowned. "That's odd," he said. "Your eyebrows are shaved. And your teeth—"

Reiko clamped her lips shut, but he pried them apart with his strong fingers.

"They've been dyed," Tamura said. "You're no peasant—you're a lady."

The actor blinked at Reiko. "And not an old one, either,"

he said, rubbing Reiko's hair between his fingers. "That isn't gray hair, it's soot. I should have known—I've used that trick myself in the theater."

"Who are you? What are you doing here?" Tamura said, hostile and suspicious.

"I'm a poor woman who has fallen on hard times," Reiko said, feigning a humble commoner's speech, desperate to conceal her true identity and purpose. "I'm here to earn my living."

Disbelief showed on the faces around her. Yasue said, "I knew there was something not right about her. It was strange that the estate manager should hire her, because I can tell she's never worked a day in her life."

Koheiji said, "I remember you waited on Okitsu and me yesterday. You seemed a little too interested in us."

"In me, too," Agemaki said. "When she brought my meal, she tried to hang around me, even though it was obvious that I didn't want her."

"She must be a spy," Tamura said.

Quiet descended. Reiko felt as if Tamura's words had depleted all the air from the room. But at least she'd managed to learn a few things about the members of the household. Now she sensed them wondering how much she'd observed, to their detriment.

"Whose spy are you?" Tamura demanded. He seized Reiko's chin in a painful grip, wrenching her face upward and glaring into her eyes. "Are you working for Lord Matsudaira? Did he send you to report on Senior Elder Makino's household?"

Startled by his erroneous assumption, Reiko kept silent. His hands quickly felt along her body. He found the dagger strapped to her thigh under her skirts, tore it off, and threw it aside. A dreadful moment passed while Tamura contemplated her.

"Well, it doesn't matter whose spy you are," he said. "Whatever you've seen or heard here, you won't be telling anyone."

He drew the short sword at his waist. Panic shot through

Reiko. He meant to kill her! Yasue grabbed her hair, tilting back her head, exposing her throat for Tamura's blade. As Tamura advanced on her, Okitsu and Agemaki watched, their faces vacant with shock or confusion. Reiko felt her heart racing fast and hard, and the vertigo that heralded a bad spell. Through her mind flashed images of the ambush on the highway; screams echoed in her ears. Aghast that this should happen when she most needed her strength and wits, Reiko fought the evil magic. She jabbed her elbow into Yasue's stomach. The old housekeeper grunted and let go. But even as Reiko lunged for the door, Koheiji caught her.

"Hey, Tamura-*san*," he said, "how about if I have a little fun with her before you kill her?"

His cheerful voice was edged with malice. He yanked on her clothes. The flimsy cotton fabric tore, exposing her shoulders and bosom. As she struck out at him, Koheiji laughed and dodged. He seized her in a crushing embrace, grinding their bodies together. His snarling face was close to hers. As Reiko turned her head, pushed on his chest, and strained away from him, she saw the others ranged around her and Koheiji.

Okitsu pressed her knuckles to her mouth and closed her eyes. Tamura frowned in disgust but said nothing; Agemaki's expression was blandly indifferent. Yasue's beady eyes glittered with vicarious lust and excitement. None of them intended to stop Koheiji.

"Help!" Reiko shouted, in the desperate hope that Sano's detectives were near and would come to her rescue.

"When you watched me with Okitsu yesterday, you wanted some of what you saw, didn't you?" Koheiji said, panting with his effort to quell Reiko's thrashing arms and legs. "Well, I'll give it to you now. You can die happy."

Reiko felt the hardness in his groin pummeling her. She dug her fingernails into his arms, but he held fast; he was too strong. The liquor on his breath and the heat of his body revolted Reiko. She screamed in terror as he forced her down on the floor. This was what she'd feared most of all—a reprise of that terrible scene in the Dragon King's palace.

The actor's handsome, cruel face above her dissolved into the Dragon King's strange, crazed visage. The thought of Senior Elder Makino, savagely beaten to death, flashed across Reiko's dazed consciousness.

Had Koheiji killed Makino? Was this man ravishing her the murderer she and Sano sought?

Koheiji tore open her skirts. The panic and vertigo dizzied Reiko, weakening her as she fought him. But her instinct for survival ignited her resistance. Her wish to see her husband and child again, and her determination not to surrender to evil, infused her with new strength. She heaved forward and slammed her head into Koheiji's face. Pain exploded through her brow. Her vision went momentarily black. Koheiji yelled, and the sound revived her. The vertigo was gone, her mind clear. She saw Koheiji recoil from her. Blood poured from his nose and mouth.

"Hey, you like to play rough?" Koheiji said, grinning and licking the blood on his swollen lips. "Well, so do I."

As he remounted her, Reiko shoved her knee hard into his groin. He howled in agony, rolled off her, and lay curled around his injured manhood. Reiko jumped to her feet. Tamura stepped between her and the door, his expression murderous, his sword held ready to slash.

"Get her!" Yasue shrilled.

Reiko saw a charcoal brazier on the floor near her. She snatched it up and hurled it at Tamura, striking him across his knees. He staggered. Soot and live, glowing coals flew out of the brazier. Fire blackened Tamura's robes where the coals touched them. He dropped his sword and beat his hands against himself to extinguish the flames. Reiko raced toward the door.

"Stop her!" Tamura shouted, coughing amid a cloud of smoke.

Okitsu collapsed, but Yasue and Agemaki chased Reiko. Agemaki caught her sleeve. Reiko grabbed Agemaki by the arm, whipped her around, and flung her away. Agemaki tumbled knees over head. Yasue charged at Reiko, hands spread, screeching like a crow gone berserk. Reiko picked up a lacquer tray table and bashed her across the face. The housekeeper fell, stunned. Tamura had his sword back in hand. Out the door Reiko raced.

"She's getting away!" Koheiji cried in a strangled voice.

Reiko heard Tamura's footsteps pounding after her as she sped down the corridor. She burst through the door and ran down the steps into the garden. Trees, shrubs, and boulders were monochrome shapes beneath the dull silver sky of late dusk. Icy rain lashed her; the cold instantly chilled the skin bared by her torn robes.

Tamura shouted for the patrol guards. He called to Reiko, "It's no use running. You won't get out of Edo Castle alive."

Fortunately, Reiko didn't need to get out of Edo Castle, only to reach her home in the official quarter, a few streets distant. Answering shouts came from the patrol guards; their hurrying footsteps drew close. Reiko dashed between buildings, around corners, groping in near darkness. Across a courtyard she spied a crooked pine tree. Behind it loomed the outer wall of the estate. Reiko launched herself up the tree's low branches and climbed through cold, prickly needles. She crawled onto the top of the wall, lowered herself feet first over the outer side, then dropped down.

In the private quarters of his estate, Sano sat drinking hot tea with Hirata in his office. Outside, temple bells tolled, summoning priests, monks, and nuns to evening prayer rites; the distant gunfire subsided as darkness fell. The watchdogs had left Sano to make their reports to Lord Matsudaira and Chamberlain Yanagisawa, but their men still occupied the house. Through open partitions that divided several rooms adjoining his office, Sano watched the maids feeding Masahiro his supper in the nursery. Two thugs sat near Masahiro, guarding him. The little boy didn't chatter or laugh as usual; he and the maids were quietly somber. Detectives stood in the corridor, ready to protect the household from the unwanted guests. An ominous gloom infected the estate.

"What have you learned?" Sano asked Hirata in a low voice that wouldn't carry to the thugs in the nursery or elsewhere on the premises.

Hirata also kept his voice low as he described his visits to Tamura and Koheiji. "After I left them, I checked their stories about what they were doing at the time of Daiemon's murder. The other actors at the Nakamura-za say that Koheiji left the theater for more than an hour during the rehearsal last night. He didn't tell them where he went, or why."

"Then he lied when he told you he was at the theater the whole night," Sano concluded.

"Yes. He was gone long enough to kill Daiemon," Hirata said. "And Tamura's alibi is almost as weak. His men confirmed that he went to the army camp, but I think they were lying."

"Did you find out whether anyone in the camp saw him?"

"By the time I got there, all the troops had gone to the battlefield. But neither Tamura nor Koheiji admitted anything about the night Makino died. And there doesn't seem to be any evidence to connect either of them to Daiemon's murder."

Disappointment and fatigue, combined with his fears for Reiko, weighed upon Sano. "The same can be said for the women as for the men." Sano told Hirata the results of his inquiries. "Agemaki stuck to her story about sleeping through Makino's murder without seeing or hearing anything. Okitsu changed hers to include a glimpse of Daiemon standing over Makino's corpse with the murder weapon in his hand, but I think she invented that."

"By herself, or with help from someone?" Hirata said.

"The latter, I suspect, and I have a good idea who that someone is."

Hirata nodded in accord. Sano continued, "I spent the afternoon establishing the women's movements of last night. Agemaki's palanquin bearers say they carried her around town for a while, then took her to a teahouse. She went inside and drank, while they went to a gambling den around the corner. They picked her up and took her home about an hour later. The teahouse isn't far from the Sign of Bedazzlement."

"She could have sneaked over there while the bearers were away gambling," Hirata noted.

"When I questioned the owner of the teahouse, he said Agemaki is a frequent customer. She went out to the alley for a while, but he assumed she'd gone to the privy," Sano said. "Later, I visited the Sign of Bedazzlement, under protest from the watchdogs. The proprietor didn't recognize her name or my description of Agemaki. If Agemaki is the woman Daiemon met, she took care to conceal herself. But here's an interesting fact I uncovered: A girl who matches Okitsu's description was seen at the house by a maid who works there."

"Then Okitsu could be Daiemon's mistress," Hirata said.

"The girl came in a palanquin," Sano said. "She went inside one of the rooms—the maid isn't sure whether it was Daiemon's. But the maid is sure the girl was gone by the time Daiemon was found dead and the police came."

"What do Okitsu's palanquin bearers say?"

"They took her to four different houses last night," Sano said. "At each place, she went inside, then came out a short time later. They don't know what she was doing, and they're not sure of the locations." Edo was a maze of houses similar in appearance, where even a person who knew the city well could become confused. "Tomorrow I'll send a detective out with the bearers to retrace their route and see if they can point out the places Okitsu visited. The best thing that happened to me today is that I exhausted Otani and Ibe while leading them around Edo and resisted letting them rush me into a premature arrest."

Sano exhaled through his teeth. "I'm more certain than ever that the women are withholding information about what happened the night Makino died. And their movements the night of Daiemon's death are as suspect as Koheiji's and Tamura's. But if there's any evidence that they're guilty of either murder, I've yet to find it."

"I did find one lead," Hirata said, and he reported learn-

ing about the house Daiemon kept. "After I finished investigating Tamura and Koheiji, I went there and had a look. It
seemed empty, but I didn't go in. I decided I should tell you
first."

"Well done," Sano said. A glimmer of hope at a potential
source of new clues brightened his spirits. "And a wise decision." The fact that Hirata had chosen to consult him instead
of rushing ahead on his own meant that Hirata was learning
self-discipline. "I want a look inside that house, but the
question is how."

He and Hirata looked across the connecting rooms at the
men watching Masahiro eat. Otani and Ibe would never allow Sano to investigate a clue concerning Daiemon that
might lead to Lord Matsudaira or Chamberlain Yanagisawa.
And if Sano left his house without them, his men would tell
them.

Just then, Sano heard footsteps pelting down the corridor,
accompanied by rapid, labored breaths. Reiko burst into the
office. Her eyes were wild, her hair and clothes in disarray.

"Reiko-*san*!" exclaimed Sano. He was so glad to see his
wife that at first he barely noticed her condition. "Thank the
gods!"

He leaped up and enfolded her in his arms. She was cold,
wet, and shivering. A closer look at her told Sano why his
detectives hadn't been able to find her at Makino's estate:
She'd disguised herself so well that they'd not recognized
her. Now concern for her encroached upon Sano's joy.
"What happened to you?" he said.

Reiko was so winded after her mad dash through
the official quarter that she couldn't speak. As she struggled
to catch her breath, she clung to Sano, overjoyed to be with
him again, relieved to be home. Then she heard Masahiro
call, "Mama!" and saw the little boy run toward her through
the adjoining rooms. With a cry of delight, she pulled away
from Sano and rushed to meet their son. The sight of two
strange samurai in the nursery halted her. Masahiro collided

against Reiko and threw his arms around her knees. Embracing him, she turned to Sano and Hirata in puzzlement.

"Who are those men?" she said. "What are they doing here?"

"I'll explain," Sano said, but first he gently detached Masahiro from her. "Go and get ready for bed, Masahiro. Mama will come to you soon."

The boy toddled off with his nursemaids. The two strangers followed them. Sano seated Reiko by the charcoal brazier in his office and wrapped a warm quilt around her. Hirata poured her a bowl of tea. As she sipped the hot, invigorating liquid and warmed her icy hands on the bowl, Sano told her what had happened since she'd left home. Reiko listened in shock.

"But what happened to you?" Sano repeated with anxious concern.

"I had to leave Senior Elder Makino's estate because his people figured out that I was a spy," Reiko said.

She described how Yasue had caught her eavesdropping. But she didn't say that Koheiji had tried to ravish her, Tamura had meant to kill her, or she'd fought her way out of the estate. Nor did she mention that she'd barely reached her own gate before Tamura's troops came rushing up the street after her. If Sano knew, he would never let her spy again. Not that Reiko was eager to repeat the experiment, but she might need to in the future.

"Did the suspects find out who you are, or that you were working for me?" Sano said.

"No," Reiko said. "And I managed to observe some interesting things before I left."

While Sano and Hirata listened avidly, Reiko told them about finding Makino's trove of sexual paraphernalia and seeing Tamura replace the jade phallus that she thought was the murder weapon. She described the conversations she'd witnessed.

"It could be that Tamura was hiding evidence that implicated him in Makino's murder," Sano said. "And the affair between Koheiji and Okitsu is the strongest reason we've found for them to want Makino dead."

"That Agemaki is jealous of Okitsu and was afraid that Makino would throw her out and marry his concubine gave her a reason, too," Hirata told Reiko. "What you heard contradicts the image she presented to us."

"And there surely is a conspiracy of silence involving Koheiji, Okitsu, and Agemaki," Sano said.

"It's looking more and more as if the killer was someone in Makino's household," Hirata said. "Maybe they were all in the murder together."

"I don't think so. There's so much bad feeling among them that I can't imagine them cooperating in anything. Maybe some of them together, but not all."

"We might have suspected all this but not had any verification, except for you," Sano said to Reiko.

His warm, praiseful look rewarded Reiko for the hardships she'd suffered. She said eagerly, "Does my information help you identify the killer?"

Sano and Hirata pondered, then told Reiko what their investigations had uncovered while she'd been away. She realized with a sinking heart that although each of them had found pieces of the puzzle, the picture didn't add up to a solution to the crime. They had an abundance of suspects, motives, and theories, but no culprit.

"I wish I could have spied longer," Reiko said.

"You might have spied forever and not proved that someone from Makino's household is guilty," Sano said in an attempt to console her. "Remember that Lord Matsudaira, Chamberlain Yanagisawa, and their factions are still suspects. We haven't ruled them out of either murder."

"If Ibe and Otani have their way, we won't be able to rule them in, even if they are responsible," Hirata said glumly.

"What shall we do?" Reiko asked, thinking how hopeless the situation appeared.

Sano told her about Hirata's discovery. "That Daiemon had quarters outside the Matsudaira estate suggests he had a private life that may be related to his death."

"But you can't investigate Daiemon's business with Otani

and Ibe shadowing you," Hirata reminded Sano. "Do you want me to search the house by myself?"

After a long moment's thought, Sano said, "I have an idea."

He confided his plan. Reiko and Hirata nodded in approval, yet Reiko despaired because she couldn't do more to help. Then sudden inspiration elated her.

"Even if Otani and Ibe forbid you to look for Daiemon's missing woman, I can look," she said. "They won't even notice me."

Sano regarded her with consternation. Reiko knew he was wondering what more had happened to her at Makino's estate than she'd told him, and he was hesitant to further involve her in the case. "What do you propose doing?" he said.

"I'll ask around and see if any of my friends can tell me who was Daiemon's mistress," Reiko said. "Women talk. The romantic affairs of an important man like him are hard to keep secret. Someone is bound to know."

"All right," Sano said. "That sounds harmless enough for you. But be careful this time."

28

Sano found Otani, Ibe, and their troops waiting for him outside his gate the next morning. The rain had stopped, but moisture still darkened the walls and buildings of the official quarter. The sky showed pale blue streaks between bands of cloud, but the air still had a frosty tang. Overnight, the portals of the estates had sprouted banners bearing the Matsudaira or the Yanagisawa crest. The banners snapped in the wind. Only Sano's gate was unadorned. Up through the passages of Edo Castle reverberated the pounding of hooves and footsteps as troops marched off to battle.

"What's he doing here?" Otani said, frowning as he spotted Hirata among the detectives who accompanied Sano.

"He's helping me with my inquiries today," Sano said.

"No, he's not," Ibe said. "We banned him from the investigation."

"If you want any more cooperation from me, you'll let him come along," Sano told the watchdogs.

He thought Hirata had earned his reinstatement in the investigation. As Ibe and Otani began to protest, Sano said, "My son is your guarantee of Hirata-*san*'s good behavior as well as mine."

"I don't care. I want him gone," Otani said, angry that Sano would defy him.

But Ibe said, "I'm tired of arguing over everything. Let him come. What does it matter?"

Otani subsided with a grudging nod. "Today you'll arrest either the widow or the concubine for the murders of Senior Elder Makino and Daiemon," he told Sano. "You've run out of reasons to delay."

"Not quite," Sano said. "There's another clue that I must investigate before arresting Agemaki or Okitsu. Last night, I received this message."

He handed Otani a folded paper. Otani opened it and read aloud, "'If you want to know who killed Senior Elder Makino, go to the middle house on the west side of Tsukegi Street in Kanda.'" He said, "There's no signature. Who sent this?"

"I don't know," Sano said, although he'd written the message himself. "The letter was slipped under my gate sometime during the night. No one saw who did it."

Last night Sano had devised this ploy to investigate Daiemon's house under Ibe's and Otani's very noses. If they didn't know the house belonged to Daiemon, or how Sano had learned of it, they might not object to going there, and they couldn't blame him for whatever he found.

Ibe took the paper from Otani and inspected it suspiciously. "Anonymous messages are not to be trusted."

"True, but I can't ignore this one," Sano said. "That would be neglecting my duty to the shogun."

A silent consultation ensued between the watchdogs. Sano waited, hoping that if fear of their lord didn't sway them, curiosity would.

At last Otani said, "Very well."

"But if this is a trick, someone will pay." Ibe's glance at Sano proclaimed exactly who that someone was.

Reiko knelt at the dressing table in her chamber, preparing to call on the friends whom she hoped would tell her the identity of Daiemon's mistress. A good night's sleep had restored her spirits and strength. Having washed the soot out of her hair, applied makeup to her face and black dye to her teeth, and donned clothes appropriate for the wife of an important *bakufu* official, she looked like herself instead of the hapless servant she'd been yesterday. But her return to normal didn't assuage her worries.

The watchdogs' men never let Masahiro out of their sight. They'd hovered near while Reiko dressed and fed him this morning. She hated to leave him with them, even though Sano's detectives stood ready to defend him. And she feared for Sano, navigating through the war zone that Edo had become, alone except for his own retainers now that he'd refused to join either faction. Reiko saw the anxiety on her face reflected in the mirror. She deliberately smoothed her expression. She'd risen and put on her cloak, when a maid came to the door.

"Fetch my palanquin, bearers, and guards to the courtyard," Reiko said.

"Yes, mistress," the maid said, bowing, "but I must tell you that Lady Yanagisawa is here to see you. She's waiting in the reception hall."

Dismay, coupled with anger, flashed through Reiko. No sooner had she arrived home than Lady Yanagisawa was after her again! Reiko decided she could no longer tolerate Lady Yanagisawa's destructive madness. She must put an end to their friendship once and for all—now.

She hastened to the reception room and there found Lady Yanagisawa. "Reiko-*san*!" Lady Yanagisawa cried, hurrying to greet her.

The woman's usually pale cheeks were flushed; her eyes glittered with unnatural intensity. "At last we're together again," she said. Her rapid breathing was audible as she clasped her hands at her bosom and gazed yearningly at Reiko. "It is so good to see you after our long separation."

"It's good to see you." For the last time, Reiko thought.

"I have something important to tell you," said Lady Yanagisawa.

"Oh? Well, I have something important to tell you, too."

Because Sano had already repudiated and offended the

chamberlain, Reiko thought she could do little more harm with his wife. Reiko prepared to say exactly what she thought of Lady Yanagisawa, and good riddance.

"I bring a message from my husband," Lady Yanagisawa said.

"For me?" Reiko said, taken by surprise. A message from the chamberlain was not to be ignored. "What is it?"

Lady Yanagisawa grasped Reiko's hands and drew her downward until they were kneeling opposite each other. Reiko felt Lady Yanagisawa trembling; the woman's hands were damp and feverishly hot. Something more than usual was wrong with Lady Yanagisawa. A warning note sounded inside Reiko.

"My husband asks two favors of you," Lady Yanagisawa said. "First, you must convince your husband to declare that Senior Elder Makino was murdered by Lord Matsudaira's nephew Daiemon."

Amazement stunned Reiko. That Lady Yanagisawa had done various shocking things hadn't prepared Reiko to expect what she'd just heard. Reiko said, "I can guess why the honorable chamberlain wants Daiemon blamed for Senior Elder Makino's murder." That would exonerate Chamberlain Yanagisawa, disgrace the Matsudaira clan in the eyes of the shogun, and give the chamberlain a political advantage. "But why ask this favor from me, of all people?" He'd never deigned to notice her before.

"He knows you have much influence over the *sōsakan-sama*," Lady Yanagisawa said. "And since you and I are such close friends, he sent me on his behalf."

Reiko's mind was still reeling from astonishment. "But why does he think I would ask my husband to do such a thing?"

"He knows you love your husband and want what is best for him. What's best for him is to name a dead man as the murderer of Senior Elder Makino. Who's to say whether Daiemon is really guilty or not? And he can't be punished or cause trouble. Surely you can persuade your husband to do right by himself and by you and your son." Lady Yanagisawa spoke as if presenting the most reasonable views in the world. She smiled, anticipating Reiko's agreement.

That the woman could imagine she would even consider asking Sano to cooperate in this scheme to subvert justice and ally himself with the corrupt chamberlain! Reiko sat stupefied by the audacity of Lady Yanagisawa.

"What's the second favor your husband wants?" Reiko asked.

Lady Yanagisawa glanced out the door toward the corridor, along which detectives and servants passed. She beckoned Reiko to lean close. When Reiko unwillingly did, Lady Yanagisawa whispered in her ear: "He wishes you to assassinate Lord Matsudaira."

Reiko had thought herself already surprised beyond the point where anything else that Lady Yanagisawa said could surprise her. But now, as she recoiled in shock from Lady Yanagisawa, she saw that she'd underestimated the woman—and the chamberlain as well. It appeared that Lady Yanagisawa had worked her way into her husband's life and become his partner in evil. The request was so outrageous, it seemed absurd. Involuntary laughter burst from Reiko.

Lady Yanagisawa laughed, too, in delight. Her plain, dour features grew animated, almost pretty. "Isn't that a wonderful idea?" she said, misinterpreting Reiko's reaction. "If Lord Matsudaira were to die, his faction would fall apart. The trouble would end."

She spoke as if reciting words the chamberlain had told her. "And you are the perfect person to rid us of Lord Matsudaira. You're so clever, and so adept with swords, and killing is nothing new to you." Reiko had killed, in self-defense, some of the men who'd ambushed and kidnapped them, and Lady Yanagisawa had seen her. "My husband says he'll disguise you as a prostitute and sneak you into the camp near the battlefield where Lord Matsudaira meets with his generals. You can stab Lord Matsudaira, then run." Lady Yanagisawa caught up Reiko's hands and clasped them to her bosom. "My dearest, precious friend! I am so glad that you will grant my husband these favors!"

The conversation had taken on a nightmarish quality, and it had lasted long enough. "I will not!" Reiko exclaimed, wrenching her hands from Lady Yanagisawa. "That the chamberlain expects my husband to conspire with him, and me to kill for him, is an insult! We would never violate our honor by doing those things. I would never commit such a crime. You can tell your husband I said so!"

Surprise erased the delight from Lady Yanagisawa's face. She seemed to falter and her mind to change direction. "Allow me to mention a certain murder inquiry in Miyako," she said. "The chamberlain killed a man in order that your husband would live. If not for the chamberlain, you would be a widow. You owe him a death."

This justification had a certain logic. Society operated on favors and obligations, and Yanagisawa must be desperate enough to think it reasonable that she should pay him for Sano's deliverance. Reiko supposed that he'd been waiting for the right opportunity to call in the debt.

"Killing to save a life is one thing," she said. "Assassination is quite another, even if the chamberlain doesn't make the distinction. I won't do it."

Dismay clouded over the glitter in Lady Yanagisawa's eyes. "But—but he wants these favors from you." She sounded less fluent and sure of herself. "And what he wants . . . he must have."

"Not from me, nor my husband," Reiko said. Her anger at all the evil that Chamberlain Yanagisawa had done to Sano boiled up inside her. "The honorable chamberlain can do his own dirty work and leave us out of it." Reiko was beyond caring about the danger of saying no to such a powerful man. "That's my answer to his request, although it hardly deserves the courtesy of an answer."

"But if I tell him you won't do what he wants . . . my husband will be very angry with me." Fear crept into Lady Yanagisawa's voice.

"That's your problem, not mine," Reiko said.

"If you won't do it for the chamberlain . . ." As Lady

Yanagisawa hesitated, her eyes pleaded with Reiko. "Will you do it for me? Because we're friends?"

Reiko's anger boiled higher and hotter at the thought of everything Lady Yanagisawa had done to her under the guise of friendship. "You think I should do you a favor, after you tried to kill my son and then me? After that, you call yourself my friend?" Reiko uttered an incredulous, disdainful laugh.

An astounded look came over Lady Yanagisawa. She sat rigid, her mouth open, gazing blankly at Reiko. Either the woman had forgotten her attempts at murder, or she'd never admitted them to herself.

"Well, here's what I meant to tell you," Reiko said, carried along by the tide of her emotions. "We're not friends. We never have been. I've put up with you and your attacks on me only because I was afraid you would do even worse if I didn't. But now I've had enough of you." Reiko surged to her feet. "Get out of my house, you evil, jealous madwoman!" she shouted. "Take your husband's request and throw it back in his face. Never come near me or my family again!"

Lady Yanagisawa blenched as though Reiko had slapped her. Her flushed cheeks turned pale with shock. Tears brimmed in her eyes. She rose, groping as though blinded. Reiko felt a pity that spoiled her pleasure at finally speaking her mind to Lady Yanagisawa. Her harsh words had clearly hurt the woman by shattering her illusions about their relationship.

Then a strange, internal energy transformed Lady Yanagisawa. The hectic color returned to her complexion. Her body seemed to swell and undulate, like a serpent readying to strike. The eyes that she now focused on Reiko blazed with hatred and rage. She looked as if all the madness and evil hidden deep inside her had come to the surface.

"I am sorry that you feel so badly toward me," Lady Yanagisawa said. Her gruff voice had a vindictive, threatening undertone. An eerie smile hovered upon her lips. "But you must do as my husband wishes."

"I already told you I won't," Reiko said, although suddenly frightened by Lady Yanagisawa.

"If you don't," said Lady Yanagisawa, "I will tell your husband everything that happened between you and the Dragon King."

"What?" Confusion unbalanced Reiko.

"I'll tell him that you fell in love with the Dragon King," Lady Yanagisawa said. "I'll tell him that I saw you and the Dragon King making passionate love together in the palace."

"But you didn't see that." Reiko's confusion turned to disbelief. "It didn't happen."

Lady Yanagisawa's eerie smile stayed fixed in place. "Who is there besides you to say that it didn't? The Dragon King is dead. Your husband can't know what happened on that island because he wasn't there. But I was."

Now Reiko understood Lady Yanagisawa's intention. "You're trying to bend me to the chamberlain's will by threatening to tell my husband lies about me," Reiko said. Complete revulsion toward Lady Yanagisawa increased Reiko's determination to stand firm. "Well, don't waste your breath. It won't work. My husband knows I've always been faithful to him."

A rusty, unpleasant laugh issued from Lady Yanagisawa. "Are you so sure? Would you risk your wonderful marriage on the chance that he would believe you instead of listening to me?"

"Of course he would believe me."

But horror dawned as a shard of doubt lodged in Reiko's heart. She'd never told Sano what had happened between her and the Dragon King. He'd hinted several times that he wanted to know, but she'd always evaded answering. She'd been so loath to relive that awful time, and to confess the things she'd done in an attempt to win her liberty, that she'd left Sano free to imagine whatever he chose. Now she wished she'd told him the whole story, because it was nowhere near as bad as the one Lady Yanagisawa proposed to tell. Reiko's secrecy had bred suspicions in Sano's mind, which malicious slander from Lady Yanagisawa would feed.

"I think I could persuade your husband to believe me," Lady Yanagisawa said. "Men are possessive and jealous. They don't like to think that their woman has given her favors to someone else. And they're suspicious. One hint of infidelity can break their trust. But we needn't argue about whether you're right or I am. I'll just tell your husband my story about you and the Dragon King, and we'll see what happens."

Aghast, Reiko blurted, "You stay away from my husband!"

Lady Yanagisawa laughed again. "Perhaps you're not so sure of him after all. Do you think he'll be so angry that he'll divorce you for cheating on him? Do you fear that he'll throw you out of the house and you'll never see your son again?"

Reiko did. Although Sano was a reasonable man, she couldn't predict how he would react to Lady Yanagisawa's claims. He knew Reiko was hiding something about her experiences at the Dragon King's palace. There was no one besides herself to refute Lady Yanagisawa. Midori and Lady Keisho-in hadn't seen what had happened between Reiko and their kidnapper. The Dragon King's henchmen, who'd witnessed much of it, were dead. And Sano's trust of Reiko's fidelity had never been tried before. He might be quick to suspect and retaliate. Even if he didn't, their marriage would never be the same. Reiko vowed never to keep a secret from Sano again. But her vow came too late to help her now.

"I'll take the chance that my husband will listen to you and punish me," Reiko said, pretending confidence. She folded her arms across her chest. "I won't coax him into conspiring with the chamberlain. I won't assassinate Lord Matsudaira, not even to protect my marriage."

"Why not?" Lady Yanagisawa's gaze, alight with madness, burned into Reiko. "Lord Matsudaira seeks to usurp power from the shogun. He is a traitor to his own cousin. He deserves to die. Isn't your marriage worth his life?"

"Nothing is worth manipulating my husband or killing in cold blood," Reiko said.

Yet as she floundered amid this nightmare, a voice deep inside her mind whispered that Lord Matsudaira's life as well as his clan's good name were but small prices to pay for protecting her marriage. She didn't know the man, or care about him. Her own attitude horrified Reiko. But a primitive, selfish part of her would sacrifice almost anyone or anything to keep the husband she loved. It reasoned that Lady Yanagisawa was right, and Japan would be better off without Lord Matsudaira; it inclined her toward believing that she should do the shogun a favor by killing his overambitious cousin. It argued that Lord Matsudaira's death would prevent a big civil war and save many lives. Reiko pictured herself disguised in the gaudy clothes of an army camp whore, stealing into Lord Matsudaira's tent, a dagger clutched in her hand.

Lady Yanagisawa smiled a sly, nasty smile. "You're smart enough to assassinate Lord Matsudaira and not get caught. Your husband will never have to know. The chamberlain will never tell. Nor will I."

The moral, rational part of herself told Reiko that if she did kill Lord Matsudaira, she must always live with the knowledge that she was guilty of murder even if she got away with it. And killing a member of a Tokugawa branch clan was treason even if Lord Matsudaira could be considered a traitor himself. Furthermore, Reiko knew better than to trust Lady Yanagisawa or the chamberlain. Bowing to blackmail would only put her under their power for the next time they wanted a favor.

"I won't obey. Leave my house at once," Reiko said.

Her voice lacked force and conviction. Lady Yanagisawa greeted her wavering with a look that was almost affectionate. "I'll go now and give you some time to think things over," Lady Yanagisawa said. "I'll expect your decision by tonight."

Clearly, she believed that Reiko would capitulate. Shaken and terrified, Reiko faced the choice between committing murder and treason or losing everything that mattered most to her. "But even if I should decide to give in to you, my husband will resist pinning Senior Elder Makino's murder on Daiemon. How am I supposed to persuade him?"

"That's your problem, not mine." With a triumphant smile, Lady Yanagisawa turned and walked out the door.

29

Lady Yanagisawa arrived, breathless and excited, outside her husband's office. Her heart throbbed wildly; exhilaration dizzied her. She flung open the door and staggered across the threshold. The chamberlain, seated at his desk, and some eight or ten officials kneeling around him, all stared with disapproval at her. But then the ire on her husband's face gave way to anticipation. He quickly dismissed the officials, shut the door behind them, and turned to her.

"Have you something to tell me?" he said.

"I did it," Lady Yanagisawa said, gasping. "I did everything you asked."

His keen, luminous eyes inspected her for signs of falsehood. Then a deep breath seemed to replenish his spirit and release a flood of anxiety from him. "I now have a foothold in the future," he said. "And my control over the present is strengthened." His face relaxed into a gloating, exultant smile. "The advantage is mine. Victory is possible."

Lady Yanagisawa savored his pleasure. With giddy, almost unbearable expectation, she waited for her reward.

Sudden doubt shadowed the chamberlain's features. "But are you sure that Lady Reiko will cooperate?"

"I'm sure," Lady Yanagisawa said, for she believed that a wife who loved her husband would do whatever was necessary to keep his love. Reiko would soon forget her objections and assassinate Lord Matsudaira. The *sōsakan-sama* would declare Daimon a traitor and murderer. Lady Yanagisawa would share in the chamberlain's triumph. That made worthwhile everything that had happened to her.

Lady Yanagisawa had suffered agonies of doubt and misery before her visit to Reiko. She'd known that by forcing Reiko to do something so wrong she would lose Reiko's friendship. How alone she would feel without Reiko! Her nerve had almost failed her. Then Reiko had said such terrible things to her. Hatred had gained ascendancy over Lady Yanagisawa's love for her friend. Reiko deserved to suffer.

"Very good," the chamberlain said, reassured. "All I need do is wait for events to take their course."

His gaze drifted away from Lady Yanagisawa, as if he were looking at the future when he would rule Japan. "Was there something else you wanted?"

He'd forgotten her reward, Lady Yanagisawa realized with dismay. "You said that if I . . ." she stammered. "You promised me that you would . . ."

"Ah. What a good memory you have." Irritation showed on the chamberlain's face. Lady Yanagisawa sensed him thinking about all the things he had to do that were more important than spending time with her. "Very well," he said. "A promise is a promise. You deserve your little treat. Come along."

Lady Yanagisawa was too desperate to quibble with his attitude. As desire swelled hot and urgent in her, she followed her husband to his bedchamber. It was dim and cold, but Lady Yanagisawa barely noticed. She watched, trembling in a torment of eagerness, while the chamberlain opened a cabinet, hauled out his futon, and threw it open on the floor beside her. Facing her, he stroked her cheek, her lips, her neck. Lady Yanagisawa didn't mind that his caresses seemed perfunctory. Her lips swelled and her skin tingled at his touch. As the desire flowed its heavy, liquid weight through her breasts and loins, she moaned.

The chamberlain loosened her robes and dropped them

from her. The cold raised bumps on her skin. Heat rising within her steamed from her pores while his hands moved over her. "Please," she whispered, clutching at him.

He let her untie his sash and stroke his bare, smooth, muscular chest. With fumbling hands she removed his loincloth. His manhood hung flaccid. His obvious lack of desire for her didn't discourage Lady Yanagisawa. She sank to her knees. She fondled and sucked his manhood. As it curved erect, she relished its velvet-skinned hardness that pulsated under her tongue and fingers. The chamberlain groaned, and pleasure lowered his eyelids. He let her worship him until she fell back on the futon, gasping with need, her arms outstretched for him. He straddled her and caressed her shoulders; he tongued her nipples; his fingers rubbed hot, wet circles between her legs.

Inarticulate cries arose from Lady Yanagisawa as he raised her toward the heights of sensation that she'd approached with him two days ago. She went mad with pleasure. Her gaze devoured him; her hands frantically roved his body in an attempt to experience him to the full. To her delight, she saw her need reflected in his eyes, although they didn't meet hers; she heard his breathing quicken. She eagerly spread her legs wide. He lowered himself, held her, and entered.

The tight, slick friction when he slid into her! The feel of him moving inside her for the first time in the ten years since they'd conceived Kikuko! Sobbing with rapture, Lady Yanagisawa heaved and writhed under him. Through her tears she saw his face. His eyes were closed, his head tilted back as he thrust. She understood that he didn't want to look at her and thereby spoil his enjoyment. But her hurt quickly faded. Her insides were melting and unfurling in a blossom of flames, blood, and desire. Her pleasure reached its zenith. Violent waves of ecstasy pulsed through her. She screamed with a joy and release she'd never thought possible. Afloat in a world of fulfillment, she sobbed in gratitude and embraced her husband.

"Come to me," she murmured, craving his release as much as she had her own. "Come to me now."

He thrust harder and faster, his jaws clenched, every muscle straining. Suddenly he reared back on his knees. His manhood whipped out of Lady Yanagisawa. He moaned, arched his back, and spurted hot, wet semen onto her stomach. As he shuddered and gasped, Lady Yanagisawa realized why he'd withdrawn before his climax: He didn't want to breed another idiot child.

Happiness yielded to humiliation. The room seemed cold now, as the heat from their coupling dissipated and her bodily sensations waned. Lady Yanagisawa felt slighted by her husband. She regretted the friendship she'd ruined for his sake. Now she couldn't even turn to Reiko for comfort. And the bloody stain of her guilt would never go away. To please this man who treated her so deplorably, she had doomed her soul to burn forever in the fires of the netherworld.

Then the chamberlain lay down beside her. Propping himself on his elbow, he smiled into her eyes. "That was good," he said, and she knew that he meant the service she'd rendered him as well as the sex they'd just had. He whispered, "I love you."

Those words compensated Lady Yanagisawa for all the pain he'd caused her. Now she wept for joy. At last she'd won his love! All the evils she'd done seemed worthwhile; all she'd risked or lost was nothing. A radiant future beckoned. The chamberlain would become a real husband to her and a real father to their daughter, just as he'd promised. He would rule Japan; she would help him whenever possible and necessary.

At this moment, not even Reiko could boast such good fortune as Lady Yanagisawa enjoyed.

The Kanda district verged upon the northeast boundary of Edo Castle. It was convenient to the seat of political power, yet a world away, and mostly populated by merchants who'd come from central Japan to seek their fortunes. Dyers, blacksmiths, carpenters, plasterers, swordsmiths, and candle makers inhabited various quarters in

Kanda, but not all the residents engaged in profitable or legal commerce. Along the bank of the Kanda River were hovels for beggars and outcasts, and a field known as a haunt of the lowest class of prostitutes, the itinerant "nighthawks." Here, a nobleman could find a haven from the Tokugawa court; he could exist anonymously among people beneath his class and too occupied with the struggle for survival to pay him much notice.

Sano arrived with Hirata, a squadron of detectives, Otani, Ibe, and their men, in Tsukegi Street. The street was named for the product sold there—charms against fire, Edo's worst natural hazard. Shops displayed the little figurines made from wood and sulfur. Above the shops were living quarters. These had latticed windows and rickety balconies sheltered by overhanging eaves. Sano and his companions dismounted and secured their horses outside the middle building on the west side of the street, where Daiemon had maintained a secret establishment.

Its entrance was located in an alley festooned with laundry on clotheslines. Sano and Hirata climbed a creaky wooden staircase to Daiemon's quarters while the other men waited below. Although Hirata had determined the house to be unoccupied, Sano knocked on the door because Ibe and Otani were watching and he must act as if he knew nothing about the house or who might be there. Nobody answered. Sano tried the door and found it locked, but when he and Hirata shoved hard against it, the catch gave way. Ibe and Otani hastened up the stairs and followed them into the house.

The first room was a kitchen furnished with a hearth and a few dishes and utensils. "Whoever lives here doesn't do much cooking," Ibe remarked.

They passed beyond a sliding partition, into a chamber that contained a *tatami* floor, built-in cabinets, and an elaborately carved black wooden chest. Charcoal braziers filled with ash stood about the room; a red lacquer table held a porcelain sake decanter and cups. A silk cushion sat before a writing desk made of black lacquer and decorated with floral gold inlays. In one corner, a screen decorated with a painting of a waterfall enclosed a metal tub large enough for a man to bathe in. Such luxurious decor seemed out of place in humble Tsukegi Street.

"He makes himself comfortable," Otani said as he opened a cabinet to reveal folded silk bedding and robes.

Ibe examined the screen. "This wasn't cheap. He has money."

Sano wondered uneasily whether Ibe and Otani would discover whose house this was and what would happen if they did. But Daiemon seemed not to have left any obvious clues to his identity. Sano and Hirata found two smaller rooms, both unfurnished. They returned to the main chamber, where Otani had opened the chest. This held a pair of swords on a rack.

"Whoever he is, he's a samurai," Ibe said.

Otani lifted out the long sword and frowned in puzzlement. "This dragon design on the hilt looks familiar," he said. "I'm sure I've seen it someplace before . . . but where?"

Sano gave Hirata a look that said they'd better finish inspecting the house before Otani recalled that he'd seen his lord's nephew wearing the sword. While Hirata began searching the cabinet, Sano opened the lid of the desk. Inside he found writing supplies and a pile of gold coins alongside a stack of white rice paper. Sano riffled the sheets and found them all blank except the last, which bore scrawled black writing.

"What's that?" Ibe said, leaning over Sano's shoulder.

The paper read:

> Makino
> One hundred *koban* beforehand
> One hundred afterward
> Final payment the next day, at the Floating Teahouse

Elation vied with apprehension inside Sano. "Unless I'm mistaken, this means that somebody hired somebody else to assassinate Senior Elder Makino," he said.

And if Sano was correct, the person who'd hired the assassin had to be Daiemon. Yet Sano was less pleased with the thought that he'd solved the crime than concerned about the consequences of the solution. If he exposed Daiemon as the person responsible for Makino's death, what then? Chamberlain Yanagisawa would be delighted to have the Matsudaira clan disgraced. Lord Matsudaira would come raging after Sano's blood . . . if Sano first survived defying his watchdogs' orders against investigating Daiemon or involving their lords in the crime.

"But who's the assassin?" Ibe said. "And who hired him?"

A creaking noise outside froze everyone into alert silence. Somebody was coming up the stairs. Sano and Hirata drew their swords and stood to one side of the doorway leading through the kitchen to the entrance. Ibe and Otani also unsheathed their weapons and positioned themselves on the other side. Suspense hushed the room. Sano heard the door open. The footsteps crossed the kitchen. Into the parlor walked a samurai.

"Halt!" Sano ordered.

He lunged, his blade pointed at the samurai. Hirata, Otani, and Ibe followed suit. The samurai yelped. His eyes widened and his mouth gaped in horror as four blades impinged on his throat. He fumbled for his own weapon.

"Don't even try," Sano said.

The samurai gulped, nodded, and held his hands palms up in surrender. He was in his twenties, with a heavy jaw and a square, short, muscular build. His silk garments and expensive swords declared him a member of the upper social ranks.

"Who are you?" Sano asked.

Before the samurai could answer, Otani said, "Kubo-*san*?" Startled recognition marked both men's faces. "What are you doing here?"

"Otani-*san*," the samurai said with obvious relief at seeing someone he knew. "Please don't hurt me! Please allow me to explain!"

"How do you know each other?" Sano said, surprised

himself, as he and Hirata and the watchdogs sheathed their weapons.

"He was a retainer to Daiemon," said Otani. Then he addressed the young samurai: "By all means explain."

Sano saw Hirata's leery expression. He braced himself for what he knew was coming.

"I came to get some money and swords that Daiemon left here," said Kubo. "I thought I should give them to his family."

"This was Daiemon's place?" Otani demanded, as he stared at Kubo, then around the room.

"Well, yes," Kubo said nervously. "Only a few of his men know about it. We weren't supposed to tell. But now that he's dead, I guess it doesn't really matter . . . does it?"

A brief silence, fraught with tension, ensued while Otani and Ibe grasped the meaning of the news they'd just received. Otani spoke in a tone of dumbfounded revelation: "Those are Daiemon's swords. I knew I'd seen them before." He snatched the note from Hirata. "It was Daiemon who wrote this?"

Kubo peered at the note. "That looks like his writing."

Ibe's face showed dawning enlightenment, then a calculating look. "Daiemon hired the assassin. He was behind Senior Elder Makino's murder."

"No!" Otani exclaimed, aghast. "It can't be!"

"This place belonged to Daiemon. He wrote the note," Ibe said.

"But—but maybe we've misinterpreted the note," Otani said.

"What other interpretation is there?" Ibe said.

Otani opened his mouth, then shook his head.

"Did I say something wrong?" Kubo said in a small voice.

"Just take the money and swords and go," Sano told him. "Forget what happened here."

Kubo went. "Wait until Chamberlain Yanagisawa hears about this," Ibe gloated. "How glad he'll be to learn that Lord Matsudaira's nephew was the guilty one. That should strengthen him and weaken his enemy."

"But . . ." Shaken and confused, Otani said, "We're not

going to tell the chamberlain. We agreed to leave our superiors and the factions out of the murder investigation . . . didn't we?" His eyes implored Ibe. "And we agreed that one of the women should be blamed for both crimes. We can't expose Daiemon as the killer and traitor!"

Sano saw that Otani was terrified of Lord Matsudaira's displeasure and the shogun's wrath. Since Daiemon was dead and beyond punishment, his clan and its associates would pay for his crime.

"This changes everything," Ibe said, wresting the note from Otani's grip. "I agreed to our pact because I thought it would serve our mutual interests, and I thought one of the women was as likely to be the culprit as anyone else. But now that we know different, I can't let the wrong person be punished for killing my lord's friend and ally while the Matsudaira clan goes free. Nor can I hide such important information from Chamberlain Yanagisawa."

The man did have some sense of honor and duty after all, Sano saw; but only if it favored his interests. A divergence of interests had shattered the alliance between Sano's watchdogs. Otani stood frozen by horror that his partner had not only cut him loose, but meant to strike a crippling blow at his lord.

"Congratulations on solving Senior Elder Makino's murder," Ibe said to Sano. "Let's take the news back to Edo Castle."

"No!" Otani shouted as fury roused him to life. He turned to Sano in desperation. "I order you to never speak of what we found here. I order you to arrest Okitsu or Agemaki!"

His words fell into dead quiet. Nobody moved. "Are you coming?" Ibe asked Sano.

"Not yet," Sano said.

As Ibe regarded him with puzzlement, and Otani with sudden hope of a reprieve, Sano said, "There's not enough evidence to prove Daiemon is guilty."

"What are you talking about?" Ibe said. He waved the note. "There's this, written by Daiemon, describing the arrangements he made with the assassin. What more do you want?"

"Verification that the note is what it appears to be," Sano said.

"That it appears to be in Daiemon's handwriting, and it was found in his house, doesn't mean anything," Otani said eagerly. "Someone could have forged the note and planted it here."

"Do you question the evidence because you're afraid of how Lord Matsudaira will react?" Ibe asked Sano.

"No," Sano said, although the idea of Lord Matsudaira's wrath was good reason to hesitate before incriminating Daiemon. And he wasn't eager to help Chamberlain Yanagisawa come out on top. "I want to be sure that I've identified the person truly responsible for Makino's murder. Even if the note is genuine and it means what we think it means, there are too many questions left unanswered."

"Such as?" Ibe said.

"Such as, who is the assassin?" Sano said. "If indeed he exists, he's out there somewhere. He can confirm that Daiemon hired him. And he's just as guilty as Daiemon. He must be caught and punished."

"And how did he get into Makino's estate and kill him without anyone noticing?" Hirata said.

"And what are the other suspects hiding about the murder?" said Sano, convinced that they'd played roles in whatever had really happened that night. "Where does the perfumed sleeve fit into this?"

"What does any of that matter," Ibe protested, "when you can finish your investigation and discharge your duty to the shogun? And why should I care, when we can please my master by deciding that Daiemon was responsible for Makino's death?"

"Something might happen later to prove that he wasn't," Sano said. "Do you want to take the chance and risk that Lord Matsudaira will retaliate against you as well as Chamberlain Yanagisawa for smearing his clan's reputation?"

Ibe hesitated and sucked his lips. Sano bet that the man's cowardice would prevail. Ibe said, "All right—you win. But how do you propose to find the evidence you need?"

"The Floating Teahouse is a place to start," Sano said.

"Let's go, then." Ibe headed for the door with Sano and Hirata.

"I forbid you," Otani said, grasping at the shreds of his authority.

"You can come with us if you want," Ibe said, "but you can't stop us."

Otani reluctantly followed them out of the house.

30

Reiko rode in her palanquin along the passage that led uphill from the official quarter to the palace. While her bearers negotiated turns and paused at checkpoints, her mind went over and over her conversation with Lady Yanagisawa. She desperately sought a way to evade blackmail and ruination.

The moment when she'd considered obeying Lady Yanagisawa had passed; conscience had overridden self-interest. Reiko couldn't interfere with Sano's investigation on the chamberlain's account. And she could never bring herself to assassinate Lord Matsudaira. Having realized that, Reiko must somehow protect her marriage from Lady Yanagisawa.

The simplest way would be to tell Sano the truth about what had happened between her and the Dragon King, before Lady Yanagisawa got to him. But if Reiko did, he might still believe Lady Yanagisawa. Even if he didn't divorce Reiko, he would never trust her again. Their love would be damaged beyond repair. Although Reiko knew that their love should matter less than resisting the evils that Lady Yanagisawa had asked of her, it was the most important thing in her life besides her child.

Next, Reiko thought of discrediting Lady Yanagisawa in order that Sano wouldn't believe anything she told him. But

Sano already knew from Reiko that Lady Yanagisawa was a jealous, treacherous madwoman, and even that didn't seem enough to counteract her lies. Sano hadn't witnessed Lady Yanagisawa's attempts to kill Masahiro or Reiko. One hint of suspicion about Reiko's veracity might goad him to think that Reiko had invented the murder attempts, as well as her version of the story about the Dragon King. Yet despite these problems, discrediting Lady Yanagisawa—and getting the woman permanently out of her life—still seemed the best defense to Reiko. But how to do it?

She rode through a gate and a garden of cherry trees whose bare, black limbs seemed unlikely to ever blossom in the spring. The bearers set down her palanquin outside the Large Interior, the wing of the palace where the shogun's concubines, female relatives, and their attendants lived. Reiko forced herself to forget her personal problems and concentrate on the murder investigation. She climbed out of the palanquin and hurried up to the two guards stationed outside a door to the half-timbered, tile-roofed complex of interconnected buildings.

After identifying herself to the guards, she said, "I wish to see Madam Eri."

Soon Eri came out the door. "Honorable Cousin Reiko!" she said with a friendly smile. A thin, middle-aged woman, she had hair dyed black and a gaunt face. Once a concubine to the previous shogun, she was now a second-rank palace official in the Large Interior. She wore a padded cloak thrown over the blue kimono of her rank. "How nice to see you!"

"I need your help," Reiko said, forgoing pleasantries in the interest of haste. "Can you spare a moment to talk?"

"Certainly," Eri said.

Reiko beckoned Eri, and they walked among the cherry trees in the deserted garden. "I need to find out the name of the woman that Lord Matsudaira's nephew Daiemon was having an affair with. Can you tell me?"

Eri's pleasant expression turned uneasy. She halted on the path. Averting her gaze from Reiko, she said, "I'm sorry. I don't know who she is."

"I think you do," Reiko said. "You know everything about the personal business of high society." Eri was a notorious gossip who gathered news from the wives, concubines, servants, and other women associated with prominent men. "Who is she?"

"All right. I do know." Eri faced Reiko, her eyes troubled. "But I can't tell you."

Reiko was surprised because Eri had often helped her with investigations. "Why not?"

"The woman is beholden to a jealous, violent man. I don't want to cause trouble for her."

"If she met Daiemon at the Sign of Bedazzlement and killed him, she deserves trouble."

Eri shook her head. "I can't believe she killed him."

"Then help her clear herself," Reiko said. "Tell me who she is so I can talk to her. If she convinces me that she didn't kill Daiemon, I'll tell my husband she's innocent. Her affair will never become public."

"But what if she doesn't convince you?" Eri said, defensive and obstinate. "You'll drag her into the *sōsakan-sama*'s investigation. Her man will punish her for cheating on him. She'll be a dead woman."

"As might I be, if my husband doesn't find out who killed Daiemon," said Reiko. "Would you shield Daiemon's mistress at my expense?" In her desperation, Reiko had no qualms about using whatever means necessary to coax Eri. "Would you sacrifice your own cousin to protect a woman who may have murdered the shogun's heir apparent?"

Guilt and uncertainty colored Eri's features. She clasped her hands and bowed her head over them, as if praying for good judgment. Then she leaned close to Reiko and whispered in her ear, "The woman's name is Gosechi. She's Lord Matsudaira's concubine. Now do you understand why the affair had to be kept secret?"

The Floating Teahouse was a boat moored on the Kanda River. It had a long, flat, wide hull enclosed by a cabin made of bamboo blinds and a plank roof. A red lantern painted with the characters of its name hung from a pole at the bow. Up and down the river were other, similar boats that contained brothels, drinking places, and gambling dens. The pleasure seekers who frequented these businesses during warm months were scarce today. Outside a floating brothel, a frowzy young woman greeted an old samurai. A trio of male commoners joshed and laughed on a bridge that led to warehouses on the opposite bank. Ferries and barges plied the muddy, rippling water.

Sano, Hirata, Ibe, and Otani walked the path down the riverbank to the Floating Teahouse. Their troops waited on the slope above. A hunchbacked man wearing a gray kimono and leggings came out of the teahouse and hurried toward Sano and his companions.

"Greetings," he said, beaming at the prospect of customers with money to spend. "Welcome to my humble establishment. Come in, come in!" He shooed them toward the boat.

"I could use a drink," Otani said grumpily.

They entered the boat's cabin, which contained sake urns, a smoking charcoal brazier, and a tray of cups. Sano, Hirata, and the watchdogs knelt on a frayed tatami mat. Inside the boat was almost as cold as outside, but the bamboo blinds provided shelter from the wind. The proprietor served sake heated on the brazier. He hovered near Sano and the other men as they drank.

After Sano introduced himself as the shogun's *sōsakan-sama,* he told the proprietor, "I'm looking for information on two men who may have come here three days ago. One was a samurai." He described Daiemon.

"Oh, yes," said the proprietor, "I remember them. The samurai was the only one I've had here in a while, until now."

"I'm particularly interested in the other man," Sano said. "I want to find out who he is. Did you hear his name?"

"No," the proprietor said, "but I can tell you. He was Koheiji, the Kabuki actor."

"Koheiji?" Sano felt his surprise shared by his companions. "How do you know?"

"He's my favorite actor. I go to all his plays. I recognized him the moment I saw him." The old man's eyes shone with delight. "To think that such a great star drank in my teahouse!"

Sano shook his head as his surprise reverberated through it. He'd expected at best a vague description of the assassin. His mind seethed with speculation. "Are you sure it was Koheiji and not just someone who looked like him?"

"Absolutely sure, master. I'd swear on my life."

"Do you know who the samurai is?"

The proprietor shook his head. "He didn't say. And I'd never seen him before."

"Tell me what the two men did."

"The samurai was already here, waiting, when Koheiji came." The proprietor's expression said he wondered why Sano was interested in the pair's meeting but didn't dare question a *bakufu* official. "They each had one drink. They talked so softly I couldn't hear what they were saying. The samurai gave Koheiji a pouch. Koheiji opened it. He poured out gold coins. I'd never seen so much money in my life." Awe inflected the proprietor's voice. "There must have been a hundred *koban*!"

"What happened next?" Sano pictured Daiemon and Koheiji seated where he sat now, the coins glinting between them.

"Koheiji counted the money. He put it back in the pouch and tucked the pouch inside his cloak. Then they left."

Sano thanked the proprietor. He paid for the liquor that he and Hirata and the watchdogs had consumed. They joined their troops on the cold, windy riverbank.

"It was Koheiji whom Daiemon hired to kill Senior Elder Makino," Hirata said in a tone of amazed revelation.

"So it appears," Sano said, "if the samurai Koheiji met was indeed Daiemon." Ingrained caution prevented him from drawing conclusions even when evidence supported them.

"The murder was committed by someone inside Makino's household, on the orders of someone outside," Hirata said.

"Who was in a better position to assassinate Makino than a man he trusted, who lived with him?" Sano remarked.

"Daiemon must have thought of that when he chose Koheiji," said Hirata.

"He might have known that Koheiji wanted money and could be bribed into killing his master," Sano said.

"Maybe Daiemon promised to become his patron after Makino was gone," said Hirata.

"Daiemon's story that Makino defected was a lie," Ibe said with conviction. "Obviously, he'd failed to persuade Makino to join Lord Matsudaira's faction. He had the actor assassinate Makino to get him off the Council of Elders and weaken Chamberlain Yanagisawa's influence over the shogun."

Otani looked at the ground, his head bowed, humiliated by further evidence that his lord's nephew had died a criminal. His expression was stoic, but fear for his own fate emanated from him like a bad smell.

"That Daiemon appears to have conspired with Koheiji to assassinate Senior Elder Makino sheds a new light on Daiemon's murder," Sano said.

"Daiemon was a threat to Koheiji because he knew Koheiji assassinated Makino," said Hirata. "Maybe Koheiji killed Daiemon to keep him from telling."

"But if Koheiji got accused of the murder, all he needed to do was say that Daiemon hired him," Ibe objected. "Neither of them could have incriminated the other without endangering himself. They'd both have been in trouble."

"Koheiji would have been in deeper trouble than Daiemon," said Hirata. "If we hadn't found the note and come to the Floating Teahouse, it would be Koheiji's word against Daiemon's. The shogun wouldn't believe that his heir apparent had conspired to murder his old friend Makino."

"Perhaps Koheiji thought that if there was any chance he might take the blame for the crime, Daiemon should share the punishment, and therefore he stabbed him just in case,"

Sano said. "And perhaps Koheiji didn't act alone, even if he was the one who got paid to kill." Sano recalled the scenes that Reiko had witnessed between the suspects in Makino's household. "Perhaps he had an accomplice."

"If so, was it Okitsu?" said Hirata. "Or Agemaki?"

"They're both possibilities," Sano said. "But this is all unfounded speculation. To learn the truth, we need to talk to Koheiji." He addressed the watchdogs: "In view of everything that's happened, may I assume that you'll no longer prevent me from investigating him?"

"I won't," Otani said, subdued by dejection. "If he killed my lord's nephew, he deserves to be exposed and punished no matter how many high-ranking friends he has."

"Nor I," said Ibe. "Do with him what you will."

"May I also assume that you'll now remove your troops from my house?" Sano asked.

"You may not," Ibe said with a derisive laugh. "I still want assurance that the outcome of your investigation doesn't put my master or me at a disadvantage. Don't push your luck. Now let's go see what the actor has to say for himself."

31

The search for Daiemon's mistress led Reiko to Zōjō Temple.

After leaving her cousin, she'd gone to the Matsudaira estate. Eri had said that a certain lady-in-waiting there, who owed her a favor, would get Reiko inside to see Lord Matsudaira's concubine, Gosechi. But when Reiko had arrived, the lady had said Gosechi had gone to the temple. After Reiko had explained that she had urgent business with Gosechi, the lady had sent a servant along with Reiko to help her locate the concubine.

Reiko now traveled in her palanquin through the Zōjō district, administrative seat of the Buddhist Pure Land sect. Zōjō was the Tokugawa family temple, where the clan worshipped and its ancestors lay entombed in lavish mausoleums. This vast district encompassed hills and pine forest, more than one hundred buildings of Zōjō proper, and many smaller, subsidiary temples. Here lived some ten thousand priests, monks, nuns, and novices. As Reiko and her entourage passed through the crowded marketplace along the approach to the temple, her spirit darkened with memories of violence.

During the disaster at the nearby Black Lotus Temple last autumn, she'd faced evil and narrowly escaped death. Seven hundred people had lost their lives. Today, while the factions warred outside Edo, a new shadow hung over Zōjō Temple. Reiko found the precinct crowded with pilgrims seeking blessings to protect them from misfortune. They flocked around the pagodas and shrines. The grand main hall appeared under siege by the hordes that streamed around and through it. Alighting from her palanquin near the huge bronze bell, Reiko wondered how, amid so many people, she would ever find the one woman she sought.

"I want to see Koheiji," Sano told the detective who met him outside the door to Senior Elder Makino's mansion when he arrived with Hirata, the watchdogs, and all their troops.

"Koheiji went to the theater," said the detective.

"Then we'll get him there," Ibe said, turning to leave.

"Not so fast," Sano said.

Ibe regarded him with surprise. "I thought you were so eager to confront Koheiji. Why hold off now?"

"Koheiji is sure to deny everything. While I'm here, I may as well get some more ammunition to use against him besides the note and the teahouse proprietor's story." Sano asked the detective, "Where is Agemaki?"

"She's in the family chapel."

The chapel was located in a wing of the mansion built over a pond fringed with reeds. Inside, a niche contained a Buddha statue on a dais. Narrow alcoves each contained a *butsudan*—a memorial shrine in the form of a small cabinet—and offerings of food and flowers that honored a Makino clan ancestor. Agemaki knelt before a table that held a painted portrait of Senior Elder Makino, a funeral tablet bearing his name, incense in a brass burner, and a lit candle that would burn for seven days after his death. She wore plain gray robes; a white drape covered her hair. Her head was bowed, her face serene as she murmured the prayers that would ease her husband's transition to the spirit world. When Sano and his companions entered the chapel, Agemaki started; her voice broke off. She rose, and caution hooded her gaze.

"Please excuse us for interrupting your funeral rites," Sano said, "but we have important news. We've found evidence that Koheiji killed Senior Elder Makino."

Shock tightened Agemaki's elegant features. Her hand went to her mouth.

"It seems that Lord Matsudaira's nephew Daiemon hired Koheiji to assassinate your husband." Sano showed Agemaki the note, explained what he thought it meant, and told her that he had a witness who'd seen Daiemon pay the actor. He waited while she stood rigid and mute. Hirata and the detectives, Ibe, Otani, and their troops watched her in silence. Outside the chapel, footsteps creaked as someone hurried down the corridor.

"Have you anything to say?" Sano prompted Agemaki.

"I thank you for finding out who killed my husband." Her toneless voice hid whatever she was thinking. But Sano sensed that she was wondering whether she could relax now that he'd determined that someone else was guilty, or whether she still had cause for fear. "Now his spirit can rest in peace."

"Not quite yet," Sano said. "First the people responsible for his death must be brought to justice." When she made no response, Sano said, "Perhaps you can help me."

She glanced sideways at him, her hand still clasped over her mouth. He felt her wondering what he expected of her.

"A witness heard you and Koheiji talking. Each of you promised to say nothing about what the other did in connection with your husband's death." Sano heard Agemaki's breath catch with a small, ragged sound. "That suggests you conspired in the murder that Koheiji was hired to do. If he's guilty, then so must you be—as his accomplice."

Sano saw the watchdogs frown, trying to guess where and how he'd gotten the evidence that he hadn't discovered while with them. Agemaki dropped her hand from her mouth. Her lips parted and the gaze she lifted to Sano was filled with dismay.

"That maid who ran away last night . . . I was afraid she'd been eavesdropping on me. She was your spy." Panic crept into Agemaki's voice as she said, "But I never conspired to kill my husband. I wasn't an accomplice. I had nothing to do with his death. That's not what Koheiji and I were talking about."

"Then what were you?"

Agemaki pressed her lips together. They twitched and strained, as though with the effort to contain her knowledge.

"Your pact with Koheiji is worthless now," Sano said, playing the widow against the actor in the hope that she would affirm Koheiji's guilt. "There's no point in protecting him. Do you think he'll protect you when I tell him that I know he killed your husband?" Sano infused his voice with pitying disdain. "Of course not. He'll spill whatever information he thinks will save him. He'll put the whole blame for the murder on you. While you go to the execution ground, he'll spend the money Daiemon paid him."

A visible shudder passed through Agemaki as she saw the threat of death approaching. She crumbled to her knees.

"Why let Koheiji go free while you suffer?" Sano said. "Tell me the truth, and I'll be as lenient toward you as I can."

She breathed a long, tremulous sigh of resignation. Fear and distrust pooled in her eyes, but she nodded. Sano experienced relief because he'd broken her at last, and without violence. His heart beat fast with the thought that the solution to the crime was imminent.

"That night, I took my sleeping potion before bed," Agemaki said. "I always did, so I wouldn't be disturbed by the sounds."

She paused, and Sano said, "What sounds?"

"The sounds of my husband playing sex games with Koheiji and Okitsu." Revulsion twisted Agemaki's mouth. "Usually the potion made me sleep no matter how loud they got. But that night, I woke up. And I heard them. I heard that little whore Okitsu giggling, while Koheiji uttered filthy, obscene talk and my husband moaned."

Koheiji and Okitsu had lied when they'd said they hadn't

seen Makino that night, Sano thought. He watched Agemaki curl her hands into claws. Her bitter expression not only confirmed what Reiko had said—that Agemaki was rabidly jealous of the concubine—but also that she'd hated her husband for his infidelity and his depraved amusements.

"I couldn't bear to think of what they were doing, but I had to know. I couldn't help myself." Agemaki's tone conveyed the torment she must have felt. "I got out of bed and crept down the passage. I peeked through the door to my husband's bedchamber."

She expelled her breath in a shivering hiss. "I saw the three of them. My husband and Koheiji were naked. Okitsu wore the embroidered ivory silk kimono that my husband bought her. She was crouched on her hands and knees. My husband was kneeling in front of her, panting like a dog while she sucked his manhood and Koheiji coupled with her from behind."

Outrage shone in Agemaki's eyes. "I wanted to rush in and scream at my husband and Koheiji and their whore to stop. I wanted to pull them apart. But I knew my husband would be furious if I did. Instead, I went back to my room. I took more sleeping potion. I got back in bed and dozed off, but I awakened again while it was still dark. The house was quiet and peaceful. But there was no peace in my mind. I lay in bed, worrying about the future."

Agemaki spoke in a tone fraught with distress: "My husband had barely bothered to speak to me these last few months, and when he did, he dropped hints that he was tired of supporting me. 'That kimono you're wearing was awfully expensive.' 'Do you really need so many servants?'" She mimicked his crabby voice. "I knew he was going to divorce me. And I knew that when he did, he would cut me off without a single copper. I would have to go back to Asakusa Jinja Shrine. I wouldn't inherit the money he promised me when we married. I would have nothing. I would *be* nothing."

Fresh outrage blazed from her. Sano could almost see flames consuming the serene, prim guise she'd worn. "That night I decided I wouldn't let my husband get away with humiliating me and reneging on his promise. I decided that if I must be ruined, then so must he. I got up and lit a lamp. I fetched a paper-cutting knife from my writing desk. I took the lamp and knife and crept into my husband's bedchamber. I meant to cut his throat while he slept. But his bed was empty. I saw something glittering in the corner. It was Okitsu's sleeve. It must have gotten torn off her kimono. My husband was gone. So I went looking for him. I found him in his study."

She stared downward, her expression startled, as if reliving the moment. Sano pictured her standing in Makino's study, the burning lamp in one hand, the knife clutched in the other. "He was lying on the floor," Agemaki said. "There was blood on his head, his face, and his clothes. His eyes and mouth were open. He looked like he'd had a bad shock." Her gaze darted, as if taking in the scene impressed on her memory. "There was a bloodstained wooden pole on the floor near him. Papers were scattered everywhere. There was cold air coming through the open window. I bent over my husband and touched his face. It was cold. He wasn't breathing. I knew he was dead."

Sano conjectured that Koheiji had staged Makino's assassination to look like an attack by an intruder and thereby hide his guilt. But how had Makino ended up lying in his bed as though he'd died of old age while asleep? Postponing his questions, Sano let Agemaki continue her story.

"At first I was thankful," Agemaki said. "Someone had broken into the house, killed my husband, and saved me the trouble. He couldn't divorce me. I would inherit my legacy." Her eyes glowed briefly with happiness, then darkened. "But I was still filled with anger toward him. I wanted him to suffer even more than he had. And I'd lost my chance at revenge.

"That was when I decided that I would humiliate him as best I could. I opened the partition that separates my husband's bedchamber from his study. I dragged him into the bedchamber."

This at least explained how Makino had gotten there, Sano thought, if not everything.

"I took off his clothes and rolled him over on his stomach. Then I fetched a jade phallus from a collection he had. I rammed the phallus into his rear end. I wanted him to look as if he'd died while playing one of his games. I wanted all the people who curried his favor to see what a disgusting fool he was. And I wanted Okitsu blamed for his death. That would be my revenge on her, for stealing my husband. I fetched her torn sleeve. It stank of sex and her incense perfume. I laid it beside him."

She smiled fleetingly at her cleverness. "But I worried that someone might guess that an intruder had killed him. I hurried back to the study and closed the window, but the latch was broken. I couldn't fix it."

And she hadn't noticed the trampled bushes outside, Sano deduced.

"Then I thought I heard someone coming. I didn't want to be caught. So I blew out my lamp. I carried the wooden pole through my husband's room to my own. I waited until the house was quiet, then went outside and threw the pole into the water." Agemaki gestured, indicating the pond beneath the chapel. "Then I went back to bed. I fell asleep at once. The next thing I knew, Tamura came into my room. He told me that my husband had died in the night. I pretended to be surprised. But when Tamura took me to him, I really was surprised."

A soft, incredulous laugh issued from Agemaki. "He was lying in his bed, dressed in a clean night robe, as peaceful as could be. I couldn't figure out what had happened to him."

Hirata said, "Tamura must have fixed him up."

Sano nodded. He could imagine Tamura duped into thinking Makino had died during a sex game and wanting to preserve his dignity. Tamura must have removed the phallus from Makino, then dressed him and put him to bed, breaking his bones in the process. He'd overlooked the torn sleeve and the signs that an intruder had broken into the study, and he'd been unable to hide Makino's injuries; yet if not for Makino's letter to Sano, the murder would have gone undetected. So would the rearranging of the crime scene.

"Then Koheiji came into the room," said Agemaki. "He said, 'When a man as important as Makino dies, people may suspect he was murdered. There may be questions asked. You and I need to get our answers ready.'

"I said, 'What are you talking about?' And he said—" Agemaki paused, obviously afraid to say what had happened next.

"You'd better tell us the whole story before Koheiji tells us his version," Sano warned her.

Agemaki inhaled a deep breath for courage. "Koheiji reminded me about a banquet held in this house a month ago. I'd given him wine to serve to my husband. He said he'd seen me pour some powder into the cup, and he'd guessed that I'd poisoned the wine. He knew I wanted him to serve it to my husband, and he would die, and Koheiji would be blamed. Well, my husband didn't die then. I'd always wondered why not. Koheiji said he'd given the wine to a servant and told him to throw it away. But instead, the servant drank it. He became very ill the next day. He almost died."

This was her guilty secret, Sano understood. She'd tried to kill her husband long before his murder.

"Koheiji said, 'If I were to tell what you did, you could get in a lot of trouble. People would think you'd succeeded in killing your husband this time,'" Agemaki said. "I asked him, 'What do you want?' He said, 'You know that Okitsu and I entertained Makino last night. You must have heard us. I could get blamed for his death just on account of being near him. I want you to promise that you won't tell anyone. In exchange, I won't tell anyone you tried to poison Makino.'"

"And you agreed," Sano said, remembering what Reiko had overheard.

"What choice did I have except to protect Koheiji so that he would protect me?" Agemaki's voice was plaintive with self-justification. "That's why I lied to you. It wasn't because I'd done any harm to my husband. I desecrated his body, but he was already dead when I found him."

In her eagerness to persuade, she leaned toward Sano. Her features sharpened with the cunning that had raised her from her humble station as a shrine prostitute to the rank of wife to a high *bakufu* official. "Koheiji assassinated my husband. You said so yourself. He's the murderer, not I. That's why he was so anxious to keep me silent. If he had an accomplice, it was that little whore Okitsu. She was with him and Makino that night."

Agemaki's eyes gleamed with malevolent pleasure at the chance to incriminate her rival. "She must have helped Koheiji kill my husband. She should be punished along with him."

"Arrest the actor first," Ibe told Sano. "The girl can wait her turn."

Sano envisioned the murder case as an onion whose layers he'd peeled only to find more layers concealing the solution at the heart. What Agemaki had told him, and the evidence that Daiemon had hired the actor to assassinate Senior Elder Makino, wasn't the whole story.

"The girl has information I need," Sano said, then addressed his detectives: "Bring in Okitsu."

32

Reiko found Gosechi in a minor, seldom-used sanctuary inside the main hall of Zōjō Temple.

Lord Matsudaira's concubine knelt alone before the altar, a roofed enclosure with carved gold columns. Her bronze silk cloak and long, lustrous black hair gleamed in the light from the candles burning in front of the gold Buddha statue. She was small and slender. With her back to the door and her head bowed, she seemed isolated in private thought, oblivious to the chanting of other worshippers in the main sanctuary or gongs pealing outside. Reiko quietly approached her, through shadowy dimness saturated with the odors of incense and burnt wax.

"Gosechi-*san*?" Reiko said.

The woman turned. Reiko saw that she was very young and stunningly beautiful. Her face was wide at the brow and tapered at the chin, blessed with petal-soft skin and dainty features. Reiko could understand how she'd attracted both Lord Matsudaira and his nephew. Her eyes, as open and innocent as a child's, brimmed with grief, and confusion because a stranger had addressed her.

Reiko introduced herself, then said, "I'm the wife of the shogun's *sōsakan-sama*." She knelt beside Gosechi. "I'm sorry to bother you, but there are urgent matters that I must discuss with you."

Wiping tears on her sleeve, the girl murmured, "Perhaps some other time . . . if you would be so kind." Her voice was raw from weeping. "Please don't take offense, but I'm very upset right now."

"I understand," Reiko said with pity. "You're mourning for Daiemon." She hated that she must disturb Gosechi after she'd just suffered what appeared a devastating loss.

The alarm in Gosechi's eyes confirmed that she'd had an illicit affair with Daiemon and still feared the consequences should Lord Matsudaira find out. "No—I mean, yes, I'm sad because he died. He was my lord's nephew."

"He was more than that to you, wasn't he?" Reiko said gently. "You and he were lovers."

Gosechi shook her head in vigorous denial, but her face crumpled. She wept into her hands while her body convulsed in paroxysms of grief. "I loved him more than anything else in the world," she said between sobs and gasps. Reiko sensed relief in her, as though she found solace in speaking at last to someone who knew her secret. "I can't bear that he's gone!"

Reiko put her arm around Gosechi while she continued weeping. After a long while, Gosechi grew calmer. She said in a soft, desolate voice, "I knew I was wrong to love Daiemon. I should have been faithful to Lord Matsudaira. I owe him so much. My parents couldn't afford to support me. They sold me to a broker who supplies women to the pleasure quarter. If Lord Matsudaira hadn't bought me, I would have become a prostitute. He's kind and generous to me. He loves me. He deserves my loyalty."

Lord Matsudaira was also thirty years older than Gosechi and probably more like a father than a lover to her, Reiko thought.

"But Daiemon was so handsome, and so charming," Gosechi said. "I fell in love with him the first time we saw each other. And he was smitten with me, too. We couldn't help ourselves." Her face briefly shone with the memory, then saddened again. "We used to meet in secret. If Lord Matsudaira had known, he would have killed me. He would have expelled Daiemon from the clan. But every moment we spent together was worth the danger."

Fresh tears flowed down Gosechi's cheeks. "But now that Daiemon is gone, I feel so alone, so lost. I feel so guilty because I deceived Lord Matsudaira. I'll never be happy again until my death reunites me with Daiemon. That I must hide my love for him makes the pain of missing him even worse."

Reiko hated to exploit a suffering, vulnerable woman, but she was bound by love, honor, and duty to help Sano solve the crime. She said, "There's a way that you can make amends to Lord Matsudaira for deceiving him and honor your love for Daiemon."

"Oh? What is it?" Gosechi looked puzzled but hopeful.

"Help me find out who killed him," Reiko said. "Help my husband deliver his killer to justice."

Gosechi nodded, brightening as a new sense of purpose distracted her from her pain. "But how can I?"

"You can answer some questions," Reiko said. "Did you and Daiemon meet at the Sign of Bedazzlement?"

Gosechi's face crumpled again at the mention of the place where her lover had been murdered. "Yes. Sometimes."

"Did you meet him there the night he died?"

The girl shook her head. "We had no plans to see each other then. I was at home with Lord Matsudaira."

"Then why would Daiemon have gone to the Sign of Bedazzlement?"

"The only reason I can think of is that—" A sob wracked Gosechi.

"He was meeting another woman?" Reiko said.

Gosechi fixed her desolate gaze on the altar. The tears sliding down her cheeks glistened in the candlelight. "I didn't want to believe that Daiemon was unfaithful to me. I couldn't believe he'd found someone else. But recently . . ." She sighed. "We didn't see each other as often. He said he was busy with politics, but I couldn't help being suspicious."

"Have you any idea who the other woman is?" Reiko said hopefully.

"None," said Gosechi, "although I tried to find out." She

covered her face with her hands, then dropped them onto her lap. "I'm ashamed of what I did. It makes me look so jealous. I asked a bodyguard of mine to follow Daiemon if he should leave the estate that night. I told my bodyguard to spy on him and the woman, discover who she was, and tell me."

"Did the bodyguard obey your orders?" Reiko said as excitement burgeoned inside her.

"I don't know," Gosechi said. "After I learned that Daiemon was dead, I couldn't bear to ask who'd been with him on the last night of his life."

"Can we ask now?"

"I suppose we must." Gosechi rose lithely to her feet. "Come with me."

She led Reiko from the sanctuary. In the dim passage outside loitered a young samurai, who bowed to Gosechi, then stood as tall as his meager height allowed. He had a homely, good-natured, intelligent face that looked upon Gosechi with slavish devotion. Reiko understood at once why Gosechi had assigned him the task of spying on her lover. He was obviously in love with her and would do anything she wanted.

"Hachiro-*san,* this is Lady Reiko. I want you to tell us if you followed Daiemon as I asked you to do," Gosechi said.

The young man hesitated, his expression worried. "Yes— I followed him. But I'm afraid that what I saw will upset you."

"It's all right," she said with a sigh of resignation. "I must hear."

Hachiro nodded and began his tale. "Daiemon left the estate on horseback soon after the hour of the boar that night. He seemed in a big hurry. I had to ride fast to keep up with him, but I stayed far enough behind that he wouldn't notice me." Reiko envisioned one horseman shadowing another through the torchlit passages of Edo Castle. "He went into town," continued Hachiro. "He rode around and around, looking over his shoulder, as if he wanted to make sure nobody was watching him. Finally, he ended up at the Sign of Bedazzlement. I knew the place because . . ."

The bodyguard paused, blushing unhappily. Reiko deduced that he'd recognized the house of assignation because he'd escorted Gosechi there to her trysts with Daiemon.

"Daiemon left his horse in an alley, then went into the building," Hachiro said. "I was afraid to follow him in there because he might see me, so I watched from a teahouse across the street."

"Did you see him meet a woman?" Reiko asked.

"No," Hachiro said. "I had a drink and waited a few moments. Then I saw a samurai on horseback gallop down the street. He went by me so fast, I couldn't see him clearly. I thought he was Daiemon. I didn't know until the next morning that he'd never left the house alive. I thought maybe he'd decided not to stay, and he'd gone out a side door, gotten his horse, and was heading back to Edo Castle. I would have followed him, but just then a woman came out of the house."

Hachiro squinted, peering into space, as he must have done while observing the woman emerge. "She was wearing a dark cloak, and a dark shawl that covered her head and face. She hurried over to a palanquin that was standing down the street. She climbed inside, and the bearers carried her away. I had a hunch that she was the woman Daiemon had come to meet."

Reiko saw Gosechi close her eyes as if in pain: She must have been hoping desperately that her suspicions had misled her and there had been no other woman in Daiemon's life. But Reiko was hoping the woman would turn out to be a valuable witness.

"I wanted to find out who the woman was," Hachiro said, "so I got on my horse and rode after her."

"Where did she go?" Reiko said eagerly.

"To Edo Castle. The guards at the gate let her right in. I followed her to Chamberlain Yanagisawa's compound."

Reiko felt shock and amazement catch her breath. She'd connected the chamberlain with the murder! The woman seen leaving the Sign of Bedazzlement must have been sent by Yanagisawa to assassinate Daiemon. Probably she wasn't a woman at all but one of Yanagisawa's men dressed in female garb. Yanagisawa must have found out that Daiemon was having an affair with Gosechi and where they went to tryst. He must have seen a perfect opportunity to strike at the rival faction.

"How did you and Daiemon arrange your meetings?" Reiko asked Gosechi.

"Whenever I knew that Lord Matsudaira would be busy and he wouldn't want my company at night, I would send Hachiro to slip a piece of red paper under Daiemon's door," said Gosechi. The bodyguard hung his head, sheepish at his role as go-between. "I would travel that evening to the Sign of Bedazzlement. Daiemon would come to me."

Yanagisawa must have learned their habit, Reiko deduced. A spy he'd employed in the Matsudaira house must have given Daiemon the signal to meet Gosechi that evening. Unaware that she was spending the night with Lord Matsudaira, Daiemon must have gone to the Sign of Bedazzlement expecting amorous pleasure, only to find Yanagisawa's assassin lying in wait.

"Did you ever get another look at the woman?" Reiko said, although without much expectation that Hachiro had.

"Yes," Hachiro said. "When her palanquin went in Chamberlain Yanagisawa's compound, the guards were slow to shut the gate. I rode up and looked inside. There were torches lit in the courtyard. A little girl jumped out of the palanquin and ran off. A woman climbed out and followed her. That's all I saw because the gate closed then. But I heard the woman call, 'Kikuko, wait for me,' and the little girl call, 'Hurry up, Mama.'"

His words collided against a wall of disbelief and astonishment inside Reiko. Her heart began to thunder with excitement. As far as she knew, there was only one little girl named Kikuko who lived in Chamberlain Yanagisawa's compound. And there was only one woman whom Kikuko called "Mama."

It was Lady Yanagisawa who'd left the Sign of Bedazzlement soon after Daiemon had arrived.

"Merciful gods," Reiko said as she clutched the wall for support.

"What's wrong? Who is the woman?" Gosechi cried, her face avid with fearful curiosity. "I can see that you recognize her. I thought I didn't want to know, but now I must, so I can see her and understand why Daiemon wanted her instead of me. Please tell me who she is!"

"I can't tell you," Reiko said, for innate caution warned her to keep her discovery to herself at least until she'd decided what to do about it. Fortunately, neither Gosechi nor Hachiro had guessed Lady Yanagisawa's identity. Lady Yanagisawa seldom ventured into society, and few people knew that the chamberlain had a daughter because he was ashamed of her. "But I can assure you that this woman wasn't having an affair with Daiemon. She didn't go to the Sign of Bedazzlement to make love to him."

There could be no other explanation: Lady Yanagisawa had gone to assassinate Daiemon, on the chamberlain's orders. Lady Yanagisawa had no lover to meet in secret. She cared nothing for any man except her husband. And she would do anything to please him.

A chill of horror descended upon Reiko. Lady Yanagisawa was even more mad, desperate, and cunning than Reiko had ever suspected. Blackmailing Reiko was the least of the evils that Lady Yanagisawa had recently done. She'd stabbed Daiemon to death, thereby ridding her husband of a rival, weakening the Matsudaira faction, and clearing the way for the chamberlain's son to inherit the Tokugawa regime and become the next shogun.

Gosechi, Hachiro, and her surroundings faded from Reiko's perception as she marveled at what Lady Yanagisawa had done. The sound of gongs and chanting barely impinged on her consciousness. Yet even though revolted by Lady Yanagisawa's crime, Reiko realized that her own luck had turned. Exhilaration dazzled her, for Lady Yanagisawa had unwittingly rendered herself vulnerable to a counterattack.

"Thank you for your help," she told Gosechi and Hachiro. "Excuse me, but I must go."

She left them gazing after her in puzzlement and hurried out of the temple hall. Her palanquin and entourage waited amid the crowds in the precinct. As Reiko jumped into the palanquin, she ordered her bearers, "Take me to Edo Castle."

There she would have her final confrontation with Lady Yanagisawa.

33

At Senior Elder Makino's estate, Hirata led Okitsu into the chapel where Sano waited with Agemaki and his watchdogs. "I found her hiding in the coal storehouse," Hirata said.

Some two hours had passed since Sano had told his detectives to bring Okitsu to him for interrogation. They'd discovered that the concubine was missing, presumably because she'd heard that Sano had come back and she'd run for her life. Now, as Hirata propelled her toward him, Sano saw that her face and clothes were smudged black with coal dust. Her terrified gaze lit on Agemaki, who knelt where Sano had forced her to confess her actions the night of Senior Elder Makino's murder. Agemaki had calmed herself, but her poise looked brittle and thin, like ice near a fire. Okitsu ran to her and collapsed beside her.

"I'm so glad you're here," Okitsu whimpered, clutching Agemaki's arm. "You'll protect me, won't you?"

Agemaki pulled away from Okitsu. She brushed grime from Okitsu's hands off her sleeve. The concubine stared at her, then everyone else, in uncomprehending fright.

"Every time I've talked to you about Senior Elder Makino's murder, you've lied to me," Sano said. "Now is your last chance to tell the truth."

"But I—I did tell the truth," Okitsu said breathlessly. "I

was with Koheiji that night . . . we didn't see Makino." Her
forehead wrinkled and her eyes darted as she tried to remember everything she'd said. "I saw Daiemon in the
study."

"You lied," Agemaki said in a voice that dripped acid.
"You and Koheiji were playing games with my husband. I
heard you. I saw you. And I told them." She flung out her
hand, indicating Sano, Hirata, and the watchdogs.

Okitsu turned to Agemaki. Her expression displayed confusion, then hurt. "You told them? But how could you? I
thought you were my friend."

"I'm not." Agemaki snarled. "Only someone as stupid as
you are would think I could like a woman who stole my husband." While Okitsu shrank away, as though struck a wound-
ing blow, Agemaki said, "Well, your fun is over. These
people know that Koheiji was hired to assassinate Makino.
They think you helped. I can't wait to watch you lose your
head at the execution ground. I'll laugh while you die, you
dirty little whore!"

A mewl arose from Okitsu. "Please, please spare me,"
she begged Sano, throwing herself on hands and knees in
front of him. "Koheiji and I didn't kill Makino. We're innocent. You must believe me!"

"If you expect me to believe you, then you have a lot of
explaining to do," Sano said. "Begin with the sex show that
you and Koheiji performed for your master."

Okitsu scuttled away on all fours. "I can't!" she cried. "I
promised Koheiji I wouldn't tell."

"That you lie to the shogun's detective for Koheiji shows
what a fool you are," Agemaki said with withering disdain.
"He doesn't love you. He'll never marry you. He's just leading you on so you'll protect him."

"You're wrong! He does love me! We are getting married!"
Okitsu reared back on her heels as she shouted at Agemaki.

"I caught him making love to a woman in his dressing
room at the theater," Hirata said.

"No! He didn't! He wouldn't!" But the quaver in Okitsu's
voice belied her defiant words.

"Koheiji is due to take the punishment for Senior Elder Makino's murder," Sano said. "Unless you want to share it with him, you'd better start talking."

For a moment Okitsu sat silent, her face bunched into a pout. Then she wilted under the knowledge that her friends had betrayed her and she was on her own. She uttered a querulous sob.

"You and Koheiji performed for Makino that night . . ." Sano prompted.

Okitsu nodded. "We did our usual routine," she said in a weary, toneless mumble. "I gave Makino some cornus berry tea." This was a potent aphrodisiac. "Then he watched Koheiji and me while we undressed and started making love. Pretty soon he joined in with us."

Sano imagined Makino eagerly sipping the aphrodisiac, watching the amorous couple, then the grotesque entwining of sleek young bodies and the wrinkled, emaciated one.

"But Makino couldn't get excited," Okitsu said. "No matter what we did, he stayed limp as a dead worm. Koheiji even tried playing rough. He tore my clothes off me and tied my wrists and pretended to hit me. That usually got Makino going, but this time it didn't. He asked for more cornus berry tea. I gave it to him. We started the game again. I sucked on Makino while Koheiji took me from behind."

She spoke without shame, as if discussing the weather. Sano recognized the scene Agemaki had told him she'd witnessed while spying on the trio.

"Pretty soon, Makino was as hard as iron," Okitsu continued. "He said he was ready. Koheiji lay down on the bed. I got on top of him and took him into me. Makino stuck himself in my backside." Okitsu leaned forward, knees apart, balancing on her hands, and unconsciously pantomimed the mating. "Makino went wild. He was moaning and ramming me so hard and fast that it hurt. All of a sudden, he made a sound like he was choking. Then he fell on top of me." Okitsu dropped flat on the floor, her voice and expression conveying the surprise she must have felt when crushed between her two partners. "Koheiji said, 'What happened?' We pushed Makino off us. He flopped onto the bed. We sat up and looked at him."

Okitsu suited action to words. Sano pictured Koheiji beside her, both of them gazing in puzzlement upon their inert master. "He didn't move," Okitsu said. "There was spit oozing out of his mouth. His eyes were open, but they had a sort of empty look. Koheiji called his name, but he didn't answer. I shook him, but nothing happened. Koheiji said, 'He's dead.'"

Sano heard in her voice the echo of Koheiji's, replete with horror. Amazement filled Sano. If she was telling the truth—and he thought she was this time—then this death he'd been investigating wasn't a murder. Makino hadn't died by foul play, a victim of his enemies, as his letter had claimed. Nor had Daiemon hired Koheiji to kill him. Someone had planted the note in Daiemon's secret quarters and the story at the Floating Teahouse to make Daiemon appear responsible for Makino's death. And Sano could guess who. Chamberlain Yanagisawa, with all his spies, must have discovered the secret quarters. The scheme to incriminate his enemy fit his devious nature. He must have expected Sano to find the false evidence during the course of the investigation. Sano was certain that if he hadn't, Yanagisawa would have devised an alternate plan for bringing the note to light. But Yanagisawa couldn't have known that his false evidence would lead Sano to the truth.

"I thought Makino had died because he'd strained himself too hard," Okitsu said. "Koheiji said it was the extra cornus berry tea."

Or perhaps his death had resulted from a convulsion due to both aphrodisiac poisoning and strenuous sex, Sano conjectured.

"But we didn't kill him," Okitsu said, hysterical with her need to convince. "We didn't mean to hurt him. It was an accident!"

Relief showed on Otani's face, and chagrin on Ibe's. Hirata looked disappointed. Agemaki beheld Okitsu with loathing, obviously upset that her husband's death wasn't her rival's fault. Sano shook his head. That the investigation should turn out like this! He'd crossed Lord Matsudaira and Chamberlain Yanagisawa, and risked his wife and son's safety, all because Senior Elder Makino had succumbed to his own lust. Yet the investigation wasn't over. A gap in the story divided the moment of Makino's demise and the instant when Agemaki had found his corpse in the study.

"What happened after you discovered that Makino was dead?" Sano asked Okitsu.

"I told Koheiji that we should get help, we should tell someone," Okitsu said. "But Koheiji said, 'No! We can't!'" She grabbed her arm, as he must have done. "He said there was nothing anyone could do to save Makino. He said people might blame us for Makino dying. We could be put to death." Her eyes grew round with the fear Koheiji had instilled in her. "I said, 'What shall we do?' Koheiji said he had an idea. He told me to get dressed fast. The sleeve of my kimono had gotten torn off during our game, and he wiped himself on it before he put on his clothes."

Sano saw the actor carelessly tossing aside the sleeve, which would later turn up in Makino's bedding.

"Then he told me to help him dress Makino." Okitsu shivered and grimaced. "It was weird, like dressing a big doll. Afterward, we moved him to the study. You wouldn't think a skinny old man like him could be so heavy, but it took both of us to carry him. We laid him on the floor. Koheiji broke the window latch. He said that would look as if someone had sneaked into the house and killed Makino. Then he ran outside and trampled the bushes."

That explained who had planted the signs of an intruder and why, Sano noted.

"When he came back, he brought a wooden pole," Okitsu said. "He told me to mess up the room. While I was throwing papers and books around"—Okitsu winced—"Koheiji was hitting Makino with the pole, to make it look like he'd been beaten to death."

Sano wondered if, when Makino had written his letter, he had considered the possibility that his death would result from a natural or accidental cause rather than assassination. Probably he had. Makino had been an opportunist who must have viewed his own inevitable death as a final opportunity to exploit, a last chance to make trouble for the enemies he left behind. A murder investigation by Sano would have suited his purpose. He'd have relished the thought of his enemies harassed and persecuted as suspects, even if nobody was ever punished for his death because it turned out not to be a murder. He couldn't have known that his death would involve his sexual games and the suspects would include his two partners.

"Koheiji hit Makino's head. It bled all over the floor," Okitsu said.

Her words reminded Sano of what he'd learned while examining corpses with Dr. Ito at Edo Morgue. He also remembered the bruises they'd found on Makino's corpse. His idea of what had happened to Makino, which had changed time after time throughout his inquiries, suddenly shifted again.

"Koheiji put out the lanterns in Makino's chambers," Okitsu said. "He took me to his room. He said we should stay there until morning, and if anyone asked, we should say we'd been together the whole night and we hadn't been near Makino at all. I said, 'What if Agemaki heard us? She'll know we're lying.'"

Okitsu gave Agemaki a peevish look. Agemaki smirked. Okitsu said, "Koheiji told me not to worry about her because he could keep her quiet. So we did as he said. We pretended we didn't know how Makino died. Later, Koheiji told me to say I'd seen Daiemon in the study." She lifted her clasped hands, then let them plop apart on her lap. Disillusionment and tears clouded her charcoal-grimed face. "Things didn't work out the way we planned. But we didn't kill Makino." She addressed Sano in a timid, pleading voice: "I swear it's the truth."

Hirata, Ibe, and Otani nodded, accepting Okitsu's confession. But although Sano believed that she'd finally revealed all she knew—and she truly believed all she'd said—

Makino hadn't died the way Okitsu claimed. She and Koheiji weren't as innocent as she thought.

"Makino's death was nothing but an accident brought about by his own lust," Otani said with relief. "And Daiemon didn't conspire to assassinate him. Lord Matsudaira will be glad to know that he and his clan are no longer under suspicion."

"Because Makino wasn't murdered," Ibe said, disgruntled. "The investigation has proved that no one is guilty."

"I disagree," Sano said. "Makino didn't die when he collapsed during the game. He was alive until Koheiji hit him with the pole. The dead don't bleed." Nor do their bodies bruise when struck. "He must have had a fit and passed out while having sex. Koheiji's beating finished him off."

Okitsu gasped. "I didn't know," she wailed. "I thought he was already dead!"

Otani blew out his breath through pursed lips with an expression that said, What next? A smile glimmered around Agemaki's mouth. "So Koheiji did do it," she said triumphantly. "And Okitsu helped him cover up what happened. I told you she was an accomplice. I was right."

"Makino's death was murder after all," Ibe said in a tone of stunned comprehension.

"Accidental murder," Sano said. "Koheiji didn't realize Makino was still alive when he beat him. He didn't intend to kill Makino; he made a mistake. So did Okitsu."

"A mistake that cost Makino his life," Ibe said. "If Koheiji hadn't beaten Makino to a bloody pulp after he fainted, if this stupid girl had fetched a doctor instead of going along with that no-good actor, Makino might have survived."

"Okitsu is guilty of interfering with an official investigation at the very least," Hirata told Sano.

"And Koheiji is guilty of killing Makino whether he meant to or not," Ibe said. "He should pay for Makino's death and all the trouble it's caused."

"Someone has to," Otani added.

They were right, Sano knew. Although he hated to punish anyone for an honest error of judgment, the shogun would

expect retribution for Makino's death from everyone involved. Sano summoned four of his detectives. As he told
them to take Okitsu to jail, she wept. Agemaki watched with
delight.

"You're going, too," Sano told her. "You're just as guilty
of interfering with the investigation as she is. And you'll be
tried for the murder of Makino's first wife."

She fumed and Okitsu sobbed as the detectives led them
away. Sano experienced a massive relief because the end of
this difficult investigation was in sight. Soon the only task
left to him would be to solve the murder of Daiemon.

"Let's catch Koheiji's last performance at the theater," he
said to Hirata and the watchdogs.

        "I want to see Lady Yanagisawa," Reiko said to the
guards stationed outside the chamberlain's compound.

The guards opened the gate. Reiko marched in, followed
by four of Sano's detectives she'd brought. She hungered for
her clash with Lady Yanagisawa as a warrior headed into
combat hungers for blood. Attendants led her and her escorts
to a reception hall in the mansion. Here, on painted murals
along the walls, lightning bolts pierced clouds that floated
above the expanse of *tatami* floor. Reiko could hear gunfire,
war drums, and conch trumpets echoing from the distant battlefield. Soon Lady Yanagisawa hurried into the room.

"Welcome, Reiko-*san*," she said breathlessly.

Reiko stared at Lady Yanagisawa. The woman had under-
gone an astonishing transformation. She wore a satin kimono printed with orange and crimson flowers instead of
her customary drab garments. Its neckline and the white
under-robe dropped low around her shoulders, exposing
creamy white skin. A blood-red flush colored her cheeks and
lips. Her bearing was sinuous instead of rigid as usual. She
looked almost pretty, but she gave off an air of corruption
that repelled Reiko.

"Have you come to tell me your decision?" Her gruff
voice had acquired a strange, husky sweetness.

"Yes," Reiko said, wondering what in the world had happened to Lady Yanagisawa since the previous day.

Lady Yanagisawa's broad lips moved in a sensual smile. "May I assume that you will do as my husband wishes?"

"You may not," Reiko said.

For a moment Lady Yanagisawa looked disconcerted. Then cruelty radiated like poison from her. "You'll live to regret your defiance. If you'll excuse me, I have something to tell your husband." She moved toward the door.

Reiko stepped in front of Lady Yanagisawa. She said, "I, too, have something to tell my husband. He'll be very interested to hear that you were at the Sign of Bedazzlement the night Lord Matsudaira's nephew was murdered there."

Lady Yanagisawa's features jerked, as if someone had sneaked up behind her and startled her. She said, "I don't know what you're talking about."

"I know you do," Reiko said. "I have a witness who saw you coming out of the house shortly after Daiemon went in."

"It must have been someone else who looks like me." But Lady Yanagisawa's eyes shifted away from Reiko's, as if they were windows through which she feared Reiko might glimpse the dark places in her mind and her memory of the crime she'd committed.

"The witness followed your palanquin home," Reiko said. "He saw you in the courtyard with Kikuko."

Lady Yanagisawa's face acquired a look that Reiko had seen when she was cornered once before. The skin tightened around her eyes, narrowing them. She resembled a cat with its ears pricked back in alarm.

"You stabbed Daiemon because your husband told you to, didn't you?" Reiko said. Lady Yanagisawa wheeled in a circle, avoiding Reiko's scrutiny. Reiko shifted her own position, keeping them face to face. "There's no use denying it."

Suddenly Lady Yanagisawa flung up her head. "You think you're so clever." Sardonic amusement and naked malice shone in her eyes. "You must be congratulating yourself because you think you've found out something that you can use against me. What good fortune you always have!"

Quickening breaths hissed from her like steam; her cheeks flushed redder. She moved closer to Reiko. "But you're not the only clever, lucky one." A reckless daring swelled her countenance. "Would you like to know how I did it?"

34

A mob was gathered outside the Nakamura-za Theater when Sano arrived with Hirata, a squadron of detectives, the watchdogs, and their troops. People surged, yelling and shoving, toward the entrance, where police officers tried to hold them back. As a chorus of wild shouts issued from the building, more crowds hurried down the street, eager to join the excitement. Sano and his companions leaped off their horses and pushed their way through the mob toward the theater.

"What's going on in there?" Sano called to the police.

"Some crazy samurai jumped on the stage during the play," the officer said as he shoved at men trying to scramble through the door. "He's up there threatening one of the actors."

Sano had planned to walk into the theater, wait until the show ended, and make a peaceful arrest of Koheiji. Now his smile mocked his notion that anything about this investigation should turn out the way he'd expected. The mob pressed in on him. Nearby, Hirata and the detectives jostled boisterous spectators; the watchdogs and their men floundered at the edges of the crowd.

"Let us in," Sano told the police. "We'll restore order."

The police fought back the mob long enough for Sano and his companions to slip through the door. The theater was jammed with people. Sano couldn't see the stage because the audience was standing up on the dividers between the seating compartments, craning their necks, blocking his view. The cavernous room thundered with their shouts. The smells of liquor and sweat mingled with the acrid tobacco smoke that hazed the dim atmosphere. Sano tasted violence, intoxicating and contagious, in the air. He leaped onto the walkway, the only unimpeded path to the stage.

As Hirata and the other men hurried after him along the walkway, the audience waved at them and cheered their arrival. The noise clamored in Sano's ears. Faces distorted and ugly with bloodlust surrounded him. On the stage Sano saw two men facing each other. One held a sword raised high. The other cowered, his palms lifted. Nearing the stage, Sano recognized the cowering man as Koheiji. He wore samurai costume; wide trousers, two swords at his waist, surcoat, and flowing kimono. Shock and fright showed on his painted face. The other man, dressed in black, was Tamura. Surprise halted Sano at the rim of the stage.

"I've come to avenge the death of my master, the honorable Senior Elder Makino!" Tamura shouted. He pointed his sword at Koheiji. "You who murdered him shall pay with your blood!"

The spectators roared. Maybe they thought this was part of the play, but Sano knew Tamura was carrying out the vendetta he'd sworn on Makino's killer. Suddenly Sano recalled hearing someone outside the chapel of the Makino estate while he'd interrogated Agemaki. It must have been Tamura, eavesdropping.

Hirata exclaimed, "He overheard you saying that Daiemon hired Koheiji to assassinate his master!"

"You're insane," Koheiji told Tamura. "I didn't kill Makino." But his fear quaked under his scornful tone. "You've got the wrong man."

While the audience cheered, Tamura said, "No more lies!" Rage and determination hardened his stern, masklike face. His blade glinted in the sun that shone through the skylights. "Admit your guilt before you die, you coward!"

Although Sano understood the honor involved in a vendetta, and he hated interfering with a fellow samurai's duty to avenge his dead master, he couldn't let Tamura take the law into his own hands. The shogun had the first right to deliver Koheiji to justice if he wanted. Sano stepped onto the stage.

"Tamura-*san*," he called.

The noise from the audience subsided into an expectant hush. Tamura turned, glancing at Sano but keeping his attention focused on Koheiji. "*Sōsakan-sama*," he said, his manner amused as well as hostile. "Many thanks for discovering that this worthless gob of filth murdered my master. I suppose I owe you an apology for underestimating you. Now, if you'll stand back, I'll save you the trouble of arresting him."

He lunged and slashed his sword at Koheiji. The actor vaulted backward, narrowly escaping the blade. The onlookers cheered. Their hunger for thrills exceeded any concern that their favorite's life was in peril.

"I'm not the murderer." His desperation obvious, Koheiji said, "Ask Okitsu. She'll tell you."

"She has," Sano said. "She told me the whole story."

"Louder!" came shouts from the audience. "We can't hear you! Speak up!"

Sano glanced over his shoulder and saw hundreds of avid faces looking at him: He'd become part of the drama. "You did kill Makino," he said to Koheiji, then addressed Tamura: "But he's not a murderer."

Both men stared at him. Tamura halted on the verge of another attack. Disbelief and confusion showed on both their faces.

"Tamura-*san*, you listened to only part of the story," Sano said. "You overheard me tell Agemaki that Koheiji had been hired to assassinate your master. If you hadn't rushed off so fast, you'd have heard there was no assassination plot, and Makino's murder was an accident."

"What?" Tamura exclaimed. The audience quieted, eager to hear the conversation.

"Makino collapsed during a sex game," Sano said.

Koheiji exhaled a puff of relief that the truth had come out. "That's right," he said. "Makino dropped dead on Okitsu and me while we were giving him a little fun."

"Quiet!" Bent on pursuing retribution, Tamura slashed his sword at Koheiji.

The audience gasped a collective breath. Koheiji drew his weapon and parried strikes; the audience cheered him on. But his sword was a mere theater prop. Tamura's sword hacked off its wooden blade. Koheiji stared in dismay at the useless stub that fell from his hand.

"I don't believe you," Tamura said angrily to Sano. "You're just trying to trick me out of my vengeance."

"This is no trick," Sano said. "The assassination plot was a fraud."

Tamura glowered and raised his sword at Koheiji, who cried in desperation, "Get him out of here, will you please?"

Sano gestured for Hirata and the detectives to surround Tamura. As they moved in on him, Tamura ordered, "Get out of my way. Let me at him." But indecision flickered in his eyes. Sano had shaken his certainty that Koheiji had murdered his master.

A gang of samurai jumped onto the walkway. Clad in tattered clothes, they appeared to be *rōnin.* Sano saw that they wanted to join the action, and they were too excited—or too drunk—to worry about the consequences of interfering with *bakufu* business. Ibe's and Otani's men held them back from rushing onstage. Their leader, a brute with an unshaved face and a red head kerchief, yelled, "Fight! Fight!"

The audience took up the chant. The rhythm, accompanied by stamping feet and clapping hands, rocked the theater.

"Makino drank too much aphrodisiac and overexerted himself," Sano said. "He's as responsible for his death as anyone else is."

Tamura stood paralyzed. His face reflected shock, then disgust, then acceptance that lustful habits, not murder, had been his master's undoing.

"Now that you know I'm innocent, can you all just go?" Koheiji whined. "Can I please finish the play?"

"Fight! Fight!" chanted the audience. The brute in the red head kerchief wrestled with Otani's and Ibe's troops as they tried to force him and his gang off the walkway.

"I'm afraid not," Sano told Koheiji. "You see, Makino wasn't quite dead when he collapsed. You shouldn't have tried to make his death look like murder by an intruder. The beating you gave him is what really killed him."

Koheiji stared in open-mouthed, silent horror. Sano could almost see his face turn pale under its makeup. "Merciful gods," he whispered. "I had no idea . . ." He shook his head, ruing his mistake. Sano watched him realize that someone must shed blood for Makino's death, and he was that someone. He staggered under the knowledge that he'd come to the end of living by his impulses and wits, and this was one scrape from which they couldn't save him.

"Then Makino's death was a stupid blunder by this fool," Tamura said. "It's not worth avenging. And a fool isn't worth bloodying my sword." Crestfallen, he lowered his weapon. But Sano discerned that he was relieved—he lacked the heart to enjoy killing. Now he sheathed the weapon. "I renounce my vendetta," he said and jumped off the stage.

The audience and the gang of *rōnin* booed, furious to be cheated out of the carnage they wanted to see. Police moved through the theater, forcing the mob to clear the seats. Sano nodded to Detectives Marume and Fukida. They moved to Koheiji and grabbed his arms. He didn't resist; he appeared too shattered by his misfortune.

"You're under arrest," Sano said.

"My husband had discovered that Lord Matsudaira's nephew and concubine were having a love affair," Lady Yanagisawa told Reiko. "He'd learned about the signal that Lady Gosechi used to arrange secret meetings with Daiemon. He lured Daiemon to the Sign of Bedazzlement and sent me there to assassinate him."

Lady Yanagisawa seemed unfazed that the detectives, as well as Reiko, were listening to her incriminate herself.

Shocked by her admission even though already aware of what Lady Yanagisawa had done, Reiko said, "Weren't you afraid? How could you do it?" A reason occurred to her. "What did the chamberlain offer you in return?"

"His love," Lady Yanagisawa said.

Her mouth curved in a secretive smile; she sighed with pleasure. Reiko saw her suspicion confirmed. The chamberlain had taken advantage of his wife's passion for him and promised to make the crime worth her while. After she'd rid him of his enemy, he'd rewarded her by bedding her as she had longed for him to do.

"I disguised myself as Gosechi. I wore my hair down," Lady Yanagisawa said, stroking the black tresses that flowed down her bosom. "I put on the kind of bright, pretty clothes that Gosechi wears." She touched her orange kimono. "I covered my head with a shawl. I carried a dagger that my husband gave me." Her fingers curled around the hilt of an imaginary weapon.

"Why did you take Kikuko with you?" Reiko said.

Guilt shadowed Lady Yanagisawa's features. Even if she didn't care that she'd killed a man, she felt she'd done wrong by bringing her daughter on such an errand. "Kikuko has been difficult lately. When I tried to leave the house, she screamed and clung to me. She wouldn't let me go. I had no choice but to take her along."

Lady Yanagisawa shook her shoulders, casting off blame for her lapse of maternal responsibility. "We rode in the palanquin to the Sign of Bedazzlement. When we arrived, I told the bearers to wait for me down the street. I told Kikuko that she must stay inside the palanquin and be very quiet. She thought it was a game. I left her and hurried into the Sign of Bedazzlement." Lady Yanagisawa drifted across the room as if in a trance, following the path along which the chamberlain had sent her that night. "There were other people in the house—I could hear them in the rooms. But the doors were shut. The corridor was empty. No one saw me."

Reiko pictured Lady Yanagisawa's furtive figure sneaking through the house of assignation, the dagger clutched hidden under her sleeve. Her eyes must have glittered with the same determination as they did now.

"I went to the room where my husband had told me that Daiemon and Gosechi met," Lady Yanagisawa said, drifting to a stop in a corner. Lightning bolts painted on the mural converged toward her head. The detectives watched, impassive. "I covered the lantern with a cloth to make the room dim. I took off my cloak but kept my shawl over my head. Then I sat on the bed and waited for Daiemon. I began to worry that something would go wrong." A spate of trembling disturbed her composure. "I almost got up and ran out of the house."

The image of her huddling in her shawl, beset by last-moment anxiety, the knife shaking in her hands, filled Reiko's mind.

"But I'd promised my husband. And it was too late to turn back. He was coming down the passage." Lady Yanagisawa whipped her head around. Reiko could almost hear Daiemon's footsteps echoing in Lady Yanagisawa's memory. "He entered the room. He said, 'Here I am.' He sounded happy because he thought I was Gosechi. I didn't answer. I was praying for courage and strength."

Fear coalesced in her eyes; she mouthed silent words. "He knelt beside me on the bed and said, 'Why are you so quiet? Aren't you glad to see me?' I turned toward him, willing myself to do what I must. He lifted the shawl off my head before I could stop him." In Lady Yanagisawa's eyes seemed to float a reflection of Daiemon, surprised to find a stranger in place of his beloved. "He said, 'Who are you? What are you doing here?'

"I drove the dagger into him." Lady Yanagisawa held her fists one behind and touching the other; she thrust them violently forward. A crazed, inhuman expression distorted her face. "Daiemon opened his mouth to speak, but no sound came out. The dagger was stuck in his chest. I saw that he realized he'd been tricked. He was furious. But then his eyes went blank. He fell against me. He was dead."

This was more satisfactory a confession than Reiko had expected to get.

Lady Yanagisawa recoiled as if from the corpse dropping on her. "I pushed him away and stood up. His blood was all over me." Her throat contracted as she swallowed her rising gorge. She rubbed her hands against each other and down her robes, as if feeling the warm, slick wetness of Daiemon's blood. "I covered it with my cloak and shawl. Then I ran out through the secret passage to my palanquin. I climbed in with Kikuko. We rode away."

Soon thereafter, the chamberlain's men—who'd have followed Lady Yanagisawa—must have tipped off the police that Daiemon was dead.

"I started shaking. I couldn't stop." A visible tremor rippled through Lady Yanagisawa. "I vomited until there was nothing left to come up."

Perhaps she did feel some guilt, Reiko thought.

"My sickness frightened Kikuko," said Lady Yanagisawa. "She cried and hugged me and said, 'Mama, what's wrong?' I said I would be all right soon, and she mustn't worry. I told her that someday I would explain to her what I'd done. Someday she would understand that I'd done it for her as well as myself, so that her father would love us both. I promised her that everything would be wonderful from now on."

"That's a promise you won't get to keep," Reiko said with a twinge of vindictive joy. Soon Lady Yanagisawa would reap her punishment for all her evils. "You killed Daiemon. You'll pay for his death with your life."

And when Sano learned of her treacherous crime, he would think the worst of Lady Yanagisawa. He would never trust anything she said about Reiko and the Dragon King.

Lady Yanagisawa smiled. Her happiness at winning her husband's favor apparently outweighed both her guilt and her fear of repercussions. "But you can't prove I killed him. If you publicly accuse me, I'll deny my confession. I'll claim that you forced me to say what you wanted me to say. My good character has never been questioned before. No one will believe that I am a murderer."

Her confidence seemed invincible, but Reiko said, "We'll see about that." She turned to the detectives: "Arrest her."

The detectives moved toward Lady Yanagisawa. Dissonant laughter emanated from her. "Don't bother," she said. "My husband will set me free. He won't allow me to be punished for killing Daiemon."

"Your husband won't lift a finger to save you," Reiko said. "He'd rather let you take the blame for the murder than continue living under suspicion himself. When you're accused, he'll say that you acted on your own, and he had nothing to do with Daiemon's murder. He'll sacrifice you to protect his own position."

"No. He would never do that." Although Lady Yanagisawa emphatically shook her head, sudden fear glinted in her eyes. "He loves me. He said so."

"You're a fool to believe him," Reiko said. "During all these years, he's neglected you and cared nothing for you. Now, all of a sudden, he loves you?" Reiko raised her voice to a scornful, incredulous pitch. "Doesn't that strike you as odd?"

"People change," Lady Yanagisawa said, her manner adamant yet uncertain. The color drained from her cheeks. "He's just realized how much he cares about me."

"He realized how useful you could be," Reiko said. "His enemies are on the attack, he needs all the help he can get, and he knew you'd do anything for him. So he manipulated you into doing his dirty work. What you think is his love for you is nothing but an act. And you fell for it."

"It's not an act," Lady Yanagisawa whispered. A sob broke her voice. "He meant what he said. If you'd heard him—if you'd seen him making love to me—you would know."

"You should know that sex isn't the same thing as affection." Reiko pitied as well as disdained Lady Yanagisawa's naïveté. "Your husband took his pleasure while assuring that you were his devoted slave."

Tears of angry hatred glittered in Lady Yanagisawa's

eyes. "That's not true. You're just jealous because my husband is superior to yours. You hate for anyone to have more than you do."

"Speak for yourself," Reiko said. "Your husband won't even miss you when you're gone. And what will become of Kikuko after you're dead? Who will take care of her? Her father will neglect her just as always. She'll die of grief and loneliness for you."

Lady Yanagisawa stared, clearly appalled by this grim depiction of Kikuko's future.

"But maybe you don't mind sacrificing yourself for love of your husband," Reiko said. "Maybe you don't mind that he'll climb to power over the corpse of your beloved child."

Horror welled in Lady Yanagisawa's eyes. Her lips moved in silent, inarticulate protests as her illusions shattered. Reiko watched her absorb the dreadful fact that she'd been duped and the chamberlain couldn't care less if she and Kikuko paid the price for his triumph. She uttered a broken-hearted moan.

"Don't let him get away with it," Reiko said. "He doesn't deserve your loyalty or love. Come with us." Standing amid the detectives, Reiko beckoned Lady Yanagisawa. "Tell the world how you were tricked into assassinating Daiemon. Let the chamberlain take his rightful punishment. Then maybe you'll be allowed to live, and Kikuko won't lose her mother."

Lady Yanagisawa breathed in painful, accelerating wheezes, then began to shake her head and stamp her feet. She wailed and tore at her hair. Her eyes rolled, wildly seeking some remedy for her anguish or target for her wrath. They lit on Reiko.

"This is all your fault." Her voice emerged in a growl from between gnashing teeth. "You always have to get your own way, and you don't care whom you hurt." She glared at Reiko through the tangle of her hair. Hatred ignited in her eyes. "You always win. But not this time."

With an ear-splitting screech, she flew at Reiko, her hands outstretched and curled into claws. Reiko leaped away, and the detectives moved to stop Lady Yanagisawa, but she was too fast. She grabbed Reiko's neck. Her momentum knocked them both to the floor. As they crashed together, Reiko screamed. Lady Yanagisawa squeezed her throat. Reiko tried to pry away Lady Yanagisawa's hands, but they seemed made of iron. Reiko coughed, gasping for breath. Lady Yanagisawa's face, twisted with rage and madness, loomed above hers. Continuous shrieks and yowls burst from Lady Yanagisawa. Hot, acrid breath flamed Reiko's face. She heard the detectives shouting as they fought to pull the woman off her. They raised Lady Yanagisawa, but she held tight. Reiko felt herself lifted up from the floor by Lady Yanagisawa. She kicked Lady Yanagisawa and clawed her wrists, all the while choking and gagging. Panic surged through Reiko. Dark blotches spread across her vision. The thunderous pounding of her heartbeat drowned out all other sounds.

Suddenly Lady Yanagisawa's hold broke. Reiko collapsed onto the floor, gulping air, moaning with relief; she clutched her sore, bruised throat. As her vision cleared, she saw the detectives holding Lady Yanagisawa, who screamed curses as she thrashed in their grip. But the pounding in Reiko's ears continued, and she realized that her heart wasn't the cause.

"What's that sound?" she said.

The detectives listened. Lady Yanagisawa fell silent; she ceased to struggle. The pounding stopped. Running footsteps outside signaled a horde entering the estate. Men's voices arose in furious shouts amid the clash of steel blades. The noise resounded through the mansion. Into the reception room marched a brigade of samurai troops clad in armor, brandishing swords. Reiko staggered to her feet. She saw the Matsudaira clan crest on the troops' armor, and astonished comprehension filled her.

The Matsudaira faction had invaded Chamberlain Yanagisawa's domain. The pounding she'd heard was a battering ram, breaking down the gates.

The invaders faced off against the detectives. Their hostile stares took in Reiko and Lady Yanagisawa. The leader of the Matsudaira troops demanded, "Who are you?"

A detective explained that he and his comrades were the *sōsakan-sama*'s retainers. He identified the women, then said, "What's going on?"

"Chamberlain Yanagisawa's army has retreated from the battle," the leader said. "Most of his allies have defected to our side. And Lord Matsudaira has convinced the shogun to throw the chamberlain out of the court. We're here to capture him."

A wail of horror arose from Lady Yanagisawa. Reiko could hardly believe that the corrupt, wily chamberlain had finally fallen from power. But now she heard blades ringing, loud crashes, and screams of agony as his guards tried in vain to defend him and his territory against the invaders. Down the corridor, past the reception room's doorway, filed Matsudaira troops, leading Yanagisawa's officials. Then came the chamberlain himself. Two of his rival's soldiers held his arms. His posture was proud, his expression fierce; he gazed straight ahead. Behind him stumbled Kikuko, escorted by another soldier. She saw Lady Yanagisawa and cried, "Mama, Mama!"

"No!" shrieked Lady Yanagisawa.

She broke away from Sano's detectives. Weeping, she flung herself toward her child and husband as they disappeared from view. The leader of the Matsudaira troops seized her. He said, "We have orders to take the chamberlain's whole family. Come along quietly now."

Dazed by too many emotions to comprehend, Reiko watched her enemy borne away from her.

The detectives led a meek Koheiji offstage beyond the backdrop. The curtain fell. Outside it, the audience booed louder while exiting the theater. Hirata, walking alongside Sano as they followed the captive actor, experienced a tremendous letdown.

The investigation was over. The man he'd dismissed as a

trivial nobody had killed Senior Elder Makino. And Hirata had done nothing to win back Sano's trust, prove himself a worthy samurai, or salvage his reputation. Playing by the rules hadn't helped. The best clue he'd discovered— Daiemon's secret quarters—wasn't enough. Nothing that had happened had required heroics from Hirata. He must wait for an opportunity to redeem himself that might never come. If only he could have one more chance, now, at restoring his honor!

Suddenly, loud yells and scuffling erupted nearby on the other side of the curtain. The gang of *rōnin* burst through the curtain, waving their swords, chased by Ibe, Otani, and their troops. Hirata barely had time to realize that the *rōnin* meant to have their fight, the consequences be damned, when the leader with the red kerchief came charging toward Sano. Bellowing with maniacal abandon, the *rōnin* raised his sword in both fists.

"Look out!" Hirata yelled.

At the same moment, Sano turned and his eyes perceived the attack impending. His hand flew to his sword. But Hirata drew his own sword first. He leaped in front of Sano. In the instant that the *rōnin* arrived within striking distance of them, Hirata slashed him across the belly.

The *rōnin* roared. He faltered to a stop. Pain and madness blazed in his eyes. He began to crumble, the sword still raised in his hands. With his last strength he swung the blade violently downward as he died.

It happened in a flash. Hirata had no time to dodge. The blade sliced down his left hipbone, then deep into his thigh. He cried out as agony shot through muscles, veins, and sinew. Letting go his sword, he toppled hard onto the stage. Throbbing spasms of pain wrenched his features into a grimace.

He heard Sano exclaim in horror and alarm, "Hirata-san!" He glimpsed the *rōnin* lying dead nearby and the detectives and the watchdogs' troops fighting the gang. They all dissolved into a blur as he saw the blood spurting from his thigh, out of the tear in his clothes, and spreading around him. Hirata's pulse raced; gasps heaved his lungs as dizziness weakened him. Terror pierced the depths of his spirit. Many times he'd fought and been injured; always, he'd survived. But he recognized that this wound was different.

Now Hirata saw Sano, his face aghast, bending over him. Sano was alive, unhurt. He seized Hirata's hand in his strong, warm grasp. He shouted, "Fetch a doctor!"

Even as Hirata moaned in pain and horror of impending death, triumph dazzled him. He'd taken the fatal sword cut meant for Sano. He'd performed his heroic act and achieved the ultimate glory of sacrificing himself for Sano.

"You're going to be all right," Sano said urgently, as if willing himself as well as Hirata to believe it. Hirata felt someone binding his thigh, stanching the flow of blood. "Just hold on."

"Master," Hirata said. His cracked, barely coherent whisper conveyed all the respect, obligation, and love he felt toward Sano. Pain and lethargy prevented him from speaking more. Sano's image grew dark, indistinct.

"You've proved yourself an honorable samurai," Sano said in a voice raw with emotion. It seemed to echo across a vast distance. "For saving my life, you have my eternal gratitude. The disgrace you brought upon yourself is gone. I'll never doubt your loyalty again."

Hirata reveled in the words. As he felt himself raised up from the hole into which his disgrace had sunken him, he was dimly aware of his physical and spiritual energy fading. Any effort to save him seemed futile. He thought of his wife Midori, who would grieve for him, and his daughter Taeko, who must grow up without him. Sadness pierced Hirata. He thought of Koheiji and felt brief amusement that the actor had turned out to be an agent of his fate. He remembered his hunch that Tamura would figure into the solution of the mystery. Instinct had proved correct one last time.

And now Hirata heard a rushing sound, like a tidal wave coming to carry him into the black emptiness obliterating his vision. He sensed legions of samurai ancestors awaiting him in a world on the other side of death. Sano's hand holding his was all that tethered Hirata to life.

35

The passage of three days brought milder weather, rains that engulfed Edo, and tentative peace to the city.

Legions of mounted troops and foot soldiers marched along the highways, heading beyond hills cloaked in mist, back to the provinces from whence they'd come to fight the war between Lord Matsudaira and Chamberlain Yanagisawa. Under the murky, clouded sky, the battlefield lay abandoned, strewn with trampled banners, fallen weapons, and spent arrows. The rain gradually washed away the blood where men had died.

In the official quarter within Edo Castle, the estates no longer sported the crests of the rival factions. But troops patrolled the streets in case trouble should break out again. Officials scurried furtively between the mansions. Behind closed doors there and in the palace, the Tokugawa regime had begun the delicate, volatile process of reorganizing itself in the wake of major changes within the political hierarchy.

Far from the castle, Lord Matsudaira's soldiers escorted Chamberlain Yanagisawa down a pier raised on pilings above the rain-stippled gray water of the Sumida River. Ahead of him, at the far end of the pier, stood Police Commissioner Hoshina. Beyond Hoshina loomed a ship with an enclosed cabin and protruding oars. Its mast supported a square sail that bore the Tokugawa crest. The crew waited silently aboard. Behind Yanagisawa toiled a handful of servants carrying baggage. Then came his wife and daughter, huddling together beneath an umbrella. Four of his sons and more troops trailed after them. On the riverbank, along docks that extended across the Tokugawa rice warehouses, a crowd stood gathered to watch the departure of the man who'd once commanded the shogun's power as his own.

Yanagisawa strode proudly; his face under his broad-brimmed wicker hat showed no emotion. But inside him, his spirit raged against his bitter fate.

Now he and his escorts reached Hoshina, who waited by the gangplank leading to the ship. Hoshina bowed to Yanagisawa with elaborate, mocking politeness.

"Farewell, Honorable Chamberlain," he said. "Have a pleasant journey. May you enjoy your exile. I hear that Hachijo Island is quite a charming place."

Humiliation, fury, and anguish howled like a storm through Yanagisawa. That his exalted political career should end with his banishment to a tiny speck of land in the middle of the ocean, and the scorn of his lover turned enemy!

"You probably thought you could finesse your way out of this," Hoshina said.

Indeed, Yanagisawa had cherished hopes that even though most of his allies had deserted him, and his army had dissolved, all wasn't lost. He'd felt certain that he could rely on the shogun's protection and he would soon mount another attack on Lord Matsudaira, defeat his rival, and reclaim his position.

"Too bad the shogun refused to see you after you were captured and imprisoned." Hoshina's smile expressed cruel delight that Yanagisawa had been thwarted. "Too bad that while you were busy trying to raise more troops for the battle, Lord Matsudaira convinced the shogun that you are responsible for every misfortune that's ever befallen the Tokugawa regime, and you should be eliminated."

Hence, the shogun had exiled Yanagisawa forever and allowed him to take only his wife, his daughter, his sons, and these few attendants as company during the long years until he died.

But now, as Yanagisawa mounted the gangplank, his hope of a return to Edo and eventual triumph burned like flames inside his heart. The shogun had spared his life, although Lord Matsudaira must have tried hard to coax their lord into executing him. Yanagisawa deduced that the shogun still bore him some affection and had honored their longtime liaison by banishing him instead. As long as Yanagisawa lived, he had another chance at victory. Already his mind nurtured new schemes.

He paused at the top of the gangplank, turned, and looked back toward Edo. Rain spattered his face as he gazed up at the castle. There, in the heart of the shogun's court, he'd left a remnant of himself, a door open for him to enter when the time was right.

"You haven't seen the last of me," Yanagisawa said, then stepped aboard the ship.

Inside Sano's estate, Reiko and Midori sat vigil in the chamber where Hirata lay unconscious in bed. His eyes were closed, his face pale and without expression. A quilt covered his motionless body and its terrible wound. Nearby, the Edo Castle chief physician mixed medicinal herbs for a poultice. A Shinto priest chanted spells and waved a sword to banish evil, and a sorceress jingled a tambourine to summon healing spirits. Reiko hugged Midori, whose tear-stained face was haggard with woe. Midori hadn't left Hirata's side since Sano had brought him home from the theater.

"He's going to be all right," Reiko said, trying to reassure Midori and herself even though Hirata's chances of survival were meager. Sano had told her that Hirata had lost much blood before a local doctor had arrived at the theater, sewn up his wound, and applied medicine to prevent shock and festering. "We must have faith."

"He's young and very strong," said Dr. Kitano, the Edo Castle chief physician. "That he's still alive after three days bodes well for his recovery."

A sob shuddered through Midori. "I love him so much," she wailed. "If he should die . . ."

"Don't dwell on the thought," Reiko said, tenderly wiping Midori's tears. "Be strong for the sake of your daughter."

But Midori wept harder at the thought of Taeko, whom she'd left in the care of a wet nurse. She couldn't bring Taeko into Hirata's room, for fear that the evil spirits might contaminate their baby. "Why did this have to happen?" she cried.

"It was fate," Reiko said, having no better answer. "We're all at its mercy." Then she saw Hirata stir and his eyes slowly open. "Look, Midori-*san*! He's awake!"

Midori exclaimed. She clasped Hirata's hand as he blinked up at her and Reiko. His blurred, empty gaze came into focus, as though his spirit had returned to his body after wandering in the netherworld between life and death.

"Midori-*san*," he said. "Reiko-*san*." His voice was hoarse and weak. Amazement dawned on his face. "I'm alive? That *rōnin* didn't kill me?"

"Yes, you're alive," Midori cried, weeping for joy now.

"And his wits are intact," Dr. Kitano said as he knelt beside Hirata. "That's a good sign." He felt the pulse points on Hirata's body. "His energy is stronger. I think he will make good progress."

While Midori sobbed and laughed, Hirata breathed a weary sigh and closed his eyes. "Let him sleep," Dr. Kitano said. "Rest will help cure him."

The physician went back to his potions. Midori and Reiko sat quietly beside Hirata. "Oh, Reiko-*san*, I forgot that your husband is still in danger," Midori said contritely. Now that Hirata's condition was improved, she could take an interest in other things. "What's to become of Sano-*san*, with all the changes since Lord Matsudaira defeated Chamberlain Yanagisawa?"

"I don't know," Reiko said.

The one definite good thing that had happened was the exile of Lady Yanagisawa as well as the chamberlain. Reiko regretted that the woman had escaped worse punishment for the crime of murdering Daiemon, but Reiko's marriage was safe for the time being. Perhaps, Reiko hoped, Lady Yanagisawa would never return to plague her again. But this blessing didn't compensate for the other repercussions that Lord Matsudaira's victory and Chamberlain Yanagisawa's downfall threatened for Sano.

"Lord Matsudaira has been meeting with the highest-ranking officials in the government," Reiko said in a low voice that the doctor, priest, and sorceress couldn't hear. "He's been deciding who will stay and serve under his new regime and who will go. He has said nothing to my husband yet."

Fear bit cold and hard within Reiko. "Rumors are flying, but nobody seems to know what will happen to us. Lord Matsudaira may not forgive my husband for refusing to bend to his wishes during the murder investigation. When his reorganization of the *bakufu* is done, my husband may no longer have a post."

"But the shogun will want Sano-*san* to stay, won't he?" Midori whispered anxiously. Reiko saw she'd realized that if Sano went, Hirata would also lose his station with the Tokugawa. He and Sano would both be *rōnin,* their families' home and livelihood gone, their honor destroyed after years of faithful service and much personal sacrifice. "Won't the shogun keep Sano-*san* and his detective corps no matter what Lord Matsudaira thinks?"

"The shogun has secluded himself in the palace for the past three days," Reiko said. "He's just summoned my husband to an audience with him and Lord Matsudaira. I suppose we'll soon find out whether we're safe—or ruined."

A cadence of doom reverberated through Sano as he walked up the length of the audience hall toward the dais on which the shogun sat. The shogun waited in impassive silence as he approached. Lord Matsudaira, kneeling in the position of honor to the shogun's right, regarded Sano with a stern expression. The four members of the Council of Elders gravely watched him from their two rows on the upper floor level below the dais. Guards standing around the room and secretaries seated at desks along the walls avoided his gaze. This cool reception convinced Sano that his tenure as the shogun's Most Honorable Investigator of Events, Situations, and People would end this very day.

As he knelt on the lower level of the floor and bowed to the assembly, he noticed the young man who knelt near the shogun's left. What was Chamberlain Yanagisawa's son Yoritomo doing here? Surprise almost eclipsed Sano's dread. He'd heard that Yanagisawa's whole family had been exiled. Why had Lord Matsudaira spared the boy? Sano could only guess that Yoritomo had seduced and charmed the shogun so thoroughly that the shogun had insisted on keeping the boy in Edo despite Lord Matsudaira's opposition.

"Greetings, Sano-*san*," the shogun said in a weary voice. He looked older and frailer than Sano had ever seen him. "It seems that, ahh, an eternity has passed since we last met."

"Indeed it does, Your Excellency." Sano had spent an agonizingly long three days suspended between his dread of losing his post and his honor, and his fear that Hirata would die. At least he could soon stop waiting for one blow to fall.

"I, ahh, have something important to tell you," the shogun said.

He looked toward Lord Matsudaira, as if for permission to speak. Sano saw that even though Lord Matsudaira might not always have his way with the shogun, he now had their lord as firmly under his thumb as Chamberlain Yanagisawa ever had.

"All in due time, Honorable Cousin," said Lord Matsudaira. "First we must hear Sano-*san*'s report on his investigation."

His gaze commanded Sano. As everyone watched him and waited for him to speak, Sano felt as though he'd been granted a stay of execution that only made his doom more unbearable to anticipate. "Senior Elder Makino's murder was an accident," he said, then explained what had happened. "The actor Koheiji has been executed. Makino's concubine Okitsu was sentenced to work as a courtesan in the Yoshiwara pleasure quarter." Since she'd been an accomplice in covering up the murder but not directly responsible for it, she'd been given the usual punishment for female petty criminals.

"Makino's wife Agemaki has been tried for the murder of his first wife," Sano said, "but there was insufficient evidence to prove her guilt. She, too, has been sentenced to Yoshiwara." She now lived in the same brothel as Okitsu, her rival. Sano had told its owner to keep a close watch on her, lest she inflict her murderous tendencies on her companions or clients.

"Have you also solved the murder of my nephew?" Lord Matsudaira said.

"I have," Sano said. "Chamberlain Yanagisawa's wife assassinated Daiemon, on orders from her husband."

He could have mentioned that he'd finally accounted for Koheiji's, Okitsu's, and Tamura's whereabouts on the night Daiemon had died. Koheiji had admitted leaving the rehearsal to dally with a lady love, and Okitsu had gone out looking for him at the Sign of Bedazzlement, among other places where he'd been known to conduct romances. Tamura had had a secret meeting with a retainer of Lord Matsudaira, during which he'd pledged to join Lord Matsudaira's faction. But these details didn't matter anymore.

Lord Matsudaira nodded, appearing satisfied with Sano's report, especially since it cleared him of blame for the death of Senior Elder Makino and confirmed that Yanagisawa had been responsible for the murder of Daiemon. Yet Sano doubted that Lord Matsudaira had forgotten that Sano had offended him during the investigation. Sano thought surely his fate was already decided.

The shogun also nodded, like a puppet operated by Lord Matsudaira. "Well, I am glad that we, ahh, have dispensed with the matter," he said as if the murders and the investigation had been a vexing but minor inconvenience to him. He

seemed not to care anymore that his dear old friend and his
onetime heir apparent were dead. "But one problem remains."

He turned to Sano. "I have, ahh, lost my chamberlain."
The shogun sighed in fleeting regret that Yanagisawa was
gone. Sano realized that Tokugawa Tsunayoshi didn't understand exactly why; he still didn't know about the war between the factions or the circumstances that had led to
Yanagisawa's exile. "I need a new chamberlain. After, ahh,
much deliberation, I have, ahh decided that it will be you."

Sano's jaw dropped. At first he thought he'd not heard
correctly. He had to repeat the shogun's words in his mind
before he could believe them. Shock rendered him speech-
less. Instead of losing his post, he'd gained a promotion to
the highest office in the *bakufu*! The forces that had plunged
Chamberlain Yanagisawa to his downfall had propelled Sano
in the opposite direction. Now Sano saw the shogun, and the
assembly, waiting expectantly for his reply.

"Your Excellency, this is a most unprecedented honor,"
Sano said, breathless and dizzy from his sudden, inexplica-
ble, and rapid ascent. "A thousand thanks." He was aware
that the post represented the pinnacle of a samurai's career,
but was too stunned to think what the job entailed or how he
felt about it. "May I ask . . . what made you choose to grant
me the privilege of serving as your chamberlain?"

"You've never done me wrong as far as I know," the
shogun said. "And your, ahh, company is tolerable to me.
Therefore, you are, ahh, as good a choice as any."

This was faint praise and inadequate reason. Sano looked
to Lord Matsudaira for an explanation.

"All of us have agreed that you are the right man for the
post," Lord Matsudaira said, indicating himself and the elders. He gave Sano a sardonic smile. The elders nodded in
approval that seemed grudging yet resigned. Yoritomo gazed
upon Sano with an expression that combined fear with hope.
"Your conduct during the investigation was the deciding
factor."

Belatedly, Sano noticed the seating arrangement occupied by Lord Matsudaira, the elders, and Yoritomo. Elders

Uemori and Ohgami, allies of Lord Matsudaira, sat nearest him. Elders Kato and Ihara, once beholden to Chamberlain Yanagisawa, sat nearest his son. Although the battle had ended, the war had not. The remnants of Yanagisawa's faction had regrouped around Yoritomo, proxy for his absent father. They were using him—and his position close to the shogun—as a means to challenge Lord Matsudaira for control over Japan. Already they'd gained a foothold in the new order. And at last Sano understood why both sides had chosen him as chief administrator of the *bakufu*.

His skills, accomplishments, loyalty to the Tokugawa, and wisdom had nothing to do with the decision. During his investigation, he'd proved that he could work with both factions while letting neither control him. His independent mind and his imperviousness to coercion had made him the only man whom both sides found acceptable. Neither side would choose someone connected with the other. He'd won the post of chamberlain by default.

"Congratulations, Honorable Chamberlain Sano," said Lord Matsudaira. "I wish you the best of luck in managing the affairs of the nation." He added in a warning tone: "May you use your authority wisely."

Sano suddenly realized what a burden had landed on him. As chamberlain, he must oversee the government's numerous departments, although he was woefully unfamiliar with their operations. He, who had only ever been responsible for the hundred men of his detectives corps, must now supervise countless feuding bureaucrats. He must keep the huge, unwieldy, and corrupt Tokugawa machine running. He must make important decisions for the shogun and keep him happy. And as if that weren't enough, Sano must also navigate the narrow, dangerous zone between the two rival factions, trying to please both while offending neither.

This was Sano's glorious reward for maintaining his impartiality during the murder investigation.

"Come, Chamberlain Sano." The shogun beckoned. "Sit here." He pointed to a place on the floor below the dais, between Yoritomo and Lord Matsudaira.

Sano rose. He knew he couldn't refuse the position; he couldn't go back to what he now realized had been a comfortable existence as the shogun's *sōsakan-sama*. Duty and honor propelled him up the room. Sano took his seat at the helm of the *bakufu*.

Twilight descended upon Edo. Throughout the castle, lanterns and torches burned in watchtowers, atop the walls, along streets, and outside gates. The misty drizzle formed glowing haloes around the lights. Hoofbeats echoed through the passages as troops patrolled and officials headed homeward. Temple bells pealed across the city, where more lights flickered. But Chamberlain Yanagisawa's compound was dark and silent as a tomb. The sentries were gone from the gate, the archers from the roofs, the guards from the towers. Rain dripped from the trees into shadows that filled the labyrinth of vacant buildings.

Up the road toward the compound came a procession composed of a palanquin, eight mounted samurai bearing lanterns, and a few servants carrying trunks. The procession halted outside the gate. Sano leaped off his horse. Reiko climbed from the palanquin. They stood together and gazed up at the compound's stone walls that rose before them.

"Welcome to our new home," Sano said.

When Sano had told her that he was the new chamberlain, Reiko had almost fainted from shock. But now her mind began to accept the reality of Sano's amazing promotion—and the changes it would bring to their lives.

"How generous the shogun was to give you Chamberlain Yanagisawa's compound," she said.

Yet she hated to leave the estate where she and Sano had lived the entire four years of their marriage, where she'd borne their son. The compound seemed inhospitable, forbidding, and tainted by the evil spirits of Yanagisawa and his wife. Reiko was reluctant to begin moving her household into the place.

"This is one gift I wish I could refuse," Sano said, echoing Reiko's thoughts.

"I can still hardly believe that an accidental murder could have such huge consequences," Reiko mused.

A rueful, bitter smile twisted Sano's mouth. "The political power hierarchy has been drastically altered. My chief retainer and dearest friend is fighting for his life. I've achieved the height of glory. None of these things might have happened if not for Senior Elder Makino and his playmates and their game."

Reiko thought of the perfumed sleeve, a symbol of female sexuality that is soft and pliable, yet a potent force of nature that can topple and destroy the strongest men.

"Even though he couldn't have known how he would die, Makino would have been pleased by the big stir that he caused by his death and his letter to me," Sano said.

"Will you mind so much, being chamberlain?" Reiko asked.

"Not if I can use my authority to do good," Sano said. His smile softened as their gazes met. "Will you mind being the chamberlain's wife?"

Reiko loved him for his readiness to make the best of a daunting situation and serve his duty to noble purpose. She postponed thinking about what she would do from now on. "Not as long as we're together."

Sano called the detectives to open the gate of the compound. They flung apart the thick, heavy, ironclad doors. Inside, darkness extended as far as Reiko could see. Sano took a lantern from one of his men. He and Reiko walked into the chamberlain's compound.

Read on for an excerpt from
Laura Joh Rowland's next book

THE ASSASSIN'S TOUCH

Coming soon in hardcover from
St. Martin's Minotaur

A gunshot boomed within Edo Castle and echoed across the city that spread below the hilltop.

On the racetrack inside the castle, five horses bolted from the starting line. Samurai riders, clad in metal helmets and armor tunics, crouched low in the saddles. They flailed their galloping mounts with riding crops; their shouts demanded more speed. The horses' hooves thundered up a storm of dust.

Around the long oval track, in wooden stands built in tiers and shaded from the sun by striped canopies, officials urged on the riders. Soldiers patrolling atop the stone walls of the compound and stationed in watchtowers above it waved and cheered. The horses galloped neck and neck until they reached the first curve, then crowded together as the riders jockeyed for position along the track's inside edge. The riders struck out at their opponents' mounts and bodies; their crops smacked horseflesh and rang loud against armor. Fighting for the lead, they yelled threats and insults at one another. Horses whinnied, colliding. As they rounded the curve, a rider on a bay stallion edged ahead of the pack.

The sensations of power and speed thrilled him. His heartbeat accelerated in rhythm with his horse's pounding hooves. The din resounded in his helmet. Through its visor, he saw the spectators flick by him, their waving hands, col-

orful robes, and avid faces a blur in the wind. He whooped
as reckless daring exhilarated his spirits. This new horse was
well worth the gold he'd paid for it. He would win back its
price when he collected on his bets, and show everyone who
the best rider in the capital was.

Hurtling along the track, he drew a length in front of the
rest. When he looked over his shoulder, two riders charged
up to him, one on each side. They leaned forward and lashed
their whips at him. The blows glanced off his armor. One
rider grabbed his reins, and the other seized his tunic in an
attempt to slow him down. Ruthless in his need to win, he
banged his crop against their helmets. They dropped behind.
The audience roared. The leader howled with glee as he
veered around the curve. The pack rampaged after him, but
he coaxed his horse faster. He increased his lead while racing toward the finish.

In his mind there suddenly arose an image of a horseman
gaining on him, monstrous in size, black as night. Startled,
he glanced backward, but saw only the familiar horses and
riders laboring through the dust in his wake. He dug in his
heels, flailed his whip. His horse put on a burst of speed that
stretched the gap between him and the pack. Ahead, some
hundred paces distant, loomed the finish line. Two samurai
officials waited there, holding red flags, ready to signal the
winner.

But now the monstrous horseman grew larger in his perception, storming so close that he could feel its shadow lap-
ping at him. He felt a sharp, fierce pain behind his right eye,
as though a knife had stabbed into his skull. A cry burst from
him. The pain began to pulse, driving the blade deeper and
deeper, harder and faster. He moaned in agony and confusion.

What was happening to him?

The sunlight brightened to an intensity that seared his
eyes. The track, the men at the finish line, and the spectators
dissolved into a blinding shimmer, as if the world had
caught fire. His heart beat a loud, frantic counterpoint to the
pulses of pain. External sounds melted into dim drones. A

tingling sensation spread through his arms and legs. He couldn't feel the horse under him. His head seemed very far away from his body. Now he knew something was dreadfully wrong. He tried to call for help, but only incoherent croaks emerged from his mouth.

Yet he felt no fear. Emotion and thought fled him like leaves scattering in the wind. His hands weakened; their grip on the reins loosened. His body was a numb, dead weight that sagged in the saddle. The brilliant, shimmering light contracted to a dot as the black horseman overtook him and darkness encroached on his vision.

The dot of light winked out. The world disappeared into black silence. Consciousness died.

As he crossed the finish line, he tumbled from his mount, into the path of the oncoming horses and riders.

Above the racetrack, past forested slopes carved by stone-walled passages that encircled and ascended the hill, a compound stood isolated from the estates that housed the top officials of the Tokugawa regime. High walls topped with metal spikes protected the compound, whose tiled roofs rose amid pine trees. Samurai officials, wearing formal silk robes and the two swords, shaved crowns, and topknots of their class, queued up outside. Guards escorted them in the double gate, through the courtyard, into the mansion that rambled in a labyrinth of wings connected by covered corridors. They gathered in an anteroom, waiting to see Chamberlain Sano Ichirō, the shogun's second-in-command and chief administrator of the *bakufu*, the military government that ruled Japan. They passed the time with political gossip, their voices a constant, rising buzz. In nearby rooms whirled a storm of activity: The chamberlain's aides conferred; clerks recorded business transacted by the regime, collated and filed reports; messengers rushed about.

Closeted in his private inner office, Chamberlain Sano sat with General Isogai, supreme commander of the army, who'd come to brief him on military affairs. Around them, colored

maps of Japan hung on walls made of thick wooden panels
that muted the noise outside. Shelves and fireproof iron
chests held ledgers. The open window gave a view of the
garden, where sand raked in parallel lines around mossy
boulders shone brilliant white in the afternoon sun.

"There's good news and bad news," General Isogai said.
He was a bulbous man with a squat head that appeared to
sprout directly from his shoulders. His eyes glinted with intelligence and joviality. He spoke in a loud voice accustomed to shouting orders. "The good news is that things
have quieted down in the past six months."

Six months ago, the capital had been embroiled in political strife. "We can be thankful that order has been restored
and civil war prevented," Sano said, recalling how troops
from two opposing factions had clashed in a bloody battle
outside Edo and three hundred forty-six soldiers had died.

"We can thank the gods that Lord Matsudaira is in power,
and Yanagisawa is out," General Isogai added.

Lord Matsudaira—a cousin of the shogun—and the former chamberlain Yanagisawa had vied fiercely for domination of the regime. Their power struggle had divided the
bakufu, until Lord Matsudaira had managed to win more allies, defeat the opposition's army, and oust Yanagisawa. Now
Lord Matsudaira controlled the shogun, and thus the dictatorship.

"The bad news is that the trouble's not over," General Isogai continued. "There have been more unfortunate incidents.
Two of my soldiers were ambushed and murdered on the
highway, and four others while patrolling in town. And yesterday, the army garrison at Hodogaya was bombed. Four
soldiers were killed, eight wounded."

Sano frowned in consternation. "Have the persons responsible been caught?"

"Not yet," General Isogai said, his expression surly. "But
of course we know who they are."

After Yanagisawa had been ousted, scores of soldiers
from his army had managed to escape Lord Matsudaira's
strenuous efforts to capture them. Edo, home to a million

people and of countless houses, shops, temples and shrines, afforded many secret hiding places for the fugitive outlaws. Determined to avenge their master's defeat, they were waging war upon Lord Matsudaira in the form of covert acts of violence. Thus, Yanagisawa still cast a shadow even though he now lived in exile on Hachijo Island in the middle of the ocean.

"I've heard reports of fighting between the army and the outlaws in the provinces," Sano said. The outlaws were fomenting rebellion in areas where the Tokugawa had less military presence. "Have you figured out who's leading the attacks?"

"I've interrogated the fugitives we've captured and gotten a few names," General Isogai said. "They're all senior officers from Yanagisawa's army who've gone underground."

"Could they be taking orders from above ground?"

"From inside the *bakufu*, you mean?" General Isogai shrugged. "Perhaps. Even though Lord Matsudaira has gotten rid of most of the opposition, he can't eliminate it all."

Lord Matsudaira had purged many officials because they'd supported his rival. The banishments, demotions, and executions would probably continue for some time. But remnants of the Yanagisawa faction still populated the government. These were men too powerful and entrenched for Lord Matsudaira to dislodge. They comprised a small but growing challenge to him.

"We'll crush the rebels eventually," General Isogai said. "Let's just hope that a foreign army doesn't invade Japan while we're busy coping with them."

Their meeting finished, Sano and General Isogai rose and exchanged bows. "Keep me informed," Sano said.

The general contemplated Sano a moment. "These times have been disastrous for some people," he remarked, "but beneficial for others." His sly, knowing smile nudged Sano. "Had Yanagisawa and Lord Matsudaira never fought, a certain onetime detective would never have risen to heights far above expectation . . . isn't that right, Honorable Chamberlain?"

He emphasized the syllables of Sano's title, conferred six months ago as a result of a murder investigation that had contributed to Yanagisawa's downfall. Once the shogun's *sōsakan-sama*—Most Honorable Investigator of Events, Situations, and People—Sano had been chosen to replace Yanagisawa.

General Isogai chuckled. "I never thought I'd be reporting to a former *rōnin*." Before Sano had joined the government, he'd been a masterless samurai, living on the fringes of society, eking out a living as a tutor and martial arts instructor. "I had a bet with some of my officers that you wouldn't last a month."

"Many thanks for your vote of confidence," Sano said with a wry smile, as he recalled how he'd struggled to learn how the government operated, to keep its huge, arcane bureaucracy running smoothly, and establish good relations with subordinates who resented his promotion over them.

As soon as General Isogai had departed, the whirlwind outside Sano's office burst through the door. Aides descended upon him, clamoring for his attention: "Here are the latest reports on tax revenues!" "Here are your memoranda to be signed!" "The Judicial Councilors are next in line to see you!"

The aides stacked documents in a mountain on the desk. They unfurled scrolls before Sano. As he scanned the papers and stamped them with his signature seal, he gave orders. Such had been his daily routine since he'd become chamberlain. He read and listened to countless reports in an attempt to keep up with everything that was happening in the nation. He had one meeting after another. His life had become an unceasing rush. He reflected that the Tokugawa regime, which had been founded by the steel of the sword, now ran on paper and talk. He regretted the habit he'd established when he'd taken up his new post.

In his zeal to take charge, he'd wanted to meet everyone, and hear all news and problems unfiltered by people who might hide the truth from him. He'd wanted to make decisions himself, rather than trust them to the two hundred men who comprised his staff. Because he didn't want to end up ignorant and manipulated, Sano had opened his door to hordes of officials. But he'd soon realized he'd gone too far. Minor issues, and people anxious to curry his favor, consumed too much of his attention. He often felt as though he was frantically treading water, in constant danger of drowning. He'd made many mistakes and stepped on many toes.

Regardless of his difficulties, Sano took pride in his accomplishments. He'd kept the Tokugawa regime afloat despite his lack of experience. He'd attained the pinnacle of a samurai's career, the greatest honor. Yet he often felt imprisoned in his office. His warrior spirit grew restless; he didn't even have time for martial arts practice. Sitting, talking, and shuffling paper while his sword rusted was no job for a samurai. Sano couldn't help yearning for his days as a detective, the intellectual challenge of solving crimes, and the thrill of hunting criminals. He wished to use his new power to do good, yet there seemed not much chance of that.

An Edo Castle messenger hovered near Sano. "Excuse me, Honorable Chamberlain," he said, "but the shogun wants to see you in the palace right now."

On top of everything else, Sano was at the shogun's command day and night. His most important duty was keeping his lord happy. He couldn't refuse a summons, no matter how frivolous the reason usually turned out to be.

As he exited his chamber, his two retainers, Marume and Fukida, accompanied him. Both had belonged to his detective corps when he was *sōsakan-sama*; now they served him as bodyguards and assistants. They hastened through the anteroom, where the officials waiting to see Sano fretted around him, begging for a moment of his attention. Sano made his apologies and mentally tore himself away from all the work he had to do, while Marume and Fukida hustled him out the door.

Inside the palace, Sano and his escorts walked up the long audience chamber, past the guards stationed against the walls. The shogun sat on the dais at the far end. He wore the cylindrical black cap of his rank, and a luxurious silk brocade robe whose green and gold hues harmonized with the landscape mural behind him. Lord Matsudaira knelt in the position of honor, below the shogun on his right. Sano knelt in his own customary position at the shogun's left; his men knelt near him. As they bowed to their superiors, Sano thought how similar the two cousins were in appearance, yet how different.

They both had the aristocratic Tokugawa features, but while the shogun's were withered and meek, Lord Matsudaira's were fleshed out by robust health and bold spirits. They were both fifty years of age and near the same height, but the shogun seemed much older and smaller due to his huddled posture. Lord Matsudaira, who outweighed his cousin, sat proudly erect. Although he wore robes in subdued colors, he dominated the room.

"I've requested this meeting to announce some bad news," Lord Matsudaira said. He maintained a cursory charade that his cousin held the power, and pretended to defer to him, but fooled no one except the shogun. Even though he now controlled the government, he still danced attendance on his cousin because if he didn't, other men would, and he could lose his influence over the shogun to them. "Ejima Senzaemon has just died."

Sano experienced surprise and dismay. The shogun's face took on a queasy, confused expression. "Who did you say?" His voice wavered with his constant fear of seeming stupid.

"Ejima Senzaemon," repeated Lord Matsudaira.

"Ahh." The shogun wrinkled his forehead, more baffled than enlightened. "Do I know him?"

"Of course you do," Lord Matsudaira said, barely hiding his impatience at his cousin's slow wits. Sano could almost hear him thinking that he, not Tokugawa Tsunayoshi, should have been born to rule the regime.

"Ejima was chief of the *metsuke*," Sano murmured helpfully. The *metsuke* was the intelligence service that employed spies to gather information all over Japan, for the purpose of monitoring troublemakers and guarding the regime's power.

"Really?" the shogun said. "When did he take office?"

"About six months ago," Sano said. Ejima had been appointed by Lord Matsudaira, who'd purged his predecessor, an ally of Chamberlain Yanagisawa.

The shogun heaved a tired sigh. "There are so many new people in the, ahh, government these days. I can't keep them straight." Annoyance pinched his features. "It would be much easier for me if the same men would stay in the same posts. I don't know why they can't."

Nobody offered an explanation. The shogun didn't know about the war between Lord Matsudaira and Chamberlain Yanagisawa, or Lord Matsudaira's victory and the ensuing purge; no one had told him, and since he rarely left the palace, he saw little of what went on around him. He knew Yanagisawa had been exiled, but he wasn't clear as to why. Neither Lord Matsudaira nor Yanagisawa had wanted him to know that they aspired to control the regime, lest he put them to death for treason. And now Lord Matsudaira wanted the shogun kept ignorant of the fact that he'd seized power and virtually ruled Japan. No one dared disobey his orders against telling the shogun. A conspiracy of silence pervaded Edo Castle.

"How did Ejima die?" Sano asked Lord Matsudaira.

"He fell off his horse during a race at the Edo Castle track," Lord Matsudaira said.

"Dear me," the shogun said. "Horse-racing is such a dangerous sport, perhaps it should be, ahh, prohibited."

"I recall hearing that Ejima was a particularly reckless rider," Sano said, "and he'd been in accidents before."

"I don't believe this was an accident," Lord Matsudaira said, his tone sharp. "I suspect foul play."

"Oh?" Sano saw his surprise mirrored on his men's faces. "Why?"

"This isn't the only recent, sudden death of a high official," Lord Matsudaira said. "First there was Ono Shinnosuke, the supervisor of court ceremony, on New Year's Day. In the spring, Sasamura Tomoya, highway commissioner, died. And just last month, Treasury Minister Moriwaki."

"But Ono and Sasamura died in their sleep, at home in

bed," Sano said. "The treasury minister fell in the bathtub and hit his head. Their deaths seem unrelated to Ejima's."

"Don't you see a pattern?" Lord Matsudaira's manner was ominous with insinuation.

"They were all, ahh, new to their posts, weren't they?" the shogun piped up timidly. He had the air of a child playing a guessing game, hoping he had the right answer. "And they died soon after taking office?"

"Precisely," Lord Matsudaira said with surprise that the shogun remembered the men, let alone knew anything about them.

They were all Lord Matsudaira's trusted cronies, installed after the coup, Sano could have added, but didn't.

"These deaths may not have been as natural as they appeared," said Lord Matsudaira. "They may be part of a plot to undermine the regime by eliminating key officials."

While Lord Matsudaira's enemies inside and outside the *bakufu* were constantly plotting his downfall, Sano didn't know what to think about a conspiracy. During the past six months, Sano had watched him change from a confident leader of a major Tokugawa branch clan to a nervous, distrustful man insecure in his new position. Frequent sabotage and violent attacks against his army by Yanagisawa's outlaws fed his insecurity. Stolen power could be stolen from the thief, Sano supposed.

"A plot against the regime?" Always susceptible to warnings about danger, the shogun gasped. He looked around as though he, not Lord Matsudaira, were under attack. "You must do something!" he exclaimed to his cousin.

"Indeed I will," Lord Matsudaira said. "Chamberlain Sano, I order you to investigate the deaths." Although Sano was second-in-command to the shogun, he answered to Lord Matsudaira, as did everyone else in the government. In his haste to protect himself, Lord Matsudaira forgot to manipulate the shogun into giving the order. "Should they prove to be murders, you will identify and apprehend the killer before he can strike again."

A thrill of glad excitement coursed through Sano. Even if

the deaths turned out to be natural or accidental, here was a welcome reprieve from paperwork. "As you wish, my lord."

"Not so fast," the shogun said, narrowing his eyes in displeasure because Lord Matsudaira had bypassed his authority. "I seem to recall that Sano-*san* isn't a detective anymore. Investigating crimes is no longer his job. You can't ask him to, ahh, dirty his hands investigating those deaths."

Lord Matsudaira hastened to correct his mistake: "Sano-*san* is obliged to do whatever you wish, regardless of his position. And you wish him to protect your interests, don't you?"

Obstinacy set the shogun's weak jaw. "But Chamberlain Sano is too busy."

"I don't mind the extra work, Your Excellency." Now that Sano had his opportunity for action, he wasn't going to give it up. His spiritual energy soared at the prospect of a quest for truth and justice, which were fundamental to his personal code of honor. "I'm eager to be of service."

"Many thanks," the shogun said with a peevish glare at Lord Matsudaira as well as at Sano, "but helping me run the country requires all your attention."

Now Sano remembered the million tasks that awaited him. He couldn't leave his office for long and risk losing his tenuous control over the nation's affairs. "Perhaps His Excellency is right," he reluctantly conceded. "Perhaps this investigation is a matter for the police. They are ordinarily responsible for solving cases of mysterious death."

"A good idea," the shogun said, then asked Lord Matsudaira with belligerent scorn, "Why didn't you think of the police? Call them in."

"No. I must strongly advise you against involving the police," Lord Matsudaira hastily.

Sano wondered why. Police Commissioner Hoshina was close to Lord Matsudaira, and Sano would have expected Lord Matsudaira to give Hoshina charge of the investigation. Something must have gone wrong between them, and too recently for the news to have spread.

"Chamberlain Sano is the only man who can be trusted to get to the bottom of this matter," Lord Matsudaira declared.

It was true that during the faction war Sano had remained neutral, resisting much pressure to take sides with Yanagisawa or Lord Matsudaira. Afterward, he'd loyally served Lord Matsudaira in the interest of restoring peace. And long before the trouble started, he'd earned himself a reputation for independence of mind and pursuing the truth even to his own detriment.

"Unless the murderer is caught, the regime's officials will be killed off until there are none left," Lord Matsudaira said to the shogun. "You'll be all alone." He spoke in a menacing voice: "And you wouldn't like that, would you?"

The shogun shrank on the dais. "Oh, no, indeed." He cast a horrified glance around him, as though he envisioned his companions disappearing before his eyes.

If Lord Matsudaira allowed attacks on his regime, he would lose face as well as power, and Sano knew that was worse than death for a proud man like him. "Then you must order Chamberlain Sano to drop everything, investigate the murders, and save you," Lord Matsudaira said.

"Yes. You're right." The shogun's resistance wilted. "Sano-san, do whatever my cousin suggests."

"A wise decision, Your Excellency," Lord Matsudaira said. A hint of a smile touched his mouth, expressing contempt for the shogun and pride at how easily he'd brought him to heel. He told Sano, "I've sent men to secure the racetrack and guard the corpse. They have orders that no one leaves or enters until after you've examined the scene. But you'd better go at once. The crowd will be getting restless."

Sano and his men bowed in farewell. As they left the room, Sano's step was light, no matter what calamities might strike during his absence from the helm of the government. Never mind how much work would accumulate while he looked into Chief Ejima's death; he felt like a prisoner released from jail. Here was his chance to apply all the might and resources of his new position to the cause of justice.

WOODFORD RESERVE BAR & GRILL
LOUISVILLE AIRPORT
LOUISVILLE, KENTUCKY

4183 Matika

1 38/1   4491   GST 1
NOV09'05 10:17AM

***** SEAT 1 *****
1 COFFEE   1.99
  DONT MAKE
1 BOURBON TRAIL   8.49
1 WATER   0.00
  SUBTOTAL   10.48
TAX   0.63 AMOUNT   11.11
******** ********

SUBTOTAL   10.48
TAX   0.63
10:56 AMOUNT $11.11

**$4 OFF DAY PASS @ ALTITUDE CLUB
WOODFORD RESERVE BAR & GRILL
LOUISVILLE AIRPORT
LOUISVILLE, KENTUCKY
THANK YOU FOR VISITING US